T0162674

Travels

❧ On The ❧

ROAD

To

AMERICA

Travels
On The
ROAD
To
AMERICA

KENNETH C. GARDNER, JR.

iUniverse

TRAVELS ON THE ROAD TO AMERICA

iUniverse books may be ordered through booksellers or by contacting:

iUniverse
1663 Liberty Drive
Bloomington, IN 47403
www.iuniverse.com
1-800-Authors (1-800-288-4677)

ISBN: 978-1-4917-7283-6 (sc)
ISBN: 978-1-4917-7284-3 (e)

Print information available on the last page.

iUniverse rev. date: 07/31/2015

Books by Kenneth C. Gardner, Jr.

Novels

>*The Song Is Ended* (2011)
>*The Dark Between The Stars* (2012)

Collections

>*Meatball Birds and Seven Other Stories* (2013)
>*"And All Our Yesterdays…" and Nine Other Stories* (2014)

Non-Fiction

>*Echoes of Distant School Bells: A History of the Drayton Public School, 1879-1998*, Volume 1 (1994); Volume 2 (1999)

For my Golden Friends—Doug, Ardis, Wanda, Jerry, Larry, Bobby, Danny, and Archie...unfading memories.

DAY ONE

You know how it is. Summer comes orange over the horizon. Plans form in your mind. The days shorten and most of them don't work out. August steps out of the trees and leaves shadows so different from those of July. The green seed pods on the caraganas have aged to a deep brown; the deep purple chokecherries bend their branches toward the earth; the mother wren, free of her brood, chats and scolds in the hedges. The year is aging. Soon the winter cold will conquer the summer, so you'd better do something.

Custodians Tommy Dodge, Clyde Colvin, and I had been working in the school since graduation in May. Tommy had taken his two weeks and gone fishing in June. Clyde never took any time off, claiming he couldn't afford to at his age. For me it was August or never.

That had been a bad year.

Vietnam, the fighting and the demonstrations; *Apollo 13* just about didn't make it back to Earth; Kent State, demonstrations and shootings; Ulrike Meinhof helped Andreas Baader escape from jail in West Germany, where they would go on to form the Red Army Faction, a terrorist organization.

Sunday dew glistened in the grass and glossed up my boots as I wheeled the Honda CB750 out of the large lean-to addition at the rear of my house. When Miss Mae Larson owned the house right next door to my parents' place, the addition had been a storage area; it served me the same way. Miss Larson had been our school and city librarian until she died alone in bed, the way she had slept her entire adult life. She hadn't done much with the house since she had inherited it from her folks, so I got it cheap.

The Honda cost me $1500, almost as much as the house. I bought it at Be-Bop's Cycles on the west side of town. There were three colors available: Candy Blue-Green, Candy Gold, or Candy Ruby Red. It wasn't the red color that sold me; it was Be-Bop explaining the advantages of the electric start, the front disk brake, and the quality engineering.

Be-Bop had fought in the European Theater, from Normandy to the Ardennes, without so much as a scratch. He came home full of "piss and vinegar," as they say, and took up with the Crusaders, a group of vets and a couple high school dropouts who rode Harleys.

They weren't a motorcycle gang as such, just a bunch of guys who would ride to neighboring towns on Friday and Saturday nights; try to drink the bar or bars dry; get into some knuckledusters, nothing too serious; and weave their way home.

Be-Bop bought a big two-story house on the west side of Menninger, converted the first-floor into a repair shop with two large doors, and lived on the second floor. He had a way with motors, small engines, anything mechanical, so he started taking care of the Crusaders' bikes. Eventually, he started selling Harleys.

Through attrition—marriages, moving away, health issues, and one death when Jimmy McTag drove drunk right into the side of a GN freight stopped at Benton—the number of Crusaders dwindled from a high of thirty-five to five before they disbanded.

Be-Bop's business suffered accordingly, and he had to go to work as a mechanic at Menninger Motors, but working the weekends in his own shop. Then in the late Sixties Harley quality dropped and nobody wanted to buy them. Be-Bop had to do something, so he turned Japanese.

Honda saved his shop, but lost him his friends. The four ex-Crusaders hated the "rice-cycles" and refused to let Be-Bop work on their American bikes, preferring to trailer them to Caseyville when they went bad.

I didn't like the treatment Be-Bop was getting, and I didn't want to be burned buying the shoddy workmanship Harley was putting out, so I had Be-Bop order a CB750.

He test-drove it for me, and he made certain it wasn't a sandcast model because their chains could stretch out, get caught up in the sprockets, and whip through the cases, making for a nasty repair problem.

The first time I took it out on the East Highway, its inline four banging away between my legs got me up to a hundred before I eased off. I hadn't even hit top-end.

I strapped my gear on the back of the seat and went into the house for a final check. When I saw the record player, on a whim I decided to play a couple songs.

I put on the Dot 45 of Roy Clark's "Yesterday, When I Was Young." Whenever I felt gloomy, I'd listen to the lyrics—"Yesterday when I was young, the taste of life was sweet as rain upon my tongue…There are so many songs in me that won't be sung; I feel the bitter taste of tears upon my tongue"—and reflect on my life about being young "yesterday" with happy songs to sing, but without happy songs now and get to feeling sorry for myself, how I was getting older and hadn't accomplished a blamed thing of importance.

After I was thoroughly depressed, I pulled Tommy James and the Shondells' "Crystal Blue Persuasion" out of its Roulette Records sleeve. Every time I heard that opening bongo joined by the guitar it made me feel good. Some of the druggies were saying it was a veiled reference to drugs, maybe acid, but I just thought of it as a very optimistic, maybe naïve, song about what life could be like: "A new day is comin', people are changin', ain't it beautiful, Crystal Blue Persuasion."

Mom and Dad were having bacon for breakfast; I could smell it as I walked into the house where I grew up. Mom was at the stove, scrambling eggs. Dad was seated at the table.

"I'm gonna take off."

Mom put the bacon, eggs, and toast in front of Dad. "Eat, Lige, before it gets cold." But he got up, came around the table, and shook my hand.

"Be careful, Chris; let us hear from you."

"I will, Dad."

He had given me a stack of postcards and wanted me to write a little each day, find a mailbox, and drop it in. He was sixty-five years old and had just retired from the insurance business. I could tell by his face and his voice he wished he were coming along.

Mom, on the other hand, didn't want me to go—"What if some crazies attack you?" "What if you have an accident hundreds of miles away?" "What if you get in trouble with the law again?" I knew she was thinking about Chicago, 1968.

I could have said, "Mom, life is made up of 'what if's'," but I just said, "Mom, don't worry; I'll be fine. I'll be home before you know it."

They walked me to the door. We hugged and Mom's eyes started to wet-up, just like I knew they would.

They stood on the steps while I went around to the east side of my house.

I slipped on my helmet, made certain the fuel tap was on and I was in neutral, reached down and lowered the kick starter, turned the throttle, stood on my left leg and used my right to kick down the starter. It caught. I revved the engine twice, used my heel on the kickstand, clutched, and eased the shift lever into first.

My parents were still on the steps. We exchanged waves. Down the hill the cars of the Catholics at early Mass were parked, but there was no traffic. I pulled onto Lamborn.

Mom and Dad would get dressed and go to church. Afterward he'd read the *Fargo Forum* and she'd get out her Bible. And I'd be riding.

At the corner I turned and headed south, crossing Villard and glancing at the Hall residence. In high school I'd had a crush on Alix Hall and asked her out, only to discover that she and Joey Carson were going steady. Recalling that, I could feel my face getting hot, even though it had been ten years prior.

A few houses to my right stood the home of the O'Connells—Aunt Mildred, Uncle Daniel, and my cousins Maureen, Kevin and Theresa: their brothers and sisters Rory, Mary-Margaret, Liam, and Kathleen all grown up and gone, as would Maureen when college started.

Theresa would be starting junior high. I hoped that would go well. She was so withdrawn and shy, it was difficult for her to try anything new. I felt anger surge into my heart as I remembered when she had been molested at the age of three and her vibrant personality was replaced by timidity and suspicion, especially of men. She still wouldn't hug me.

I turned left on Tilden and headed up the Hill inhabited by the prominent members of Menninger society. About halfway up I passed the home of Dotty and Earl Wright. I slowed, hoping to see my friend Dotty in the yard, but the Wrights rarely made it to church, so they wouldn't be up yet. She was pregnant with her fourth child in less than seven years of marriage. I said a little prayer for her.

I passed the brick hospital. Too many bad memories.

At the Gold Star Highway I waited for a southbound red and white "flat nose" Peterbilt pulling a cattle trailer to pass.

The Good 'n' Hot Drive-In and the Cock-a-Doodle Drive-In stood on the east side of the highway, both dark on an early Sunday morning.

The Cock-a-Doodle was my favorite. When I was in high school, the owner Angel Annie, a widow lady, was full of energy and plans, and my friends and I had plenty of good times talking to her at the counter or as she stood by our table. Then her daughter Shirley got into a car accident, broke her back, and ended up in a wheelchair. Her husband divorced her and she came home. Angel Annie took care of her, but she lost her enthusiasm, became old, and her business was up for sale. I couldn't remember how long it had been since I had eaten there, but I did remember the food hadn't been very good.

While I was eating, Angel Annie had come over and sat down, something she never did in the past, and started talking about how much she had enjoyed it when I'd come in when I was in high school. From somewhere in the back Shirley started yelling that she was hungry, followed by some filthy language. Angel Annie got a sour look on her face, got up, and shuffled her way past the counter and disappeared down a hallway.

I didn't think I would have treated Mom the way Shirley treated her mother, but I'd never had a broken back, so I guess I didn't really know.

I pulled onto the Gold Star, shifting smoothly with the scuffed toe of my left boot. At the top of the overpass, I was already at sixty-five and had to slow it down to make the curve. The Gold Star straightened out and I throttled up.

I was in an old melt-water channel left over from glacial days. My high school science teacher Prof. Walter Gruening had stirred an interest in geology which had never left. He thought the channel was an early version of the Jacques River which had formed along the margin of the glacier while it had been melting back and which drained the water to the southeast. As I studied the geology of the land, I became convinced the professor was right.

He was also right when he said, "We live on water-created land." Most of the surface of North Dakota was the product of running water and glacial ice.

As I climbed up the south side, I turned and got a last view of Menninger, at least of the trees, a few houses, the grain elevators, the old and new water towers, and the railroad.

The remains of the Midnight Star Drive-in Theater—the projection-concession building, the raised concentric semi-circles where the cars parked, and the screen with several panels missing—a weathered monument to faded youth, passion, and changing times, loomed up on my left and disappeared.

There was a rural Lutheran Church off to the west. I couldn't see it, but dust was rising from the cars of the faithful on the gravel road taking them to worship. Mom and Dad would soon be heading down Lamborn to our church.

When I was a kid, there was a "Cradle Roll" hanging in the church basement. It was a large piece of pasteboard depicting a bassinet, and there were ribbons of blue and pink hanging from it. Names of all the babies and pre-schoolers in our congregation were printed on small cards and the cards were attached to the ribbons, the boys on the blue and the girls on the pink.

The "Cradle Roll" had shrunk and didn't have half the names it once had. No more big families were one reason, of course, but another was that many of the younger parents no longer saw any necessity for church. There were at least four such families that should have been members of our congregation, and although some of them might show up on Easter and Christmas, they didn't make a habit of church attendance.

Our preacher, Rev. Alvin Underwood, was a sincere man of faith; he and his wife Myrtle had grown gray serving our church. They had the ladies host a coffee and pastry hour after the Sunday service; they were involved in all kinds of community projects and urged all of us to join in; they had service-oriented groups for the men, for the ladies, and for the teenagers. Still, church attendance tailed off. Except for the elderly, people attended less frequently. Me included.

The church had slowly evolved into a social club; the ancient message of human imperfection, sin, sorrow, and redemption faded, to be replaced by the spirit of togetherness: "How are you this fine morning? Would you like another Danish? God loves you, brother; God loves you, sister."

Christianity used to be a tough religion: "repent you sinners." Many of Christ's followers turned away when the message of all-consuming faith interfered with their daily lives. Now being in the church required no sacrifice, no need to change anything in your life.

I figured if I wanted to help people in need, I could donate to the Red Cross or some disease-fighting organization, and if I wanted companionship and something to eat, I could join the Eagles, the Masons, or play some poker. Evidently, a lot of the younger people believed that, too. The difficult way to salvation was no longer to be found in the churches.

The barn-smell hit my nose as I caught up with the Peterbilt. No oncoming, so I whipped out and opened her up. The cows might as well have been in a pasture as I topped 110, the driver honking his horn. I figured I'd better keep two hands on the bike, so I didn't wave.

I also figured if I lost control at that speed what good was a helmet going to do me?

On the left stood a shelterbelt where Dotty and I had parked just after I got my driver's license and discovered we'd rather be friends than lovers.

I passed over some sloughs which in high water ran off east to the Jacques River three miles away.

The land was turning August-brown. The barley was ready to harvest, and the wheat was turning to gold. The weeds in the ditches and fence lines were sun-browning, but the vegetation in the sloughs and the shelterbelt trees were still green. The blackbirds were solitary or in small groups; they hadn't flocked up yet.

When I came to the spot where the cottonwood we called the Lonely Tree had once stood, I gave it the horn, just like we used to do in high school for luck.

I passed the Hearth, a steakhouse owned by the father of Sherilynn Carlson, a Caseyville girl I knew, but her name was Sherilynn Bauer, having married her long-time boyfriend Johnny Bauer. She had a heart-shaped birthmark just below her left breast.

The Gold Star dipped into what they called a slough, but was really a creek hiding in the cattails. When I was a kid, there used to be an old pumping station for the Caseyville Water Department on the south side. Coming up the hill the smell of barnyard hit me—the calling card of a feed lot and some pens belonging to a cattle auction barn.

Caseyville showed to the south, and soon I was on the overpass spanning the Soo Line; a red and white locomotive was parked on a sidetrack to the west.

I couldn't count the times I had been on that overpass when I was going steady with BethAnn Borgan. We were in high school and pretty new to the feelings we had for each other.

Yesterday, when I was young, the taste of life was sweet as rain upon my tongue.

I thought of turning off and going by BethAnn's old home, but she was married and living in Coffeyville, Kansas, with a couple of kids, I'd heard.

I passed the Big Norski Café and the F&A Drive-In, good eating.

Unlike Menninger, there were no hills in Caseyville. It wasn't built on a river or lake; its location was due to the fact that one winter it was the railhead for the branch line. Back in the 1890s before adequate wells were dug for the town, circuses that stopped in Menninger would bypass Caseyville because there wasn't enough water available for their elephants, horses, and other animals.

The Northwest Highway joined the Gold Star at Caseyville, and together they went south and then southeast. I picked up the railroad on my right. The wooden "T's" of the telegraph line stood along the tracks as they had for almost ninety years, but the telegraph wasn't used anymore, and the lines were down in some spots, hiding in the weeds.

Off to the west I could see the blue-black blister called Red-Tail Ridge, one of the buttes the Yanktonai used as navigation guides

I sped through little towns and villages spaced between six and eight miles apart. The railroad had put in sidings at those distances so farmers would have easy access to grain elevators. It was the Northern Pacific Railway back then, but in March the NP had merged with its rival the Great Northern, the Burlington, and a small railroad on the West Coast to form the Burlington Northern. The old Roughrider Teddy Roosevelt, North Dakota's favorite President, must have rotated in his grave when that happened since he had fought against the merger of the NP and GN in the Northern Securities Case in 1904.

The first two—Newport and Prairie City—were on my left; the other two—Needham and Pierce—were on my right. They were all waking up to a sleepy Sunday, but life in those towns was getting sleepier as the abandoned buildings began to outnumber the occupied ones. They all had depots and elevators trackside, a bar or two, a post office, and some stores. An occasional steeple spired up. Most of the buildings and almost all the houses were painted white. They reminded me of Jesus talking about "whited sepulchers" in the book of Matthew, not that the residents were any worse than other humans, but that their white towns, shimmering in the Sunday morning sun, were hiding the fact that they were dying. The little towns had lost half their populations in the Sixties.

The land was gently rolling until I hit a rougher couple miles southeast of Prairie City and even more southeast of Pierce, the remnants left by melting at the terminal edge of glaciers.

North of Kingston the railroad and the highway diverged. The railroad siding at that point had never developed, but it was easy to tell why—it had been named Arctic.

I slowed coming down the hill into Kingston, knowing the Gold Star curved left. A gravel road went off to the right, climbing through the highway cut. It ended at the site of old Ft. King, but there was nothing left of the fort.

The Crippled Children's Home was set back on my right. They did good work there: I saw it in action when I attended MHS: a couple of polio victims received services at the Home.

I crossed a bridge over the Jacques River and soon I was downtown, nestled in the valley formed by glacial runoff in what became the valleys of the Jacques and Sand Piper Creek. I crossed the BN mainline, several grain elevators announcing to everyone that agriculture was king.

One of the Catholic Masses had just ended, and people in their "Sunday Best" were leaving the Basilica, many of the older women with their heads covered. There were a lot of people: maybe the Catholics still believed in miracles.

I crossed the Jacques River Bridge and headed up the hill to the Interstate, which had replaced Highway X. Sweeping down the cloverleaf onto the double lanes, I felt like I was in the TV show *Route 66* in which Martin Milner and George Maharis as Tod Stiles and Buz Murdock traveled the country in a Corvette, finding adventures. After Maharis was replaced by Glenn Corbett in 1963, I lost interest in the program, but the idea that adventures awaited never left me.

East of Kingston I dipped into a wide coulee carved deep into the land by water rushing from a melting glacier before Christ, before Moses, before Stonehenge, before the pyramids, before any humans walked that land. I gunned the bike up the other side. I could see Tod and Buz doing the same thing in their convertible, the wind in their hair, but a motorcycle was even freer than a convertible. I was like a Yanktonai brave riding a supercharged pony, the wind not just in my hair, but all over my body. I throttled up and over a hill.

Just beyond the crest, sitting on the shoulder, was a vehicle with a cherry on the roof and a picture of an Indian in profile with a full eagle feather headdress—Red Tomahawk, the man who shot Sitting Bull.

What the heck is the Highway Patrol doing out on a Sunday morning?

I cut the gas—75 m.p.h.—it was too late. I went by at 70 and waited for the cherry to light up. Nothing. I cut back to 65 and waited. Nothing. I dipped into another melt-water channel and checked my rear view as I topped the other side. No cherry. Thank you, St. Christopher or whoever watched over travelers.

Old Highway X and the Northwest Highway had merged at Kingston and what was left of them ran a couple miles north of the Interstate, the small towns on them growing smaller since the traffic was all on the super highway.

At first the land to the north of the Interstate was hillier, a moraine which was the remnants of deposits from the re-advance of a glacier; then the concrete curved north and when it straightened out the hills were on the south. I had passed over the north-south Continental Divide, but there was no sign to mark my passage. It was one of the spines of the continent and it was unremarkable.

Back in 1960 author John Steinbeck had crossed North Dakota on the trip he made famous in his book *Travels with Charley*. He made no mention of the Continental Divide, but he did remark about the east-west divide on the return portion of his travels. He crossed the Colorado River, raced through Arizona, and camped in a canyon on the Continental Divide in New Mexico, where he realized he had been avoiding people and had stopped seeing the country on that leg of his trip. He made a birthday cake for his poodle Charley, even though he didn't know the actual date when Charley was born, out of four hotcakes, syrup, and a candle. They explored a trail along the side of the canyon together, finding a pile of thousands of broken whiskey and gin bottles and a piece of mica, which Steinbeck put in his pocket.

The Interstate concrete was smooth, smoother than the asphalt of the Gold Star. In high school I had argued the merits of asphalt with Lanny Berg, who supported concrete. Now I had to admit he was probably right.

Worthington was in the Divide River Valley, which was the product of water from melting glaciers and from a large glacial lake far to the northwest ripping a trench into the earth. A glacial lake had formed in the valley when it was blocked about ten miles south of where I was by a glacier that intruded from the east; now a man-made lake, used for fishing and flood control, occupied the valley north of the town behind a large dam.

Old Highway X had gone straight down the valley wall into the town, making for an exciting ride on icy winter pavement. The Interstate skirted around to the south in a long curve with a more gradual entry into and exit from the valley. I eased around the first part of the curve and throttled up to climb the other side of the valley.

Four miles later I rolled over a north-south glacial moraine and then onto more rolling country. A small dry coulee went through Ellsbury and ducked under the highway which angled to the southeast for three miles, then it headed directly east on an almost perfectly straight line to Fargo.

A mile or so later the highway dished slightly, and I crossed a gash in the earth at the bottom of which the Maple River stagnated. Ten years earlier Steinbeck had camped on the banks of the Maple in a copse of what he thought were sycamores, but which probably weren't: sycamores aren't hardy enough for our winters.

Steinbeck had driven on old Highway X west out of Fargo, so his turnoff would have been three miles north of where I was, and I wasn't going to take the time to find it. If it had been Hemingway...

Steinbeck had been very disappointed in Fargo. He had never been there, and the name "Fargo" had conjured up the mythical abode of the Old West, of overwhelming summer heat, of bone-cracking winters of despair, of towering dust storms that brought night during the day. Instead, he had found a typical small (46,000) American city with traffic problems, garish neon signs, and an outskirts of old metal and broken glass.

The Maple River camp was a pleasant place to rethink Fargo. As he reflected, he found that the name "Fargo" still brought with it stagecoaches, blizzards, summer heat, and huge dust clouds. His being there hadn't changed the myth and he liked that.

Steinbeck had always prided himself on knowing Americans, but at the age of fifty-eight, he discovered that he hadn't been in touch with his country and its people for twenty-five years, a separation that was suicidal for a writer.

He got a three-quarter ton pickup with a V-6 engine, put on a camper top, filled it with modern conveniences, and painted "Rocinante" (Don

Quixote's horse) on the side. He filled it with a shotgun, two rifles, some fishing gear, food, a thirty-gallon water tank, writing materials, books, booze—beer, Scotch, bourbon, gin, vodka, brandy, and aged applejack— and a bleu French poodle named Charley.

First, he traveled through New England, enjoying the roadside stands of pumpkins, squash, and apples; the neat and unchanging villages; and the fiery hues of the autumn.

Drinking some applejack, he and a farmer discussed the Soviet leader Nikita Khrushchev, who had taken off his shoe and pounded a table with it during a speech at the United Nations. The farmer thought the U.S. should be more aggressive in its stance against the Soviets. When Steinbeck asked him peoples' opinions about the upcoming Kennedy-Nixon presidential election, the farmer said no one talked very much about it: no one seemed to want to share an opinion, unlike his father's and grandfather's generations. Steinbeck wrote that he found that attitude throughout the nation.

Eating breakfasts in early-open restaurants failed to give him much information about the nation: the men were there to eat, not to talk.

He learned to love the radio; he said it had taken the place of the old local newspaper.

Every so often he would pull Rocinante into a rest stop, make some coffee, and let Charley do his business while Steinbeck contemplated whatever he wanted to contemplate—nature, where he had lived, books he loved. Sometimes while waiting he would read a little.

He described himself as a six-footer, with blue eyes and grizzled gray hair, beard, and mustache. He shaved his cheeks. He wore a beard as pure decoration; he said it was the one thing a man could do better than a woman, unless she was in the circus.

He wore a blue serge naval cap with a small visor, but after seeing the attention the cap brought in the non-sea faring states of Wisconsin, North Dakota, and Montana, he bought a small Stetson which he wore until he got to the West Coast.

Steinbeck stopped occasionally at auto courts or motels for one express purpose—a hot bath.

He saw the Aurora Borealis, which he had seen only a few times, and thought it majestic. He condemned casual hunting because the hunters didn't need the food; they were trying to prove their masculinity. French Canadians were picking potatoes; Steinbeck worried that the United

States might be overwhelmed someday by people who were not too proud to harvest the things Americans would eat, but no longer sweat for. He deplored the denuded countryside and rural villages as people fled to the big cities, changing our national character.

Steinbeck said he was "born lost." He got lost in Bangor and Ellsworth, Maine; in a small town near Medina, New York, in a rain storm; in Chicago; in St. Paul-Minneapolis (he wasn't sure which one, but four hours later at a German restaurant the people told him it was Minneapolis).

He described the America that he saw, but wouldn't guarantee that anyone else making a similar journey would see the same America.

He went to church every Sunday, a different denomination each week, but only heard one hell fire and brimstone sermon, in a New England Presbyterian Church.

He read road signs and historical markers.

He claimed to admire every nation, but to hate all governments.

He avoided the Interstates until he fell behind schedule and picked up I-90 because he feared getting caught in a blizzard in North Dakota. On the Interstates he missed too much of the country, and he didn't like the spotless and overly sanitary rest stops, gas stations, and restaurants. He did enjoy talking to the truckers, whom he liked, and listening to them, but he didn't learn much about the country from them because they almost always talked about the road and driving, much like Mark Twain's riverboat pilots who always talked about the Mississippi.

He took I-90 across northwest Pennsylvania and into Ohio, where he took U.S. 20. He cut north into Michigan, Pontiac and Flint, and back down to 20, through Indiana and into Illinois.

He was fascinated by the mobile homes and the people who lived in them, symbols of the restlessness of Americans.

The Midwest was more populated and busier than the last time he was there. The people friendlier than those of New England. He remarked on the rich soil and the abundant trees, especially in Michigan.

He thought radio and TV were eliminating local and regional speech patterns from American English, except in Montana, a state he loved.

Three times a week he called his wife back in New York State.

In Chicago he stayed at the Ambassador Hotel. His room hadn't been made up yet, so while waiting he looked at what the previous occupant had left and tried to piece together his story. From laundry tags, hotel stationary, a letter he had started to his wife, an empty bottle of Jack Daniels, some soda bottles, an ashtray full of cigarette butts, the lingering scent of perfume, and a bobby pin, he concluded he was from Connecticut, was on a business trip, was married, but had entertained a woman who had not stayed the night. Then his stomach acted up, based on Tums wrappers and he had a hangover—empty Bromo Seltzer tubes. He thought the man was very lonely.

Steinbeck's wife joined him briefly in Chicago.

Wisconsin he thought of as a magic land of abundance, richness, and cheese. Two things disturbed him: he stayed on a hilltop where truckers scraped out the residue of manure from their truck boxes, creating mountains of fly-blown excrement; and in the valley below he saw a moving black mass, which, upon inspection, proved to be turkeys, milling about. He thought turkeys were stupid, excitable birds.

He was caught up in a mass of truck traffic and drove through the Twin Cities without noticing anything, except the traffic around him. He drove on U.S. 52 to Sauk Center because he wanted to see the birthplace of Sinclair Lewis, a writer he respected, but inexplicably, once he got there, he turned north on U.S. 71 and drove to Wadena, caught U.S. 10, and went to Detroit Lakes, where he spent the night.

After driving through Fargo, Steinbeck made his mid-morning stop on the Maple River, not far from Alice, a small village of 124 souls. I didn't know what he meant by "not far." To get to the Maple River he would have passed through another town, Buffalo, which was somewhat bigger than Alice, and driven another couple miles. Buffalo was three miles north of where I was. To get to Alice, Steinbeck would have had to drive eight miles south of where I was and then take a county road two-and-a-half miles to the Maple. It didn't make sense to me when I first read it and it still didn't.

Steinbeck took some time to wash clothes and dry them on some bushes. While he was waiting, he wrote a few notes on the qualities of being alone.

Charley nosed around and started shaking a discarded paper bag. A rolled-up piece of heavy white paper came out and Steinbeck picked it up. It was an order from a court in an eastern state to some guy to pay his alimony or face the consequences. Steinbeck took out his Zippo and burned the order, with no sense of guilt.

He took off his boots and socks and put his feet in the Maple, which was running icy cold. It was just after noon, but he decided to stay next to the river. He began to think of what he'd learned about America and found that whatever it was, it wasn't much: food along the highways was bland and not very good, except for the breakfasts, which were especially good if they contained bacon or sausage, eggs, and pan-fried potatoes; the predominant newsstand fare was comic books and trashy paperbacks; local radio stations played the same homogenized music and announcements everywhere; no one seemed willing to talk politics, except against the Russians, whom it was safe to hate.

Out of nowhere an old sedan pulling a small trailer parked fifty yards away. After awhile the stranger wearing a leather jacket and a cowboy hat with a brim curled up on the sides and held by a chin strap sauntered over.

He was a down-on-his luck actor of older middle age and thought Steinbeck might be an actor also because the author knew what the man referred to when he used the term "the profession."

They enjoyed some coffee and enjoyed some whisky even more. The actor explained that for almost three years he and his partner, a dog, had been traveling the country, doing performances at churches, service clubs, schools, any place he could find an audience. Before that, he hadn't worked for over a year. He enjoyed performing Shakespeare in front of audiences that seemed to appreciate his work, although they were far from Broadway.

Steinbeck asked a lot of questions and would have asked more, but the actor didn't wish to wear out his welcome and made a mid-afternoon exit to his own trailer.

Steinbeck had a restless night because a powerful wind came up, strong and steady, a wind he had never experienced before on either seacoast. He was concerned he would wake up to snow or that a tree would fall on Rocinante. In the morning there was a crust of frost that Charley and he crushed with their feet. The actor's trailer was dark as they drove away on an uneventful portion of the trip until they passed Bismarck.

Crossing the Missouri, Steinbeck felt he was crossing into the American West, leaving the green Bismarck side for the Mandan side of brown grass, scoured ravines, and small crops of buttes.

Coming to the Badlands, he turned off the highway onto a road of broken shale. He met two Badlanders: a not very talkative man leaning on a fence with a .22 rifle and a scrap heap of dead rabbits and small birds at his feet, and an old woman who gave him some water and talked the entire time he waited until he could make his escape; she was not a native and was terrified of the quiet desolation in which she lived.

Leaving her, Steinbeck felt afraid also, afraid of the dry land, cut and gouged, afraid the night would catch him there. Then the late afternoon sun showed him all the layered colors of the earth and his fear left. That night the stars seemed brilliantly close. The temperature plunged and he had to get out his insulated underwear, but the next morning he realized he had developed a fondness for the Badlands.

I was a long way from the rugged Badlands. Instead, a vast plain stretched out in front of me.

Steinbeck skimmed across the "thumb" of Idaho, where he thought the air was milder due to the inland travels of the wind over the Japanese Current. While waiting for Charley to do his business, Steinbeck tried to recall hearing or seeing anyone on his travels so far who wasn't afraid to show some guts or display his convictions in public. He could only recall two things—both fistfights and both over women.

He stayed at a cabin and ate ham and beans in the owner's kitchen where he found himself in the middle of an argument: the twenty-year-old son wanted to go to New York City to be a hairdresser; his father was opposed. Steinbeck handed the father a line about how he had studied hairdressers and discovered how important and powerful they were in a community because they knew all the women's secrets. The father then became enthusiastic about his son's chosen career. That night Steinbeck felt guilty for interfering in something not his business.

Charley became ill during the night, so the next morning Steinbeck rushed him to a vet in Spokane, who gave him some pills, but whose attitude made Steinbeck disgusted.

Steinbeck smelled his ocean—the Pacific—long before he hit Seattle. He remembered a much smaller Seattle that was almost quaint in comparison to the bustling, building, bulldozing, busy metropolis the city had become. He found solace in the old port section which hadn't changed that much, but he was afraid it represented what most modern American cities had become: a vibrant outer ring surrounding the older inner city which was foundering into decay and despair.

He stayed in a modern motor court until Charley felt better.

On a rainy Sunday afternoon in Oregon, his right rear tire blew, and while changing it, he saw a huge bulge on his left rear. After creeping along at five miles per hour for what seemed like forty years, Steinbeck pulled into a little town where everything was closed, but one old service station. The owner didn't have his size, but made several phone calls and located two tires. Another call sent his brother-in-law into the rain to get them, and after four hours Steinbeck was on his way. He gave the owner a large tip.

In southern Oregon he stopped in a grove of giant redwoods, thinking the huge trees would be a dog's paradise. Charley ignored them, sprinkling a weed, a sapling, and a bush. Even when Steinbeck pointed Charley's face up along the trunk, the dog showed no interest. Finally, Steinbeck cut a small willow twig, placed it against the redwood's trunk, called Charley over, and the dog did his business to the great satisfaction of the author.

They stayed two days in the land of the woody giants. Steinbeck ruminated over their age and thought that perhaps the reason people were so quiet in their shadows was because the trees reminded them of the great age of the earth and the slow passage of time which was oblivious to humans.

Northern California was his native country, and as he saw all the detritus of human development that littered the landscape of his boyhood, he felt resentment toward the newcomers who had created it.

San Francisco had been "The City" to him ever since he was a child, and he lingered to drink in its magnificent setting—the hills, the Bay, the Golden Gate—before hurrying south to cast his absentee ballot in Monterey.

His family had been Republican, but Steinbeck had been a Democrat since the 1920s, and his conversion caused problems with his sisters who still supported the GOP. After arguing politics bitterly with his sisters, he explored the town where he had spent part of his young adulthood. Eventually, he went to Johnny Garcia's bar. Johnny wanted him to leave New York and come back to Monterey, but Steinbeck told him it was too late for that—most of the places he had known were too changed, and most of the people he had known were dead. He quoted author Thomas Wolfe's statement as a true one: "You Can't Go Home Again."

He drove up Fremont's Peak and viewed the Salinas Valley, where he grew up; the town of Salinas, Mount Toro, and Monterey Bay. As a boy had had wanted to be buried on Fremont's Peak to be close to the things he loved. On that day, he saw that as a boyish romantic inclination and fled down the mountain and hurried out of California as quickly as he could go, via Fresno, Bakersfield, and the Mojave Desert.

Taking stock of his journey (which he viewed as a personal and unique experience) at that point, he claimed that he had met no strangers: he saw his own American qualities reflected in every geographical and ethnic group he met; Americans are like other Americans more than they are like any other group; despite sectionalism and ethnic diversity, we had become a single American nation, unlike any other under the sun.

He decided to cut the time he would spend on the second half of his journey and limit his in-depth time to Texas and the Deep South.

Driving the dry Mojave Desert was a frightening experience. The heat, the lack of moisture, the secret places, the struggle for life were all terrifying. Perhaps if Man destroyed most of the Earth with his bombs and other weapons, life could begin again in the desert, maybe it could be engendered again just as the great thoughts of the monotheistic religions and the impressive thoughts of order and unity might push out of the sands, just as they did in older times.

He crossed the Colorado River into Arizona, and camped in the canyon on the Continental Divide in New Mexico, where he found the pile of thousands of broken whiskey and gin bottles and the piece of mica, which he pocketed.

The Interstate passed between some glacial leftovers: some snaky eskers to the north and some mounded kames to the south.

I hadn't read much of Steinbeck until I went to college. Grandma Margaret had a collection of his short stories with a brown cover called *The Long Valley*, and several years after her death I read the stories. Some of them were hard to understand—"The Murder" described Jim Moore, who married a Slavic woman named Jelka, who didn't seem to have much time for him. He caught Jelka and her cousin in bed together and shot and killed the cousin. He got off because of the "unwritten law," went home and beat his wife with a bullwhip, after which she made him breakfast and paid more attention to him. What kind of woman was that? "St. Katy the Virgin" was about a pig that became a Christian. Some I didn't care for—"The Snake" in which a doctor and a tall woman watch a rattlesnake kill a rat in a cage, and "The Raid" in which Dick and Root, a couple of Marxist labor organizers, attempt to hold a meeting of workers and are beaten up by a mob, even though Root calls them "Comrades." Dick quotes Marx: "Religion is the opium of the people," which upset me. The stories I liked had vivid descriptions of the geography of the places involved—"Flight" was about Pepe Torres, a nineteen-year-old who rides into town from his home on the Monterey coast on an errand for his mother and ends up killing a man with his knife. His mother gives him provisions and he tries to escape by heading into the mountains. Steinbeck's description of the mountains, rocks, vegetation, and animals seems so real it's like you are there riding alongside Pepe; or "The Red Pony," a sad, three-part story of a boy, ten-year old Jody, his love for his pony and his relationships with ranch hand Billy Buck and with his father. I liked the authenticity of Steinbeck's description of the ranch and life on it.

I should have read more Steinbeck. Mom and I had watched the 1940 Henry Fonda-John Ford film *The Grapes of Wrath* on late-night TV. In college the History Department and the English Department collaborated in showing the film in the Student Union, and that piqued my interest in reading the novel.

When I taught in western North Dakota, one of my students told me her Dad had known Steinbeck in California. When he was writing *The Grapes of Wrath*, he would grab a bottle of wine, go sit under a tree, and write. Whether that was true or not, any drinking he did seemed not to have affected his work. It all seemed so authentic to me, probably because he had lived with the Oakies to experience what they had experienced in their trek from Oklahoma to California. When the Joads put a con-rod in the engine of a car, Steinbeck's description is so vivid, it's like you are there, handing Tom a wrench.

I liked much of the book: the opening description of the effects of the drought in Oklahoma, the wind, the sun, the dust; the way Muley Graves decides to stay behind in Oklahoma and fight the authorities; the scene when Ma Joad had to burn some of her little trinkets and treasures because she couldn't take them to California; the descriptions of the abandoned houses and how they were disintegrating; Highway 66 and the people traveling on it; the story of Mae the waitress and Al the cook who helped out some Okies, and how the truck drivers overheard and left Mae big tips; the way Tom told the one-eyed man to quit feeling sorry for himself, to get cleaned up, and leave the job and boss he hated; the terrible conditions that caused little kids to die of malnutrition; and the way Uncle John sent the body of Rose of Sharon's dead baby down the river to send a message about how bad things were in America.

I agreed with Tom when he said, "I'm just tryin' to get along without shovin' nobody around" and Casy the preacher: "On'y one thing in this worl' I'm sure of, an' that's I'm sure nobody got a right to mess with a fella's life."

I didn't care for Steinbeck's pantheism: the preacher, "Maybe all men got one big soul ever'body's a part of." Tom tells Ma about Casy, "…he foun' he jus' got a little piece of a great big soul. Says a wilderness ain't no good, 'cause his little piece of a soul wasn't no good 'less it was with the rest, an' was whole." The belief in pantheism says God is everything. So is evil in God, or isn't it evil at all, but some kind of good? Casy says, "There ain't no sin and there ain't no virtue. There's just stuff people do. It's all part of the same thing. And some of the things folks do is nice, and some ain't nice, but that's as far as any man got a right to say."

So severe child molestation "ain't nice"?

Steinbeck was wrong in his left-wing view that capitalists caused the Great Depression and that the federal government was the answer. The intervention of the federal government via Hoover and later FDR and the New Deal exacerbated and lengthened the Depression far beyond what it would have been under laissez-faire capitalism.

I had been traveling over ground moraine, smoothed to some extent by the glacier, but which still had some rolling features. Then there was a slight decline on either side of the Interstate, and I had passed over an ancient beach of Lake Agassiz.

Lake Agassiz was the largest fresh-water lake ever formed. The Red River Valley in North Dakota and Minnesota was covered by the southern arm of the lake; the vast majority of the lake spread out in what became Manitoba, Ontario, and Saskatchewan.

The glaciers of the Wisconsin glaciation slid down the already-made valley and as they melted back, a lake was formed behind the ice that acted as a block. The melt-back continued and the lake grew. Icy water spilled off the glacier; rivers poured in silt-laden water. Eventually, drainage overcame the addition of water, and the lake shrank in size. The glacier re-advanced, then retreated, leaving an end moraine, which was now a small rise between Grand Forks and Fargo. Storms on the big lake blew the icebergs calved from the glacier generally in a northwest to southeast direction, the bergs dragging bottom as they reached shallow water and leaving deep drag-gouges in the earth.

Hundreds of years of clayey silt settled on the lake floor; sand and gravel beachlines were thrown up by storms and wave action. The glacier melted back to the north and the lake began draining more furiously. It eventually left the Red River Valley and slowly vegetation moved onto the clay.

Thousands of years of dying vegetation formed a rich, dark humus on the clay base; more vegetation moved in, but the grass was predominant. Not the puny grass I saw in the ditches, but six-foot giant spears, thick enough to hide a buffalo.

I crossed four more beachlines, the last one the most prominent, and I was in the Red River Basin, "Valley" being too restrictive a term for the vast flat expanse of some of the world's richest farmland that surrounded me.

The fondness Steinbeck felt for the Badlands was nothing compared to his feelings for Montana, which he loved—its grandeur, its mountains, its grasslands, its people, who still spoke with a regional speech and lived in towns of neighborliness. He visited the Little Big Horn battlefield, Yellowstone National Park (where Charley went crazy whenever he saw or smelled a bear), and crossed the Great Divide.

Well, I loved the flatlands where the view from horizon to horizon was unobstructed, except for some shelterbelts and farm buildings. I liked to see what was coming at me. I had taken a trip to California, and I felt trapped in the Rockies, hemmed in by granite and evergreens, sometimes a cloven rock wall on one side and a sheer-drop chasm on the other. Not seeing, not knowing, what was around the bend left me uneasy, and I could hardly wait to leave the peaks and drops behind.

I raced east on the flat basin floor where the tallest "trees" were the power poles, and the highest "hills" were the cloverleaf bridges on the highway, averaging about one every two miles. Shelterbelts were thick and still green, the farm yards were filled with substantial buildings, and the crops verged on harvest. Even during the Dust Bowl years, when the western part of the state was covered in wind-sifted dirt, farmers in the

Valley never knew a crop failure. Six inches of black humus laid down over the lake clay and propitious rainfall saw to that.

Ahead I could see the outlines of West Fargo and then the "Queen City of North Dakota," Fargo. I curved south of West Fargo, hanging like a five thousand-soul growth onto its larger neighbor, past what once was South West Fargo, and then onto a small stretch of the north-south Interstate, turning off on University into a south-side neighborhood. I took a right to Lindenwood Park and another right down 5th Street until I saw my brother Boy on a ladder repairing the soffit on his ranch-style house. Sunday rest didn't mean much to him.

When he heard my bike in the driveway, he looked over and yelled, "Chris!" He dropped off the ladder and walked over, extending his hand. Even at forty-one he was still a handsome man. We shook. "What's wrong?"

"Nothin'. I'm headin' for New Orleans and thought I'd just stop by."

"Wait a minute." He headed for the house. "Sandy, come on out here."

A blond woman appeared in the doorway. "Why, Chris!" She came out, followed by her daughters, Cheryl, who would be a sophomore at NDSU, and Christine, who was seventeen and was about to begin her junior year at Fargo South. Their son Dennis had graduated from NDSU and was working as an engineer in St. Paul.

Boy said, "He's headed for New Orleans."

"What? Isn't that a little dangerous, Chris?" There was concern in Sandy's voice.

"I'll be careful."

Always shy, Cheryl and Christine just smiled.

"How's the folks?" Boy asked.

"Good. Dad's gettin' a little slower, but good."

A couple cars went by, and the neighbor family came out with a picnic basket and walked across 5th into the park.

"Are you hungry? Do you want to eat?" Sandy was still concerned.

"No. I've got to get goin'. I want to stop at Tom's."

Boy gave me a hug. "Good luck, Chris."

Sandy and the girls followed suit, but silently.

I fired up the bike and rolled down the driveway. "God bless you," Sandy called over the sound of the motor.

I waved and four hands went up. I didn't look back.

I turned west opposite the entry to the park and passed the comfortable homes of south Fargo, some with fenced lots and some bragging about their well-kept lawns they showed to the public. I crossed University, not very busy on the day of rest. I passed an elementary school on my left, Fargo South on my right, and turned south onto another comfortable street.

Fargo South was a new school, built in 1966 after Fargo Central up on 2nd Avenue South, caught fire and burned. Luckily, there were no casualties even though it was April and school was on.

My brother Tom, his wife Joan, both in their mid-thirties, and their kids—Debbie, sixteen, Linda, fifteen, and Karen, thirteen—were just getting into their 1968 Matador Red Chevy Impala with the recessed triple horseshoe taillights and the 396 c.i. V-8 engine, which Joan thought was too much power for a family car, but knowing Tom, I thought she was lucky he didn't buy the 427.

Tom's pride was his yard, just as Boy's was his house. The grass, drying a little with the spare rain of August, was still a generous green, testimony to fertilizer and sweat. Three red barberry shrubs were spaced out in front of the house and two shrubs which Tom had told me were called burning bush sentineled the driveway; in the fall the red foliage would stand out amidst all the yellows we have in North Dakota.

When Tom saw me, he got out and called my name. "What're ya doin' here? Is everything all right?"

"Sure. Fine. I'm on my way to New Orleans."

"You're kidding!" Joan, her white teeth set off by her dark brown hair and a tan, smiled.

The girls came up and greeted me, looking over the Honda with faces that ranged from "You're nuts!" to "Wish I was going, too."

After explaining that Mom and Dad were fine, I said I had to get moving.

"Have you eaten?" Linda asked. "The Bowler has a Sunday special and we're going. You're welcome to come, too."

"Thanks, but I just stopped to say hello. I want to make Sioux Falls by dark."

Tom said, "You'd better get movin' then" and gave me a hug. Joan and my nieces followed, which was somewhat awkward since I was straddling my bike. I waved as I pulled out of the driveway, and they returned it and headed for the Impala.

In many ways Boy and Tom were my idols. They had both served in Korea and still kept in the same shape they had in the Army. When my cousin Theresa had been molested by a neighbor almost ten years prior, Boy and Tom had been instruments of justice, exacting punishment on the molester when the law had failed, and allowing me and Theresa's brother Rory to be a part of it. I would be forever grateful.

Theresa was twelve now, a delicate girl. I would do anything for her. Especially if it would make her well.

Back on University I turned into a Standard Station and gassed up. It took me north, out of my way, but I liked supporting the company founded by John D. Rockefeller, a man vilified as a "Robber Baron," but who brought cheaper kerosene and gasoline to the public and whose company greatly reduced the slaughter of whales by reducing the demand for whale oil used for lighting.

Rockefeller's Dad, William Avery Rockefeller, had a screw loose and abandoned his family. He traveled the country as a con artist, mountebank, bigamist, and charlatan and once had lived in northeastern North Dakota under the name of Dr. William Levingston, claiming he could cure cancer. Rumor had it that Rockefeller sent detectives to North Dakota, where they kidnapped "Big Bill" Rockefeller and kept him hidden under a false name and out of the public limelight until he died in 1906 in Illinois.

After I read about John D. Rockefeller's family life, I was glad Dad wasn't anything like his Dad.

North Dakota's Sunday-closing law allowed restaurants and gas stations to remain open on the Lord's Day. I didn't have time to eat in a restaurant, so after I filled my tank, I went into the station and got some cookies, chips, and pop. While I was eating, a song came on the radio.

Whenever Tommy, Clyde, and I were working, we had a small radio always on in the boiler room. In late June a song came on just as we were finishing our lunch. The other two left, but I stayed and listened to Karen Carpenter singing "(They Long to Be) Close to You" for the first time.

Now she was singing it again. What a voice, and what inspired instrumentation. "Close to You" was number one on the charts that I still kept, ones that I started in high school.

After the song finished, I shoved off into some moderate traffic, heading south. There was no Interstate south of Fargo, so I would have to take the regular U.S. highway. I crossed over the east-west Interstate, which had been completed all across North Dakota, but which ended just to the east of Moorhead, and up ahead on my left loomed the Bowler. I picked out Tom's Impala in the parking lot.

Fargo was starting to build south of the Interstate, but there wasn't much beyond the Bowler. A dark line of trees marked the river to the east. I passed over a creek almost obscured by the reeds along its sides. The Red River snaked in bends east and west, sometimes within eighty yards of the highway. The fertile farmland spread out, waiting to be gobbled up by the city. The unused Milwaukee Road right-of-way ran beside the highway. It continued into South Dakota and then tailed off into Minnesota through Wheaton and Graceville to Ortonville, where it tied into the main line.

"Close to you." Boy and Tom were both married and raising families. My sister Barbara and her husband Jim were the parents of seven-year old twins, and my sister Marjorie and her husband Mike were raising a five-year old and were expecting a second child.

Everyone was close to someone, except me.

Alix Hall was a freshman when I developed a deep crush on her. She was so small, she looked like a tiny princess when she walked down the halls of Menninger High School, always dressed up in fine clothes and driving me crazy with her deep brown eyes and russet hair, which was always precisely arranged. Finally, I got up enough courage to ask her out, but when I called her, she told me she was going steady with Joey Carson. My humiliation was complete when her girlfriends started laughing at me in school.

She had gone to the University in Grand Forks and gotten married a month after she graduated. She and her husband were living in Fargo, and I had seen in the *Menninger Messenger* that they had a son. A least I had the satisfaction of knowing that she hadn't married Joey Carson, whom I still disliked.

I crossed the Folles Homme River with trees crowding the bridge.

I'd had a crush on Dotty, too, but it had grown into a friendship that continued even after her marriage to a guy I knew wasn't worthy of her. Then there was BethAnn, a flame that burned, flickered, and died.

Off to the west I saw a sign advertising a bar and pointing to a huddle of buildings which was Otisville a half mile away. Like the other villages on the old Milwaukee, Otisville was being sucked dry by Fargo.

At Minot State College I became friendly with Patty Lloyd, a blue-eyed blonde who was the most politically oriented woman I ever knew. Her Dad was an organizer for the John Birch Society and ran the American Opinion Bookstore on Main Street South.

I was double majoring in English and History, and she was a History major, so we had several classes together, lively classes because she was always challenging the professors, while in most of my classes the students tried to emulate the three wise monkeys by being blind, deaf, and mute.

I finally got up enough nerve to ask her out, and she said yes, but I had to meet her father. That was an ordeal I hadn't gone through before because BethAnn's father was dead.

Dad had told me to stay clear of the John Birch Society because of their accusations that many prominent Americans, such as Dwight D. Eisenhower, were tools of the Communist Conspiracy.

Bricker Lloyd was a young-looking man in his forties. After we got through the small talk—where I was from, my family, my major—we got down to the important stuff.

"What do you think of Communism?"

Patty had warned me to be ready.

"Communism, especially in its Marxist variety, is a heinous philosophy of godless materialism blended with an unworkable and ignorant economic theory and attached to a false theory of history which, if it ever were fully implemented, would lead to a dystopia of mass starvation and monumental oppression."

Bricker Lloyd stared at me for a long time.

"Son, I like you. 'Heinous philosophy', huh? I'll have to remember that one."

Patty was beaming.

"You believe in a Communist Conspiracy, don't you?"

"You mean where they infiltrate a society before taking it over? Yes."

"That's good. Not too many your age do. Has it happened in the U.S.?"

"Yes." When I was a kid I had listened to Fulton Lewis, Jr., a Mutual Broadcasting commentator on KRSW in Sacred Water at 6 P.M. just about every weekday, and he was big into the Communist Conspiracy. I was even more convinced after Mom and Dad gave me *Witness* by Whittaker Chambers for my sixteenth birthday. Chambers was a *Time* magazine editor who had been a Soviet spy in the Thirties, but who had defected. In 1948 he testified under oath that Alger Hiss and some others who worked in the federal government had spied for the Soviet Union. He backed these claims in his memoir *Witness*, which became a best-seller in 1952. It took me six months to wade through the book, but I came away convinced that Communists had been active in the federal government

"What do you think of Dwight Eisenhower?"

"Well, he was a great administrative general. I don't think he won any battles himself, but he organized things so other could win them."

"No, I mean was he a Communist?'

That was the question I had been dreading. "No, I don't."

He gave me the stare again. "What about his brother Milton?"

I'd never heard of him, but I answered, "No."

"Chief Justice Earl Warren?"

"No."

"Ambassador to the United Nations Adlai Stevenson?"

"No."

He stared again. "I thought you said you believed in the Communist Conspiracy?"

"I do."

"Well, I just named some of its biggest members, and you don't believe any of them are Commies. Either Commies or fellow travelers."

Patty looked distressed.

"Don't you believe there were Communists in the federal government?"

"Yes."

"Who?"

I thought back to Fulton Lewis, Jr. "Alger Hiss, the Rosenbergs, and that guy in the Treasury."

"Harry Dexter White."

"Yes."

"And how do you know they were Commies? They certainly didn't carry membership cards in the Communist Party."

I thought for a moment. "By what they did."

"Such as?"

"Hiss passed State Department documents to the Soviets, the Rosenbergs gave our atomic secrets to the Soviets, and White advised

FDR at the Yalta Conference, where we gave Eastern Europe over to Soviet domination."

"Good. So 'by their works ye shall know them,' as St. Matthew says."

"That's right."

"Then look at the works of the Eisenhowers, Warren, and Stevenson. Do they help or hurt the Commies? Are the Reds stronger now or when Eisenhower took office in 1953? Plus, Eisenhower appointed Warren as Chief Justice, and the Warren Court has consistently voted to strengthen the federal government as opposed to the state governments so the Commies will have an easier time with their subversion—just one government instead of fifty. The Court has allowed the federal government to intervene, not just in school desegregation cases like it did in *Brown*, but in search warrant cases. It also extended the right not to testify before a congressional committee in the *Watkins* case, so Commies will be shielded. Now in *Engel vs. Vitale* Warren's court said that prayer in school is unconstitutional. What more proof do you need Warren's an atheistical Communist?

"When Stevenson was governor of Illinois, he vetoed a bill that would have required public employees to sign a loyalty oath to the United States, and he was a character witness for Alger Hiss."

It all seemed to make a sort of convoluted sense to me, but it was a kind of Alice in Wonderland logic.

"Who's your hero?"

I wondered if that was a trick question. "Mickey Mantle."

"No, I mean a political hero."

"Barry Goldwater."

"That's not bad. Could be a lot worse. What about Senator Joe McCarthy?"

Again it was Fulton Lewis, Jr., to the rescue. "I think he pointed out, correctly, that Communists had infiltrated the federal government and were acting as Soviet agents, but he also tarred some people with a very wide broom, people who weren't Communists."

"What else?"

"He was a veteran, World War II; he got in trouble with the U.S. Army over his charges of Communism and finally the Senate voted to censure him; he drank himself to death."

I could see Patty cringing.

"Well, son, he was a war hero; the Army with Eisenhower's connivance did attack him; the Senate condemned him; it wasn't a censure; and someone poisoned him, but it wasn't alcohol. I think you should do more reading on McCarthy and maybe it will elevate him in your estimation. Right now, I think we've talked long enough. I can see you young people are ready to leave on your date."

Patty let me go out to the car—a 1949 Ford a friend had sold to me for a dollar when he was leaving Menninger. Mom didn't think it was reliable enough for me to drive to Minot and back on a regular basis, so I didn't have a car for the first few weeks of college, but then Dad had a mechanic at the Ford dealership go over everything and convinced Mom it would be all right.

I waited and opened the car door for Patty. When I got in, she smiled. "Dad likes you." That was a relief; I thought he hated me.

"How can you tell?"

"He said so."

"What did he say?"

She hesitated a second and then said, "Well, he said you were a cut above most of the boys I had brought home and at least you knew something about politics."

"Anything else?"

"Yes. He said you would be a major reclamation project before you would be fully politically developed."

We were going over the Broadway overpass. I decided to let that remark die. We found a parking spot just off Main and walked to the Empire Theatre, where I bought tickets for *Dr. No*, the first of the James Bond films and starring Sean Connery, the best Bond ever.

I was surprised that Patty liked the movie; I didn't think most girls would because of the killing. I enjoyed the movie—the action, the scenery, the way Bond carried himself in any society, and Ursula Andress as "Honey Rider," but I was disappointed that the Soviets weren't shown as allies of Dr. No, so that Bond's victory over No would have been a victory over the Soviets, too.

In the Ian Fleming novel the movie was based on, Dr. No and the Russians are allies. I hadn't read any of the Bond novels, but two of my college friends—Robert Dahl and Red Scoby—had, and Robert loaned me his copy when we heard the movie was coming to Minot.

I didn't even attempt to kiss Patty goodnight, afraid her Dad was lurking behind the living room curtains. We had several other dates, and I would have pushed our relationship further, but she said she liked me as a friend, but was not going to get serious about any boy while she was in college.

Christmas came and went and when there was no talk about presents, I knew we were friends and nothing more.

Besides something happened during that Christmas break which had me thinking about a girl other than Patty.

North Dakota had been petrified by an Arctic blast, and vehicles had been immobilized in campus parking lots by the glacial temperatures. I could walk from Forge to Old Main through a tunnel, but if I had classes in any other building, my lungs would be burning with cold fire before I went ten feet.

The '49 wouldn't start after I'd packed up to go home, but Robert and Red brought a can of ether, pulled off the air filter housing, and squirted the ether into the carburetor. After some coaxing, the motor fired up.

I thanked them, wished them Merry Christmas, and sat behind the wheel, waiting for the car to warm up.

Robert and Red ran back to start their own cars. Usually, only one of them would drive home to Banks and then they'd trade off the next time, thus saving on gas. Sometimes other students from Banks would ride with them, but they liked it when they had only one passenger, Suellen Chaffee.

Suellen always rode between them, and after they had talked for awhile and were out of the Minot-area traffic, she'd yawn, say she was tired, and go to "sleep." Soon Robert's and Red's hands were exploring second base, and that kept up until the boys got tired of it. They never dared attempt to steal third. A minute or so after they quit, Suellen would "wake up," and the trip would continue as if nothing unusual had happened. The same thing occurred on the way from Banks to Minot; it never got old.

I stopped by Rose Hall and picked up two girls from Calvin City and another two from Menninger at White Hall. Charging them two dollars apiece would pay for my gas.

A couple days after I got home, I was in Amazon Lanes when Phil Archer, a high school classmate, came in. After we compared notes (he was going to Fertile Valley State Teachers College) and reminisced a bit, he said he was going to Caseyville to buy a present for his girl, Janelle Leland, who was a senior at MHS. I didn't even know they were going together.

We took the Gold Star, and he honked at the Lonely Tree, keeping up the tradition, as the other-worldly sound of "Telstar" by the Tornadoes came from the radio. It was an O.K. song, but couldn't compare with some others we heard: "Return to Sender" by Elvis, "Love Came to Me" by Dion, "He's a Rebel" by the Crystals, and "Half Heaven— Half Heartache" by Gene Pitney. However, it was significantly better than Lou Monte's "Pepino the Italian Mouse" and David Seville's "The Chipmunk Song."

Phil pulled off Main and stopped in front of Webb's Department Store; he said it would be about twenty minutes, so I told him I'd be back then. I walked to Main and crossed over. There was a huge stone bank on the corner and a drug store one door down. I headed for the drug store for no conscious reason.

The door was an old-fashioned heavy wood and glass affair, and just as I got ready to shove on it, someone opened it. My heart crashed out of my chest, careened back into place, and my breath slowly returned.

The "someone" was BethAnn Borgan, a girl I had gone with for part of my senior year. Our parting was not pretty.

Her brown eyes smoldered. My breathing failed me, but I managed to croak out a hello. She held the door open for me. "Hello." Her voice was firm. I walked inside and the door closed. I watched her green winter coat turn west and disappear.

I wandered over to the counter. BethAnn was a girl I had almost loved, maybe I had loved her. Maybe she'd give me another chance. I had fifteen minutes to find out. I ran to the door. Two steps and I was on the sidewalk. No green coat; no BethAnn. I looked in the Ice Cream Shoppe, Jack's Café, and every store, but the Cloverleaf Bar, then I crossed the street and repeated the process.

BethAnn was gone and I was alone.

I climbed into Phil's car and waited. We hardly spoke on the way home.

I thought a lot about BethAnn after that—what our lives would have been like if we had stayed together. I dreamed about her several times, but the dreams faded. What didn't fade were the memories when I heard certain songs: "April Love" by Pat Boone, which had been "our song"; "Cry, Baby, Cry" by the Angels, which we had listened to on our first date; "Johnny Angel" by Shelley Fabares, which she had dedicated to me on the radio. Those songs would bring up a picture of BethAnn, her brown hair and eyes and memories of how nice a person she was.

And she was always smiling.

All the survey history classes were taught by my advisor, Professor Edwin Nord. In American History 101 we studied from the beginning to the Civil War, so Patty didn't have much to challenge the professor about, but in American History 102 we went from the Civil War to World War II and in American History 103 from the end of the war to the present. That's when Patty hit her stride.

She attacked the Progressives as proto-Communists, went after President Woodrow Wilson and his shadowy advisor Colonel House, and when we came to FDR and the New Deal, it was Katy-bar-the-door. When she called Franklin Roosevelt a "crypto-Communist," Professor Nord forbade her from speaking in class.

Bricker appealed to the faculty council, and they supported him, reluctantly, forcing Nord to back down in the name of academic freedom. However, Nord had the last laugh because he refused to acknowledge Patty whenever she raised her hand with a question or comment.

That spring something happened that drove a wedge between us for awhile, and it wasn't anything political—it was hormonal.

There were four dorms on the campus—Forge Hall and Great Plains Hall for the men and Prairie Rose Hall and Nancy R. White Hall for the women. Forge and Plains were open twenty-four hours a day, but they did have a faculty resident and his family on the first floor and two student proctors on each of the other floors to maintain decorum. Rose Hall and White Hall were open from 7 A.M. to 10 P.M. and then locked by the house mothers. Female students could still get admitted by ringing a bell until 11 P.M. Sunday through Thursday and 1 A.M. on Fridays and Saturdays.

Male students could be escorted to the lounge area and converse with a young lady if at least one other female was in the room. No one of the opposite sex was allowed in any room in any of the dorms. Virtue ruled.

The indiscrete college women were virtuous enough to keep their indiscretions off-campus, but most of them maintained their virtue to the point their Daddies would be proud—no drinking, no smoking, and nothing beyond second base.

That situation worked well for the girls who felt little or no pressure to give in to a guy who may or may not be "the one," but it played havoc with the libidos of the boys. During the long cold winter, things seemed to be under control, but when spring came, the sap began flowing in the trees and the boys simultaneously.

In early May the hormonal sap reached its boiling point. Word was passed the jocks, especially the football players and the wrestlers, were planning something big.

A week or so later the word took shape—panty raid!

Now every guy on campus had seen bras and panties before—in ads, in the laundry at home—but there was just something so illicit and exciting about bras and panties carefully laid away in dorm room drawers by virgins (that's how we implicitly saw the girls, warranted or not) that a fever swept over the contingent of love-starved males. We couldn't wait for the signal.

Finally it came: tonight!

At first-dark the jocks sauntered out onto the porch of Forge, then slowly the rest of us gathered below them. We stood around, anticipating, but nothing happened. The jocks milled around on the large porch, sometimes whispering among themselves. We lesser beings waited; we weren't going to do anything without the jocks.

Waiting wore a hole in the fabric of time; our enthusiasm started to drain.

I was in a group—Robert and Red; Bradley from the Pine Tree Ranch down on the Garrison Reservoir; Pete, the son of a postmaster from Nutting south of Minot; and my roommate Tommie Hart from Divide ten miles north of Menninger. We called ourselves the "Forge Five plus One," but could never decide who the "One" was.

Robert said, "Let's get goin'."

Red chipped in, "Yeah, this is boring."

No one answered. The waiting continued; dark time crawled by. Finally, Pete said, "I'm leavin'" and started to move to the porch steps. He was passed on the first step by a large shape which the jocks greeted with subdued cheers.

It was the "Big Goose," the center on the football team. Jimmy Dean sang about "Big Bad John," who stood six-foot six and weighed two forty-five. Well, Big Goose stood six-foot six and weighed two ninety-five.

Two minutes after his arrival, Big Goose was leading a charge of cheering, yelling, howling, testosterone-filled boys across the campus toward the girls' dorms. The Forge Five plus One ran as a unit; my stomach was electric. Rebel-yells came from some of the Southern boys.

Across the west leg of the semi-circular drive that went from 9th Avenue to Old Main and back to the street. Pounding the spring grass past the flag pole, Old Main to our left, seeming to glare down on our escapade. Across the east leg of the drive and the NORMAL SCHOOL bench, and there it was, our El Dorado of sexual fantasy.

Of course when we reached Rose Hall, the front door was securely locked, and Big Goose was not about to shoulder it open: he may have lacked some intelligence (Robert and Tommie had to tutor him in Biology), but he had enough good sense not to jeopardize his scholarship.

When the elderly house mother came to the door and saw him just outside and several hundred young men backing him up, she yelled through the glass that we had to leave; her girls were trying to sleep.

Actually, that might have been true on a normal school night, but the girls had gotten wind of the raid, and they were not about to sleep through it. Looking up, we saw windows open and young women fluttering their "unmentionables" in the breeze and yelling for us to come and get them.

The leaders of a smaller group of raiders that had gone on to White Hall reported the same prison-like situation. It appeared that our raid was a flop.

It didn't help when the girls stopped yelling for us to get their underthings and began taunting us with names like "chickens," "dummies," "dip sticks," and from some of the more daring ones, "candy asses."

Necessity may be the mother of invention, but humiliation, especially by the opposite sex, produces results, too.

Rose Hall appeared invulnerable, but White Hall was newer and had a chink in its anti-male armor. Steel awnings projected over the doorways, offering some slight protection from the rain. There was a window above each awning.

Robert had wrestled in high school and was solidly muscled, but he stood just 5'7" and was smaller than most of the crowd. When Big Goose saw his tutor, he came over. "Hey, Toot, I need you. C'mere." They walked over to the awning and Goose boosted Robert up. "Now try the window."

Robert tried. "It's locked." Goose let loose an expletive. "Wait, there's someone coming... It's a couple girls...They're opening the window." A couple seconds later Robert disappeared inside.

All of us cheered, then the cheers died out as we waited. Suddenly, the door flew open, and Robert emerged with bras and panties hanging from his arms, neck, hands, and stuffed in his pockets. Right behind him was the house mother, who fetched him a blow across the back with a broom that sent him sprawling.

Seizing the opportunity, several raiders sprinted past the woman, who must have been a muleskinner earlier in life, based on the language she was screaming. A line formed, pushing past the apoplectic woman and into the dorm, but before I got inside, a police car pulled into the parking lot and a couple officers and the Dean of Men emerged.

They were met by quite a sight: a hysterical house mother clutching a broom; male students rushing into forbidden zones, running rampant, and emerging looking like bizarre lingerie mannequins; female students waving and tossing their underthings out of windows; and worst of all, girls outside the dorms after curfew.

The Dean was a nice man with kids of his own. He had addressed us at our freshman convo the previous fall and had come across as genuinely caring about us and our successful acclimation to campus life at the same college he had attended. But that night he was out of his depth, and the meager police presence was no deterrent.

He got out a bullhorn and spoke into it, but no one listened. For another five minutes he made repeated attempts to no avail.

Most of us didn't go into the dorm, preferring to cheer on those who did. Besides, the Rose and White girls were joining us outside.

Even freshly laundered, multi-colored lingerie loses its appeal eventually, so things would have quieted down on their own, but after while we could hear the Dean's bullhorn-enhanced voice telling us we were breaking the law and that we had to return to our dorms. When he began calling out the names of the individuals he recognized, there was a murmur, especially among the jocks, fearful of repercussions that could threaten their athletic careers, and many of us began to move.

Some headed back to Forge and Plains; however, most of us moved through the trees to Broadway. That was our mistake: we had left behind the protection of the campus and began brazenly to challenge the Minot Police Force on their own turf.

Several hundred of us sauntered down Broadway toward the business district. There were even dozens of the braver girls.

As we got closer to the viaduct over the Mouse River and the railroad tracks, we saw lights and police cars at its crest. The cops were making a stand.

Some of the weaker-hearted turned back to the campus. Others milled around at the base of the viaduct, talking about what to do next. Around fifty of us headed east to a wooden footbridge that led to downtown.

After we crossed over, we divided into smaller groups. The Forge Five plus One stayed together. Two cop cars screamed around the head of the block and screeched to a sliding halt some fifty yards from us. Two officers piled out of each car.

I thought I saw Patty go into a restaurant two doors ahead, but when I looked in the window, I saw it wasn't.

I looked across the street and two of Minot's finest were chasing down a couple college students. Then I saw the two other cops bearing down on us—only there was no "us."

When I turned to say something to my friends, I saw they were high-tailing it back down the block. Then someone slammed me against the restaurant, and a raspy voice growled, "You're under arrest, dickhead." It was then I realized I was the "One."

The cop jerked my right arm behind me and snapped on some handcuffs; then he did the same to the left. He pushed me toward the cop car.

Downtown Minot was infested by flashing lights and police sirens.

The cop shoved me in the backseat and waited as his partner did the same with a student I didn't know. The doors slammed and the cops took off running down the street. We could hear sirens, but didn't speak to each other. I was trying to figure a way out of what I'd gotten myself into. There were no handles on the doors.

The cops came back with two more handcuffed prisoners. Once they were safely inside, the cops got in the front seat, and the car screamed to the end of the block and turned left onto a cinder road paralleling the tracks.

Raspy Voice turned and glared through the cage. He smacked his billy club into his hand. "I pity the next young punk that tries to run away from me." We prisoners were silent.

The car left the cinders and squealed up the pavement to the police station, where it skidded to a halt.

"Get out and don't try anything!" Raspy Voice struck his palm with the billy again.

The four of us meekly entered the station, which was a chaotic mess with kids and officers all over the place. Some girls were crying. The boys looked shell-shocked. We were fingerprinted and booked; our possessions, including our belts, were itemized and placed in containers.

The arresting officers had left, to pursue more victims. The jailer led us down a corridor and put us in the bull pen with two passed-out drunks and a couple dozen college students. He was an elderly man who kept shaking his head. The only sounds he made were his shoes on the tile and "tsk! tsk!" He locked the door and left without a word. The girls were locked up somewhere else.

Everyone was explaining why they shouldn't be there. I didn't have any sympathy for those who had stayed on the campus and were arrested either in White Hall or running from it or for those who had been arrested while in the act of vandalizing property, but I thought that anyone, like me, who had merely been walking the streets of Minot had a legitimate gripe.

Four students—two boys and their dates—had just gotten out of the late movie at the Empire and were arrested walking to their car. Another four were just driving back after a double date at Skateland in south Minot when they were stopped on Broadway at the barricade and arrested when the cops found out they were college students.

Another dozen arrests were brought in and after they had told their stories, usually filled with youthful bravado, everyone began cursing the cops and then sank into silence, fighting off various fears. The drunks slept placidly on, lying on the steel bunks, snorking and snarking in their alcohol dreams.

The jailer returned and called out some names. When one of them asked why, he said, "Bailed out."

Friends of the imprisoned had come to the rescue. The dozen or so girls were bailed out first, in true gentlemanly fashion, and then they started on the boys.

At first it went quickly, but as the hours dragged by, the more popular walked through the door with words of encouragement to us lesser lights, while we waited, thinking our situation couldn't be worse. Then almost simultaneously the two drunks wet their pants, and the odor permeated the bull pen. Two of the weaker-stomached puked in the toilet.

The small hours saw one or two of us bonded out at a time until there were just three of us left. Then two. Then just me.

I decided I'd have to wait it out, so I climbed onto an upper bunk. There were no blankets or mattresses on the bunks, just the steel bed. When I put my hands on the metal bed, it was sticky with an unknown substance. I jumped down, washed my hands, and determined I'd stand for the duration. The drunks slept on.

The Forge Five didn't have the fifty dollars among them, so they angered a lot of people by pounding on doors in Forge and Plains and then over to the fraternity and sorority houses, begging for any amount. A sleepy co-ed gave them a final dollar at 6 A.M. and they were off to the police station in Robert's car.

After I signed for and picked up my personal belongings, I walked out of the booking room into the waiting room and the Forge Five and a dozen other people burst into applause. All I could do was mumble a thank you. I was so grateful I forgot to be mad that my friends had taken off, but then I realized it was my own stupid fault. I had learned a lesson: when the cops come, you run.

Pete asked me how it was, and I answered, "Not so bad." And it wasn't, except for the urine-reek, the sticky hands, and the loneliness after everyone else was gone.

We pulled up to Forge Hall and Red said, "Look." High on the flagpole, flapping in the breeze, was a white bra. When I was in high school, my friend Ronnie, my cousin Rory, and I had devised a scale to indicate the size of a girl's breasts. It ran between cherry and watermelon. The white bra was between a cantaloupe and a watermelon. We stood at attention, saluted, and ran into Forge laughing.

At 11 o'clock I wasn't laughing. Every arrested student was in a room in Old Main. First, the Dean of Men and the Dean of Women addressed us with sad looks and words of disappointment. I felt bad that we had caused them so much distress, but I wasn't that fearful. Then the college president got up.

He was an elderly gentleman who lived with his wife in a residence just across from Rose Hall. During the Raid, the house remained strangely dark, but not as dark as the look he gave us. I half-expected lightning to flash out of his forehead.

He had a ruddy complexion that went right up into his thinning hair. As the deans spoke, his complexion deepened and when he stood, he had the skin of a Pontiac potato.

"Ladies and gentlemen, and I use the terms loosely. Last night you brought shame and disgrace, not only on yourselves, but to this college. I can't do much about how you choose to live your lives, but as long as you remain a member of our campus community, by Gad, you will follow our rules."

As he warmed to his task, his voice followed suit.

"Next week finals begin. By all rights I should bar you from taking any examination and expel you from Minot State."

For the first time real fear filled my soul. Sniffling sounds told me some girls were crying, but the president was unrelenting.

"However, the deans have asked me to be lenient. I have spoken to the municipal judge and we have come to an agreement. You will appear before him, plead guilty to unlawful assembly, and he will accept your plea. As a group you will then pay restitution to any resident who suffered property damage, and you will do community service to the extent the judge requires. After completion of your sentence, your records will be expunged. This agreement is contingent on one hundred per cent cooperation. If any of you has determined to fight the case in court, the deal is off, and each of you is on your own and will be subject to the mercy of the court, which, I can assure you, will not be merciful. In addition, each of you will contact your parents and inform them of your actions. You have five minutes to give me your answer."

The three walked out of the room, which emerged from a stone-cold silence into a heated chaos of voices and tears.

I was certain of my innocence: walking on a public sidewalk, even in a small group, was not unlawful assembly. I had planned on hiring Amy Alice Buczkowski, Minot's most notorious attorney. When she and her husband divorced after she caught him and his secretary in the Parkview Motel, she took him for everything he had, including his ten-year old Golden Retriever, Andy. For several years she would take Andy for a walk in front of the rooming house where her husband lived until Andy's death. Her husband died two weeks later. She cried at Andy's funeral.

There were several others, including the couple arrested in their vehicle and the movie-goers, whose families had already hired lawyers, but the pleading and the tears wore us down.

When the three administrators walked back into the room, fragrant with sweat and fear, they knew they had won.

The hardest part of it all was calling my folks. My mother cried; my father was mostly silent; I felt sick inside.

They were there for the hearing. Each of us had to stand and admit our guilt, then the seventy-five dollars for vandalism was handed over and our punishment was handed out: we had to clean the ditches along the highway that ran up North Hill.

On the appointed Saturday morning I walked up the hill with a jug of water and a load of guilt. Once everyone was there, the police officer who seemed sympathetic (he probably had kids) and the state highway worker passed out the bags and work gloves. We divided into two groups and began working our way downhill. I was in the west ditch.

At first no one talked, still aware of our shame, but as the morning warmed, conversations developed within small groups, then between groups. At first when passing drivers honked, we ignored them, but then a few of us began to wave, and pretty soon everyone was yelling and waving, often with the "V for Victory" sign.

Except for the ache that developed in my back, the punishment was turning into fun. About half-way down, the group ahead of mine stopped and were looking at something. When we caught up, we walked over. It was a rained-on copy of *Juggs*, a skin magazine. The girls took one look, made sounds of disgust, and walked away. We guys took some time to enjoy the revealing photos of the opposite sex before the magazine went deep into a bag.

Someone found a cat, dead since the previous night, and someone else found some bones of a small animal, but no one knew what. The cat and bones remained where they lay.

By the time we reached the bottom of the hill, no one was acknowledging the honks. We threw our bags in the box of a state truck.

The Forge Five had been cruising the area for awhile, and when they saw that I was done, they stopped and I jumped in. We drove up to Harold's Hamburgers and enjoyed ten cent-burgers, but I made certain I washed my hands in scalding water and soap.

I had tests to study for so I had plenty to keep me busy. The sense of guilt faded. I began to feel that I'd had a great college experience.

Patty didn't. After our History 103 final, she was walking ahead of me. I called out for her to wait. She slowed, but didn't stop. I caught up.

"What's wrong?"

"I suppose you think you're pretty hot stuff, getting arrested on a mindless panty raid. Well, I think you are just infantile." She hurried away and I could tell she didn't want to be around me.

I had been zipping along in a straight line south over the old lakebed for a little over four miles when I went into a right-hand curve and through the village of Tyler, another stop on the old Milwaukee being drained of souls by Fargo.

Norby showed up in the distance as a couple elevators hugging the old Milwaukee right-of-way. The flat land ran away to the horizon.

I got a summer job at the Jackson & Robertson Wholesale Grocery warehouse just off the railroad tracks and only two blocks from where I had been arrested. I lived in a small walk-up apartment, and my landlords were an elderly couple who were mostly deaf, so I could play my radio as loudly as I wanted to, only I worked the graveyard shift, so when I got home a little past seven A.M., I just needed to eat breakfast and hit the sack, tuning the radio low to help me fall asleep.

To get to work, I walked across the same footbridge I had used on my fateful night.

Other than work, I did get to go to a Sun Dance on the Ft. Sully Reservation which involved one of my high school classmates known as the Horse.

I didn't see Patty at all that summer, I avoided her Dad's bookstore, and I went home to Menninger just about every weekend.

It wasn't until that fall that Patty wanted anything to do with me.

When I signed up for Journalism 250, the instructor Mrs. Heath asked me to be a political columnist for the college paper of which she was the advisor. Of course, I'd already be helping with the paper as part of the class, so I agreed.

When my first column came out, Patty suddenly reappeared. It became obvious that she wanted to have some input into my column, but I was willing to be used if I could be with her. Soon Pete, who was an officer in the College Young Republicans, joined us as we planned our next anti-Kennedy, anti-New Frontier, pro-Goldwater journalistic foray.

Although Mrs. Heath, like almost all my college professors, was a Liberal Democrat, she never censored anything that I wrote. She actually believed in the free marketplace of ideas.

The memory of my arrest receded into a deep pocket of my mind which I rarely visited. I liked my classes, my column made me a recognizable figure on campus, I enjoyed my friends, and Patty and I began dating again.

On the Friday before Thanksgiving break, I was on the second floor of Old Main, taking my American Literature final. Professor William Wallace Ross, white-haired and wrinkled, but still sharp at the age of seventy, presided.

A couple minutes after the test had started, Professor Rooney came into the room and whispered something to Professor Ross, who got up and walked with Rooney to the door, where they whispered for a few minutes.

Everyone had to remain for fifty minutes, during which time Ross sat up front, staring around the room with vacant eyes.

Just before the time was up, Rooney came back and whispered something to Ross that caused the old man to visibly jerk in his chair. Rooney hurried out. At the close of the fiftieth minute, all the tests were done and Ross collected them. Before he let us go, he announced in a quavering voice, "I have distressing news. The President has been shot. Cronkite has reported that the President is dead."

No one spoke as we left the room. There were no sounds on the second floor, except for the shoes on the stone floor. People hurried along with their heads down.

There was noise on the first floor: a professor had a television set on and there was a crowd outside the office door. I walked to the big doors, wondering if people in Lincoln's time felt as I did. Except for his stand in Vietnam and his facing off with Khrushchev over Cuba, I didn't like Kennedy's policies, but he was the President, and I felt a loyalty to the office.

Two young women on the newspaper staff came down the concourse, mascara-streaked faces twisted with pain. Both of them had framed pictures of the young President on their desks.

They caught me before I got to the door.

"I hope you're happy now he's dead!"

"It's people like you who're to blame!"

They headed for the TV room. I hesitated while the bitter-ice feeling dwindled in my stomach. I pushed my way through the big doors, between the four Doric columns, down the fifty-year old steps, and onto the sidewalk.

I met the president of the Young Republicans, always dressed in a suit and tie. He was supporting Nelson Rockefeller for the Republican nomination for President, but we were cordial to each other.

He asked, "Have you heard?"

"Yeah."

"This is gonna be tough." He hurried away.

The lounge in Forge was packed with everyone's attention focused on the television. Remembering the girls in Old Main, I quietly climbed the stairs to my room and lay down, praying the assassin wasn't a Goldwater supporter.

I was lucky: when Pete was walking to his room, two football players grabbed him, cursed him for Kennedy's death, and slammed his head into the wall a few times to demonstrate their patriotism.

I dozed and then Tommie came in. I woke up and he said, "They think they got the guy who killed Kennedy. He also killed a cop."

He left, but came back several times with reports. At suppertime he drove up to Harold's and brought back some burgers, fries and a drink because he knew I wasn't going down to eat.

Everything was quiet in the dorm on Saturday, except the TV in the lounge. I stayed in my room until Tommie came in and said, "The guy's a Commie. His name is Oswald and he killed the President and he's a Commie."

I felt relieved. I still felt bad for the Kennedy family and for the country, but I was relieved it wasn't a right-winger who had pulled the trigger. I even went down to the lounge and no one seemed to notice me.

Pete came in a little while later. The two football players who had bounced his head off the wall apologized to him, and he said it was all right, but he moved out of the dorm at the start of the winter quarter.

That made us the Forge Five plus One again because we had been the Forge Five Plus Two after Bradley's younger brother Greg had joined us that fall. With seven it made riding in a car somewhat difficult, but with six it was just right.

That weekend the entire campus grieved; the entire country grieved.

The one bright spot was that the Commie rat Oswald got what was coming to him when Jack Ruby shot him as they were transferring him from the Dallas city jail to the county jail.

Later it turned out that in April, Oswald had tried to shoot Major General Edwin Walker, a right-wing military officer, as he sat at his desk, but the bullet was deflected when it hit the window frame. That was another indication of Oswald's political slant.

After President Kennedy was laid to rest, Pete, Patty, and I turned our attention to the new President, Lyndon Johnson, who proved himself much more dangerous than Kennedy: he got things done, things we thought were detrimental to the United States.

Patty and I kept on with our casual dating, but she made certain things never got too passionate.

That summer I worked at the J&R again, but Patty and her Dad were gone on a recruiting trip, preparing for the fall presidential election.

As soon as school began, Patty, Pete, and I began setting up a Goldwater for President campaign, but Pete was voted out as Young Republican treasurer because of his support for the Arizona Senator.

Most of the Young Republicans had favored Nelson Rockefeller for the nomination until he lost the California primary in June, then they turned to Governor William Scranton of Pennsylvania as part of a Stop-Goldwater Movement. With Goldwater heading the Republican ticket, their support ranged from tepid to non-existent.

On the other hand, some Minot Republicans headed by a former National Committeewoman were wildly enthusiastic for Barry, and we passed out material and put up signs we obtained from them.

Just beyond Norby the highway swung southeast. About halfway to Hutchison, I noticed a black patch on the shoulder of the highway. As I approached, it exploded into six crows flapping themselves out of danger.

It looked like someone had taken a bucket of grape juice and splashed it on the pavement. Then there were chunks of meat, and I passed a doe lying beside the road, staring with unseeing eyes and with her guts strung out six feet over the grass.

At Minot State there was no pretense of political diversity among the faculty. Oh, there was the occasional moderate Republican in such departments as Health and Physical Education, Business, Education, and Science, but there were no conservatives or even libertarians.

In the English Department the faculty was straight Liberal Democrat, except for two old maids who hadn't been active in politics since William Jennings Bryan.

The History Department was solidly Liberal, either Democrat or Independent.

The most radical department was that of Forensics. It was small—only two professors—but they made certain that those they recruited for the Speech and the Debate teams were actively loyal to the Left.

Professor Fred Traven's office had three framed pictures on the wall: radical union organizer Eugene Victor Debs, who was a five-time candidate for President on the Social Democratic and then the Socialist Party tickets from 1900 to 1920; "Mr. Socialism" Norman Thomas, who ran for President six times on the Socialist Party ticket between 1928 and 1948; and Upton Sinclair, who was a Socialist muckraker and wrote the novel *The Jungle* about conditions in the Chicago meatpacking industry and who ran for Governor of California in 1934 as a Democrat.

Professor Ronald Cornell didn't pussyfoot around: he had one picture on his wall—an oversize one of Chairman Mao of Red China—and two of Mao's quotes in smaller frames: "Political power grows out of the barrel of a gun" and "A revolution is not a dinner party."

As the November election approached, the members of the Debate Team issued a challenge: they would meet any and all Goldwater supporters at a public debate in the Student Union.

On the appointed evening several hundred students filled the ballroom. The top three debaters were on the stage seated in chairs. Three empty chairs were on the opposite side. We Forge boys, Patty, and a couple seniors, John Timblin and Ross Torelli, who were stationed at the air base north of town and working on their degrees, stood together.

At seven o'clock the three chairs were still empty. The three debaters glowered at the audience.

Finally, August Arlington Kinsey IV arose. He weighed over three hundred pounds and the floor creaked as he headed for Down Stage Center. He never went anywhere in public without a suit, tie, and vest. His coat alone could have been used as a tent for a small Arab family, and a light plane could have landed on his tie and parked on the Windsor knot.

Gus asked for a Goldwater supporter to come on stage and present any arguments he or she had for the Arizona Senator. Robert and Red nudged me, but I wasn't about to let myself be publicly destroyed and humiliated by three semi-professional talkers.

After a minute Gus shrugged and waddled back to his chair. I was hoping it would collapse, but it didn't.

Next, Eldrick Offterdinger got up and issued his challenge. He was trying to grow a beard, but was failing, so his face looked like a half-weeded garden of hair. When no one ventured on stage, he shot a look of disgust at the audience and sat down.

Randolph Claunch remained seated, his feet barely touching the floor. Because of his black hair, his dark bushy eyebrows, the black clothing he usually wore, and his four-feet something height, he was known as the Black Dwarf. He never said a word, but his dark eyes shot fire as they searched for an opponent.

The three talked among themselves until 7:15, then Gus got up.

"I would like to thank all of you for coming tonight. It's a shame that the Goldwater supporters refused to argue for their candidate, but I guess that speaks volumes in itself." He went back to his chair.

Hunching forward, the Black Dwarf snickered.

The evening would have ended with the snicker, but for Eldrick. He moved to the front of the stage. "A man should have the courage of his convictions, so I see we have no men here in the opposition tonight." Red stuck a knuckle in my back, but my conviction was to stay put. "I don't like to call names, but you Goldwater supporters are the same stuff I step on when I walk in front of a chicken coop."

The knuckle doubled in force; so did my resistance.

From Stage Left there was a movement: it was Patty. Overcoming our shock, half the audience burst into applause and cheers. When Gus asked if she had a team, she looked at the audience. I hid behind Bradley. No one moved.

It wasn't a real debate. Patty stated her views, touching on Goldwater's domestic program, but focusing on the need to stop the Communists in South Vietnam. Gus answered her domestic policy arguments, denouncing Goldwater as a modern-day Scrooge who would destroy the Social Security System and throw twenty-one million elderly Americans into the street. Goldwater was a throw-back in his opposition to certain sections of the Civil Rights Act of 1964; he was a veiled racist and a darling of the KKK.

Randolph didn't respond to anything Patty had said. He hopped off his chair and attacked Goldwater as a fascist, a closet-Nazi, and as a nut case who was psychologically unfit to be President. Further, if the psycho-Senator ever got the chance, he would use nuclear weapons in Vietnam and maybe even against the Soviet Union and the Peoples' Republic of China. A group of us booed as he boosted himself back into his seat. He wasn't used to that; his black look at us was out of the Old Testament.

Eldrick took on her foreign policy statements, attacking each one with arguments that could be summed up as the voters had to reject allowing a madman to have his finger on the nuclear trigger. Goldwater would pull the U.S. out of the U.N. ("the last best hope for mankind to avoid nuclear annihilation"), resume above-ground atomic bomb testing, and invade Cuba which would lead to a confrontation with the Soviets with the threat of nuclear weapons hanging over the world like a Sword of Damocles.

To my surprise the audience seemed divided fifty-fifty in their applause, but was it because of the strength of the Goldwater platform that Patty had laid out (she had avoided bringing in any John Birch positions) or because half the people found the three debaters to be arrogant SOBs?

Patty then had the opportunity to challenge their support of the Great Society programs, including the War on Poverty. She didn't fare too well since she knew far less about domestic policy than she did about anti-Communism. In her summary, her voice cracked and her cheeks glistened.

Only Eldrick spoke in summation. He paced back and forth at Center Stage, pounding home the Americanism of the Johnson program and the dangerous extremism of Goldwater. At the end he stared out at the audience and trumpeted, "I say this, if you vote for Goldwater, the United States will be involved in a land war in Asia. Within three months of his inauguration, 'Barry the Bomber' will launch a bombing campaign against North Vietnam, and it will escalate from there. A vote for Johnson-Humphrey is a vote for peace and prosperity. A vote for Goldwater is a vote for bombing and war."

Outside we waited for Patty, but she wasn't very talkative even with dozens of people congratulating her.

I walked her to her car. As she got in, she said, "I was so alone."

We were never close after that. I had let her down and it was all my fault. I was afraid of public embarrassment and I ended up hurting my friend.

In November Goldwater carried six states, five in the Deep South.

Just before quarter break Patty called me. The floor proctor knocked on my door and told me someone was on the phone. I walked down the hall to the three-phone bank on the wall.

"Hello."

"Hello, Chris?"

"Yeah."

"This is Patty."

"Hi."

"I just want to let you know that Dad and I are moving to Bismarck."

"When?"

"We're just about to leave now."

"Can I see you?"

"No, we're leaving."

"But…"

"Chris, you have a lot of potential. I wish things could have been different between us. Goodbye."

She hung up and that was that. I never even got to say goodbye.

I turned south and buzzed through the west edge of Hutchison, passing a graveyard where the first row of stones was almost on the highway shoulder and a steepled brick church, probably Lutheran. I looked beyond the old Milwaukee Road right-of-way for the old fort buildings over near the river, but they were a mile off and I wasn't sure.

After Patty, I turned to my studies more than ever. I did date some girls.

Cheryl was a cute blonde from Mouse River who was painfully shy. Getting her to say anything was like being with a puppet without a ventriloquist. Two dates was all I could handle.

Mary Anne never shut up, but it was all about her friends, her family, her makeup, her clothes, her likes, her dislikes, and the fact she had dated a guy who had made the Minnesota Vikings roster. The third time she told me that was the last.

On the morning of February 7, two surprise attacks by the Viet Cong in Pleiku province killed nine Americans and wounded another seventy-six. Finally stirred to action, President Johnson authorized Operation Flaming Dart. That afternoon forty-nine U.S. Navy planes left their carriers and bombed the North Vietnamese barracks at Dong Hoi, a very timid response.

On February 10 the Viet Cong attacked the base at Qui Nhon, killing twenty-three Americans and wounding twenty-one.

Acting upon a recommendation by McGeorge Bundy, President Lyndon B. Johnson's order to begin bombing North Vietnam went into effect as "Operation Rolling Thunder" on March 2 with one strike per week.

I kept working on the newspaper and was gratified when we ran a Letter to the Editor from John Timblin. In part, he wrote, "I was told that if I voted for Goldwater, we'd be bombing North Vietnam. Well, sure enough, I voted for Goldwater and we're bombing North Vietnam."

On March 8 two Marine divisions began landing at Da Nang. "The Marines have landed." Now we're really in it.

I've heard people, especially those who are mountain-bred, complain about the monotonous sameness of traveling the Lake Agassiz Basin, and it can be that way if you keep your eyes only on the general topography. But it's not that way on a motorcycle.

The line of undulating trees to my left, tailing off to the southeast told me the Red River of the North was there, with Minnesota beyond. An insignificant creek bed ran under the highway; there was a culvert, but no water.

The highway moved closer to the Folles Homme River and edged along the fringe of trees. The twisting water created islands and peninsulas and capes of green, then the pavement straightened out and the prairie took over again.

There were few shelterbelts in that part of the basin, but the farmyards were surrounded by trees, mostly box elder, elm, and ash, while some had old cottonwoods mixed in.

The land was green or golden or gray-black depending on the crop or if it was lying fallow.

Ditch weeds and grass were generally long, but some had been mowed. Green and light brown predominated, but there were dark brown-stemmed plants in bad soil.

A two-lane highway on a cycle made you very aware of the traffic. Even the "skateboards" or flatbeds could blow you around, and the KW's, the Macks called "Bulldogs," the GMCs that some drivers called "General Mess of Crap," or any eighteen-wheeler could really buffet your bike.

In high school I'd worked at Hank's Super Saver grocery store and twice a week a truck driver named Chuck Morse would bring in loads of supplies from Fargo. He taught me some trucker lingo, and he also told us stories of moving over closer to the centerline when he saw a motorcycle, so he could batter it with a blast of air. I thought that was funny; now I didn't.

Cars going somewhere on a Sunday drive would occasionally honk, and I'd exchange a wave with every guy on a motorcycle.

I crossed a bridge and then skirted tree-hemmed Pronghorn Creek, emerged from the trees, and entered Wilburforce a half-mile later. Once again the graveyard touched the highway shoulder, but the gravestones kept their distance. A brown Lutheran Church with an off-set steeple faced the road.

On the south edge I bumped over the Burlington Northern tracks; one set was a siding for the grain elevators where some pigeons were on the ground gathering early harvested grain.

I crossed Pronghorn Creek again and about two-and-a-half miles later came to a sign pointing left and reading "Richville." I took a left.

Almost immediately I passed a red and white IH combine and then a faded orange Allis-Chalmers tractor with a trip bucket loader. The kid driving the A-C wore a blue baseball cap. We waved, and as I checked my rear view mirror and swung back into line, I yelled, "Take that, Jack."

In July 1947 aspiring writer Jack Kerouac bussed and hitchhiked from his aunt's house in Paterson, New Jersey, to Denver to meet his friend Neal Cassady. In September 1957 Kerouac's book *On the Road* describing that trip and three other cross-country adventures was published, with Kerouac appearing as the narrator-character Sal Paradise and Cassady as the irrepressible Dean Moriarty.

At Gothenburg, Nebraska, Kerouac as Sal Paradise was picked up by two young Minnesota farmers driving a flatbed truck. The flatbed already had a half dozen or so hitchhikers, among them two North Dakota farm boys. Kerouac wrote that they were wearing red baseball caps, which he claimed was "…the standard North Dakota farmer-boy hat…."

When my friend Ronnie Kerr and I discovered the Signet paperback edition of *On the Road* in Hayward Melby's newsstand at the front of the Burger Baron…and Fries. We chipped in and bought it. Within four days we both had read it, and both of us agreed that the standard farm hat in North Dakota was a blue baseball cap.

In 1947 the most popular teams would have been the Yankees, the Dodgers, the Cubs, and the Cardinals, the first three of which had blue caps. Even with the addition of the Minnesota Twins in 1961, the blue caps would still predominate, although some Twins caps were red.

With *On the Road* on our minds, our freshman year saw Ronnie and me become "Beats" although we weren't quite sure what that was. All we knew was that life on the road as described by Kerouac was the life for us when we got older.

Like Kerouac we could go cross-country, eating just apple pie and ice cream, especially rich in Iowa, where he claimed the prettiest girls in the world lived in Des Moines. (He also said something similar about the girls in Los Angeles.) Or maybe cherry pie and ice cream in Nebraska. Or bread and salami. Sometimes just toast and coffee, if that was all we could afford. And we'd be enthusiastic about everything. Of course, we wouldn't drink the whiskey and beer and wine, smoke, or swear like the men in the book did or steal cars

We'd learned about sex from the *Reader's Digest* and some older boys, but we wouldn't tumble into bed with the strange, sleazy women Kerouac seemed to.

What we wanted was, like Kerouac, to "…go and find out what everybody was doing all over the country." We'd meet people on the road like Kerouac did—Mississippi Gene, Montana Slim, Ponzo, the Ghost of the Susquehanna, Hyman Solomon.

Plus, after we had an adventure, we could write about it in easy-to-read prose that seemed to flow unadulterated out of Kerouac's brain, although sometimes we'd have to look up words like Dostoevski, Modigliani, Schopenhauer, Nietzschean, Oedipus, weed, hasheesh, Benzedrine, whore, huaraches, Pachuco, lugubriously, peremptory.

We didn't know what sex-parties and pornographic pictures were, but they sounded interesting.

When Kerouac mentioned bop, we were attracted and even had our parents buy us some hard-to-get albums with Charlie "Bird" Parker blowing alto sax on "Ornithology," "Scrapple from the Apple," and especially "Anthropology" and "Bird Gets the Worm," where Parker is driving his sax faster than the cars that hurtled Sal and Dean back and forth across the U.S.

We started speaking "Beat" like "You gone daddy," "Let's go, man," "I dig it." Instead of saying "Let's get dressed up," we'd say "Let's sharp up." We'd say "I dig you, man" if we agreed with someone. If something was important, it was "crucial, crucial." If we could do something, we were "hotrock capable." Just like Dean, we said "Yes! Yes! Yes!" a lot and called each other "cat." Talking that way to each other gave us a bond, but it distressed the high school boys to such an extent that they would attempt to make us see the error of our ways by introducing a locker door to our heads or throwing us into a scalding hot or a freezing shower after Phy. Ed.

I crossed the Folles Homme River for the last time, its volunteer trees supplemented by those of a farmyard. The Burlington Northern was angling into Richville on my left. A small dry creek bed, then another one which was tree-choked, and then Steinbeck's detritus of motels, gas stations, implement dealers, and small businesses whose owners had decided to chance it on the highway rather than downtown.

I didn't need gas, but I pulled into a station, used the facilities, and bought a Snicker bar, a small bag of Old Dutch chips, and a Dr. Pepper. As I was finishing, a car pulled up beside me. Four shining faces of teenagers—two girls and two boys—gleamed out. The driver leaned over. "Hey, dude, wanna go to a party." The girls giggled. The car emitted a pungent, slightly skunky, burned odor.

"No, maybe later."

"Your loss, dude." Off they went to get higher, if that were possible.

The highway turned south. A yellow plane was taking off from the airport. I tried to imagine the checkerboard fields from the air. There were more tree-sheltered farmyards per mile than I had seen on my trip so far.

On the far side of the airport, there was a small cemetery. A stone replica of a shattered Big Top tent pole complete with a carved rope and chain stood off by itself on the grounds, a dedication to two men killed around the turn of the century when a thunderstorm passed over Richville and lightning struck the main tent pole of the Ringling Brothers Circus as they helped to raise it. The men were buried in pauper's graves that afternoon. I had seen the stone shaft up close, but I couldn't see it from my cycle. Many times the Black Shadow strikes you unaware.

After Sal Paradise met up with Dean Moriarty in Denver, there were parties, drinking, dancing, singing, and trips into the mountains, but eventually it all came to an end. One morning after he had a breakfast of stale beer, Sal decided he was itching to leave for San Francisco. He also realized he was slowly joining the new beat generation. In San Francisco he got a job as a night watchman, then left for Los Angeles by bus on which he met a cute little Mexican girl named Teresa, who had left her husband because he beat her. Terry and he hitchhiked to Bakersfield and then went to Sabinal to work in the fields, but it was too hard for Sal, so he left Terry behind and hitched and bussed back to New York.

A dozen miles of lake-bottom flat; well-kept fields dotted with prosperous-looking farmyards, some of them hugging the highway; the old Milwaukee and the river off to my left; and my tires singing on the warming road. I bumped over some tracks and bypassed DeVillo, which at one time bragged of having four railroads and now had one.

About a year after Sal Paradise had returned to New York, he met Dean again, when Moriarty and his first wife Marylou arrived in Virginia where Sal was celebrating Christmas with relatives. Dean had left his second wife Camille and two-month-old daughter behind. They drove to New York City, had a huge New Year's Eve party, and went to hear the blind British piano player George Shearing jazz out some hot numbers at Birdland. In a dive called Ritzy's Bar, Dean proposed that Sal make love to Marylou, but when all three were in bed together, Sal said he couldn't do it.

The three of them and a friend, Ed Dunkel, left for New Orleans in Dean's 1949 Hudson; Sal said they were performing their "one and noble function of the time" which was to *move*. They got their kicks listening to full-blast radio, fast driving, and the "purity of the road." They got a twenty-five dollar speeding ticket in Virginia on the day Harry Truman was inaugurated as President, leaving them fifteen dollars. They kept going, looking for the pearl in the oyster, and picking up hitchhikers. They stole gas and cigarettes. In New Orleans they met morphine-addled Old Bull Lee and his wife Jane, who was using Benzedrine three times a day. Old Bull had experimented with all kinds of drugs and hated Washington bureaucrats, liberals, unions, and cops. Ed Dunkel's wife Galatea was there and mad at Ed for having left her behind. Dean, Sal, and Old Bull went barhopping while Jane stayed home and used three different drugs and drank. Back at his house Old Bull shot up with morphine. The next day in a Graetna bookie joint Sal won fifty dollars betting on a horse named Big Pop because it reminded him of his father.

Old Bull told Sal that when someone dies, his brain mutates into something no one knows anything about, but never explained how he knew that.

Dean, Ed, and Sal hitched a ride on a freight train for half a mile, while Marylou and Galatea waited in the car. The men got back an hour later, having rambled around the freight yards; the women were mad.

"In a sad red dusk" Sal, Dean, and Marylou headed for San Francisco. They stole food and cigarettes. It began raining in Texas and when he was driving, Sal was forced into the ditch by a carload of drunken field workers and got stuck. The other car kept going, so it took Sal and Dean a half hour to push the Hudson loose. They were covered with mud and then it began to snow. Cowboys drifted by in baseball caps and earmuffs.

Dean had them take off all their clothes and they drove through west Texas buck naked. Truckers looking into the car would swerve at the sight. A young hitchhiker with a crippled hand said if they took him along to Tulare, California, he could get some money from his aunt. He got in. They ran out of money, so Sal hocked his watch. In Tucson a writer friend of Sal's gave them five dollars after which they went to his house and ate noodles from a great pot.

They picked up an Okie cowboy musician, who said if they took him to Bakersfield, he'd get them some money from his brother. They went up the Tehachapi Pass, and Dean turned off the ignition, pushed in the clutch, and they coasted down the other side, gaining speed and passing cars like they were standing still, into the San Joaquin Valley.

They found the Okie's brother, got some money, and gunned it out of town. In Tulare the crippled hitchhiker found out his aunt had shot her husband and was in jail, so there was no money. They dropped him off at Madera, so he could continue to Oregon after having experienced "the best ride he had ever had."

They crossed the Oakland Bay Bridge into San Francisco with its "eleven mystic hills" and where Dean left Sal with Marylou on O'Farrell Street and went to find his other wife Camille. Sal and Marylou got a cheap hotel room on credit and spent their time looking for food money. With Dean gone Marylou had no interest in Sal. In bed Sal told her stories of the great serpent that lived in the earth. Its name was Satan, and someday it would emerge and devour everything in sight; but Dr. Sax, a saint in an underground shack, was developing a secret herb blend which would kill the serpent, and large clouds of gray doves would fly out of the snake and bring peace to the world. Marylou ran off with a female nightclub owner.

Sal saw her a few days later with the owner and a rich old man. They got into a Cadillac. Sal realized Marylou was a whore and he was alone. Hunger was driving him close to insanity. He saw that life was recurring, that he had experienced death and rebirth numerous times, and that they were like ripples created by the wind on still water. He thought he would die, but instead walked four miles to the hotel, picking up ten cigarette butts on the way which he smoked in his old pipe and thought of all the meat, fish, and fowl there was to eat in San Francisco, that he didn't have.

Dean came and got him, and he lived with Dean and Camille while Dean tried to sell pressure cookers door-to-door until he lost interest and quit. Dean and Sal went to hear Slim Gaillard, a Negro who played piano and sang and liked to end what he said with "orooni," such as "right-orooni," and Lampshade, a big Negro blues singer.

Sal had wanted it to be a "magnificent trip," but except for the bar-hopping and listening to the crazy musicians who really blew the sound, Sal finally admitted he didn't know why he was there. Camille didn't want him around and Dean didn't seem to care if he went or stayed. He made ten meat sandwiches and went out one last time to the Negro jazz joints with Dean, who had picked up Marylou.

At dawn they went to the bus stop. As Sal was boarding, Dean and Marylou asked for some sandwiches. Sal said no, and that was that. The bus chugged away for New York.

A large drainage ditch went under the highway, an artificial attempt to clear water off the flat fields for an earlier spring plowing. Some of the land appeared a little scabby. Off to the right a Lake Agassiz beach ridge angled slowly toward the highway. I passed an old shelterbelt. The trees ended, a large sign in my rearview welcomed people to North Dakota, a road ran off to my right, and I was in South Dakota. An even larger sign welcomed me. The topography and vegetation were exactly the same; the only difference was political. I had passed seamlessly from the administration of Democratic-NPL Governor Bill Guy to the jurisdiction of Governor Frank Farrar, Republican.

I began to smile, recalling when in *Tom Sawyer Abroad*, Tom, Huck Finn, and Jim are kidnapped by a mad professor and taken aboard a hot air balloon. As the wind blows them east, Huck insists they are still over Illinois even though Tom tells him they must be over Indiana. They argue and to prove his point, Huck says he knows they are over Illinois because he saw a map once which showed Illinois in green and Indiana in pink and all they could see below was green.

The beach ridge closed on the highway from the west and I passed over it; the land looked unhealthy. A sign directed me east to White Rock, where the old Milwaukee had passed over the river (now called the Bois de Sioux) into Minnesota; I ignored it. On my left a graveyard appeared, its sign obscured by a tree. Other trees surrounded the cemetery in a square as though they were a stockade protecting the old stones.

I was in the central spillway of Lake Agassiz where the water had gushed out when the lake would drain to the south. I knew the beaches were a tangle of low ridges to my right, but I didn't have time to investigate.

I passed a large water-filled depression, the water green with algae, curved around a large farming operation, then straightened out with some long lakes to my left. A sweeping curve and I was headed for Rosholt, passing onto the Sisseton-Wahpeton Reservation, but not knowing when since there was no sign.

In the spring of 1949 on his third road trip, Sal Paradise rode a bus to Denver, where he got a job lugging crates around a fruit market until he quit because the work was too hard. He began to wish he were a Negro or a Mexican or a Jap, anything but a disillusioned white man.

A rich girl he knew gave him a hundred dollars, and he and two other men drove a travel bureau car to "the fabled city of San Francisco." During the trip Sal saw God appear as massive gold clouds over the Utah desert. Dean was married to Marylou and Camille simultaneously and Camille now had a baby. She and Dean fought all the time and Marylou was whoring around. Dean couldn't stand that. He smoked some green marijuana, got a gun, and told Marylou to shoot him. She thought about it, but didn't. A few months before Sal arrived, Dean had hit Marylou in the forehead and broken his thumb. It got infected and he lost the tip. It was infected again and almost useless, hiding in a huge bandage. He was suffering leg, foot, and nose problems, and Marylou had married a used car dealer.

The morning after Sal arrived, Camille threw both Dean and him out. The men decided to go to Italy, but first they had to cruise the streets and listen to "the great jazz of Frisco." Ed Dunkel had left his wife Galatea and was in Denver. As Galatea berated Dean for abandoning Camille and his daughter while Dean giggled and his dirty bandage unrolled, Sal saw that Dean had become "BEAT—the root, the soul of Beatific." He was a "HOLY GOOF." They went to "Little Harlem" on Folsom Street and hopped all the jazz joints, grooving on the hot and soulful music, with Dean in ecstasy. They were in the midst of "the pit and prune-juice of poor beat life itself in the god-awful streets of man...."

They slept in "a sad old brown Frisco hotel," got a travel bureau car, and headed for Sacramento. Sal had been in San Francisco some sixty hours.

The car was a Plymouth and there were three other people riding in it—a homosexual and a couple. The homosexual drove to Sacramento way too slowly for Dean and Sal, so they sat in the backseat and told stories about their childhood. Dean drove out of Sacramento and goosed that Plymouth as fast as it would go, shifting in and out of danger and scaring his passengers to death.

He pulled over on a hill that looked down on Salt Lake City, collapsed, and went to sleep. After Dean woke up, the young couple insisted on driving, but in eastern Colorado Dean took over again. The couple fell asleep and Dean punched the accelerator and they flew toward Berthoud Pass, which Dean coasted down, never touching the brake and weaving past other vehicles. In Denver Dean and Sal got off at 27th and Federal. New York was a long way off, but they didn't care because "the road is life."

Dean told Sal he was getting old and Sal blew up. Dean walked out of the restaurant and started to cry, so Sal apologized. They stayed with an Okie family in a house overlooking Denver and at night looked at all the lights below them. Dean searched for his father, but didn't find him. He did find a cousin who said the family didn't want to have anything to do with Dean again.

At night Dean would get drunk and throw pebbles at the bedroom window of a girl who lived across the alley, hoping she'd come out. Instead, her mother got a bunch of high school boys who threatened to beat Dean up. Sal cooled everything down.

They went out drinking and Dean stole a car to go joyriding, then came back with a better one. Some cops came into the bar and said there was a stolen car outside. While the cops were there, Dean stole a convertible and took off. Sal went to the Okie house and soon Dean showed up in a stolen coupe and passed out. After Sal got him awake, Dean drove the coupe a half mile into a field and ditched it there.

They got a job transporting a 1947 Cadillac to Chicago. First, Dean picked up a waitress he knew, and they had sex in the Caddie at the back of a parking lot, then Dean drove back. He picked up Sal and two boys heading for an eastern Jesuit school and took off. He drove over a hundred and ten miles per hour even in the rain, slowed down to seventy when he hit some mud, and ended up in the ditch. A farmer pulled them out. They ate at the home of a rancher Dean knew and took off, blasting across the night in Nebraska at 110, telling stories while the Jesuit boys slept.

Dean was speeding through a hot July morning in Iowa when a man in a Buick passed him. They began to race, taking brutal chances on the curves, and endangering dozens of lives as they weaved in and out of traffic. Finally, the Buick pulled into a gas station and the man waved goodbye.

Dean kept the accelerator on the floorboards, 110, and passed four slow cars and a semi on a bridge so narrow it was one-way traffic. Sal and the two Jesuits all got in the back seat. Dean picked up two hobos and they screamed into Chicago. After letting the hobos and the Jesuits out, Dean said that he and Sal had "gotta go" and not stop until they got there. Sal asked where they were going. Dean said, "I don't know but we gotta go."

In a saloon they listened to a bunch of young bop musicians play Chicago-style with saxes imitating Lester Young and Charlie Parker, a bass, drums, and a piano some Italian kid played like Thelonius Monk. When the musicians went to Anita O'Day's club, Dean and Sal followed.

At intermissions they'd drive off in the Cadillac to look for girls, but Dean was drunk and wrecked the car backing into hydrants and smacking into various objects. The rods and the brakes were already shot from the trip.

Back at the club George Shearing appeared and blew everyone away with his piano. He played for an hour; everyone else played until nine o'clock in the morning.

They dropped off the severely damaged Caddie and took a bus back to downtown Chicago before anyone could call the authorities.

They took a bus to Detroit and stayed in an all-night theater, watching a double feature six times. At dawn they went to look for a lift and caught one with a middle-aged man who charged them four dollars apiece for a ride to New York. In Pennsylvania Dean took the wheel, but they made it to the big city without incident.

About a week later they went to a party where Dean met Inez. He started calling long distance to Camille asking her for a divorce so he could marry Inez, even though Camille was pregnant. Then Inez got pregnant. Dean had no money. The trip to Italy fizzled out.

A silver water tower announced Rosholt, a little town of several hundred souls, unremarkable as I slowed and passed the gas stations, bars, implement dealers, and other businesses along the highway. Although the town was on a reservation, all I saw were white faces. A brown brick Quincy-box school waited for students still enjoying summer. When they returned, it would be as Raiders, according to a sign. A single diesel locomotive with "SOO LINE" on the side and the older paint scheme of maroon and gold instead of the more modern one of white and red tugged a dozen box cars and gondolas into town. An ancient red caboose trailed behind.

Beyond, the land was more rolling. A small knob with long brown grass appeared on the right and then a well-cared-for cemetery with straight rows of stone.

I was starting a slow climb to the west and went up and down the first real hill I'd been over since gliding onto the Agassiz Basin in North

Dakota. Little farms passed by and little dirt roads ran off at right angles to places unseen. A gopher scurried across the pavement; I felt right at home.

Coming over a rise, I saw a lake extending to the south in a large depression that curved to the east after the highway passed over it. The water was as clear and blue as the sky. I wished I knew the geological history of South Dakota better.

Riding up the far side of the depression, I met a car. The driver honked and I waved. A yellow diamond sign with a black arrow told me of an approaching curve, so I slowed a little, not knowing how sharp the arc would be.

A sign identified a small cluster of buildings and trees to my right as Victor. I went into a long lazy curve and there was the railroad. We ran in parallel for half a mile and then the rails turned west, while I kept going southwest for another half mile when another curve pointed me to the west.

A paved road led off to the north a short way where the village of New Effington lay hidden among the trees. I needed gas, but I thought I could make it to Sisseton, which was maybe twenty miles away. I tried to recall the map I had consulted before I left, but it was in my sleeping bag.

The rolling prairie continued in all directions with most of the trees far from the highway. The pavement dipped and rose in union with the land. An occasional drying slough skirted by. The highway contractors had shaved through a north-south ridge; I rode the pavement, looking up at the wheat. The highway bisected a large lake. My passage disturbed some coots and red-winged blackbirds. The red-wings were upset, but I couldn't hear them.

Some of the land looked uneven and some of it was scabby. Several long rows of shrubs, bushes, and a few trees obscured farm buildings to the south. I saw a long ridge ahead and began ascending. A double line appeared on the middle of the highway. I crested the ridge with trees on both sides of the road. On the flat I opened her up, but on another rise I had to slow as I got behind a Ford pickup.

On the flat again I pushed her a little above the speed limit, zipping past a haying operation near a small pond on my left. Crossed more water with both sides of the highway riprapped and then up again. More reed-fringed water; trees either alive or dead; more climbing and dipping; more trees; dirt roads perpendicular north and south; more climbing and dipping; fields cropped or uncropped; pastureland; flat road. Far off in the distance I saw the Coteau des Prairies, the plateau underlain with shale so tough that it forced Pleistocene glaciers to divide and pass on either side, which were sheered and trimmed by the advancing ice that acted like water when it comes to an immovable object and took the line of least resistance. It appeared as a long gray line bulging out of the prairie and showing spots and streaks of dark green which were trees in the eroded sides of the Coteau.

I curved south, passing a slough, shrinking in August, with its south shore reed-choked, a band of thick trees, and a small farmstead with a white house. Foxtails waved beside another slough. I raced along with a telephone line supported by single poles to my right. How lonely farm women must have been before Bell's invention. Hay bales in the ditches. More small sloughs. White farm buildings. Red farm buildings. A scraggily shelterbelt. Cropland. A sign reading "Continental Divide" and the highway as flat as a griddle and the sign full of bullet holes. A magnificent shelterbelt. Pastureland. A stunted shelterbelt. More traffic than I'd been used to. And the Coteau ever closer.

Over and down a rise: the Coteau more prominent. Cropland, hay land, grassland, sun land, flat-riding, then the mild up and down of small rises, shelterbelts against the wind, blue sloughs with green fringes, and always the enduring Coteau edging closer to the highway.

Combine dust in the distance with a priestly dispensation about Sabbath work if the farmer was Catholic, but just a prayer to God if he was Protestant. Or maybe no prayer at all, even though most farmers are religious. A run over a bridge spanning a steep-sided gash in the prairie, but where was the water? A long ridge ahead with a man-made saddle for the highway and a farmyard on the crest with pieces of equipment scattered in no apparent order, as if a giant had just dumped them there.

Into a left-hand curve and over another waterless prairie gash. Maybe the trees had sucked the little stream dry or maybe it needed rain. Then a curve to the right, then straight, then Sisseton.

The fourth time Sal Paradise took to the road, he left Dean Moriarty behind in New York. Dean was a parking lot attendant living with Inez and smoking a lot of weed. Sal had some money from the sale of his book, *The Town and the City*. Just before he left, he and Dean were looking at some snapshots of Dean's family and friends when Sal thought his own life had become a hell, a "senseless nightmare road…endless and beginningless emptiness." A bus took Sal to Denver, where he met Tim Gray and Stan Shephard, and they spent a week of afternoons in Denver bars and nights in Negro jazz joints, then Sal learned that Dean was coming to team up again, a situation that made Sal uneasy. Dean told Sal he had come to Denver to accompany Sal to Mexico, where Dean would get a divorce from Camille. Dean, Sal, and eleven friends went to the Windsor Hotel bar and got rip-roaring drunk on wine, beer, and whiskey. Seven of them spent the night in a basement drinking wine and talking. Dean, Sal, and Stan took off south in a wreck of a 1937 Ford with the front seat broken down on the right side.

They told life stories as they drove through Colorado, New Mexico, and the endless plains of Texas. They stopped in San Antonio for a grease job and to get penicillin for Stan, who had been stung by a bee or some other insect. They watched a crippled midget shoot pool, not very well.

At 3 A.M. they crossed at Laredo into Mexico, "the magic land at the end of the road," where they got their kicks with beer, weed, and whores and reveled in the jungles; the mountains; the smells; the Indians; the sense of air, jungle-rotten or keen blue until they reached Mexico City, where they feasted and drank until Sal got dysentery. Dean obtained his divorce, went to New York, and left Sal in his misery. Sal realized Dean was a rat, but that was his nature, and Dean had to get back to "his wives and woes." Dean married Inez, but that night left for San Francisco, Camille, and his two baby daughters.

That fall Sal arrived in New York, met a girl named Laura, and planned to move to San Francisco. He wrote to Dean, who read Proust and used a railroad pass as he came across the country on cabooses to help them move, but Sal didn't have the money. Dean decided to go back to San Francisco and take Inez with him. He'd have one place for Camille and the girls and another place for Inez, but when she heard his plan she threw him out. Sal had no money to help him and left him standing on a street. Watching Dean walking in the cold, Laura almost started to cry, but Sal told her that Dean would be all right. Sal spent a lot of time thinking of where he'd been, what he'd done, and about Dean Moriarty.

Most of Sisseton was west of the highway. I passed a gas station, thought of going back, but figured there'd be others. I followed the highway signs west toward the Coteau, but then the road went south. Where were the gas stations?

I kept going, bumped over the Milwaukee Road tracks, and saw a combination gas station-repair shop in a small grove of trees. I pulled in on the gravel and waited beside the pumps.

I didn't know if it was full-serve or self-serve, so I waited, vehicles humming by on the pavement, but not stopping. The wheels of progress had certainly bypassed the station. The white paint on the building was peeling and the steps had lost any semblance of color. I looked for a sign—Standard, Texaco, Gulf, Phillips 66, Skelly—but there was none. No one appeared, so I opened my tank, grabbed the hose, dropped the lever, and began to pump.

I was wondering what would happen to the little station when they completed the Interstate which had been surveyed a few miles to the east when a little girl came out and sat on the dirt-darkened steps. She stared at me with solemn prairie-bred eyes set in a chestnut face framed with black velvet hair. I smiled; she remained impassive.

When I went in to pay, she followed me. The interior was dark, but I was used to that because Blackie's station in Menninger was the same way. The walls had several trophy heads and one framed picture. I paid a teenage boy who had been watching TV and went over to the picture.

A young soldier smiled out at me, bright teeth in a dusky face, proud of his uniform. Crossed behind the frame were two large feathers and on a shelf beneath the picture were three small lined boxes with a silver star, a bronze star, and a Purple Heart.

"My uncle." The boy stood beside me.

"I'm sorry" and I was, as I am for all soldier-deaths.

"So were we, but he wanted to go; he volunteered. It just about killed his mother, though."

I couldn't think of anything to say, so I turned to go and almost bowled over the little girl. "Oops; excuse me. What's her name?"

"Chumani, but we call her Dew Drop or just Dewy."

I thought I'd be funny, so I asked, "Does she work here?"

"Some people drive off without paying, so Dewy gets their license number and I call some guys I know on the Indian Police and they stop the drive-away before they reach the res boundary. We get our money, plus interest, and the police get a little for their trouble."

I took a last look at the smiling soldier, thanked the young man, and said goodbye to Dewy, who just stood there, not smiling.

Vietnam is everyone's cross.

I eased away from the pumps just as a car pulled in. Dewy appeared on the steps, and I hit the pavement, accelerated, and was out of town and into a lazy left-hand curve with a hill-ridge to my right, hiding the Coteau. A dip and rise and the Coteau was closer. A lazy right-hand curve and I was heading due south. A nicely kept farmyard—or were they called ranches in South Dakota?—with some Herefords trying to scrape up water in a dry creek bed. Over and down a rise and by some scraggily trees around a mud-hole drying up and then another rise. Past some old cottonwoods that spread their branches over the left-side lane.

On the right an electrical sub-station and two teenage boys thumbing at a crossroads. No room for riders on the 750, so I swerved into the left lane, waved, got two returns, and cut back to the right. Trees partly hiding small houses and a pint-size creek. More trees, then wide-open spaces, then more trees, all the trees bracketing houses or creeks.

A road sign pointed west: Agency Village. The road was gravel. Past a small grove and the Coteau, tree-shouldered, appeared to the west and ran southeast. I saw the highway disappear against it in the distance. I passed a small corral, empty, on my right, fronting broken land. Up and down a rise and then up a long rise to a crossroads and a sign pointing left to Peever.

Up and down, up and down, over water-traced terrain. A tree-crowded hill and onto wheat land. Over and down, seeing where the highway builders had sliced through ridges. More trees crowding around evaporating creeks and more highway cuts. A long incline, a single tree by a slough, and another incline, the afternoon sun creating a mirage of water on the highway ahead.

A long thin shelterbelt guarded the left-hand ditch, then an even longer one, and then a long slope upward. Water-sculpted land, but where was the water now? An abandoned barn, white paint peeling off, but no house. A row of cottonwoods almost touching the right shoulder. Rolling land making a rolling highway. A long, lazy right-hand curve and the highway rode up the Coteau.

I had been thinking an irrational thought: not knowing the size of the incline, I was afraid the 750 wouldn't be able to make the climb. Rationally, I knew it could because I'd run it up very steep hills east of Menninger, including Buffalo Hump, but I wasn't one hundred percent convinced until I saw the highway and felt the 750 climb up without effort.

In our naiveté Ronnie and I had played at being Beat because it was fun and people noticed, but until college I really didn't understand the milieu of the true Beat.

Jack Kerouac was born in 1922 and became a founding member of the Beats, a term he later derided. Jazz or Bop, springing forth from the bands of Count Basie and Duke Ellington; the horns of Lester Young, Charlie Parker (died March 12, 1955), Miles Davis, Dizzy Gillespie, John Coltrane, Ornette Coleman; the pounding percussion of Max Roach. And the mellow-whiskey voice of Billie Holiday.

Kerouac read—Shakespeare, Thoreau, Whitman, Goethe, the philosopher Friedrich Nietzsche, Emily Dickinson, the novelist-poet Thomas Hardy, Thomas Mann, Thomas Wolfe, Jack London, the Russians Dostoyevsky and Gogol, James Joyce, Proust, the decadent French poets Rimbaud and Baudelaire, Irish poet-mystic W.B. Yeats, Aldous Huxley, New Jersey doctor-poet William Carlos Williams, Wilhelm Reich and his outlandish sexual theories, the German philosopher Oswald Spengler and his cyclical theory of history, St. Thomas Aquinas, the Bible, and books on Buddhism.

He was attracted to aspects of Buddhism with its stress on suffering, impermanence, the illusion of life, rebirth, and enlightenment. He also searched for the "Way," the "Tao."

Kerouac became alienated from his father and tied to his mother whom he cared for the rest of his life.

Kerouac almost killed himself taking Benzedrine and was hospitalized. He smoked Camel cigarettes and weed (he wrote his books *Visions of Cody* and *Dr. Sax* while grass-high; *The Subterraneans* and *Big Sur* while using Benzedrine; *Mexico City Blues* flying on weed and morphine; and *Visions of Gerard* high on Benzedrine and weed); used barbiturates, hashish, little balls of opium; and drank too much (beer, Tokay, white port, Jack Daniels, Old Crow, Johnny Walker Red, Hennessy Cognac) and too often. He was plagued with thrombophlebitis in his left leg, was beaten up in bar fights, suffered delirium tremens, nightmares, depression.

The Beats were into opium, morphine, heroin, Benzedrine, speed, psilocybin, peyote, LSD, weed, just about anything the government categorized as an illegal substance and some that weren't.

However, there was a saving grace: of all the Beats, Kerouac was the most anti-Communist.

Jack's inner circle included Lucien Carr, a handsome blonde would-be intellectual; Allen Ginsberg, a bespectacled Jewish homosexual; William S. Burroughs, a homosexual searching for thrills in every drug imaginable (his first book was called *Junkie*); and David Kemmerer, a hanger-on in love with Lucien, who rejected him and eventually stabbed him to death. Carr served two years.

In college I learned that in *On the Road* Lucien Carr appeared as Damion, William S. Burroughs showed up as Old Bull Lee, and Allen Ginsberg was Carlo Marx.

Ronnie and I had heard of the obscenity trial for the poem *Howl* written by Ginsberg. When the poem was found not to be obscene, we had Hayward Melby order a copy, although he asked us if we knew what we were doing.

The first part of the first long line—"I saw the best minds of my generation destroyed by madness…."—was enthralling, but as I read the rest of the poem, it seemed to me that the "best minds" had brought on their own problems with drugs and alcohol and all kinds of sexual encounters and then blamed society and America ("Moloch") for eating up their brains, and I never went back to Ginsberg, although some of his lines were great—"who loned it through the streets of Idaho seeking visionary indian angels"; "you walk dripping from a sea-journey on the highway across America in tears to the door of my cottage in the Western night"—they weren't enough. After we read the poem a couple times, we tossed the book into the incinerator behind the jail for fear our mothers would find it.

I gave the 750 the gun and sliced through the guardian trees, up, up, up, and then I was on top of the Coteau, cheering, and being greeted by pastures with white rocks gleaming in the sunshine. Now the rolling land. I saw the highway had added a pink tone over the blue. Climbing past a large cattle operation to the right that had to be a ranch. Pastureland with some water. A meadowlark sang from a fence post, but I couldn't hear it—only the movement of its throat.

A left-hand curve slung the road around to the south. I was on a real buffalo prairie with hay bales taking the place of the buffalo. I zipped by a faded corral, not used recently. The land was a treeless plain with some distant power poles replacing the trees, and I rolled over it in great undulating waves, the road, the bike, and I as one with the land. *Thank you, God.*

Up through a saddle created by the excavating machines of the highway builders, and wire fences looked down on me. A solitary old bull stood on a hill and finally some trees that hid an ancient white house. Except for the cars and trucks that I met, some of them honking, where were the people?

A crossroads sign told me Wilmot was ten miles to the east, and soon I saw where the coming Interstate had been surveyed and passed the place. I curved by a large pond or small lake, which had been larger, and in the distance saw a water tower and trees that marked the homes of some two hundred people in Summit. Despite its name, the surrounding land was universally flat.

Just south of town I went west, crossed the incipient Interstate, and took a left. It would be a straight shot to Watertown, twenty-five or so miles away.

In 1958 the term "beatnik" was invented and applied to the bearded, shade-wearing fringe characters and their chicks in black leotards and turtlenecks who inhabited coffeehouses, pounded on bongos, and played at being "cool." Critics metamorphosed Kerouac from a Beat into a beatnik, but it was a term and a lifestyle he abhorred. In September 1959 Ronnie and I met a beatnik, not a real one, but a Hollywood version on TV. *The Many Loves of Dobie Gillis* debuted on CBS with Dwayne Hickman as Dobie and Bob Denver as his "good buddy," the work-averse Maynard G. Krebs. For a month or so we tried to develop a persona like Maynard, trying to dress like him by wearing sweatshirts with cut-off sleeves (of course, our mothers wouldn't allow them to get as dirty and holey as Maynard's were), talk like him (when someone would say our names, we'd answer, "You rang?"; when someone said "work," we'd jump and yelp "work!"; plus expressions such as, "I'm like beat, man," "cool, big daddy," "I don't like dig it," and "like how?"), and act like him, but failing to grow any semblance of his goatee.

We thought we were real Beats, but then both of us got jobs at grocery stores and being Beat wasn't so much fun anymore. Maybe we had just grown up a little. Maynard and Kerouac, good-bye.

Up and over a lichen-encrusted concrete bridge that spanned the single-track Milwaukee Road. Most of the great American railroads—the B&O, the Burlington Route, the C&O, the Erie, the Great Northern, the Milwaukee Road, the New York Central, the New York, Chicago & St. Louis (better known as the Nickel Plate), the New York, New Haven & Hartford, the Northern Pacific, the Pennsylvania, the Southern Pacific, the Union Pacific, the Wabash, and the Western Pacific—were basically east-west lines, although some were north-south—the Atlantic Coast Line, the GM&O, the Illinois Central, the L&N, the Rock Island, and the Seaboard Air Line.

I love railroads, American railroads—as the novelist and short story writer Albert Halper said, "I've got a locomotive in my chest."

Another lichen-covered bridge crossing a creek which spilled a trickle of water into a small lake. Pastureland and a curve, then a sign with the universal bullet holes and dents, with the added novelty of the pattern from a shotgun blast, telling me I was leaving the reservation. The land turned to corn, and on the edge of many of the fields I began to see metal signs with a green and gold corncob and the name "DeKalb."

Some crops didn't look as good as others I had seen and there were pastures and meadows with no crops, but some white barns and red barns testified to the farmers' optimism in their choice of land.

I did give Jack one more chance. When Grove Press published *Mexico City Blues*, I had Hayward order me a copy. It was supposed to be 242 choruses of Jack blowing out jazz poetry the way Bird blew out the blues. Some I liked (3rd Chorus when he described cooking in a camp by a railroad; 8th Chorus about rivers; 10th Chorus about geography; 146th Chorus about trains and airplanes) or just parts, such as "Shining essences…of universes of stars…disseminated into powder…and dust—blazing…in the dynamo…of our thoughts…in the forge…of the moon" from 16th Chorus or "But I'm really a citizen…of the world… who hates Communism…and tolerates Democracy" from 34th Chorus or "I'd rather be thin than famous" from 104th Chorus. But there was too much about using drugs—"For the first time in my life…I pinched the skin…And pushed the needle in…And the skin pinched together…And the needle stuck right out…And I shot in and out…Nothin a junkey likes better…Than sittin quietly with a new shot…And knows tomorrow's plenty more"; or Buddhist absurdity, such as "Who am I?…do I exist?…(I don't even exist anyhow)"; "What I have attained in Buddhism…is nothing. What I wish to attain,…is nothing. In seeking to attain the Dharma…I failed, attaining nothing,…And so I succeeded the goal,…Which was, pure happy…nothing"; "Nirvana aint inside me…cause there aint no me"; or incomprehensible things, such as "Muck Ruby…Crystal set…Smithereen…Holylilypad…Bean—A la Pieté—Truss in dental…Pop Oly Ruby…Tobby Tun w d l…1 x t s 8 7 r e r (" or "Blook Bleak. Bleak was Blook,…an Onionchaser Hen…necked Glutinous…Huge Food monster…that you ate…with FLAN & Syrup…in a sticky universe."

And so I left Jack in his sticky universe.

I saw a railroad approaching on a diagonal from the northeast, marked in places by short lines of trees, and then I saw a red grain elevator which towered over a small village that had no highway sign, but a bar and grill indicated it was Rauville. A round yellow railroad crossing sign with a black "X" making two diameters, a couple little bumps over the Burlington Northern tracks, and the village was gone.

The land was rolling, but flat enough to be alluvial in origin; again I wished I knew South Dakota geology better. A cattle operation on my right was emphasized by stacks of baled hay. A two-and-a-half story Victorian, complete with a porch and a roof turret, appeared. Did some Wheat King build it or had it been moved in?

A farmyard stood on the crest of a rise: white farmhouse, white barn, white outbuildings. A distant water tower signaled my approach to Watertown, but the dozens of highway billboards made certain I knew where I was. I hadn't seen so many signs since heading into Fargo. Sleep here, eat here, gas up here, bank here, shop here, buy here—but I didn't have the time.

Concrete replaced the asphalt as I entered the town, commercial lots and residential lots intermixed. I needed to stop, so I pulled into a gas station and used the facilities. I bought something to eat and a bottle of pop. I leaned against the building and watched the traffic, the customers, and the big Hubbard Grain facility across the street.

The highway curved and I began to hit more and more traffic lights. I tried to time my approach with the green. Sometimes I was successful and sometimes not. I was in a residential area. I passed a huge white house with a cement retaining wall lining the sidewalk and across the street my favorite, a two-story house with a wraparound porch, a mansard roof, and a square tower on the south side, where I would have put my bedroom.

The highway curved again, and I saw the Golden Arches off to the right, but it was too early for supper. Commercial buildings went by, the trees thinned, the backs of billboards showed up, and I was out of town. I imagined how the town would reach out to the east a couple miles after the Interstate was completed.

Across a creek, and billboards showed me their backs. Up a long rise and past a barn with a cupola. Up another rise and trees began casting shadows on the highway in the afternoon sun. A semi chugged past, heading for Watertown, its red trailer proclaiming "Hyman Freightways" and "The Overniters." Squared-off farmyards hiding behind sturdy trees. More long shelterbelts and then a trinity of trees along a county road. And always the gently rolling land.

In late January 1968 Neal Cassady went to Mexico once more. On February 3 he attended a wedding party in San Miguel de Allende, where he drank too much and ingested Seconal. Leaving the party, he walked along some railroad tracks in the rain, wearing just a t-shirt and jeans. The next morning he was found unconscious by the tracks and was carried to a hospital where he died just short of his forty-second birthday. Avoiding an obvious irony, he died sprawled next to the rails, not a road. The rumor was he was counting the ties, but who knows for sure?

A two-story white farm house, two gray silos, a small red barn and then the county line (no bullet marks). Gray gravel approaches leading to small gray houses. Withering sloughs and lakes off-set from the highway. A cluster of steel grain bins crowned with dunce caps sitting on a hill. A single tree out in a field around which the farmer had carefully plowed, planted, cultivated, and harvested. More vehicles than I had seen since Fargo; I whipped around the cars and pickups; most of them sounded their horns. A junction and off to my right and down a hill, the road splitting a lake.

A long depression with reed-choked ditches, but no water. A short gray approach that ended at a rickety fence and went no further. A junction and Kones Korner, a country store that sold the Midwestern essentials—gas, food, and guns. Lakes, sloughs, and ponds—Watertown was well-named. A big right-hand curve gliding into a left-hand curve and the corn and wheat land turned into buffalo land.

Suddenly more trees than I'd seen anywhere else in South Dakota, except in the towns. A sign pointed right to Hayti. More trees, including some evergreens, fringed the highway. Then the trees thinned out and after I went over a hill were gone. I was alone on the prairie until I passed a volunteer box elder on the left and a red Dodge Charger with the bumblebee stripes on the rear came zipping up; its horn dopplered past me and the four taillights blindly stared into the sun.

Trees again; more pickups than cars; a white wooden fence fronting a white house, white barn, and gray silo; then another white wooden fence and behind it a graveyard captured by trees with all the graves to the left of the approach. An abandoned house no bigger than one of the old claim shacks sitting among some dead trees, the approach overgrown with weeds. A crossroads and a homemade black and white sign proudly proclaiming that a couple buildings and a gravel approach made it Alsville.

On October 20, 1969, Jack Kerouac was sitting in a favorite chair in his St. Petersburg, Florida, home drinking and working on a new book, when his esophagus suddenly started to hemorrhage. He was taken to St. Anthony's Hospital, where several transfusions failed to save his life, and he died at 5:15 A.M. October 21 at the age of forty-seven.

More prairie, crops, and trees, and then a lazy curve leading to a collection of small buildings—a resort—and the large lake from which it fed on my left. More buildings, cabins, some campers and trailers, a gas station, a liquor store, other businesses, another lazy curve and a boat seller. The county line and on my right some small evergreens attempted to hide a cemetery, partly on a hill.

A white house sat on a shoulder of land overlooking another large lake, then more houses along the shoreline, and a long shelterbelt guarded the east side of the highway. Traffic thickened with many boats being tugged homeward by people disappointed in the fishing, the weekend, or just to get an early start back to town. I drove faster; I weaved in and out. A sign explained "Lake Albert." The houses ran out and I could see where the water used to lap the shoulder of the road. I was in a chute of trees and then emerged onto land where the trees thinned out and reeds and willows indicated hidden water.

Up a hill. A shelterbelt ran perpendicular to the highway and a gravel road followed it west to who knew where. Down onto the level. A junction and a grove of evergreens to the right—another country graveyard. A sign pointed west—Badger—I ripped past the turn and went around a carload of teenagers. Their horn sounded and I raised my hand. A gravel road went off to a hidden farm on my left, and then a tall gray silo towered over a farmyard on my right. The highway kept going in a straight line. I passed a car which sat on the shoulder of the road. The boat trailer had a flat tire, and a man was fixing it while his family sat safely out of the way on an approach.

Farms sat closer to the highway, prosperous looking. A small yellow plane lifted off the ground from an airstrip to the left. I passed between treed farmsteads on either side and went by a little slough. Small signs announced the approach of a town, and then a highway sign made it official—Arlington. At first all I saw were trees, but a sign cautioned me to slow down. A break in the trees, a half dozen grain bins, more trees, and then the town, its streets diagonal to the highway. It was a green and white town—the trees and the houses, and the houses that weren't white were green. Almost every house was on the right side of the highway with a field extending east on the left-hand side.

I went across some railroad tracks. The Chicago and Northwestern was still an active mainline, but the Burlington Northern's traffic was slowing to the point it would probably be abandoned. I passed a low-slung Shell station and a small lake with what looked like a man-made island. Arlington's cemetery was out of town on the left. Little signs showed me their backs. Up a grade crowned by two farms and a sign that said Brookings was sixteen miles east, but first I'd meet Volga ten miles away. I slowed enough to make the turn and gunned the bike east.

Down into a long shallow tree-lined depression where the highway split a lake in two, most of the water on the right side—no sign, no resort, no cabins. Over a divide and by some smaller lakes or sloughs with low hills ranging on the far side of the water to my right. Another divide and then reeds pushing onto both shoulders of the highway.

Traffic thickened in a race to Brookings. A substantial farmyard on a little hill to the left, but the land not looking very fertile. A small slough to the right with a family of teal swimming in what was left of the water. Another white house-red barn combination connected by a circular drive. A small slough to the left with some rather large Russian Olive trees. Two pathetic shelterbelts opened on the Northwestern tracks crossing the highway with traffic protected by signals. The pavement and the tracks paralleled into the town of Volga.

I zipped by the elevators, farm supply businesses, gas stations, trailer court, and a large water tower. Water towers always reminded me of what the Martians' war machines must have looked like in H.G. Wells' novel *The War of the Worlds*, but not in the movie version in which the machines flew. Despite a blue and gold sign that proclaimed that the Sioux Valley High School was the home of the Cossacks, Volga looked like another well-scrubbed Midwestern town of about a thousand souls and not Russian at all.

Menninger had one of the finest city libraries in central North Dakota, thanks to its long-time librarian Mae Larson. Miss Larson kept up subscriptions to the *New York Times*, the *Washington Post*, the *Chicago Tribune*, the *Christian Science Monitor*, and the *Wall Street Journal* as well as several other national and regional newspapers. Although she had finally relented and accepted some assistance from the ladies of the Athena Club, she made the final selections on adding new books. I enjoyed my time at the library and had spent some of it looking at the poetry anthologies. None of them contained any of the Beat poets. Neither had the anthology we had used in my college modern poetry class. I wondered what America would be like when its anthologies started to include the Beat poetry of drugs, forbidden four-letter words, and even more forbidden sexual references, underlain with a fervid anti-Americanism. I knew Miss Larson would never have accepted them, but she was dead. The new librarian, Miss Preston, was just as prim, so I couldn't imagine she would approve of the Beats, but after her?

During the previous August I had driven out to California in my Camaro to see my sister Marjorie and her husband Michael John Wayne. She was a teacher in Panorama City, where she had lived since 1961. Their only child was Marjorie Alice.

On the way I stopped in Yellowstone, saw the Grand Tetons, crossed the Sierra Nevada range near Donner Pass, and stayed on I-80 into the Central Valley. Traffic was stopped for half an hour, and when we got going, I passed over a portion of the highway covered in blood. It wasn't really blood—a flatbed loaded with tomatoes had overturned and tomato juice and flesh crimsoned the pavement.

After seeing the "blood," I slowed down, so it took me a little longer to get to San Francisco. Miles before I reached the city, I could smell the sea, and then I was on it, or at least a portion of it, as I crossed the San Francisco-Oakland Bay Bridge. I hit the toll plaza and rolled with the traffic on the cantilevered portion of the bridge, made the turn, Treasure Island looking like a small bright city to the right, passed through the bore of the Yerba Buena Tunnel and then marveled at the great steel suspension towers draped with their cable filaments. They were so magnificent; I hoped they would stand forever.

I cut over and rode the ramp down to Fremont, took Market, but got off at Turk Street when I saw there were no parking lots. I kept going until I found one and pulled in. After making sure my car was locked, I ate supper at a greasy spoon and went back to the Camaro; I was beat.

I slept the same way I had in Chicago in 1968: I locked the doors, sat in the left-hand bucket seat, turned on my side and moved my body between the seats so most of it was in the back at a ninety-degree angle to the front. I covered my legs with a couple shirts, pulled my clothes on the travel bar over my body, and went to sleep. In the dark no one would know I was in there, and if they broke in, well, I had my machete.

The next morning I was off to the greasy spoon and then went exploring after I put my billfold in my right front pocket to avoid pickpockets.

Uncle Josh had been stationed at the Presidio just after World War I, and my Dad had visited him and his family in 1923. San Francisco had changed so much in the past forty-some years that a lot of what they had seen was gone, but I still wanted to be close to where Josh and Dad had been.

I legged it over to Market and then to Powell, where the cable car turn-table was located. I boarded a green Powell & Hyde car, and we were off with the bell clanging and the operator pushing or pulling two big levers that came up from a hole in the floor. The car wheels rumbled past businesses and we'd meet other cars rolling by to our left. Some of them carried advertisements: "I stop at the St. Francis," "Pepsi," "Rice-A-Roni, The San Francisco Treat." The car made frequent stops and passengers got on and off; most of them appeared to be tourists.

We passed the St. Francis Hotel, Union Square, and kept going uphill past the Sir Francis Drake Hotel. We hit an even steeper part of the hill, leveled off at an intersection, then it was steep again before we crossed the cable car tracks on California. Going up or down, we always leveled off at intersections.

I could see a misty hill in the distance across the Bay. We started slowly downhill between rows of apartments houses. The tracks curved left onto Jackson, and we went uphill between more apartment houses—I figured we were on Nob Hill. We leveled off and then began to descend, accompanied by more apartment houses.

The tracks curved right onto Hyde, which was tree-lined, down and then up Russian Hill, and then level with blue hills across the Bay. The operator stopped so we could see the beginning of Lombard Street, the crookedest street in the world. To the east Coit Tower pointed upward from Telegraph Hill.

We started downhill with the Bay and Alcatraz coming closer and more hazy hills in the background before we stopped at Aquatic Park. San Francisco was my favorite city; I hated to think that the San Andreas Fault just outside the Golden Gate or any of the other major faults in the area could kill it.

A round white sign made to look like the wheel of a sailing vessel and with an orange crab in the center welcomed me to "Fisherman's Wharf of San Francisco." I walked to the Hyde Street Pier, bought a ticket, and explored the various ships berthed alongside. The *Balclutha*, a square-rigger, was my favorite. I got out on the wharf as far as I could and saw the Golden Gate Bridge and behind it Mt. Tamalpais, where my Dad had a spiritual experience back in '23. I scanned the Bay and saw Alcatraz, Angel Island, and Treasure Island.

The later morning was bringing with it more seagulls and hippies. The gulls were white trimmed with black; the hippie men were invariably bearded and shaggy with odd clothes; the girls were usually plain-looking with long hair and wistful eyes. Some hippies played guitars and waited for coins or bills. The gulls flapped around, looking for scraps.

For an early lunch I went to Alioto's and had clam chowder and a couple sourdough rolls. All the time I listened to the gulls and the people. The gull seemed happy; the people less so. If they were older tourists, their health was a problem; if they were younger tourists, their kids were a problem; if they were hippies, everything was a problem— the war, the government, drugs, money, life in general.

I walked west to Ghiardelli Square and had some chocolate for dessert. It was so good I had a hot fudge sundae, too. I decided to walk the whole bayside, so I took Jefferson and the Embarcadero all the way to Kearny Street, checking out the ships and boats on the Bay, the milling people, and the great city spreading up the hills.

Slowly, I walked back to Jefferson, breathing in the sea air, an occasional smell of fish, and that of unfamiliar food. At Pompei's Grotto I chickened out on anything exotic and went with an albacore tuna sandwich with lettuce, tomato, and mayo on toasted sourdough; French fries; and a Coke.

I walked around some more, passing on the Live Baby Turtles and the Hand Blown Glass for sale, but I had to do one more thing. I walked out on a dock, sat down, and sang "(Sittin' On) The Dock of The Bay," which Otis Redding had recorded eighteen days before his death in a plane crash:

> "Sittin' in the mornin' sun
> I'll be sittin' when the evenin' comes
> Watching the ships roll in
> Then I watch 'em roll away again, yeah..."

After that, there was nothing left. My Grandfather Boss had died on a bench near Coit Tower, so I decided to walk up Columbus Avenue. As I walked along the North Beach Playground, I turned and looked downhill and the street seemed vaguely familiar. Could it be one of those used in the most famous car chase in movie history where Steve McQueen as Lt. Frank Bullitt races and rams his Ford Mustang GT all over San Francisco in pursuit of two hit men? I hoped it was. I had seen the movie at the Blackstone just a couple months before and although the continual reappearance of the same green VW Bug at least four times in the various chase scenes was a distraction, I loved the continual action.

To test my endurance, I turned on Filbert with Sts. Peter and Paul Church on my left and Washington Square Park on my right and kept going up Telegraph Hill to the Tower. Filbert was one of the steepest streets in San Francisco, and after it ended, I took the wooden Filbert Steps to the Tower. I passed the statue of Columbus and walked around, looking for the spot Boss had died, but I had no idea. There were lots of trees and shrubs and I heard the famous wild parrots, but didn't see them.

The view of the Bay, the bridges, Lombard Street straight-arrow to the west until it zig-zagged up Russian Hill, the city overrunning the hills, all were gifts which weren't improved much after I paid admission and took the elevator to the top.

There were some murals painted in an American Primitive style. Boss hated a couple of them and I didn't care for the messages myself. In one set in a library, a man reached for a book entitled *Capital* by Karl Marx. In the same picture men were reading newspapers with stories about killing, protests, censorship, fraud, and a "MORATORIUM IN NORTH DAKOTA." In another there were striking miners and people in a Hooverville being gawked at by some rich people who stood beside their chauffeur-driven limousine. A provocation to class warfare in Boss's opinion, and mine. Another mural had the Blue Eagle symbol of the New Deal, anathema to Boss, and I wasn't too thrilled myself. Leaving aside the politics, the paintings reminded me a little of Bosch or Bruegel and their complex arrangements of everyday life.

After I rested awhile, I took Kearny and Union until I found a pizza joint and ordered a large pepperoni and big glasses of milk, water, and Coke. All my walking and hill climbing had taken it out of me. I figured that anyone who had seen *Bullitt* and all the hills would sympathize with my feet.

The sun was dropping fast when I got back on the west side of Columbus. I came to a somewhat squat two-story building with a lot of books behind large windows. The sign said "City Lights Books"; I was at the cradle of the Beat Movement. Its owner was Lawrence Ferlinghetti, who had won a court battle over the censorship of *Howl*. I went in. Incense covered a more acrid smell. Paperback books shouldered each other on rows and ranks of shelves, more books than those in the Minot State bookstore and the Menninger library combined.

Most of them were left-wing, but there was a display labeled "Banned Books" which contained titles such as Whitman's *Leaves of Grass*, a couple Eugene O'Neill plays, *Ulysses* by James Joyce, *Lady Chatterley's*

Lover by D.H. Lawrence, *God's Little Acre* by Erskine Caldwell, *Strange Fruit* by Lillian Smith, *Forever Amber* by Kathleen Winsor, and dozens of others I'd never heard of.

I hacked my way through some Beat poetry—Ginsberg, of course, Gregory Corso, Philip Whalen, Michael McClure, and Ferlinghetti himself.

Ginsberg was attacking the U.S. from a left-wing point of view in "America," but he had a long poem called "Kaddish," which I kind of liked because it was about his mother. My problem was it seemed to lay her bare to the public and because of some of his language.

Corso kept proclaiming he was a great American, but just couldn't stand the society.

I liked a Whalen poem about sandpipers and willets and Mt. Tamalpais, but was this poetry:

> "RESTRICTED, SPECIAL ORDER #21 this
> HQ dd 8 FEB 1946 contained 6 Pars.CENSORED
> 3. Fol EM, White, MCO indicated, ASRS indicated,
> AF2AF, are reld fr asgmt and dy this HQ and trfd
> In gr to 37th AAFBU, Dorje Field, Lhasa, TIBET…"

Michael McClure had an interesting poem about Lion Men staring at him out of his dreams when he was a baby.

Ferlinghetti had a poem called "Autobiography," which had a lot of references to events, places, and people that would have been interesting to figure out if I had the time. The poem mentioned "…a Great Stone Face in North Dakota." Was this a reference to Mt. Rushmore and a mistake, or was it a symbol known only to Ferlinghetti? I skimmed his book of poetry called *A Coney Island of the Mind*, but when he started mocking Jesus, I put it down.

It seemed that the Beats worked in free verse, a form of poetry that has to be read many times out loud to get the cadence, and I wasn't going to do that sitting in City Lights. Whitman did free verse well, but did the Beats? Moreover, I tended to agree with Robert Frost when he said that writing free verse was like playing tennis without a net.

The Beats made news in their public condemnation of the United States, its society, and its policies, but my brief exposure to their poetry didn't show them as radical in print as their public persona did.

What it came down to was that the Beats wanted to poke America in the eye, which was probably what a lot of young men wanted to do. The trouble was what happened to the damaged eye? If it doesn't see better after the poking, what's the point? What if it sees worse?

The Beats had already passed their prime, America was probably worse off than when they began poking, and while they had kicked open the doors of poetry so that it could be about anything and nothing, it wasn't any closer to mass acceptance than classical music or ballet. I knew when I got home, I'd go back to being a swinger of birches with Robert Frost and revel in the city of broad shoulders with Carl Sandburg.

The Beats hated America. It was the cesspool they suffered in, but they knew they were powerless to change it, so they turned to drugs, alcohol, sex, and exotic religions and philosophies. Those they inspired also hated America, but they thought they could do something about it.

The Beats were pavers; they paved the way for a variety of writers and thinkers, either as inspirations or as doorways by which the other intellectuals and authors were introduced to American audiences.

Norman Mailer wasn't so much inspired by them because his first writing preceded theirs, but he gained more acceptance because of the Beats. I had read *The Naked and the Dead* because it was in a Modern Library edition, and I was trying to read all the Modern Library books; I quit after twenty-one. I thought it was a pretty good war story told by a guy who had served mostly as an army cook. The only other Mailer novel I had read was *An American Dream* in which a guy kills his wife and tries to get away with it. I saw a little irony in that Mailer was on his fourth wife at the time: he had stabbed, but did not kill, his second wife. He was known for being pugnacious in public after a few drinks and/or drugs in his system, trying to be a five-foot six version of Hemingway. Sexual, orgasmic, psychopathic, violent, misogynistic, that was Mailer.

Wilhelm Reich was an Austrian psychoanalyst and Communist who tried to marry psychoanalysis and Marxism. He believed neurosis was linked to the economic conditions in which a person was brought up. Reich claimed to have discovered the "orgone," a form of cosmic energy. Sometimes it was manifested in the Aurora Borealis and other natural phenomena. He built "orgone boxes" in which he had his patients sit naked while the orgone cured them of all diseases, especially cancer. That probably didn't attract too many Beats or the disaffected young people growing up in the post-war world, but what did get their attention was Reich's emphasis on the need for sexual intercourse, especially by adolescents. Reich gave a "scientific" license for teenage promiscuity.

Herbert Marcuse was an anti-capitalist who wrote *Eros and Civilization* (1955) and *One Dimensional Man* (1964). He was a Marxist and attempted to reconcile Marx (the optimism of Utopian freedom) and Freud (the pessimism of civilized repression) through technology so people would be free to enjoy more leisure, more pleasure, more sex. He later espoused a belief in repressive tolerance in which American-style freedom is not really the type of freedom we need to create an idyllic Utopia. In Marcuse's view it was expected that left-wing ideas would be tolerated in the public forum because they are guideposts to Utopia, but right-wing ideas are to be repressed because they are repressive themselves. There can be no toleration for the intolerant.

Norman O. Brown was a scholar who wrote *Life Against Death* (1959). He was a former Marxist professor of classics, who believed in the transformation of human nature into one entirely devoid of repression in which the adult throws off all restrictions imposed by his or her infantile nature and exuberantly embraces the pleasures of the body; i.e., sex.

Paul Goodman wrote *Growing Up Absurd* (1959), in which he claimed that American society provides no noble or enlightened places for the young who grow up to take their places in an absurd world, just the type of world the Beats saw.

Without the Beats, would the following have risen to prominence: the Black Power Movement of Huey Newton, H. Rap Brown, Eldridge Cleaver, Stokley Carmichael, Malcolm X; the profanity-laced comedy of Lenny Bruce; the "singer" Bob Dylan; Carlos Casteneda, the author of *The Teachings of Don Juan: A Yaqui Way of Knowledge* in which "total freedom" is attributed to the use of hallucinogens; the *Whole Earth Catalogue*; Hippies; Ken Kesey, author of *One Flew Over the Cuckoo's Nest* and *Sometimes a Great Notion,* friend of Neal Cassady, and experimenter with LSD; singer Janis Joplin; Jerry Garcia and the Grateful Dead; Yippies Abbie Hoffman and Jerry Rubin; radical environmentalist Barry Commoner?

I did buy something, however. I saw a thin book entitled *Trout Fishing in America*, and I wondered what it was doing in City Lights. The author was Richard Brautigan, and he appeared on the cover, standing; wearing glasses and a mustache; dressed in a high-crowned hat, open coat and vest and jeans. A rather plain woman in hippie fashion and large teeth sat beside him, and a statue of Benjamin Franklin was behind them.

The book wasn't about trout fishing, although Brautigan seemed to know a lot about it. It seemed to be about a lot of things in America that disturbed him—among them industrialization, the pollution of nature, capital punishment, Mormons, the medical profession—but I liked his quirky humor and the characters he created, such as the Kool-Aid wino, an old woman who tends a blazing wood furnace, and Trout Fishing in America Shorty, so I plunked down my $1.95 plus tax, put the book in my jacket pocket, and walked out into the hustling night.

There seemed to be a lot of people on Broadway, so I walked to the corner, and the night became a clash of neon and garish lights. Huge signs clung vertically to several buildings and proclaimed them the homes of the hungry i, the Roaring 20s, Big Al's (complete with tommy gun), and the Condor, which boated a representation of a woman with huge breasts and red lights for nipples. As I got closer, I read the name Carol Doda. There were also smaller clubs and bars and an abundance of signs: Live! Erotic! Nude! Totally Nude College Co-Eds! Naked Dance of Love! Our Girls Go All the Way! Broadway was plugged with cars and the sidewalks were jammed with people, mostly men. I had found Sodom and Gomorrah, Babylon, and Imperial Rome all on one block.

Barkers stood on the sidewalk, trying to entice people inside. A sign screamed Topless! Bottomless! It couldn't be. I let myself be enticed.

It was possible. The lighting was dim, except for the stage where young women danced as naked as Adam and Eve without the fig leaves. Some naked women circulated in the crowd selling drinks. The fetid atmosphere reeked of cigarettes, booze, sweat, perfume, sex, and was capped with voices trying to be heard, orders for booze, and catcalls at some of the girls.

The place was so crowded people kept rubbing against me, including the nude women. Some people didn't smell so good. I kept my hand on my billfold.

Not all the girls appeared to be college age, but there were a couple that were cute and reminded me of the sisters of two of my friends. I had to get out of there and pushed through to the doorway.

On the street I felt dirty.

I went up the hill, caught a cable car on Mason and rode it down to Washington, then over to Powell and down to Market. I didn't enjoy it. I walked a couple blocks to Turk and climbed into the Camaro.

I had brought the smell of degradation with me and my prayer was to be rid of it. The next morning I paid the attendant and drove to Fisherman's Wharf.

I had shrimp and sourdough for breakfast and went for a walk. I met a family wearing some Green Bay Packers insignia, so I gave them a thumbs-up and said, "Go, Pack!" The two teenage girls smiled and the father stopped. We talked about the Packers chances. In 1968 they had gone 6-7-1 and lost to the Vikings twice and split with the Bears, finishing out of the playoffs under first-year coach Phil Bengston. Neither of us was optimistic, but both girls, who had 4-H pins among their Packer gear, thought their chances were good with Bart Starr, Carroll Dale, Boyd Dowler, Donny Anderson, Elijah Pitts, Forrest Gregg, Gale Gillingham, Herb Adderley, Willie Wood, and Ray Nitschke.

They knew the team just as well as I did, and I liked them. So young. So innocent.

When the family left, I walked out as far as I could go. There was a freshening breeze creating a lot of chop, and the waves would break on the wharf and send spray like wet diamonds. The gulls stood still in the wind.

Alcatraz looked medieval with its buildings like a castle sitting on top of the "Rock." I decided to take a boat cruise around the island and bought a ticket.

Once we got out into the Bay, I changed my mind about escaping from the island prison. After I read an article on the Anglin brothers— Clarence and John—and Frank Morris and their possible escape in 1962 using a raft made of rubber raincoats, I thought they had made it. Looking at the distances and the cold water, I was certain they hadn't.

I stood so Bay water from the bow and the wind sprayed onto my face and hair. I rubbed it around. By the time we got back, I was pretty well soaked. I got in the Camaro and drove over the Golden Gate Bridge and back, so I could say I had done it. Back in '23 my Dad had crossed the Golden Gate on a railroad ferry before there was a bridge.

As I headed south, my hair and clothes were drying, and I felt clean.

A bridge over a dry streambed, a sign saying Bruce (first name? last name? nobody's name?) was eight miles north, and another bridge over a small stream that passed under a black steel truss bridge on the railroad and through some trees beyond. A long pond of water split the highway and the railroad which diverged on a diagonal to the right. A couple small bridges, a couple farmsteads, and then a larger bridge over a ditch-like stream. Something in the road ahead; I swerved. A jackrabbit, body crushed, but ears sticking up. A bridge over nothing, billboards, some shelterbelts and farms, and then a turn to the right and there was Brookings.

It was a nice ride into town with fields to my right and buildings to my left. I crossed over a little creek, a turn, and then a wide thoroughfare with Pioneer Park on the right and businesses on the left. Lots of trees and mostly older homes marked a residential section with a shopping center on the left.

A young woman who worked in the ASCS office in Menninger and a graduate of South Dakota State University in Brookings told me that it was the home of the world's best hamburgers, and that I should try one. She gave me the address—427 Main—so when I saw the street sign, I made a right, passed the VFW, the post office with its six Ionic columns, and there on the corner stood the Mecca of Hamburgers— Nick's Hamburger Shop—a single-story white building with red trim and lettering which stated "Since 1929," a peppermint awning, and two corner doors. I parked, got off and stretched, and wondered why there was no one else around.

I strode up to one of the doors, the eighteen-cent burger already melting in my mouth. The door refused to open. I tried again and then read the sign: "Closed on Sundays." I walked back to the 750, head down, hoping no one had seen my vain efforts.

A large building with two Ionic columns stood on the corner of the next block—Brookings liked its Greek architecture.

An L-shaped sign, "PIZZA KING'S" with an arrow as the bottom leg, pointed to a brown two-story brick building, smaller buildings on either side, but a larger two-story brick building on the corner. I cut across the street and parked the bike in front of a window. All the parking was diagonal.

Inside, I caught that good doughy-yeasty-cheesy smell of a place that makes its pizza from scratch. I sat so I could watch my bike and ordered, making sure to have large glasses of water, milk, and Coke since I felt dehydrated. One of the specialties was called the "Jackrabbit." It wasn't really, but I passed anyway.

Six teenagers laughed their way in and took a table not too far from mine and ordered. My pepperoni pizza was too large for me, so rather than waste some of it, I stood up and brought the pizza on the pan over to them.

"Anyone care for some pizza. I haven't touched it. Take three pieces."

As I came over, I saw the three boys move a little closer to the girls. I liked that protective gesture. The girls declined my offer, but each of the boys grabbed a piece and thanked me as I walked away, very rural nice.

As I sprinkled the hot peppers on the pizza, one of the boys—his letterman's jacket said "Rob"—came over and asked if they could sit with me.

"Sure, if there's room."

They pushed their table and carried their chairs over. I continued to eat and they asked me where I was from and what I was doing. I explained and I could tell the boys wanted to do the same someday.

Rob had a twin brother, Rod, and the other boy was Ryan. Their girls were Josie, Connie, and Faith, whose name was Lucinda, so she could have gone by "Lucy" or "Cindy," but chose her middle name instead. Four of them were from Volga, but Ryan and Faith were from Bruce, really from farms outside of Bruce. However, they were all Cossacks because the Bruce students were bussed over to Volga to the high school. They didn't know where the name "Bruce" came from.

The boys all played football and were evidently proud of it, wearing their letterman's jackets even though it was warm outside. The girls were all cheerleaders. Ryan, Faith, and Josie all belonged to 4-H and were preparing for the State Fair in Huron. They all worked during the summer, three of them on their farms and the other three as counselors at a Bible camp. They were all preparing to attend college after graduation the next spring (they invited me to attend). Four were going to SDSU (Josie was going into Veterinary Science, the boys were undecided), Faith would attend Dakota Wesleyan in Mitchell, and Connie, who would be valedictorian and blushed when the others mentioned it, was going to be a doctor and was going to USD in Vermillion, which had a Medical School.

I enjoyed talking with the Cossacks, so optimistic about their futures and so happy with their lives. Their order came when I had two slices of pizza left. I picked up one and everything went quiet. The six had joined hands, bowed their heads, and were saying silent grace. I felt like a fool. When their heads came up and a couple said "amen" out loud, the talking continued. I said a silent retroactive grace.

The door opened and three kids came in. All were wearing dark clothes and fringed leather vests. The boys had long hair and attempted beards. The girl wore a beaded headband. I guessed they were pseudo-hippies as they slouched into their chairs.

Rob, Rod, and Ryan were getting ready for football practice. Their season would be a good one if they could defeat the Flandreau Fliers. The girls discussed the classes they'd be taking, and they asked me about the Menninger School.

I excused myself and went to the men's room. Just as I finished, one of the hippie-boys came in, I brushed past him, and he turned and followed me out.

I paid and walked over to the Cossacks. I told them I had to leave, but that I had enjoyed taking with them. They said goodbye, the boys standing to shake my hand. I wished them good luck and they wished me the same. As I reached the door, I heard the table scrape as they pushed it back into place.

Just as I straddled the bike, I heard, "Hey, man, can I score some grass?" It was the hippie-boy.

I wheeled the 750 around. "Just because someone has long hair and a beard doesn't mean he's a druggie." I kick-started the bike, trying to show off, geared it, and flew down the street. I had to brake fast at the corner stop sign and the bike skidded. I hoped the hippie-boy had gone inside. Another stop sign, a wave at Nick's, and I came to a traffic light. A right turn and I was on my way, the afternoon shadows reaching for me out of the west and me being upset I had lost so much time eating, but mitigated by my meeting the six young hopefuls.

A couple old houses, a commercial area, and into a residential section with a church, older homes and trees, and sidewalks with middle-class walkers. Gas stations and restaurants clustered around an intersection. A large apartment house. Houses—some new and some very old. Business places whose owners were probably hoping they were located close enough to the new Interstate to grab some customers, just as they had gotten business off old U.S. 77. Or would the Interstate siphon too many people down to Sioux Falls? Some businesses had already moved closer.

I transferred to the right lane and went down the ramp onto the new Interstate and started gaining on the traffic. I crossed an overpass with the Northwestern tracks below stretching on into Minnesota and a spur running to a sand and gravel business to the south and passed under an overpass with no interchange exits. The late sun forced shadows onto the blacktop and made a lake on my right into yellow fire. A line of trees snaked along with a little creek.

I went under the Elkton interchange and crossed over a creek gashed into the prairie. The shaded farms were far off and any little towns were miles off the Interstate. Two-lane travel is about space—what and who you see; four-lane travel is about time—how long before I get there?

A very slight curve to the right; at least it was a variation. A county line sign and a small pond on the left were other variations. Farmyards were closer to the Interstate, but they were gone in a flash. A chute of trees sent me over the Big Sioux River, its water black in the evening light and split by an island. I flipped on my headlight. A trickle of water that went under the Interstate in a concrete culvert and then the Ward interchange.

I curved around a horse trailer, but I couldn't see if there was a horse. The land was fairly flat and croppy. A road crossed over, riding on top of four pillars. Big black water on the right with some slivery trees marking its margin. I went over a bridge that spanned what appeared to be a gravel road and came to the Flandreau interchange.

I checked my odometer. Two more bridges spanning gravel roads and five miles brought me to the Colman-Egan interchange. I imagined I could see the lights of Sioux Falls; I was running out of real estate where I could spend the night. My budget didn't allow any motel rooms. I crossed a couple bridges and the Trent interchange. I had to get off pretty soon.

Farm lights teased me along the way. A bridge passed overhead, and I went into a turn to the west and a couple miles later jogged to the south again. The air was cooling.

Lights off to the east—Dell Rapids. Daylight would have revealed signs telling me of all the wonders in which to partake along the Big Sioux River. The interchange was surrounded by buildings, so I couldn't stop.

More teasing lights, another bridge, and the Baltic interchange, again with buildings. I kept going, but an empty feeling bored a hole in my gut. I saw more farm lights, but in the distance lights that could only come from Sioux Falls. I went into a slight left-hand turn.

As I passed under a bridge, bright lights showed up ahead. I turned off the Interstate at the Renner-Crooks interchange, not really sure of what I was going to do. At the stop sign I contemplated my next move. I figured I was about three miles from Sioux Falls, and I didn't want any vagrancy charges if they found me camped out inside the city limits. To the right of the ramp leading down to the Interstate, there was a tall wooden fence and behind the fence was some type of business that was lit up like a carnival midway.

The fence would act like the stockade of an old fort, protecting me on the west, and the lights would be a safety factor, too. I crossed the road and went into the broad ditch, crushing the hip-high dry weeds under my wheels. Stopping near the fence, I paralleled the Honda to the Interstate and made camp.

I took the poncho and sleeping bag off the bike, got my two flashlights out of the bag, and set the yellow one on its swivel base, so I could see what I was doing. I emptied the bag and used the grommets to attach the poncho to the bike, then used my machete to pound two metal rods into the ground and hook the other two grommets to them. Now I had rain and dew protection. I rolled the bag out and sat for awhile listening to the traffic.

Finally, I took out my journal and wrote in the date and a verbal sketch of the day. The moon wasn't out yet and even when it did appear, it would be in its first quarter, so the stars patterned the sky with distant diamond pictures. I took out a star chart I had made, sat by the fence, and gazed upward. The constellation Lyra with its parallelogram and its bright star Vega was at the zenith. To the east was Cygnus, sometimes called the "Northern Cross," with its brightest star Deneb at the top of the cross. South of Cygnus was the great parallelogram of Aquila and its bright star Altair. To the north were gentle Cassiopeia and the Little Dipper with Polaris. I walked to the end of the fence and looked south where the elongated Scorpius and its red star Antares were barely visible and then to the west where I could just make out kite-like Bootes and the famous star Arcturus and the Big Dipper to the northwest.

I walked back to camp. Stars always made me think of God, so I got out the small New Testament that I had received at my Confirmation. It also contained Psalms and Proverbs. I knew the Psalms mentioned stars, so I slid my finger down the pages until I came to Psalm 8:3-4—"When I consider thy heavens, the work of thy fingers, the moon and the stars, which thou hast ordained; What is man that thou art mindful of him? And the son of man, that thou visitest him?" My finger slid along for quite awhile before I came to Psalm 147:4—"He telleth the number of the stars; he calleth them all by their names." Then there was Psalm 148:3—"Praise ye him, sun and moon: praise him, all ye stars of light." I knew that Arcturus was mentioned in the Bible, but that was in the Old Testament somewhere.

I wanted to believe that there were no atheists in observatories, but I knew that wasn't true.

I put the Testament away and pulled out its opposite: a book of Robinson Jeffers' poems and folded in the pages some of his poems I had copied. Robinson Jeffers had died when I was a senior in high school, but no mention was made, so far had his reputation fallen. I first came across Jeffers in college, and even though he was a somewhat nihilistic, pantheistic, pessimistic misanthrope, I was attracted to his poetry. I found "Night" to be an appropriate poem, with its lines:

> "This August night in a rift of cloud Antares reddens,
> The great one, the ancient torch, a lord among lost children,
> The earth's orbit doubled would not girdle his greatness,
> one fire…
> Truly the spouting fountains of light, Antares, Arcturus…"

In "The Epic Stars" I found the words:

> "The heroic stars spending themselves,
> Coining their very flesh into bullets for the lost battle,
> They must burn out at length like used candles;
> And Mother Night will weep in her triumph…"

"Wonder and Joy" had these lines:

> "The infinite wheeling stars. A wonder pure
> Must ever well within me to behold
> Venus decline; or great Orion, whose belt
> Is studded with three nails of burning gold…"

I ended the poetry with "Prescription of Painful Ends" with its line "Plato in his time watched Athens dance the down path" that always left in me the question: "Was America dancing the down path?"

After brushing my teeth and drinking water from my canteen, I leaned the machete against the bike; rolled my brown-fringed leather coat into a pillow; got into my bag; and said my prayers, thanking God for a safe first day, for all the blessings He had given to me, especially my family, and asking for safety tomorrow.

And so to bed…

What's that noise?

The moon was up, but no quarter moon would shine as brightly as the light around the 750. I crawled from under the poncho and peered at the ramp. A pickup sat there idling, its lights glaring right at me.

"It's a motorcycle."

"Let's get it."

A door slammed.

"You guys go; I'll watch for cars."

Two figures left the pavement and began crackling their way through the dried weeds. I grabbed the machete; they weren't getting my bike without a fight. I looked for some courage, found it, and stood up. The two figures froze.

They were two teenagers in light-colored t-shirts.

"It's a guy!"

"He's got a goddang sword!"

The one in the pickup yelled, "Get your asses back here!"

I stepped around the bike, and the two scampered up the ditch, jumped into their vehicle, and the driver gunned it down the ramp. After the taillights were swallowed by the darkness, I began to laugh.

I placed the machete beside me and lay down in my unzipped sleeping bag. Adrenalin kept me awake for awhile. But then I slept the sleep of the victorious.

DAY TWO

I was up and packed in the false dawn, not tired at all. I had a long way to go that day because I would be leaving the Interstate and using a byway to a shrine in southern Iowa I wanted to visit, so I got moving.

Sunrise revealed three signs suspended over the Interstate that informed me I-90 was coming up and I could go to Albert Lea or Rapid City or that I could continue south on I-29 to Sioux Falls. I passed over the BN tracks. I saw a tractor-trailer rig crossing over on the I-90; the semi cab was green and the trailer had a giant red "C" and green "F" on the side—a "Corn Flakes."

Late one winter day when we were unloading Chuck Morse's truck at the Super Saver, he said he had seen a "Corn Flakes" jackknifed on the Worthington hill. When I asked him if Kellogg's really had trucks, he started laughing and said, "Slim, don't be so dumb. A 'Corn Flakes' is Consolidated Freightways White Freightliner." Sean Sullivan and his brother Doyle started laughing at me, too, but I don't think they knew what a "Corn Flakes" was, either.

I started looking for a truck stop, but while there was plenty of prairie, the city's growth hadn't embraced the Interstate, so I swung off onto Highway 16, headed west, found nothing, and turned around. I passed a gas station, but decided to keep going. Empty lots, then trees, then the Big Sioux River. More trees opened onto a commercial district.

Up on the left a sign announced the Town 'n' Country Café; I pulled into the parking lot in front of a large bank of windows. I read the hours. It opened at six, but there were already lights on inside.

Cars began pulling up and after the doors were unlocked, I let the regulars file in first.

The interior was well-lighted by several gold and white hanging lights. Dark brown wooden beams slanted the ceiling toward the windows. Part of the walls were painted white and the rest were paneled in brown. There was a long strip of aqua above the windows. To the left were the opening to the kitchen and a counter with gray stools that had black seats with a strip of brass around them. Tables with black chairs took up much of the rest of the interior, right up to the windows. The floor was unusual: light gold carpeting ran in strips from the counter to the windows, but six inches of a dark wooden floor showed in between each strip.

When I took a seat by the windows in line with my bike, I put my helmet on the table. Kitchen noises had already started and so had conversations. There is nothing like a café to get people talking, in this case a bunch of farmers and ag-men who apparently worked closely with SDSU, especially when it came to corn. Steinbeck was wrong.

After the waitress took my order, I listened to the closest two tables. One was talking about insecticides and European corn borers, wireworms, seed corn maggots, seed corn beetles, corn rootworms and greenbugs; the other was comparing crops yields, concluding that the best varieties were Lancer and Scout 66 winter wheat, Von Lochow rye, and Pettis oats. Back home the talk would have been less about corn and more about wheat, but the opinions, agreements, and disagreements would be similar.

Both tables were worried about rain—both June and July had been 1.6 inches below average and August was starting out even worse—and the hotter than normal weather. Crops, moisture, weather, the farmers' world.

My order came; the waitress called me "Sugah"; and I dug into a short stack covered in butter and syrup, a rasher of crisp bacon, scrambled eggs, American fries, and a large glass of milk. After my first few bites of everything, I looked through the opening into the kitchen, and, sure enough, the cook was a woman with the look of fifty years of rural living on her. For my money you can't beat a cook with roots on the farm.

When I taught in western North Dakota, I ate almost every breakfast and supper in the town's only café. Maggie, the woman who owned it, was about sixty, but did the work with the energy of a sixteen-year-old. Sometimes if the supper crowd was slow, she'd sit with me and we'd talk. The cook was what used to be called a DP, a Displaced Person. Maggie told me her name was Katarzyna, and she had grown up on a farm near Lodz in Poland, but the invasions by Germany and the Soviet Union in September 1939 crumbled her world. Her brothers were conscripted into the German army and died on the Eastern Front. Her father and mother kept on farming, but the Germans took most of the crops. In 1945 they heard that the Russians were coming, so they moved west with tens of thousands of others. Her father died on the way; he had a bad heart. Her mother, sister, and she almost made it to the Elbe when they were captured and raped by Russian troops in a barn, despite protesting that they were not Germans.

When they were done, some Russians took the mother behind the building. The girls heard a single shot and never saw their mother again.

The girls were raped for another day. That night Katarzyna found a little door where the pigs would enter and leave the barn. She told her sister they could escape, but her sister's mind had gone and she just stared. Katarzyna crawled through the door.

Eventually, she made it to France, then to England, and then to the United States.

She didn't speak English very well. At first, Maggie had photographs of every special and every item and they were all numbered, so when an order for a #1 came back, Katarzyna would look at photo #1 and go to work. After a few months she had every number memorized, plus the little marks that meant "over easy," "well done," "no mayo" and so forth. Eventually, she learned enough English that she could do away with the photos, but still when she talked to herself while cooking, it was always in Polish.

Everything she made was delicious, and I always made certain that part of my tip went to her. When I would get up to leave, I looked into the kitchen and said "Thank you," and she would smile behind her hand and give me a little bow. As I was leaving after my last breakfast, Katarzyna came out of the kitchen. Maggie said that she wanted to say goodbye, so I said goodbye first. She came closer, bowed her little bow, gave me a hug, handed me a fresh donut, then rushed back into her kitchen. I ate it going up the hill to school; rural women are the best cooks.

I talked a little with my waitress, who was from "Missourah." When she pronounced it that way, I knew I was getting closer to the South. I took a pack of postal cards out of my inside jacket pocket and wrote about my first day. I addressed it to Mom and Dad. Dad had asked me to write and had given me the cards. I also decided to write one to Theresa. I left a good tip and walked up to pay.

When I asked the waitress for directions to the post office, one of my neighbors said I should also look over their old post office and told me its location.

I rolled east on 16. I kept going, passing eating places, all closed, and crossed over the Northwestern tracks. I went into a curve and the street split: I had to take the right-hand side, passed through a neighborhood of older homes, crossed Minnesota Avenue, and I was downtown. The First Congregational Church with a big triangle on the front and a Gothic bell tower on the side loomed up on the right. Next, stood Washington High School with its four stories and a balustrade that gave it an Italian look

I went right and down a canyon of brick and glass, past the State Theatre, and on the next block came to a massive, rose-colored, stone Romanesque building standing at least three stories. Its arches, cornice, and two octagonal corner turrets exuded power. That was my kind of post office, but it was occupied as the Federal Building and Courthouse.

I cut over on 13th and turned north onto 2nd. Almost the entire next block was taken up by an earth-tone building, very modern and very dull. I put my post cards in the mail box and got away from the new post office as quickly as I could. I went north almost to the river and turned left onto 16.

Sioux Falls traffic was awake and feeling its way downtown. I passed old and new buildings, one of the oldest being the city council office. The *Argus Leader* took up the next block in a brown brick building that looked like four boxes of different heights pushed together. After the red light, I turned left onto Minnesota. The newspaper boasted about its largest circulation in South Dakota with dozens of windows and some August-drying flowers. I passed the YMCA Anderson Youth Memorial Building and an older portion of the "Y," both in darker brown brick.

I crossed the Northwestern tracks guarded by lights hanging from an overhead arm with more lights on the poles. The red lights were not on, so I kept going.

Ahead on the left I saw an old-fashioned Standard sign, so I waited for a break in the traffic and pulled in. The building was small with two little service bay doors. It was light gray as was the tall chimney and the two cornices, one over a service bay door and one over the customers' door. It must have been quite a thriving business before the Interstate sucked away its life.

After an elderly man filled my tank, I asked to use the restroom. It was around the back. I pushed the bike over by the door and carried the sleeping bag inside. I took out what I needed; washed as much of my body as was prudent; put on clean underwear, socks, and Old Spice deodorant; washed my face, and wet my hair, through which I ran a pocket comb. I brushed my teeth and packed up. Everything done in five minutes and not a knock on the door.

I paid for the gas and added a dollar, which the old man didn't want to take, but wasn't too vigorous about resisting. I hit Minnesota again, regretting the days of the little station were numbered. Two miles later and I was on I-29. Sioux Falls had been the largest city in South Dakota since statehood and its sprawl was concreting and paving more and more of Siouxland.

Siouxland appeared on a map in the novel *Lord Grizzly* by Frederick Manfred. It referred to the land in southeastern South Dakota, southwestern Minnesota, and northwestern Iowa drained by the Missouri, Big Sioux, Rock, and Little Sioux rivers. The plot of Manfred's book *Scarlet Plume* dealt with the 1862 Sioux Uprising in southern Minnesota and played out in Siouxland, while *Conquering Horse*, which described a young Sioux warrior coming of age, was partly set there. Manfred described how Hugh Glass was attacked by a sow grizzly bear and made his epic crawl while terribly wounded across part of South Dakota to the west of Siouxland in *Lord Grizzly*. Those novels, plus *King of Spades* (set even further west) and *Riders of Judgment* (in Johnson County, Wyoming Territory), made up Manfred's series of Buckskin Man Tales.

Manfred, who stood six-feet nine inches, was born Frederick Feikema in Doon, Iowa, along the Rock River in Siouxland.

My Dad and I had read all five Buckskin Man Tales and both of us thought that *Lord Grizzly* was the best, but I didn't think it was as good as *The Big Sky* by A.B. Guthrie, Jr., which was about mountain men Boone Caudill, Jim Deakins, and Dick Summers and their exploits.

After the main character Boone fell in love with Teal Eye, a princess in the Blackfoot tribe called the Piegan, he lived with the tribe, much reduced by smallpox. I loved the action, the description of the pristine mountains, the free life—when Boone yelled "Piegan me!" in the book, I yelled it myself. I would love to have been Boone, except for the "clap" he contracted in a St. Louis whorehouse.

After I talked two Menninger senior boys into reading *Lord Grizzly*, we discussed it one day after school in the furnace room. When I told them it was based on a real person and that he actually had made the crawl described in the novel, they wouldn't believe it. Even when I showed them the account in an encyclopedia, they said it was an exaggeration and that Glass had probably made it up. I was totally frustrated.

My Dad also liked Zane Grey, but I could never get into his Westerns, even though I did enjoy the Zane Grey comic books my friend Ronnie Kerr had in his collection.

I drove down the middle of Siouxland. It was about eighty miles to Sioux City, Iowa.

I passed signs that tempted me to visit Harrisburg, Lennox, Worthing, Canton, Davis, Beresford (which I could see on my left), Vermillion; rolled over the black shadows of the interchanges and bridges that carried traffic over my head; crossed the bridges that spanned dried-up creeks and the tracks of the drying up Milwaukee Road.

There was a tiny patch of buildings called Junction City near the Vermillion interchange where the highway turned southeast, and I ran with it diagonal to the crops. South a couple miles, then southeast again around Elk Point, then past Jefferson, and then south to North Sioux City, where a sign pointed out McCook Lake, which looked like a river to me.

The Interstate turned east and a bridge took me over the Big Sioux, and I was in Iowa for the first time. Trees climbed the bluffs on my left as I paralleled the Big Sioux on my right. A break in the trees showed me the Missouri, a rather placid stream. The dams on the Upper Missouri—Gavins Point, Fort Randall, Big Bend, Oahe, Garrison, Fort Peck—had turned the once-powerful prairie rattler into a mild milk snake.

Traffic thickened. A sign said a right turn would take me across the Missouri into South Sioux City, Nebraska. I'd never been in Nebraska; I took the right and ran up the interchange. Another right and I was on a bridge. The decking was open grating and I could see the river through it. The grating made me a little nervous because it fishtailed my bike a little, but I made it across, turned around and headed back, the fishtailing not so troubling.

The bluffs had receded and I came to a little sewer of a river, the Floyd. Industrial buildings spread out to my left, and a railroad bridge crossed the river on my right. Its four truss spans rested on gigantic concrete piers, and there was a faded Northwestern emblem, but the train that was on it was a Burlington Northern.

The bluffs closed in and funneled smells onto the Interstate—a combination of Big Barnyard and toxic meat. *How can people live in such a stink?*

I kept glancing up the bluffs until I finally saw what I had read about—a white obelisk.

I continued about a mile, took an interchange, and backtracked along the bluff. The hundred-foot monument marked the grave of Sergeant Charles Floyd, who died in August 1804 on the Lewis & Clark expedition up the Missouri. Clark thought he died of colic, but I read that modern doctors thought it was from a burst appendix. Floyd was the only member of the expedition to die, which was remarkable, considering the unmapped and often dangerous terrain, the freezing winter at Ft. Mandan, and the threat posed by some of the great tribes in the West—the Sioux, the Arikara, the Blackfoot—through whose territory they moved.

There was a good view of the Missouri and flat Nebraska beyond. I tried to imagine the Big Muddy ripping huge chunks of bank away as it carried gigantic cottonwoods along in a Rockies-fed spring flood, but those days were as dead as the prairie wolves and cougars that had once hunted the Missouri bluffs.

A fifteen-stripe, fifteen-star American flag, a replica of the flag carried on the expedition, was snapping in the wind. I wondered why, if they were adding a stripe and a star for each new state, there weren't seventeen because Vermont, Kentucky, Tennessee, and Ohio had joined the Union before Lewis and Clark left St. Louis. I didn't wait around to find out. I shoved off.

I passed Sergeant Bluff, its thousand residents all tucked away nicely in a small residential area east of the Interstate. A long line of trees ran beside the highway and blocked my view. The river was off to the west, but it was a couple miles away and I couldn't have seen it anyway. I knew the Union Pacific tracks were off to the east, but I couldn't see them, either.

Tall corn country which was as flat as the Red River Valley. Signs to Salix and Sloan. I began to notice the Missouri bluffs eight to ten miles east and some over on the Nebraska side of the river. I went under a bridge and the land looked water-carved and left behind as an ox-bow. The Missouri was maybe four miles west; had it flowed here once upon a time? I went under the Whiting interchange and after half a dozen miles or so a line of trees off to the right marked a watercourse. *Is that the Missouri or is it another ox-bow?* The bluffs were less noticeable on the Iowa side. I saw a train pulling out of Onawa, so I knew I had been right about the tracks. The Onawa-Decatur interchange came and went and so did a rest stop set in more ox-bowed ground with the Missouri a couple miles away. A thin ribbon of water snaked under a bridge; its channel appeared hand-carved.

After the Blencoe interchange the Missouri bluffs on both sides of the Interstate appeared as a light gray line over the cornfields, and they got more prominent the further south I went. A curve bent the highway southeast and a tree line marked the Missouri a half mile to the west. I passed over another ribbon of water, and that time I was certain that humans had straightened it. A tree-shrouded ox-bow stuck out like a sore thumb. I bridged another man-straightened stream—the Little Sioux River—just before the River Sioux interchange. Looking down the Little Sioux, I caught a glimpse of the Missouri. To the east there were two bridges; one was a truss, so I took it to be the railroad bridge. The bluffs stood out a couple miles away; trees hid the bluffs to the west. More trees in a field signaled another ox-bow.

Another man-straightened stream, another ox-bow, the Mondamin interchange, a wide depression—the former Missouri riverbed—with two little streams marking its boundary. Another stream, then up and over the single-track UP line, then another stream, and the Modale interchange.

Traffic was slowing and I saw an approaching sign which read "Do Not Pass." I whipped around a blue Ford pickup with a couple guys in the cab and some hay bales in the box, but when I realized I couldn't beat the No Passing zone, I tucked in behind a Mayflower moving van. The pickup blasted me with its horn.

We stopped, and a flagman came along, said there had been an accident, and that we had to wait for the pilot car. I took off my helmet and could hear the traffic slowing and stopping behind me.

"Hey, you long-haired hippie freak!"

I was certain it was blue pickup man, so I ignored him.

"Hey, fag, I'm talkin' to you. Go home and get a haircut and take a bath!"

I saw the pilot car approaching. I put on my helmet.

"Hey, you son-of-a-bitch, get the hell out of Iowa!"

I sent a middle-digit message by Air Mail Special Delivery and hoped the pilot car would hurry.

I heard a door slam and then my head rocked forward as something heavy crashed into my helmet. I started to black out, but caught myself: I didn't want the bike toppling over on me. Fists pounded into my back; I held on for dear life.

The pounding stopped and hands held me up. They lifted me off the bike and sat me down beside blue pickup man, unconscious, on the ground. I looked up; I was surrounded by a biker gang.

The pilot car went by to turn around. One of the biggest bikers asked, "Son, can you ride?"

When I said I could, they got me on the 750. Several of them dragged blue pickup man and dumped him on the shoulder. His buddy was standing beside the pickup with his hands in the air. I found that funny because no one had drawn a gun. Some the bikers released the Ford's brake and pushed the pickup into the ditch.

The pilot car went by, the van started to move, and so did I. The bikers followed. The big man rumbled up beside me and yelled, "There's a rest area ahead; pull in with us!"

The accident had happened at the beginning of a construction zone. Two semis were jackknifed on their sides blocking both the north and south lanes. The pilot car led us into the ditch and then through the construction area.

The big man rode beside me and the further we went the better I felt. When he motioned me toward the rest area, I thought I could go on, but I turned in.

There were about twenty bikers, most of them in leather jackets with "DoD" in white and some kind of a red snake climbing a white sword beneath it as their colors. No helmets, but a few had black bandannas on their heads. Beards, mostly salt and pepper, looking a couple weeks old.

While I was still straddling my bike, the big man took off my helmet and another biker checked my eyes with a small flashlight. *What is this?* "No concussion." Hands took off my jacket.

"What's goin' on?" The big man showed me a big dent in the back of my helmet while the other man probed my back.

"Nothing broken."

The big man spoke. "That yokel bashed you in the head with about a five-pound rock and then started punching you. We couldn't let that happen; bikers stick together." He laughed.

"Who are you?"

"The Doctors of Doom. We're a bunch of doctors from the Cleveland-Youngstown area that were riders and gang members in our past lives. Every summer we get together and ride, get away from that city crap, and free up for a couple weeks. We don't look for trouble, but we don't avoid it, either. Charlie, how many bars have we broken up so far?"

"Sixteen."

I didn't know if that was just this summer or all their summers, but I didn't ask.

"A good fight clears the mind. Except for the dentists and the surgeons; they don't risk their hands...I'm Luke Rosen, gynecologist par excellence, but you can call me Womb Master. That's Marty Kell that's been working on you. General practice. aka Irish Red. Charlie's a surgeon; call him Butcher. Where you driftin'?"

"New Orleans."

"Been there. Those Cajuns have hard heads...Well, we're gonna roll. Good luck." He stuck out his hand and I took it. The bikes rolled by, some of the doctors revving their engines, and hit the Interstate. I had forgotten to thank them and it was too late. I used the facilities, looked over the dent in my helmet, and merged with the traffic.

I passed a rest area on the other side of the Interstate and curved south over the Missouri Valley-Blair interchange. I was rubbing shoulders with the Iowa-side bluffs. The Nebraska bluffs were indistinct. Traffic thickened.

Signs appeared for Loveland, 80N, and 680. I could have gone east and joined I-80 north of Neola; that would have been the quickest route to where I intended to go, but not the route I wanted. Another rail line, I thought it was the Illinois Central, began paralleling the Interstate; most of the time I couldn't see it, but I did see a railroad bridge spanning some dead-tree-choked water. Then for every little Interstate bridge, there was a counterpart on the railroad. Honey Creek. Crescent City. The Interstate and the railroad wedged themselves between the bluffs and the Missouri. Trees shielded me from the river and from Omaha that had sprouted up on its western bank, but I did see a couple planes above the tree line, so I thought an airport might be nearby.

I looked up at the bluffs and wondered if I went up there and could see through the trees into Nebraska would I see some of the West as Lewis and Clark had seen it. No, all I'd see was Omaha and civilization. Buffalo, prairie wolves, Indians, and grass so tall it touched a man's elbows as he rode his horse through it would live only in my imagination.

I didn't waste my time looking for the "Council Bluff" where Lewis and Clark had met with some Otoe and Missouri Indians in 1804 because I knew that spot was some twenty miles north and over in Nebraska.

I jigged around a bend to the right and started passing a residential area of Council Bluffs. Were some of those houses among the ones Kerouac had called "cute suburban cottages of one damn kind and another"? I curved to the south, the Interstate following the river like a dance partner. I-29 split and 480 ran off to the west and crossed the Missouri into Omaha.

There were all kinds of trees, a golf course, and lots of houses, but on the Interstate there was no intimacy between me and them. Everything seemed sterile even though I did see some graffiti—"BIG RED RULES"—on a traffic sign. No weird-looking buildings, no houses that would ever appear haunted, every structure done in Twentieth-Century American Sanitized.

I saw some tracks to the south—were they the Union Pacific? I ran out of real estate—road construction. I exited onto 9th Avenue and stopped when I saw a guy who looked like he knew the score. He told me to keep going east until I hit 7th, take a right to 19th, a little jog left, and I'd be on 192, which would take me to 92. When he asked where I was going, I said, "New Orleans." He started to laugh and I took off. About a block later I realized he had meant where I was going on 92, which didn't go anywhere near Louisiana.

The street was a straight line. Nature has only a few straight lines—crystals like quartz and snowflakes, some light rays—but man has produced straight lines, and on 9th I was glad he did—straight as a string would get me where I needed to go.

I hit a residential area with single-family, one-story houses, mostly white. Many of the houses were older, but none were really interesting. A number of them needed new shingles. A few yards were guarded by chain-link fences.

Some young boys on bicycles came spinning around a corner onto 9th without looking. I pulled over to the left. They saw me and decided to race. I let them stay ahead for half a block, then accelerated and pulled by them. They were laughing.

An industrial area butted up against the railroad, defended by a long chain-link fence. There were some commercial buildings on the north side of the street, but after a few blocks the houses took over again, and the industrial area turned into a broad strip of green with few trees, revealing the railroad beyond with a couple UP diesels decked out in their yellow, red, and gray color scheme. A trailer court stood on the north side of the street.

I passed a sign that said Golden Spike Monument. The monument was a golden concrete railroad spike that must have stood some fifty feet in the air near some trees. It was to commemorate the completion of the first transcontinental railroad when the Union Pacific and the Central Pacific linked up at Promontory Point, Utah Territory, in 1869. The UP had started building westward from Omaha. I didn't have time to stop.

I crossed a double railroad track into a commercial section and across a single railroad track. A dark angel appeared ahead, walking alongside a wooden board fence. When I got closer, I saw it was a rather large Negro woman carrying two dark cloth grocery bags at her sides. What I thought was a halo was an enormous straw hat. It didn't appear to be a very nice neighborhood, but the woman looked as though she could take care of herself. I came to 7th and turned, paralleling 192.

I went over another double-track crossing and hit a run-down residential area. A boy sat on his bicycle in his driveway and waved. I waved back.

I came to a stop sign. A gaggle of girls in shorts stood on a corner across the street with a drug store in back of them. Maybe they would be entering seventh grade: their legs were still calf-less, making them appear to be standing on fleshy sticks. They saluted me with their ice cream cones and sunshine smiles; I waved. I hoped their parents were keeping a close eye on them.

The brown brick Bethany Presbyterian Church stood across the street from the stop sign where I turned onto 19th. I went up an incline, waited at the traffic light, and turned south. Around a curve I picked up the railroad just to my left, and I passed a huge white grain elevator complex with large cylindrical concrete storage bins.

I slowed for road construction on what would become an I-29/I-80 duplex. The two Interstates would run as one for a couple miles until they split into separate highways again. To my right were commercial buildings; to my left was a large green space. I hit a green traffic light and went east on 92 toward the bluffs. I climbed over a railroad track, passed a tank farm, and crossed over my old companion, I-29. Off to the right stood the Iowa School for the Deaf. A movie comedian from the Twenties was from Council Bluffs. Harry Langdon? Snub Pollard? Ben Turpin? I couldn't remember.

I went up the bluffs, cut down by the highway engineers, of course. Houses looked down on me on the right, and I looked down on house tops to the left. At the summit I chanced a backward glance and saw the Missouri Valley stretching into Nebraska, where it got a little hazy; I hoped it wasn't smog. Trees obscured buildings on both sides, but I did see a few new houses.

Then suddenly I was out in the country—corn fields, pastureland— but it wasn't the flatland of the valley: it was rolling hills. I went through a highway cut, then another. A sign warned me of a school bus stop.

Down into a valley and over a tiny stream. The valley must have been created by a much larger rush of water, maybe off a glacier. The Des Moines Lobe of the last large glacier terminated in Iowa. Would I see its trademark moraine or was I too far south?

The land kept rolling, and I kept rolling with it, through the ubiquitous highway cuts and over the underfit steams. In one of the valleys I passed a small yellow house on the south; girls would have called it cute. A very broad valley with a small steam, choked with dead trees, showing it rarely flooded. White farms with gray silos. A road led off to the right and went back up to a hilltop cemetery. Another tree-choked stream. Silver City—8 miles, a sign pointed south.

Another stream, another all-white farm, and then Treynor perched on the shoulder of the valley. It was a farming community and catered to agriculture. An old-fashioned red and white gas station where the roof extended out over the pumps still proclaimed that Firestone Tires were sold there. Both the tires and the pumps were gone. I was ushered through the middle of town by a sign on my right that read "Treynor High School, Home of the Cardinals" and a cemetery on my left with nice straight rows of mostly gray stones.

The topography of southwest Iowa appeared to have been made by a giant child kneeling on mud and drawing his fingers through it from north to south, creating valleys and ridges. Then he got up, moved over and did it again. Water coursed down the valleys, smoothing them, and eventually green things brought life to the valleys and ridges. And I rode over the giant child's finger tracks.

The West Nishnatbotna River was wider than the other water courses I had passed, and the trees had the good sense not to topple into the river, or if they did, they had been swept away.

The town of Carson was ag-based like Treynor, but a little bit larger. It looked like there was an abandoned rail line stretching off to the south, but I wasn't certain. I pulled up to a gas station with two service bay doors and filled up. I used the facilities and watched the owner finish greasing a car as I drank a Coke. He was talking with the car's owner about a protest on the University of Iowa campus in Iowa City the previous May in sympathy with similar protests over the shooting of four students at Kent State by the Ohio National Guard. A building known as "Big Pink" had been burned, and the station owner thought arrests should have been made. Instead the president, Sandy Boyd, let any of the students go home that wanted to. That made it appear those who wanted to "Occupy Iowa City" had won. He thought Boyd should have been fired. The talk stopped when the men looked at me. As I was walking out, the car owner said, "At least no one was killed."

When I pulled out of town, a black and white sign informed me I was leaving the home of the Carson-Macedonia Panthers. Signs for Oakland, Emerson, and Griswold; I followed the latter. A yellow sign with a black deer. A large farmhouse with three gables and two chimneys. Weathered pavement in need of repair. Farms with white buildings nestled against the highway, but then one with a red barn. A two-story white farm house on a hill to the left and on the right sheds, barns, grain bins, corn cribs, and a faded white wooden fence strung along the highway like a little village. Always the same water-furrowed, hill-and-dale, rolling land.

A red barn with a white door not ten yards from the highway, a farmer sitting on a red tractor, his wife walking back to a two-story, faded yellow farm house. More farms. Grain bins in a field. A muddy stream, then up a hill through a highway cut. A water tower guided me to Griswold, the "Home of the Tigers," where the highway was divided as it passed through a residential area by a grassy berm with intermittent flower planters. The berm ended at the business section which had a lot of red brick buildings, some with cornices and one with a corner turret, which must have been built around 1910. One brick building on a corner had so much white decoration on top it looked like a wedding cake. At the east end of the business section, two streets—Union and Clark—were set at an angle other than the ninety degrees of the other streets. I was sure it was because a railroad had run there back in the olden times, but had been abandoned. There were still tracks that led south.

The business section ended; the grassy berm reappeared for two blocks, then ended; the highway curved to the right, and the town ended. The weather-worn pavement carried me over the rolling topography. A buttermilk sky whited the mid-day, and corn plants waved a little in the wind. Life was good.

I passed four farmyards, each one on a corner of an intersection. More farms and then a beat-up sign advertised a local oil company beside an equally beat-up gas station. I couldn't tell if it was open or not, but if it was, business wasn't very good. More highway cuts and then the two longest cornfields I had seen so far, one on each side of 92, took me right up to U.S. 71 and a collection of buildings called Lyman. It may have had a business district at one time, but no more. From the intersection I could see a couple one-story buildings, but they were abandoned, or should have been.

I turned north, followed one of my cornfields, and was joined by another one on the east side of the highway which curved around a farm. A little stream with a potholed bridge. Two miles north of Lyman I turned east on 92.

Excitement was building inside me; if I were a crow flying over the Iowa cornfields, I'd be fifty miles from the home of my hero.

There are many people who are respected, who are looked up to, who are listened to, but there are fewer who can be considered heroes, Achilles-like figures that you would want as your shoulder-companions in a titanic struggle. I had heroes—my older brothers Boy and Tom, Mickey Mantle of the Yankees, Bart Starr of the Packers, Gordie Howe of the Red Wings, Senator Barry Goldwater, economist Murray Rothbard, General Patton, General MacArthur, flyers Charles Lindbergh and Claire Chennault—but one of the greatest was Marion Robert Morrison, better known as John Wayne, the "Duke."

He was born on May 26, 1907, in Winterset, Iowa, but his family moved ten or so miles north to Earlham, Iowa, in 1911, then to Lancaster, California, in 1914 and in 1916 to Glendale, California, where he graduated from high school in 1925. He played football in high school and college and then drifted into the movies as a prop boy, extra, and bit player. The one-eyed director Raoul Walsh cast him as the lead in *The Big Trail* in 1930 and renamed him after the Revolutionary War general "Mad Anthony" Wayne. His big break came when director John Ford cast the relatively unknown Wayne as the Ringo Kid in *Stagecoach* in 1939.

The first movie in which I saw John Wayne was when our family went to *The Quiet Man* at the Blackstone Theatre in Menninger. Having some Irish blood, I was enthralled by the countryside when Dad told me the movie had been filmed in Ireland. I laughed at Barry Fitzgerald and had a crush on red-haired Maureen O'Hara for weeks afterward, but it was the Duke as ex-boxer Sean Thornton that captured me. After he emerged victorious in a bare-knuckle brawl with Victor McLaglen that seemed to cover half of Ireland, he was my hero.

A couple agriculture-related businesses, the ubiquitous cornfields, some prosperous-looking farms, the unyielding rolling landscape, but most of all the wide-open spaces. A bike, a man, and his thoughts.

Some farmyards had red equipment, some had green equipment, and never the twain did meet. That is, unless the tractor was orange or cat-puke yellow, then the other equipment was a conglomeration of colors.

On the shoulder of a hill, the remnants of an abandoned railroad right-of-way, tree-covered on the right, but strangely bare on the left of the highway. Through a couple highway cuts buffeted by the passing of two Co-Op fuel trucks. Down into a depression guided by a tree line on my left and a line of power poles on my right, many trees on the hill ahead. Across a stream and the trees resolved themselves into the small town of Massena, some of its businesses, living and dead, clinging to the highway.

The Duke fit the hero mold: strong, tall (6'4"), handsome, principled, sure of himself, living up to his own code. Whether he played fliers (*Island in the Sky*, *The High and the Mighty*), sailors (*The Sea Chase*, *Blood Alley*), cowboys or lawmen (*The Searchers*, *Rio Bravo*, *The Comancheros*, *The Man Who Shot Liberty Valance*), a cavalry officer (*The Horse Soldiers*), the frontier hero Davy Crockett (*The Alamo*), a big-game catcher (*Hatari!*), I tried never to miss a Duke picture at the Blackstone. I even enjoyed his work in light comedy in *North to Alaska*.

After my Menninger school days I continued to go to Duke movies: *The Longest Day*, *Donovan's Reef*, *McLintock!*, *In Harm's Way*, *The Sons of Katie Elder*, *El Dorado*, *The War Wagon*, *The Green Berets*, *Hellfighters*, and the greatest of them all, *True Grit*. I was watching the Academy Awards with Mom the night Duke won for his role as the one-eyed U.S. Marshal Rooster Cogburn, and when he took his Oscar and said, "If I'd known what I know now, I'd have put a patch on my eye thirty-five years ago," I stood up and cheered. Mom cheered, too, but I think it was because I was so happy.

Past a small electrical sub-station and onto the prairies again. Power lines to the left. A two-and-a-half story white farm house perched on a hill. A white farm house with a red shingled roof. Miles and miles and miles with occasional farms. A sign pointed south to Bridgewater. A line of trees ahead appeared to cross the highway, but as I got closer, I could see the pavement curved to the north. I crossed a steep-sided river and went into the curve, picking up a railroad, the old Burlington, but now part of the Burlington Northern system, on my right.

I didn't like every John Wayne movie I went to. A couple of them were *The Conqueror* in which the Duke was terribly miscast as the Mongol leader Genghis Khan; the film was less a movie than an extended bad joke; and *The Wings of Eagles*, based on the true story of Frank "Spig" Wead, a U.S. naval aviator played by Duke, who falls down some stairs and breaks his neck. Much of the film shows Wead trying to learn to walk again, which he eventually does. The story is one of the triumph of the human will, but I had a hard time watching Duke paralyzed and bedridden.

No traffic, no farms, John Wayne coming closer—I gunned the motor: seventy, eighty, then a white Mercury Monterey with an emblem on the door and a light bar on top appeared in the other lane. I hit the brakes and fishtailed, released, and hoped. *What's he doing here?* We passed each other, my eyes straight ahead. The Mercury disappeared over a hill. I obeyed the speed limit, checking the rear view, and hardly breathing. I went into a curve and shot a glance back. No vehicle; I began to breathe. I passed a farm with a two-story white house with a gable painted red, then another farmyard with a neatly-trimmed front lawn. Two gravel roads diverged to two farms; the one on my right up a hill; the one on my left in a small valley. The highway and the railroad curved into Fontanelle.

After we got television, Mom and I would watch old movies on *The Late Show*. We enjoyed Duke fighting World War II in *Flying Tigers*, *The Fighting Seabees*, *Back to Bataan*, my favorite *They Were Expendable*, and *Sands of Iwo Jima*, in which Duke did some great acting, but in which his character Marine Sergeant John Stryker was killed by a Jap sniper, so I didn't like the film that much. We saw John Wayne Westerns— *Dakota* (in which Pembina was pronounced "Pem-BEE-nah," instead of "PEM-bin-ah"), *The Angel and the Badman*, *Red River* (in which Duke's dark character Thomas Dunson even scared me), *Fort Apache* (opposite Henry Fonda), *3 Godfathers*, *She Wore A Yellow Ribbon*, and *Rio Grande*. There were also a couple of sea stories: *Reap the Wild Wind* and *Wake of the Red Witch*.

In *Blood Alley*, Duke's character Tom Wilder rescues Lauren Bacall and a couple hundred Chinese villagers from the Red Chinese and ferries them to freedom in Hong Kong. I liked the anti-Communist slant of the story, something Hollywood did too little of.

Agri-businesses and grain elevators just off the tracks indicated the type of town it was. Fontanelle showed its patriotism by naming its main drag Washington Street. Fontanelle apparently shared a high school with Bridgewater, and they fought other high schools under the name Panthers. A pleasant, tree-lined residential section, a white church with a rust-colored gable and rust-colored trim on the steeple. The business section had seen better days, but it was set off by a park and playground just to the south with plenty of shade trees. A residential section with more trees, some of them large cottonwoods and evergreens. A sharp curve to the left and I headed out of town. A right-hand curve, across the railroad tracks, and the town was behind me.

In *They Were Expendable,* Duke's character Lieutenant j.g. Rusty Ryan is in a PT boat squadron headed by Lt. John Brickley, played by Robert Montgomery, trying to hold the line in the Philippines against the Jap invaders. Duke meets Lt. Sandy Davyss, played by Donna Reed, and they have a brief romance, ended by the Japanese advance on Bataan and Corregidor. You know by his looks that Ryan would have tried to rescue Sandy if it were humanly possible.

Soon I was climbing up a long hill. There were hundreds of gravestones on the crest. A left-hand curve carried me away from the cemetery. From what I saw, it appeared the people of Fontanelle cared very well for their dead. I thought of a stanza from Carl Sandburg's poem "Cool Tombs": "Take any streetful of people buying clothes and groceries, cheering a hero or throwing confetti and blowing tin horns… tell me if the lovers are losers…tell me if any get more than the lovers… in the dust…in the cool tombs."

I passed a couple large farming operations, and a county road joined me on a right-hand curve. A red pickup at the stop sign honked and I waved. More farms and then through a highway cut into a broad valley. Across a bridge and another underfit stream and the railroad appeared on my right. A right-hand curve and I was on the outskirts of Greenfield.

In *The Searchers,* Duke as Ethan Edwards and Jeffrey Hunter as Martin Pawley search for Ethan's niece Debbie, played by Natalie Wood, who was kidnapped by Comanches. As the years drift by, Ethan begins to hate the idea that Debbie has become Comanche, and when he finally finds her decides that he has to kill her. However, his moral sense returns just in time and he and Martin take Debbie back to safety.

Hundreds of trees welcomed me into town. Some were so large their branches formed a canopy over the street. Most of the homes were older one- and two-story houses, but there were people on the sidewalks, many of whom waved at me. A white Presbyterian Church with a rust-colored gable pushed its steeple skyward. I liked churches with steeples; they weren't afraid to show people what they were. Some modern churches tried hard to look like museums or government buildings: no steeples, no crosses. A brown brick building with white trim that looked like a Quincy-box school, but was a Carnegie Library. A brief business section; most of it was located further north. More trees, more houses, a boy and girl walking and holding hands, so absorbed in each other they didn't notice anything else. Another small business section centered on the junction with Highway 25. A curve took me out of town. I guessed Greenfield was about the size of Menninger—two thousand—but there were so many trees I wasn't sure.

In *3 Godfathers,* Duke, as bank robber Robert Hightower, with Harry Carey, Jr. ("The Abilene Kid"), and Pedro Armendariz (Pedro "Pete" Roca Fuerte) as his partners, tries to escape a posse by crossing an Arizona desert. The problem is they promised a woman they would save her baby. The Abilene Kid and Pete die, but Duke with his hero's drive saves the baby.

Farms with white barns, farms with red barns, farms with no barns. Thick stands of trees, solitary trees, small ponds of water. Small hills, shallow valleys, stretches of lonely prairie now corn-covered. Gray steel grain bins. Gray gravel roads leading off at ninety degree angles. Iowa kept on and so did I. A bridge over a dried-up streambed. More farms, more ponds, more trees, a bridge over a narrow stream covered in August slime, then a curve to the left which turned into an "S," decorated on both sides by farms.

In *True Grit,* Duke is Marshal Rooster Cogburn and is hired by Mattie Ross, played by Kim Darby, to find her father's killer. He does, but in the process Mattie is bitten by a rattler and Rooster saves her life by getting her across miles of wilderness to a doctor.

A farm on the left with two battered barns and a sway-backed shed; an American flag waved from a white flagpole. Down into a wooded valley where the trees hid a tiny trickle of water that passed under a bridge. A couple more farms, a large pond, and a turnout to a brown brick building with a low chimney and a large service door—a sign said it was Stanzel. There were several dwellings in the trees to the south, a square white building that could have been a one-room school in a former life, and closer to the highway a building that apparently was roofless because I saw trees growing above the roofline from inside the building. Up a hill and Stanzel was gone.

In his World War II movies and later *The Green Berets*, Duke is fighting for the United States, its people, and its way of life. The critics savaged *The Green Berets* and the Left went ballistic; even I knew it wasn't his best movie, but Duke loved the United States. When I heard that he had rushed a group of protesters in Hollywood that were attacking the United States and its military, I could easily forgive any shortcomings in *The Green Berets*.

More rolling topography, farms, corn, streams, ponds, then a weed-filled lot with derelict tractors and farm equipment rusting in the sun, a bridge over a shallow wooded stream with two sandbars, and a curve to the north which a mile later "S'd" to the east. There were fewer trees, so the land was more open. I looked to the north, hoping to see the end moraine of the Des Moines Lobe, but I was still too far south. A meadow appeared to have golden brown cows kneeling in it, but as I got closer, they resolved themselves into rolled hay bales. A two-story white farmhouse with a porch and a red brick chimney that ran up the front of the house looked down from a hill. Ten yards off the highway stood a small white barn with a weather vane. Plenty of white farms, but less corn and more meadows and pastureland. A pond appeared on my right with a herd of Herefords grazing and drinking. A sign pointed north: Earlham, 11. A sign pointed south: Roseman Covered Bridge: I didn't have time. Four small steel bins, two of them rusted, by themselves in a field. Cornfields made a re-appearance. A farmhouse just off the highway made an architectural hodge-podge with at least four additions. More farms. A tall and a squat steel bin stood just off a cornfield with a white machine shed and green equipment. I kept my eyes on the eastern horizon, but trees blocked my vision. Increased traffic, signs, and small billboards told me I was near. Then over a hill and through the last trees and there it was—Winterset, the birthplace of John Wayne.

A Muslim on his Hajj, seeing the minarets of Mecca, couldn't have been any happier than I was when I saw the Winterset water tower. When I hit the stop sign for U.S. 169, I looked around at the land because, while the buildings were all different, the land would have looked virtually the same to Duke. In the mile to the commercial district, I passed houses (could Duke have seen any of them? some of them looked old enough), an auction barn, businesses, and plenty of trees.

Suddenly, the pavement came to an end and split north and south. A graveled street that looked like an alley continued to the east. I crossed over and parked near a long red brick building, got out a slip of paper, and checked the address—216 S. Second Street.

I wanted to see a little of the town, so I headed north past older homes, both wooden and brick, and crossed Washington Street into the business district. The large silver dome of the Madison County Courthouse looked down on the mostly brown brick stores. I passed the court house square which took up an entire block. To the south stood the Iowa Theatre, which had probably played most of Duke's films. At Jefferson I took a right and then another right at North Second. A silver water tower overlooked a rather dismal street.

Then I saw it ahead—my Kaaba, my Holy Grail, my Promised Land.

It was a small, square, white, clapboard house with a front door and porch that were diagonal to the corner. A sidewalk led up to the three porch steps. I parked the bike and took off my helmet. Immediately, I was aware of an electric-crackling chirrup from the trees, the song of the cicada. How did people ever get used to it?

I got up enough nerve to knock, but no one answered. I walked around the house, but curtains were drawn on the windows, so I couldn't see in. Someone lived there, but must have been out. There were no neighbors in their yards to talk to. I went around and touched the front door with both hands. It probably wasn't the same door that was there with Duke, but it made me feel good.

I took a couple rights and headed back uptown. Winterset was the most substantial town I had been in since Council Bluffs, which surprised me since Des Moines was only twenty-five miles northeast as the crow flies over the cornfields. I circled the courthouse square and found the Northside Café, appropriately enough on the north side, in a large two-story brown brick building. I parked diagonally and went in.

If you want to get a feel for a town, don't go to the mayor, the doctors, or the lawyers; talk to the waitresses, the store clerks, the gas station attendants. My waitress was named Deb and she made me feel good about Winterset.

The noon crowd had filtered out by the time I finished my hot beef sandwich and two cobs of sweet corn slathered in fresh-from-the-farm butter, at least that's what Deb told me. We talked briefly and she told me she had lived in Des Moines, but liked Winterset a lot better. So did her kids—two junior high boys who were going out for football and a fifth grade girl for whom she wished there was a sport like football. Winterset had everything they needed, but they did enjoy driving to Des Moines a couple times a month, just for a change.

I walked around the square, letting the sunshine manufacture some Vitamin D. The large brick buildings surrounded the square on all four sides like the battlements of a medieval castle. I walked over to a Rexall Drug Store on the west side of the square. There were two clerks, one old and one young, and a pharmacist on duty. I asked each of them if they knew if that was the same building where John Wayne's father had worked. The older clerk and the druggist didn't know; the teenage girl asked me who John Wayne was and if he went to Winterset High. She said she could ask about his Dad. I left disillusioned.

I walked the downtown, wondering if Duke had seen most of the buildings. I sat on a bench in the square, manufacturing Vitamin D, and listened to some old farmers talk about crops and rain. A weathered photographer came along and spoke with the men awhile. He was doing a spread on the covered bridges of Madison County. When he left, I got on the 750 and headed east on Court Avenue and south on Ninth until I entered the Winterset City Park, which Deb had told me about because she said I couldn't miss seeing Clark Tower. After snaking my way through the tree-covered park, I drove up to and climbed the tower.

It was constructed of limestone and was about twenty-five feet high. I hoped to see the moraine to the north, but had no luck. I went back into town and drove around the square, trying to see it as Duke had, but what did a three-year-old see?

I thought of going to Des Moines to see if Kerouac was right about girls who lived there, but the afternoon sun told me it was time to get moving and leave the land of the Winterset Huskies, as a black and gold sign informed me. I drove past Duke's house, gave a military salute, and headed for the junction with 169, where I turned south. I-35 ran some thirteen miles to the east, but I liked traveling the older roads.

I was "breezin' along with the breeze," happy in my heart that I had been where Duke was born. The rolling topography was like large swells on the ocean. Traffic thinned out. Red barns began to dominate. A sign pointed east to Peru. A bridge carried me over a steep-sided stream. A junction and then a shallow-S-curve. Trees closed in on the highway, then retreated. A sign: Union County. A curve right, then left, and then straight into Lorimor. Railroad tracks worked in from the northeast and after a right-hand curve I paralleled them through town. They had been the Chicago Great Western, the "Corn Belt Route," but had merged with the Chicago & Northwestern a couple years prior. I wasn't certain the line was still in operation.

Lorimor's elevators on the tracks told the story of why the town was there, but it had fallen on hard times—many of the buildings I saw were empty; others needed paint or a wrecking ball; the elevators would have to rely on trucks. I hit the edge of town and went into a couple shallow curves. As I crossed over the railroad bridge, I glanced in my rear view and saw motorcycles approaching. At first I thought they were the Doctors of Doom, but then I knew they weren't.

The lead bikes pulled up behind me, so I signaled for them to pass. Instead, one bike slingshot around and got right in front of me. Another pulled up on my left and another hung just back of that one. A fourth tucked in behind me.

The previous year I had seen the movie *Easy Rider*, but these bikes didn't look anything like the raked choppers that Peter Fonda and Dennis Hopper rode. While some of them had their front fenders and turn signals removed, most of the bikes looked stock—no "apehangers," no raked forks, no forward-mounted foot pegs. However, they all had sissy bars because every bike carried a "Mama."

Almost all the riders and Mamas were very large individuals. None wore helmets, but they all had colors which stated they were the Satan's Slaves M.C. On the back of their coats, black chains spelled out "S.S" over a background of red, orange, and yellow flames—very impressive. Every bike was a Harley—either an Electra Glide, Duo-Glide, or Sportster.

As Robert Burns wrote in "Auld Lang Syne," we "wandered many a weary mile." We came to a T-intersection with a stop sign; no one stopped, just wheeled to the right. A farm truck with the right-of-way on U.S. 34 lurched to a halt, but the driver didn't dare make any gestures.

Six miles to Afton, but we picked up the old Burlington to the south a couple miles out. I had just come from John Wayne's town. Duke would have made a break for it, probably disabling six bikes as he roared by, but I knew their Harleys would catch me and then what?

We turned left and went into Afton. As we passed the red brick St. Edward's Catholic Church, I thought I could throw down my bike and run for it, gaining sanctuary, except a Slave of Satan probably wouldn't honor sanctuary, even if he knew the concept. We rode on, across a railroad bridge, through the business section, and took a wide sweeping curve out of town. People on the sidewalks and in vehicles stared at us. *Help me!* But there was no help.

Out into the Iowa farmland. We crossed the CGW tracks and curved by the little community of Arispe with its elevators umbilicaled to the dying railroad. We curved south, leaving the railroad, and within a few minutes entered Ringgold County.

We met farm equipment and vehicles, went by farms, crossed bridges and streams, passed by trees—all were oblivious to my impending fate. Turnoffs to Shannon City and Tingley were ignored.

The bikers had a system of rotation so that every fifteen minutes or so a bike would pull forward and take the place of one of the guard bikes which would drop back. The only exception was the lead bike. The biker was the biggest of the lot with shiny black hair sticking out from under a blue bandana. His Mama was not quite as big, but was still a formidable woman. They always stayed out front, leading the Big Parade.

We saw Mt. Ayr in the distance and started passing lone houses in between some farms, a railroad that looked ready for abandonment stretched out to the east, and went up a little hill which I guessed was the "Mt." in Mt. Ayr. When we came to the intersection with Iowa 2, there was a stop sign. I also saw a police car slowing from the east at the same time the lead bike ran the stop sign and went west. I thought for sure that was my salvation, especially when the cop flipped on his cherry. I made the turn and waited for my savior, but after all the bikes were on 2, I glanced back and the cop had turned south.

We roared through the north edge of Mt. Ayr, blasting by businesses and houses, intimidating motorists and men who loved their families enough to stay silent. We descended from the "Mt." A mile out of town 2 continued west, but 169 split off to the south. We climbed another small hill and took 169.

We angled southwest for about a mile, went south for maybe six, then curved east and continued rolling over the land for another five. A road split off and kept going east, but 169 curved south. As we exited the bend, the little town of Redding emerged from the trees. Four blocks later it was gone. If it had ever been connected to a railroad, those days were long gone.

The highway was tree-fringed. We dipped into a depression where the spring might see water, but there was none in August. We curved into another depression where there might have been water, but the trees were so thick I couldn't see any. All of a sudden the pavement deteriorated and we were in Missouri. A small sign welcomed us. It was my first time, but I didn't feel like celebrating.

Northern Missouri looked pretty much like southern Iowa, except for a lot more black patching of the pavement. We passed a sign to Irena, which just looked like a bunch of trees to me. The further south we went, the more dry runs we crossed; most didn't have bridges, just culverts and guard rails. Sometimes there were guard rails to protect drivers from the steep drop-offs to either side of the highway. We passed some outlying buildings and then blew by Grant City, which stretched out to the west.

We crossed a small river, choked with trees and sandbars, and entered some poor land with no farms visible. Then the farms and the corn reappeared. More hills, dry runs, trees, corn, and farms. We curved right and crossed a river. The village of Gentry was tree-shielded to the right. Dozens of round hay bales lined a field. We curved left, passing a weather-beaten white barn and a single-story, blue-gray farmhouse with a neatly trimmed yard. Missouri flattened out. Suddenly, I realized the pavement was better; when did that happen?

A right-hand curve, a lot of farm equipment on the left-hand side. A curve to the left, a lot of round hay bales lined up against some trees. Missouri got hillier again. We came to a junction with 169 and 136 joining to go east and west. I had planned on taking 169 and I-29 to St. Joseph because I wanted to visit the house where Bob Ford shot Jesse James in the back. There was a stop sign which we ignored and shot ahead onto a road called "H." Jesse would have to wait. If I were still alive.

There were no real ditches on H, only weed-encrusted depressions. We crossed the West Fork of the Grand River with its sandbars showing. A soldierly line of steel grain bins. A used-to-be-white barn ten yards off the highway, a mailbox with a well-worn track where the mailman would pull up to it. We climbed a hill where dark cows grazed, dipped, and continued up to the crest where there was a farm equipment and truck graveyard to the right; rust and disintegration ruled. A dip over a dry run and then a T-junction. We went left.

We passed an abandoned farmyard with weeds and dilapidated farm equipment. Soon a few scattered buildings and then Darlington, which appeared to be mostly space occupied by trees with a smattering of buildings peeping out. The highway was like a paved lane between shallow, grass-filled ditches. Darlington was someone's dream that didn't pan out. At the junction, H went right. There was no stop sign, but we wouldn't have obeyed one anyway.

We skimmed around a narrow curve, forcing a pickup to stop; the driver stared at us, his mouth open. Over a skinny bridge and up a hill, then down and up again. The weeds brushed the pavement and choked the fields. *Where in heck are we?*

We curved left, then right, the land started to look a little better, the farms a little more prosperous. A curve went through a thick grove of trees and up a hill; the bikes went around the curve three abreast. If any vehicle had been coming, there would have been blood everywhere. I edge over to the right as far as I could go. We emerged from the trees into another curve, then another curve headed us south again.

A long stretch of straight and then into another blind curve. The Slaves fanned out covering both lanes, daring someone to hit them. No one did. Weeds were scratching the right side of my bike. A left-hand curve surrounded by corn, then straight, and a junction where Highway V ran off west to Ford City. We curved east and after about three miles turned south, took a curve, made intimate friends with a narrow bridge where the tree tops formed a canopy, raced through a wooded area for quite a distance with two more death-defying curves, ran straight, and came to a junction. I barely had time to notice there were buildings on three of the corners before we shot through, ignoring the bright red stop sign that marked the hamlet of Berlin.

We passed several hundred gravestones, many of them in colors other than white and with an arched sign that said "Berlin Cemetery." At that moment I didn't need anything to remind me of death. Half a mile later we curved left, then quickly curved right and continued south on Highway A. The land started to remind me of central North Dakota.

As we entered Fairport, a little farming community, the sign said 40; we slowed to 60. Two blocks later we were supposed to go 30; we went 50. When I saw little kids playing in the shallow ditch, I wanted to slow down, but that could cause a wreck, and the bikes might crush the kids, so I didn't.

A large, abandoned, brown brick building stood on the corner of the dilapidated business section, blinding us to the traffic coming from the west. We ignored the stop sign at 40; luckily, it was a four-way stop because a farm truck had just started to pull away. The driver smashed on the brakes. We accelerated into a right-hand curve, than into a left which was on a hill and forced a pickup into what passed for a ditch. More curves, than a long straight, and we were at Maysville.

Maysville had maybe a thousand people, so the Slaves gave it some respect as far as speed and stop signs were concerned. Most of the houses were old, but sidewalks lined the highway most of the way through town. A sign said we were now on Highway 33. We went straight for three or four miles, curved left and right, and went south another three or four miles with corn on both sides until we came to U.S. 36, which we turned onto, accompanied by vehicles skidding to a halt from both east and west.

I had planned on traveling 36 from St. Joe, so I knew approximately where we were. We went left onto a new divided highway, the sinking late afternoon sun on our backs. We went over Grindstone Creek, passed some farms, and went through the northern fringes of Cameron. Just beyond the town we passed over I-35. I hoped we would stop—I was getting hungry and thirsty—but we didn't. A town appeared on the right, and a sign proudly proclaimed in the twilight that Hamilton was the birthplace of J.C. Penney. We kept going into the Missouri evening.

Finally, the lead biker slowed as we approached a grove of trees. He pulled over slightly to the right and motioned that I should turn in. Few of the S.S. bikes had turn signals. A sign said "Wayside Rest. No Overnight Camping." The leader indicated I should go to the far end of the rest area; I complied. When I stopped, rough hands jerked me off the Honda and ripped off my helmet. "Dirty Jap lover!" A fist rocked my jaw.

"Hold on!" The leader stood in front of me—all three hundred pounds. "Cheetah" was emblazoned on his black leather jacket which probably came from three cows. When everyone had gathered around, Cheetah asked, "What should we do with him?"

The guy with the ready fists said, "I'll tie him to my hog and drag him around; if that isn't enough, I'll kill him." The name "Shark" appeared on his jacket.

There was a chorus of assent, but some dissenting voices also. Cheetah took my key, my billfold, and my pocket knife. They tied my ankles together with rope and put my hands behind my back and tied them; then they tied me to a wooden picnic table over by the cement block restrooms. They fired up their bikes and moved to the middle of the rest area where they held a confab. There were around sixty Slaves.

I thought they were a little amateurish since they didn't find my boot knife or check my gear where I had my machete. Or maybe they were so sure of themselves, they didn't care.

The sun was disappearing fast and shadows blended. A group of bikes without their Mamas took off to the cheers of the other Slaves. The arguing continued, but I missed some of it because two guys came over, untied me, and led me to the restrooms. It took me quite awhile because I knew they were right outside the door.

After I was retied, the debate continued. Soon it was apparent that three Mamas had been assigned to check on me. One would come over about every fifteen minutes and pull on the ropes. Mama #1 never said a word. Mama #2 would hawk-up in her throat and spit it in my hair, then she'd make a comment such as, "You're dead meat!" or "Damn Jap lover!" Mama #3 was the youngest and smallest, which wasn't saying much; she'd wipe the sliminess out of my hair and tell me what was going on. Her name was Squeaky.

It seemed Shark's uncle had been killed by the Japanese when he was a World War II POW, so he hated everything Japanese. That feeling spread to the whole club, so they hated Japanese motorcycles and those who rode them.

A big roar went up when the other Slaves returned with food and beverages; I saw pony kegs lashed to their bikes.

Wood was gathered and a huge bonfire blazed. A semi slowed and then geared up as the driver thought better of his intended bathroom break. His red taillights blinked and were gone, cut off by the trees, as was my hope.

The three-Mama relay continued. Squeaky didn't think the Slaves had ever actually killed anyone (that was a relief), but Shark had almost castrated a Japanese man. Cheetah stopped him (a pain developed in my groin).

After she had wiped my hair the next time she came, she said they would probably drag me around the rest area in the morning, steal my money, and take my sparkplugs, so I'd have to hitchhike into Utica or Chillicothe to get new ones.

Cheetah hadn't been able to finish his third sandwich, so he sent it to me. When Squeaky gave it to me, I saw that it was a double cheeseburger with every condiment on earth; half of it was eaten, and what remained had Cheetah's teeth marks. When I thought of his mouth, I passed on the burger, although I did eat the six or so fries. I pondered whether I should have Squeaky thank him, but by that time she was gone.

After the meal people tapped the kegs and drank up. Then saddlebags were opened and hard liquor and other recreational items made their appearance. People started dancing and staggering around the bonfire, reminding me of a painting by Pieter Bruegel the Elder of peasants cavorting in "Village Scene with Dance around the May Pole," but with the bonfire as the center, instead of the May Pole.

I don't think most of the bikers were in good shape because soon everyone who had been drinking was sitting or even lying down. Then the Mamas got up to dance, or at least to jiggle in time to some kind of beat. It couldn't get any worse.

It did—the Mamas took off their clothes to the howls of the men. I could barely watch. It couldn't get any worse.

It did—the men stripped off their clothes and joined in. I couldn't watch.

Hieronymus Bosch and his painting "The Triumph of Death" with its poor, condemned nudes twisted in an orgy of agony came to mind.

Pairs drifted off into the woods and various animal sounds and grunts emerged. Some couples just did it by the bonfire.

I hoped that the quarter moon would disappear when Mama #2 staggered over, completely naked. At first, I thought she had gotten dirty during her sexual romp, but then I realized she was tattooed. The tail of a rattlesnake started above her left wrist; the snake's body wound around her arm and onto her chest; and the head with its mouth open, its fangs bared, and its red forked tongue very prominent, appeared ready to bite her breast. Words were tattooed above each breast: "Hot" and "Cold." On her lower belly just above the pubic area were more words, either "Love Conquers All" or "Look Out Below"; I couldn't really tell because of the folds in her skin.

She tugged on my ropes and spit, but it hit my shoulder. She laughed and left. A tattoo of the Satan's Slaves logo appeared between her shoulders, the bright colors very distinct. I marveled at the patience it must have taken to endure the hours of pain while the artist worked. In the middle of her back was a red heart with "Simi Loves Wolf" in the center. Just above her butt were the words "Hot" and "Stuff" and in between a bunch of red fire crackers going off, or maybe they were flowers of some kind. The many divots in her butt winked at me as she walked away.

Squeaky came over and scraped the gob off my jacket. At least she had draped a jacket over herself. She had seen my license plate and said she was from Fargo. I kind of liked her and I wished she hadn't "done it," but I knew she had. She ducked behind the picnic table, pulled out a white pack of cigarettes with a red bull's eye, and lit a Lucky Strike.

I asked her why she rode with the Slaves, and she said, "I had to get away, away from my lame job in the mall, away from my old man and old lady, away from Fargo in general. People think there's a lot to do there, but there isn't; the Bruins-Spartans football game is the biggest thrill the town has to offer. Boredom can kill you. If I die a Slave, at least I won't have been bored. When we bust up a bar...."

"Squeaky!" A male voice called.

"Gotta go," and away she went.

No journal, Bible, or poetry that night. I said a prayer of desperation—I didn't want to be dragged. Sex sounds all around. Bathroom sounds from the restrooms. Druggie laughter.

I thought about Jerry Knapp, who lived on our block in a big house with three apartments when I was a little kid. In the construction season I didn't see him much because he worked for the Melva Cunningham Contracting Company, but in the winter he'd walk by our place on his way uptown, invariably smoking a Luckies. One day he gave me an empty pack, and on the bottom I saw "L.S./M.F.T." I asked him what it meant. He told me it was either "Let's stand, my fanny's tired" or "Loose straps mean floppy tits." Later when I told Ronnie and Rory, I was the hero of the day: I had told my first dirty joke.

Despite my peril I started to laugh at the memory and then I was asleep.

DAY THREE

A tug on my ropes and a whisper woke me up. "Shhh! Get up and be quiet!" The ropes were untied and Squeaky was handing me my key, billfold, and pocket knife. "Roll that bike onto the pavement and don't start it until you get far away. Good luck, North Dakota." She started to leave.

"Wait. Come with me; I'll protect you."

"From what? That great killer of souls, boredom?"

"When they find out I'm gone, they'll suspect you."

"I doubt it; most of them don't give a rat's ass about you one way or another. Cheetah is probably lookin' for a way to keep you from bein' dragged, and Shark will cool off after he has his first toke of the day... Get goin'; you have about ten minutes." She became a shadow.

I unlocked the front wheel and started pushing. It looks easy to push a bike, but it wasn't. I was puffing by the time I hit the pavement and though the going got easier, I began sweating. Finally, I forked the saddle, started the engine, and went full tilt away from the Slaves.

I had planned on driving 36, but I didn't know how far I was from Chillicothe, which was where I thought I could hide. I gunned that bike until I was afraid I'd outrun my headlight. I hurtled down 36, which ran straight as an arrow until I went through Utica, came to a curve just east of the town, a curve I almost didn't make. I was way over on the shoulder before I regained control of the bike. I noticed it was dawning.

I crossed the Grand River, which was the biggest I'd seen since the Missouri; a gray mist shrouded the water. I curved toward Chillicothe, knowing just how a fox must feel when he's the object of a hunt. I pulled off onto South Washington Street, drove until I came to an independent service station, parked on the far side, and waited.

Just before six the owner opened up. I asked if I could clean up in his restroom and change the oil on the Honda. "Help yourself."

It took me awhile to get clean, especially to rinse my hair of Mama #2's souvenirs. When I came out, a girl and boy who looked like twins stood there hesitantly. They were probably twelve. The owner said, "Well, go on; ask him."

The boy stared at his feet; the girl looked at me and said, "Mister, can we change the oil on your bike? We know how."

The owner said, "They do; they'll do a good job."

I handed them the key. "All right." They darted out the door.

The owner explained that they were his kids and they helped him when school wasn't in session. He was teaching them mechanics; there was always a need for a good mechanic. Stella was just as good a mechanic as Slade, and he thought she'd be able to get a job as easily as Slade would, once they graduated from tech school. Of course, he'd check out the shop that wanted her, and if the men were the wrong kind, she'd have to choose another place to work.

By the time I got outside, Stella and Slade had the bike up and were draining the old oil. I checked my gear, and it was all there, then I walked to an all-night diner and ordered a bacon-and-eggs breakfast with two larges glasses of OJ. I wrote in my journal and completed my two post cards.

Between bites I read some of the Psalms, including Psalm 22 and the words: "My God, my God, why hast thou forsaken me?...Oh my God, I cry in the daytime, but thou hearest not...For dogs have compassed me: the assembly of the wicked have inclosed me...Save me from the lion's mouth...I will declare thy name unto my brethren; in the midst of the congregation will I praise thee...All the ends of the world shall remember and turn unto the Lord."

The Slaves had me, but I was free. Was Squeaky God's instrument? I offered God a prayer of thanksgiving, but I didn't witness to anyone in the diner.

I read a little Jeffers, "Advice to Pilgrims": "Walk on gaunt shores and avoid the people; rock and wave are good prophets; Wise are the wings of the gull, pleasant her song." Even after my experience with the

Slaves, I wasn't ready to give up on people. For every Mama #2 there was a Squeaky, or at least I hoped so.

I kibitzed a little with the early-shift waitress Amy. She was from a little place called Blue Mound and was engaged to a farmer. The wedding and honeymoon were planned around his farm work. She had a bright, hopeful face, and I wished her well and left a good tip.

I filled the Honda with gas, paid my bill with a traveler's check, and kept two five dollar bills in my hand as I walked outside. Stella and Slade were wiping off the bike with soft cloths.

Slade said, "We tightened your chain."

Stella added, "We had Dad sit on your bike when we checked for slack."

I offered them the bills. They looked at their Dad standing in the doorway, and when he nodded, they reached out their hands and said "Thank you." Some guys have nice kids.

I mounted, fired up, and moved onto Washington. Stella and Slade waved; I raised my hand; they couldn't see my smile. I found a post office and then went back to the junction with 36. I figured I was a couple hours from Hannibal; I got started. Just out of town I picked up another divided highway and gunned it, keeping a watch on my rearview for approaching Slaves.

As I passed under a rusty railroad bridge, I thought about Slade and Stella. The last Stella I had known was in 1968, Chicago.

Fermentation is one way to describe 1968, as America, even the world, was changed.

The year started great for me: the Green Bay Packers defeated the Oakland Raiders 33-14 in Super Bowl II.

In January the North Koreans seized the *USS Pueblo*, an intelligence-gathering ship, in international waters; it was still being held captive in 1970. The Tet Offensive by the Viet Cong and North Vietnam ended in a Communist defeat, but politically proved to be a victory because American public opinion started turning against a continuation of the war.

In February Florida's teachers went on strike. On March 31 in the face of growing opposition and loss of public support, President Lyndon Baines Johnson announced he would not seek re-election. Protests against the war; protests for civil rights; riots after the killing of Dr. Martin Luther King, Jr., on April 4 took place in Baltimore, Boston, Chicago, Cleveland, Detroit, Kansas City, Louisville, Memphis, New York City, Newark, Washington, D.C., and other cities. Protests, mostly by the young, took place in Sweden, Yugoslavia, Poland, East Germany, West Germany, France, Italy, Great Britain, Spain, Japan, Brazil, and Mexico. On June 3, painter Andy Warhol was shot by man-hating feminist heroine Valerie Solanas, but survived. On June 5, Robert F. Kennedy was assassinated by Sirhan Sirhan, an anti-Semitic Palestinian, who hated Kennedy for his support of Israel. In August the Soviet Union invaded Czechoslovakia with tanks and infantry, ending a brief period of freedom called the "Prague Spring."

The Black Power Movement, the Black Panthers, feminism, were all on the ascendant.

In April Rennie Davis and the National Mobilization Committee to End the War in Vietnam staged an anti-war march in Chicago. The police took exception and beat some of the marchers.

News reports mentioned that Chicago would be the site of a "youth festival" organized by the National Mobilization Committee to End the War in Vietnam, the Youth International Party (Yippies), the Students for a Democratic Society (SDS), and other Leftist groups. The dates were deliberately set to coincide with the Democratic National Convention, so fireworks were not only expected, but were counted on. Chicago mayor Richard J. Daley put his police department on a war footing.

On August 5 to 8, the Republicans met in Miami and nominated Richard "Tricky Dick" Nixon for President and little-known Spiro Agnew as his running mate. The night Nixon made his acceptance speech there was a riot in which four Negroes were killed by the police a few miles from the convention. With the volatility of Chicago, I knew I had to go.

When the Joad family loaded their belongings and prepared to head west in the film version of *The Grapes of Wrath*, they asked the preacher Jim Casy if he wanted to go. He did and said "There's somethin' goin' on in the West and I'd like to find out what it is." That's how I felt about going to Chicago. What was going on and why.

The week before the Democratic Convention, the Yippies led by Jerry Rubin nominated Pigasus, a real pig, for president, then the police arrested seven people and took Pigasus into custody at the Civic Center Plaza.

Sallow-skinned Eugene McCarthy, bearer of the mantle of the martyred Senator Kennedy, flew into Midway Airport. His diminutive fellow-Minnesotan, balding Hubert Humphrey, landed at O'Hare; both were intent on gaining the Democratic nod for President.

Lincoln Park became the site for riot-training by the Yippies and other groups, and some women for peace demonstrated in front of the Hilton Hotel

I packed my Camaro and left Menninger on a weekend. Mom and Dad watched me drive away; his arm was around her waist. I drove to Kingston and ramped onto I-94. I stayed on the Interstate through Minnesota, except for some gaps, including a long one between Albany and the Twin Cities when the highway reverted to U.S. 52. I gassed up at a Texaco station overlooking the Interstate and marveled at the traffic. Until then Fargo was the biggest city I'd ever been in.

The radio news kept me informed of protests in Grant Park and a Festival of Life in Lincoln Park with the group MC-5, which I'd never heard of. At the curfew of 11 P.M., the police pushed several thousand people into Clark Street, where they reinforced their demand for law and order with billy clubs.

I continued on I-94 through the dark Wisconsin woods. The radio was blasting out "Sunshine of Your Love" by the super group Cream, consisting of Eric Clapton, Ginger Baker, and Jack Bruce; "Born To Be Wild" by Steppenwolf; "Folsom Prison Blues," Johnny Cash; "People Got To Be Free," Rascals; "MacArthur Park," Richard Harris; "Angel of the Morning," Merrilee Rush; "Sky Pilot," Eric Burdon and the Animals; "Grazing in the Grass," Hugh Masekela; "Lady Willpower," Gary Puckett and the Union Gap; "Stoned Soul Picnic," 5th Dimension; "Jumpin' Jack Flash," Rolling Stones; "This Guy's In Love With You," Herb Alpert; "Classical Gas," Mason Williams; "Reach Out of the Darkness," Friend and Lover; "Hello, I Love You," Doors; and a new song "In-A-Gadda-Da-Vida" by Iron Butterfly. Man, what songs! Whatever else the Sixties didn't have, they had music.

It was dawn when I skirted past Milwaukee; I pulled over and caught a few "Z's" in a Phillips 66 parking lot near the state line.

Working my way down 94, I hit a toll plaza, passed Waukegan, hometown of the great radio and television comedian Jack Benny, went by Lake Forest, Highland Park, then cut east and south onto the Eden Expressway and passed Winnetka, which reminded me of the Big Band

Song "Big Noise from Winnetka" by Bob Crosby and the Bobcats with its opening featuring a stand-up bass and drums while the bassman whistles, and later the drummer plays on the bass's strings.

Wilmette, Evanston, Skokie; man, I was hungry, so I pulled into a Denny's and ate a late breakfast, served by a waitress who was too busy to be friendly. I decided to spend the day sightseeing and reconnoitering.

I drove east on U.S. 14 and Bryn Mawr and went south on Lake Shore Drive. At Lincoln Park I pulled over and walked around among the Yippies, hippies, druggies, draft dodgers, priests, nuns, police spies, street people, pacifists, plotters, poets, Panthers with black berets or impossible Afros, idealists, cynics, and other assorted flotsam and jetsam from the ship of 20th Century American culture. The cleanest thing in the park was the Lake Michigan shoreline.

I bought the latest copy of the underground newspaper *The Chicago Seed* and several back issues for a quarter each and left. I looked over the *Seed* in the car: veiled references to drugs, sex, free clinics, and oppression seemed to dominate. I found a trash can.

I swung onto North Clark looking for 2122, the site of the St. Valentine's Day Massacre, a machine gun and shotgun slaughter of seven men ordered by Al Capone in 1929. I was disappointed when it turned out that the building was gone; only a grass-covered vacant lot memorialized the dead.

Back on Lake Shore I found Navy Pier Park, but the famous Navy Pier was a disappointment, neglected and dirty.

West to State Street ("that great street"), passing the Tribune Tower thrusting its gray stones skyward four hundred or more feet. The home of the World's Greatest Newspaper would not have looked out of place as part of a medieval cathedral or even a king's castle. The Wrigley Building stood across Michigan Avenue, almost as tall as the Tribune Tower, but appearing more squat. Two towers spired up from the roofline, one with a clock face on all four sides, telling me it was almost two o'clock.

I went west to Halsted Street and turned south, paralleling I-94. I went under Route 66 ("Get your kicks on Route 66") and over I-90. The University of Illinois Chicago campus was on my right, and I passed Hull House, founded by Jane Addams and Ellen Starr as a settlement house. I crossed the South Branch of the Chicago River and ducked under Archer and I-55.

The streets around the Chicago International Amphitheatre were cordoned off, but I could see the large brown brick building in the distance. I had read it could hold nine thousand people. The Democrats were already inside; the chain-link fence and barbed wire, the policemen, and the dogs hadn't bothered them. I knew I'd never get close; I just wanted to see where the protests would take place. I was wrong: protestors never got close.

Every so often I caught the wonderful aroma of Chicago's Union Stockyards just to the west.

Mayor Daley had been cleaning up his city in anticipation of the convention. At least the city departments were hiding the mess. As I drove down Halsted, city crews were still out sweeping streets and putting plyboard fences up in front of weed-filled lots or windowless houses. After I turned east, the cleansing continued until I got to South Wentworth in the heart of the "Black Belt." Daley had stopped caring there because few delegates would venture into that section. I went because on one of his adventures my older brother Boy had gone to Chicago and gotten into a fight with some Negroes at a bar on South Wentworth, and I wanted to be as brave as Boy, at least from inside my car.

I passed White Sox Park on my left and the Dan Ryan Expressway on my right and headed north through shallow valleys of dilapidated apartments and small houses that even the Indians on the Ft. Sully Reservation north of Menninger would refuse to live in. Uncollected trash buzzing with flies; the city workers were busy elsewhere. It was a Depression relived every day, but who was at fault? Suddenly, I burst out of the ghetto into the light—I was in Chinatown.

Bright colors everywhere; Chinese characters on signs, on buildings; pagoda-style rooflines; Chinese archways; people in costume; and clean—you could eat off the street. I pulled over and ate a meal of chop suey, which I knew wasn't authentic Chinese, but I liked it. My waitress was a cute little thing with midnight hair and dancing-in-the-dark eyes, but much too reserved to converse or even to flirt with me. I still gave her a nice tip.

I cut over to Michigan Avenue and the hippies and Yippies started showing up. There was quite a contrast between the well-dressed shoppers and business people on the street and the remarkable and sometimes bizarre street people. I passed the imposing Art Institute guarded by two green lions (the green was patina covering the bronze); the grand hotels; Grant Park, where there was a heavy police presence and a few young protestors milling around across the street; the Standard Oil building with a huge red, white, and blue Standard sign complete with torch on its roof; crossed the Chicago River; and drove the "Magnificent Mile" with its tall buildings, department stores, famous hotels, the Art Deco Playboy building, and Water Tower Park. I took Oak to Clark and ended up back at Lincoln Park.

The mood of the protestors was ugly: they had been driven out of Grant Park, where they had retreated after a failed march on police headquarters resulted in the arrest of Tom Hayden, a leader of the SDS, a group dedicated to radical, even revolutionary, political ideas.

I was sitting under a tree, listening to the threats of the protestors, when a man walked by. "Mr. Winters?"

He stopped, came back, and squinted at me. After a few seconds, he said, "Chris? Chris Cockburn?" And he added, "You're about the last person I'd expect to see here." He sat beside me.

Back in Menninger High School, Mr. Winters had been my history teacher, but in May 1961 he and his wife Mildred left on a Peace Corps mission to Tanganyika in Africa in response to the call of his idol, President Kennedy. We had had many political discussions and many political disagreements.

"Is Mildred here?" I didn't mean any disrespect, but his wife had been a checker when I worked at Hank's Super Saver, and I had always called her by her first name then.

He got a funny look on his face. "No, no, I think she went back to her folks in Minnesota. We have a baby, a girl, and she didn't believe in what I was doing and thought it best to go home and raise our daughter away from things like this." He waved his arm at the milling protestors. "But you just can't turn your face away from such injustice. I tried to tell her that." He looked out toward Lake Shore Drive or Lake Michigan or the far horizon.

I felt awkward and wished he'd leave, but I asked, "Are you still in the Peace Corps?"

He gave a little snort. "No, after they killed Kennedy, it didn't make much sense to stay in Africa when the real fight was here at home. We completed our mission, came home, and enrolled in a college in New York. We had to fight against Johnson and the conspirators—the FBI, the CIA—they killed Kennedy because he was going to pull out of Vietnam, and now he's gone and we can't let them win. At first, Mildred saw that, but then she got pregnant. She could have had an abortion—they were easy in New York—but she refused. She left the Movement, then she went home." When he talked, there was no emotion, just matter-of-fact; it was like his idealism and love of life that he had as a teacher had been left beside Kennedy's brain in the backseat of that black Lincoln in Dallas. After while he asked, "Chris, why did you come here?"

"I guess I just wanted to see what was going on and try to understand it a little."

"An observer from the Right, huh? Well, observe away, but unless you get involved and take up the banner of revolution against the government; against the military; against the corporations and banks; against social, economic, racial, sexual, and educational oppression; you'll never understand." He got up. "Power comes from a gun, but more power comes from a bomb." He walked away, probably the most-changed man I ever knew. He never even shook my hand.

I was hungry; I walked up Clark to a restaurant and had a burger, fries, chocolate malt, and a large Coke. It was evening, but I knew things wouldn't get going in the park until late.

I drove down to the Playboy Club and loitered around outside. I had no chance of getting in, but I thought maybe I'd see a Playmate or at least a Bunny.

When I was a freshman at Minot State, Bill Nelson had the walls of his room in Forge Hall covered with the Playboy centerfolds. He'd collected them for a couple years, so he started with twenty-four and ended the year with thirty-three. Whenever the new issue came out, we'd go to Bill's room and judge the newest addition to his art works. When he didn't come back the next fall, it was a tremendous letdown for all of us art lovers.

Once a Minot State football player from Chicago was looking and mentioned that he had gone out with a Playmate, but that her foldout picture looked a lot better than she did in real life. The rest of us sat in jealous silence until he left and then argued if what he claimed was true. I waited around by the Club, hoping I could find out. A lot of men entered, but I didn't see a single woman, good looking or not, and left.

I walked around the Loop for awhile, but every time a cop saw me, he told me to keep moving. I guess I didn't look like a tourist, or at least one with any money.

Eventually, I drove back to Lincoln Park and infiltrated the shadowy figures whispering defiance and disobedience. An official started reading the ordinance about an 11 o'clock curfew and saying that violators would be prosecuted. A police line formed off to the east and the protestors began throwing up a barricade.

It wasn't much of a barricade; after the curfew came and went, the police moved in. A squad car tried to push the barricade down and people began pelting the vehicle with rocks. The cops charged behind a barrage of tear gas. They started pushing and clubbing anyone who didn't move and many who did. I moved—out of the park and up Clark until I reached my car. When the cops come, you run—I learned that at Minot State.

Traffic was backed up; no one could move; the streets were alive with running people. Behind locked doors, I saw the battle surge past me. Kids screaming and cursing; cops swearing and clubbing. I ducked down and hoped I was invisible.

After an hour or so things settled down to the point I felt it was safe to leave. I drove north on Clark, passed Wrigley Field, and pulled onto a side street in front of an apartment house where other cars were parked. I made certain the doors were locked, turned sideways and wedged myself between the seats, pulled my clothes on the clothes bar over me, and went to sleep.

There were a few businesses along 36 and the Chillicothe Municipal Airport, then flat farmland that appeared to be fertile, but where were the trees? The topography convinced me that the land had been glaciated, but it must have been earlier than Iowa or the Dakotas. I'd have to check it out after I got home. A large cemetery appeared along the westbound lanes, then trees, then a bunch of white buildings that turned out to be the small community of Wheeling. As I moved east, trees became more numerous and in a couple places were thick along the highway. I passed Meadville, which looked about twice as big as Wheeling; it stood about half a mile north of 36. The highway reverted to two lanes for a couple miles, then returned to four. Once again trees were hit-and-miss until I came to Pershing State Park, named after the World War I leader of the AEF, General John "Black Jack" Pershing, then they were thick for a mile-and-a-half. Soon I passed Laclede, which proudly proclaimed itself the Home of General Pershing. I crossed Turkey Creek, and a solitary white barn with two windows like eyes in the hayloft stared at me from the north side of the road. I went under a railroad bridge with four large concrete supports. Billboards and signs appeared alongside the trees, so I knew a town was coming up. Two miles later the divided highway ended, and I went swinging around Brookfield to the south, meeting oncoming traffic.

I pushed my clothes aside and sat up. The sun was already up. I checked my windshield just in case I had gotten a ticket, but I was safe. I drove to Wrigley Field and walked around it. I had always wanted to see the park where Babe Ruth, a Yankee, had called his home run in the fifth inning of Game Five of the 1932 World Series, but it would have been better if I could have gotten inside.

I washed up and caught a breakfast at Denny's with a freckled, red-haired waitress that called me "Darlin'." I left her a nice tip.

At Lincoln Park hundreds of people were walking around, goofing off, preparing themselves for another night of action. I wandered north to the Zoo, but left feeling sad for the tigers. They paced back and forth in their cages, occasionally looking through the bars. Their stripes were appropriate, but their life behind bars wasn't.

Back with the protestors a couple young women in long white dresses and flowers in their hair detached themselves from a gathering of hippies and hippy-wanna-be's and came up to me. They handed me two little white flowers from bunches they carried. Their eyes were tearful and their cheeks moist.

"It's so beautiful."

"He's so beautiful."

They passed on to their next flower-recipient and I moved down to where I had first seen them. I wedged my way through the crowd and in the midst of a couple concentric circles of young people sat a balding man with a long fringe of curly black hair, a comb-over at the back of his skull, and full black beard; dark-rimmed glasses; a loose white shirt; and a peace medallion around his neck—the Beat poet, Allen Ginsberg. He was chanting some Hindu thing—"Om"—over and over with some other words that sounded like "see-my-trayah" added as a trailer. A young woman was playing thumb cymbals. Some of the girls' voices sounded nice, but Ginsberg couldn't carry a tune in a wheelbarrow. And I didn't think him beautiful. I left.

I drove down to the Loop, found a parking lot, and walked to Grant Park. Both Lincoln and Grant were beachfront parks, so you couldn't escape to the east, but Lincoln was long and narrow with plenty of running space north and south and even though buildings on Clark blocked a clean escape to the west, the side streets and alleys allowed a get-away. Grant, on the other hand, was downtown. In addition to Lake Michigan on the east, a section of Lake Shore Drive, much busier than the section at Lincoln Park, would blunt any escape in that direction. Across Michigan Avenue to the west, tall buildings and hotels acted as a barricade; the cops would see to it that any attempt to rush the hotels would come at a price. The sprawling Art Institute building acted as a partial block to the north, and there were other buildings to the south. If the cops plugged the gaps, anyone inside the park was trapped. I stood across from the Hilton, imagining the cops closing in and how Custer must have felt on that hill above the Little Big Horn

I bummed around for awhile. I walked over to Wacker Drive to see where Sears was going to build the world's tallest building and down State where the Chicago Theatre boasted the largest sign and marquee I had ever seen. The red-orange and gold sign stretched upward almost six stories with "CHICAGO" in white vertical letters. There were hippies and protestors on the sidewalks, but generally in two's and three's to avoid police harassment.

I saw a group of protestors coming down Michigan, accompanied by a young man in a dark suit and red tie with a white armband on his left bicep. I figured he was some kind of marshal and that the march had been sanctioned, which surprised me because I'd heard the only sanctioned protest was Rev. Ralph Abernathy's mule wagon. A young priest wearing sunglasses, a young man in a long gray robe, and a balding man in a suit and tie carried a large white bedsheet as a banner with words painted in black: "WE MOURN SUPPRESSION of HUMAN RIGHTS VIETNAM CZECHOSLOVAKIA CHICAGO."

If I had eaten at some of the restaurants I checked out, I would have had to float a bank loan, plus I hadn't shaved and my hair was over my collar. My appearance and my jeans and t-shirt didn't seem to go over too well with the help or the clientele. I knew when I wasn't wanted, so

I drove north and found the friendly Golden Arches of a McDonald's on Clark, where no one cared if I had purple skin with pink polka dots and dressed as Bozo the Clown. I had a Big Mac, fries, and a Coke. *McDonald's fries are the best.*

I didn't want to park too close to Lincoln Park and get jammed in as I had the night before, so I chose a large parking lot a block or so west. It was surrounded by a wall on all sides and had a wide entry on Wells.

Walking around the Park was an education. In the shadow of the huge granite Grant Memorial with the equestrian statue of Ulysses S. Grant riding on top, I saw a kid being tended to after a bad acid trip. Near the South Lagoon, in the recesses of buildings and sometimes right out in the open, the heads were "tokin' and smokin'." Also, I had to be careful rounding any shrubbery for fear I'd step on someone's bare butt. The same type of activity took place more discreetly under moving blankets.

And everywhere there were sandlot socialists and tinhorn philosophers:

"Violence is born of sexual repression. You rid the world of violence by opening yourself to the aggression-destroying power of the orgasm." This gem of wisdom was directed at a cute little co-ed wearing a University of Wisconsin shirt. She seemed impressed.

"Money is the root of all evil. After the revolution, everything will be done by barter."

"Production for use, not for profit. Profit is the skin, muscle, and bone ripped off the bodies of the workers by the capitalist pigs who have enslaved them, who have enslaved us. Production for use guarantees a good life for all, not just the bloodsucking owners."

"Vietnam is a racist war organized by the white ruling class to dupe black soldiers into killing their yellow brothers."

Some of the talk was more mundane: "If my old man doesn't come through with my check early this month, I'm goin' back home and haunt him for awhile. I had expenses comin' here; how does he expect me to live?"

Or the needy, "I need a hit; anybody got some smack; I'll do anything." Or the begging, "Anybody got some spare change; I haven't eaten for two days." Or the audacious, "Anyone here wanna screw?"

It was such hopeful, self-serving, crazy, naïve, idealistic, unreasonable, hypocritical, Utopian, full-of-crap human folly I had to leave.

I needed some reality, so I walked until I found a joint that served red hot chili, had two bowls, and drowned the fire with milk. Then I went to my car and rested awhile.

Back at Lincoln Park I heard kids talking about the Black Panther Bobby Seale. He had been in the Park and spoke to the crowd, saying they had to defend themselves against the pigs with any means necessary. The kids were ready: some of them had been collecting rocks. I needed another shot of reality.

I went into a bar with a strip revue. The early show was a peroxide blonde a shade this side of middle age. Stripping down to pasties and g-string revealed a long, jagged appendectomy scar. I left.

Back in my car I slept; it was going to be a long night.

When I woke up, I could see police cars cruising Wells, so I waited until the coast was clear and dashed across the street. I didn't want to get picked up before the action started.

I made my way to Clark. As I prepared to cross Clark, I looked over to my right and standing in the lights of a building—bar? restaurant?—was Allen Ginsberg. He was talking to a man with a long face, sunken cheeks, and a prominent nose. I searched my memory: was that the Beat writer William Burroughs, author of *Naked Lunch*, a book about drug addiction, sadism, violence, killing, child-murder, pedophilia, homosexuality, orgies, totalitarianism, cannibalism, and replete with every filthy word imaginable? After I had read it, I hid it away in embarrassment, but a lot of critics claimed that it was a great work of art. I just think they didn't want to be called "square." A little, balding man came out of the building and when he spoke to them, I figured it was the French radical writer Jean Genet, an author I had never read. The three stood and looked at the Park.

I walked across Clark and the parking lot into a couple thousand protestors, most of them young, almost all of them white. As the night wore on, most of the black faces drifted off: they had plenty of experience with cops.

In a final gesture of futility, some protestors put up a barricade down to the right of where I had determined I would stand because it had a clear line of escape to the rear, except for some permanent park benches. A picnic table, a bench, another picnic table, and more superfluous items, the kids extended them into a pathetic wooden line that wouldn't keep out a determined attack by football cheerleaders.

A parked police car emitted a rotating blue light. A little before eleven, an official used a loudspeaker to read the curfew regulation and tell the crowd they were in violation and subject to arrest, which was apparently what most people were willing to chance. He was bombarded by catcalls and curses.

A group of priests and nuns and their followers came by dragging a ten or twelve foot wooden cross and had another cross on their armbands.

Time passed; another warning was booed down.

The religious group put up their cross and sat down in two circles to my right, vowing to stay. Some of them were praying, but most were silent. I did hear, "Jesus, help us stay."

I moved to my left, away from the circles, but I heard an argument start between the pacifists in the circles and the action-oriented protestors who surrounded them.

More time passed. Some of the protestors were getting nervous. The lack of action had cooled their intensity. Black faces were non-existence in the crowd around me.

A guy about a foot shorter than I, but well-built, with curly dark hair and big ears, smelling slightly of liquor, brushed past me with another man in tow. I recognized him from the dust jackets of his novels: Norman Mailer. And he was leaving the Park.

Eventually, some action. A line of vehicles entered the Park from the south and parked across the open area to the east of us; it must have been a hundred yards or so. The police exited their vehicles and formed a line of blue (helmets and shirts) and black (pants and boots) festooned with billy clubs and confident with tear gas guns after two victorious night battles. Two city street department dump trucks pulled up with them. The crowd was in the dark of the trees, but the police line stood in the light. There was no barricade between them and me.

The protestors emboldened each other with words, and some walked out of the trees toward the cops and hurled curse-filled threats, shook their fists, and threw stones, all of which fell woefully short. Many in the crowd began smearing Vaseline on their faces; it was supposed to help with the tear gas. *I should have brought some.*

The official returned and read the announcement of impending arrest. Again there were shouts and obscenities.

A young man moved toward the cops. About halfway between the protestors and the police stood a tree. He climbed it. *What an idiot!*

I was watching the "monkey-idiot," when a shout went up, and I saw the blue line move forward. People were speaking in determined voices: "Stand your ground." "Don't give in." "We shall overcome." "Peace and freedom." "Off the pigs." "Be strong." "Don't run."

I watched as the blue line moved inexorably across the grass. The big trucks were on their left flank. It all seemed like slow motion. Two officers stopped at the tree to wait for the "monkey-boy" to come down.

The protestors were shouting, daring the cops, looking to each other for strength. "Don't break." "Don't run."

South Pond was off to the left. Someone yelled, "The pigs are going around the pond to get in back of us!" I looked beyond the pond, but didn't see any movement. Some protestors near the pond broke and ran. I got very nervous.

The dump trucks pulled ahead of the blue line and aimed for the religious circles. I was standing next to a light pole with a little white globe at the top when I saw the nozzles of hoses sticking out of the boxes.

Then the night exploded in one apocalyptic moment.

Tear gas streamed out of the nozzles directly into the priests, nuns, and others of the faithful. Their faith could not shield them: they got up crying, choking, calling out for help. The gas enveloped them like the fog of death, and they broke and made for Clark, the cross dragging behind.

Loud popping sounds came from the blue line, and tear gas canisters began hitting the ground and exploding all around me. Others smashed through branches on their way down. The cops broke into double-time, billy clubs ready. The cop-advance wrapped around some skirmishers: a protestor went down with a knee to the groin; another fell from a blow to the head. The cops broke into a sprint. Someone yelled, "Stay! Don't run!"

I ran.

I vaulted over some benches and hit the parking lot at full speed, or at least I thought it was full speed until I looked to my right and a guy on crutches was keeping up with me. Across Clark I turned south, trying to look inconspicuous. I heard a lot of noise in the park, but it was hard to hear because of the car horns—traffic was backing up.

A group of people interspersed with some of the priests and nuns came toward me. They were crying gushes of tears. I thought they had been beaten by the cops. Abruptly, I was gushing tears: I had walked into an invisible line of tear gas. I had to close my eyes; I could hardly breathe. I turned around and joined the other gas victims. And walked right into a parked car.

After that, I'd walk a few steps, open my eyes, close them, and walk a few more steps. I turned west at an alley or small street. It was crammed with vehicles, their drivers and passengers emerging with flowing eyes and obscenities. I walked around an open car door, and the exiting driver just about knocked me down.

On Wells I turned south and my symptoms lessened. Wells was lined with apartment houses and on the stoops and in the windows were black families. They just sat there and watched me and a few others pass by. A cop car came screaming by, then another. I held my breath. They turned at the corner; I kept going.

I ran across Wells into the parking lot. My Camaro was the only car there. I climbed in and scrunched down. Cop cars were busy on Wells, but none of them stopped. A large white station wagon loaded with black male faces pulled in, U-turned, and went out again. Crudely painted in black across the side was the Swahili word "Uruhu," which I knew from a Robert Ruark novel meant "Freedom." I locked up and went to sleep.

If drivers liked small towns, the forty or so miles from Brookfield to Macon, Missouri, was not the trip for them. There were plenty of hills, rivers, bridges, trees, farms, two railroads, and Long Branch Lake, but the highway avoided the little towns—Bucklin, New Cambria, Callao, and Bevier—as if they were leper colonies. I went through the northern outskirts of Macon, which was a good-size town, and began paralleling a railroad, the Burlington/BN.

The next morning I was awake just after dawn. Two police cars were blocking the exit, the four officers conversing. I kept my head low and waited. And waited. Finally, they left and I moved out as fast as I dared. I drove north to Wrigley Field, found my old parking place, and finished my sleep in peace.

When I woke up, I drove Clark and North onto Michigan and gassed up at a Standard Station across from Grant Park. A line of green—the National Guard—stretched along the Park boundary. I heard later they had moved in about three A.M. I used the restroom to clean up. Then I drove around until I found a Denny's.

I heard some of the early birds discussing the news: how the damn "hippies," "Commies," or "anarchists" (depending on the speaker) had forced their way south after being driven from Lincoln Park; how they smashed store windows, set fire to trash barrels and at least one house, broke the windows and dented several police cars; how at Clark and Division the police tried to make a stand, but only fired in the air, and so were forced to retreat by a barrage of bricks (the speaker was of the opinion the cops should have killed some of the brick throwers to show them Chicago meant business); how the crowd had rushed across the Chicago River bridges before the cops could seal them off; and how the police had tried to control the swelling number of people in Grant with tear gas, but the wind was wrong and blew it into the Hilton; then the only Republican in Chicago chimed in with, "Those Democrats deserved to be gassed."

I drove up to Lincoln and surveyed the scene. There were scraps of paper on the ground, but city crews must have been up early because I didn't see any bricks, rocks, bottles, or tear gas canisters. At the spot where the religious circles had formed, I thought I could smell tear gas, but it might have been my imagination. I stood beneath my old friend the light pole and gave it a pat. Its little white globe was unbroken.

Many of the people who had been gassed and whacked at Lincoln had made their way to Grant and were still there when I arrived. After a night on the grass and smoking grass, they were ready for another confrontation. I still didn't like the layout. Apparently they did: it was right across from the Hilton, whose windows stared down at the Park. The Hilton was where many delegates to the convention were staying. It was also the headquarters for the Humphrey and the McCarthy campaigns and for a lot of reporters. In other words, the perfect spot for some "guerrilla theater."

There were a couple hundred kids in the Park, hemmed in by the Guard, the buildings, and the traffic. It must have been a long night because most of them were sleeping—under trees, on benches, on the grass, in groups, couples, alone, with blankets, without blankets, gassed or not gassed. The serious gas cases weren't there; they were under the care of doctors.

Even in sleep the protests continued: I walked by a group asleep on their stomachs, a hand-lettered sign on the ground: "WITHDRAW TROOPS from CHICAGO BLACK AMERICA VIETNAM NOW. YOUTH AGAINST WAR AND RACISM."

I passed a girl lying on a tangle of blankets. Her long brown hair looked clean; she was wearing blue jeans and a blue sweatshirt, but her feet were bare. A yellow hard-hat lay next to her. I thought she was asleep, but she sat up and said, "Hello."

"Hi."

"What's your name? I'm Stella, Stella Starfall."

I could hardly keep from laughing, but I managed to say. "I'm Chris, but that's not your real name."

She looked hurt. "It's not the name my parents gave me, Sandra Ann Marshfield, but it's my true name. It combines my essence and my existence. Everything in the universe is connected by the essence of Love and the existence of matter. My body and a star have the same matter and Love pervades us all."

"So you love the cops."

"Yes."

"Do they love you?"

"They would…they will, once all of us gather in the Park and combine our essences to defeat the negative influence of Hate that has been formed in them. Love is the most powerful thing in the universe; once unleashed, nothing can stop it."

"I don't think the cops loved you last night."

"No, but it was because too many people met their Hate with Hate of their own. Once we unite in Love, our true essences will reach out to theirs, and they will see the universe as it is. Their Hate will be transformed into Love. It takes a concerted, a concentrated effort, beyond just a mental exercise, but it can be done. I've done it."

"Do you love me?"

"Yes."

"You don't even know me."

"I know you as part of the universe; the universe is Love; I love you."

We could have carried this conversation on for hours, but with all the twists and turns we'd end up in the same place, Love; it was like following Alice down the rabbit hole into Wonderland. Then she said, "Chris is not your true name."

"Oh, really? What is it then?"

She scooted off the blankets and sat cross-legged on the grass facing me. She closed her eyes and placed her hands flat on the ground. I half-expected her to say "OM," but she was quiet. She reached out and took my hands in hers. She closed her eyes again. Finally, she let go and scooted back on her blankets. "You have a lot of goodness inside; Love has entered you…but I feel you are lacking…you have an emptiness… you are looking…seeking something…You don't realize that what you seek is already inside you."

"O.K., but what has that to do with my 'real' name?"

"Your searching defines you—you are 'Light-seeker'."

Well, she's right: I am seeking a lot of things.

Even so, our conversation was jumping off the weird end of the diving board, so I asked, "Are you hungry? Would you like to get something to eat?"

"Sure." She started gathering her things. Stella was just too innocent; I could have been Charles Manson for all she knew. She just loved everyone. I began to feel that her essence was disaster.

We walked to my car. "Are you here alone?"

"No, one of my friends got sick, so the others took him to a doctor. I stayed here and concentrated my essence to help him, then I fell asleep."

We drove north, away from all the essences Stella had to get together to save the world, to the essence of hamburger—McDonald's.

Wouldn't you know it—she was a vegetarian, so she ordered fries and a Big Mac, "hold the hamburger." I'd never seen that before, and neither had the kid behind the counter. He looked at me; I shrugged my shoulders.

Over dinner she told me about her former life in a small town in Iowa, how she'd been raised Lutheran, and how a professor at the University of Wisconsin had opened her mind to a Universe of Love. She told me there were different gradations of essence: rocks had very little compared to their matter; plants had more, but still not a great deal (that's why it was all right to eat lettuce); animals had the most essence in comparison to matter—humans, mammals, birds, fish, lizards, frogs all had the same amount of essence, it was just that some could not express it very well, so you shouldn't eat meat because maybe the cow might have used her essence to bring about more good in the world while a lettuce leaf never could.

I talked about my family life, college life, and how I thought she needed to be more careful around people—not everyone had reached her level of Love.

When we got back to Grant, it looked like there were a thousand protestors there and more arriving. I talked Stella out of going over to the Guardsmen to try to break down their hostility by concentration and releasing the Love-essence within them. I figured if one of their officers asked her what she was doing and she said, "Releasing Love-essence," she'd be arrested for sure.

We went walking in the Park. Across Michigan Avenue were such streets as Monroe, Adams, Jackson, and Van Buren. We came to a lot of marble: two great fluted columns with torches on top and marble steps leading up to a large stone platform with the bronze statue of the "Seated Lincoln" topping a marble pedestal. Abe's face looked like he was about to have a tooth extracted, but maybe he was just thinking about the Civil War or how to find a general who could win it.

Stella took my hand and led me into some trees behind Abe. "Seeker, I've noticed how tense you are. I'll help you." We pushed into some bushes and quicker than an alley cat on a hot date, she was stripping off her shirt and using it as a blanket on the ground. She was braless. "When you make love, Love-essence infuses your whole Being. Any tenseness disappears. Come here." She pulled me down.

If thought if I had been tense before, I'd be a lot tenser of someone stuck their head into the bushes and saw my bare butt trying to release "Love-essence." I mumbled, "Maybe later," and turned my back while she slipped on her shirt.

She didn't seem to mind and took my hand as we walked back to where I had first seen her. We hadn't made love, and she didn't mind; I felt that if we had made love, she wouldn't have minded, either.

There were three guys and a girl waiting for Stella, but they weren't anything like her. She introduced us. "Seeker, these are my friends—Golden Treasure, Danny Dark-to-Dawn, Tiger-Strong, and Ollie the Brain. This is our new friend Seeker; he's from North Dakota and has come to help us release the Love-essence." That was the first I'd heard of that. We sat down and they talked to Stella about Moon Man, the friend who had gotten sick, but it was a little more complicated than that: he'd been gassed and clubbed and wasn't in good shape at all. Stella began to cry and "Goldy" put her arms around her.

I could see why Goldy had gotten her "real" name: her long hair was a ripe grain field and very clean, a least compared with that of most of the other girls around. "Tiger" was also easy: he wore a black leather vest that exposed his bare chest; a tattooed tiger was leaping from the hairless skin. Ollie was a puzzle: he was dressed in a cream-colored suit, complete with dirt spots and smudges and a matching fedora, also a little grimy; a pair of brown wingtip Oxfords; and a classic white shirt with an outlandishly wide, bright red tie. I thought he was crazy: being so conspicuous would make you a definite police target, but he smiled at everyone and seemed contented, or maybe he was just stoned.

Danny wasn't too friendly and his little rat-eyes continually darted around the crowd; I could tell he didn't trust anyone, including me. His sleeveless blue denim shirt showed about fifty tattoos on his arms, many of them crude acts of violence or sex, and some of them just single, foul, curse words. When he left—no one knew why—I asked Stella about him. He had recently been released from the state pen at Joliet, and he still carried that dark experience with him, but Stella was working to drive it out with Love, and he was responding. I wondered if she helped him relieve his tension, too, but that image was too disgusting to contemplate, so I lost it.

They had a station wagon stashed in a parking garage, and when the demonstrations in Chicago were over, they were all going to the Rocky Mountains. When Stella told me that, Goldy and Tiger joined in, and Ollie's smile got even bigger. Tiger was especially proud of the fact that he had stolen the station wagon and had rigged it with stolen plates.

There were microwave towers hidden in the mountains that the CIA and the FBI used to communicate secretly with each other. Some of the messages were information provided by informers about the whereabouts of a movement leader, and whoosh, suddenly he disappeared. There were also some prisons in the mountains that no one knew about. They contained thousands of political prisoners, some of whom were tortured. Danny and his gang were going out to Colorado or Wyoming or wherever and use some explosives that Ollie would make (his smile got so wide, it almost fell off his face) to destroy the towers and blow open the prisons so everyone could escape.

I asked if that wouldn't kill some guards, but Stella said that Danny had a special way to set the explosives so no one would die. She wouldn't go if people were killed.

I asked if violence was a part of Love. Stella said violence against humans or animals was not, but violence against property that was oppressing the full experience of Love was actually part of the essence.

I had other questions, but Danny returned as mysteriously as he had left. Everyone waited quietly, waiting for him to say something, but he just sat there. I thought I could see his "prison pallor" in between his tats.

The crowd in Grant grew to be the largest I'd seen, much larger than anything in Lincoln, so large, in fact, it had metamorphosed into a living Being intent on one thing—imposing its Will.

We stood on the outskirts of the massive protest, listening to the speakers condemn Amerika. We were on a little elevation, so we could see what was going on, except for Stella: she was sitting on the ground, cross-legged, concentrating the Love-essence.

The speakers denounced Johnson, Humphrey, and Daley; damned the capitalist, warmongering, racist system; and called for resistance. Carrying rhetoric into action, three young men climbed up a flagpole and cut down the American flag. Their patriotism aroused, some cops rushed into the crowd to arrest the three, but were repelled by rocks and bodies. Tear gas was employed, but some of it disabled a few cops and the blue men retreated, pelted with rocks.

Reinforcements charged into the melee, clubbing and kicking their way toward Rennie Davis, a bespectacled, Beatle-haired leader of the National Mobilization Committee, who had a bullhorn and was trying to regain control of the situation. He went down when a cop brained him with a club.

The SDS leader Tom Hayden's acne-scarred face was twisted in anger at what had happened to Davis. He started yelling something, but I couldn't understand what. Hayden apparently saw things deteriorating in the Park and led a group away towards the Loop; it was a small group.

Allen Ginsberg was croaking out OM's to a large contingent of true believers and innocent idealists. The tear gas had ruined his voice, but he kept up a strained-chant. I thought Stella should join them, but she preferred silent concentration.

In some areas the tear gas was overwhelming, but we had been lucky. I could see the battle's ebb and flow. Groups of more militant protestors kept trying to breach the blue and green lines of cops and Guardsmen, which had them hemmed in, just as I thought they would.

Eventually, some of them found a way out over a bridge and charged onto Michigan Avenue, where they met Rev. Abernathy's mule train protest and followed it on its way to the Convention. Distracted by the legality of Abernathy and the mules and the illegality of everyone else, the cops did nothing. That allowed thousands of others to pour out of the Park and into line.

The police who were left in the Park continued their assault, finally reaching our bastion. As they closed in, Danny and Tiger launched themselves into the mass of uniforms and went down in a pile of blue and black. Goldy and Ollie beat a retreat to the north, and I tried to get Stella up. She was heavier than she looked. Protestors were wrestling with the cops at the base of our stronghold, but soon a couple broke through and started up. Stella had her eyes closed and was oblivious. A cop charged her, club raised. I shoulder-blocked him and he tumbled down the rise. Another cop was about to club Stella in the head; her hard hat was on the ground. I threw myself onto her, knocking the wind from her lungs, and a dry fire flamed up in my shoulder. The club had found me with a glancing blow.

I looked up just in time to see a protestor and the cop tumble down the little embankment. Lucky for both of us, he was probably the smallest cop on the force.

I picked Stella up and ran. She was trying to cry, but didn't have enough air to do a good job of it. I carried her into the bushes behind Honest Abe. Then she did cry, but not for long because I told her we needed the Love-essence, so she sat up and began concentrating while all around us the world changed.

I understand the mule train protest went a couple blocks to Balbo Avenue before the cops regained their composure, ushered the mules through their lines, stopped them once they were out of danger, and renewed their attack. The protestors were driven into the Park and into small groups which were easily dispersed. Paddy wagons hauled away those who were arrested. Sirens cut through the night, an eerie sound above all the rest of the noise.

Stella concentrated and I kept watch, but if a cop had stuck his head inside the bushes, what would I have done? I wasn't going to leave Stella so my options were limited. Fight or run, but what if she wouldn't run?

Eventually, the Park calmed down. I retrieved Stella's blankets, but most of the rest of her gear was gone, including her useless hard hat.

When I found she had fallen asleep while in an upright position, I put her on a blanket, cloaked us with the other two, and held her in my arms until dawn.

A lot of the action that night took place in front of the Hilton and before the eyes of TV cameras and news reporters not at the nominating convention, which I later learned was a show of its own with Mayor Daley angry at almost losing control of what was to have been his shining hour.

Earlier in the afternoon the Convention had adopted the majority plank on Vietnam, a hawkish one, but the minority plank supporters, the doves, staged a huge demonstration on the floor of the Amphitheatre which angered Daley and much of the Democratic Establishment. When word of the vote hit the streets, it was just another example of the way the Democrats—the party of Gene McCarthy and the late Bobby Kennedy—had sold out the peace movement. Democracy had its chance; now the need was for direct action. And that's what happened.

While Michigan Avenue and Grant Park echoed with the strife of a minor American civil war, the same thing was mirrored at the Convention. When news of the clashes on Michigan reached the delegates, there was a call to postpone the Convention for a couple weeks and resume in another city, any other city: it was ignored by the chair.

The nominations proceeded: that of "Clean Gene" McCarthy, "Lonesome George" McGovern, Hubert Horatio "the Hump" Humphrey. One of those who nominated McGovern condemned the "Gestapo tactics" of Chicago's finest, which unleashed an exceptionally foul-mouthed response from Mayor Daley, who called on the delegate to do something to himself which was physically impossible. There were six other nominees, among them "Bear" Bryant, the football coach of the Alabama Crimson Tide, and former white supremacist George Wallace.

Humphrey finished some eleven hundred sixty and ¾ votes ahead of McCarthy to garner the chance to take on "Tricky Dick" in November.

The Humphrey delegates, who, by extension, were loyal to the absent President, LJB, arguably the most hated Democrat in America, demonstrated their joy. The losing delegates caucused in side rooms and decided to march to Grant Park in solidarity with the demonstrators there. They started out, but the walk hurt their feet and out-of-shape bodies, so they organized a bus caravan and drove just south of the Hilton, got out, and formed up to march proudly down Michigan.

They were joined by some of those left in the Park and set up an impromptu speaking assembly line.

I could hear the speeches, the roars of approval, and see the spotlights flooding the front of the Hilton, but I didn't care. I snuggled down holding Stella and went to sleep.

The tracks just to the south of the highway were now BN, but they were the old Burlington Route, and the long freight I caught up to just east of a few buildings called Anabel was hauled by a Burlington diesel, painted in the old color of Chinese red, with a gray roof, and white lettering and stripes on the nose. The train and I hit a little place named Clarence together, but I didn't have to slow down very much, so I came out on the other side clearly ahead. The tracks snuggled right up to the highway with trees acting as a divider. I wished I hadn't been traveling so fast because if the train and I were next to each other, maybe the engineer would have waved. The tracks and I stayed together past farms, between a motley collection of buildings known as Lentner, one of them faded-red with two chimneys which might have done a good business in the Forties. I couldn't tell if it was still open.

I slowed down at Shelbina, a town of over a thousand. Some of the store buildings on the west side looked beat up, but it had a decent central business section. I breezed through another collection of old buildings with a name—Lakenan. After curving to the left a little, the tracks and I went through Hunnewell, a village that had seen better days, although its remaining residents kept their yards and the many empty lots neat. Seven miles and I was in Monroe City, a sign stating that a few more than 2300 people resided there.

For the size of town, Monroe City had a surprising lack of curbs, gutters, and sidewalks along 36, although the residential areas had nice shade trees. I rejoined the Burlington on the east side of town; it was then I noticed another set of tracks a half mile south—the Wabash. Its motto was "Follow the Flag," and I would have loved to see one of its blue and gray diesels with the red border and the blue center with "WABASH" in white, but there were no trains, and it was too far to see a flag anyway.

On a curve stood a sign saying that Hassard was off to the south, then the highway curved back, and I went up and over the Burlington tracks. Signs appeared along the way to towns or spots on the map both north and south: Ely, Huntington, West Ely, Rennselaer, Withers Mill, places I would never see, but I liked the names. A left-hand curve brought me to a divided highway, but I cut off on the MM. Hannibal was somewhere in the trees ahead.

Concentrating the Love-essence must have been surprisingly exhausting because Stella slept late, and I let her. Once I had taken piano lessons from a very young nun at the St. Ignatius Loyola High School in Menninger. Her angel-innocent face and big eyes peeked out from her black habit like a tiny bunny just leaving the burrow for the first time. Stella reminded me of her, Sister Mary Agnes, but I knew Stella wasn't as innocent; she just looked like it as she slept.

We walked across Michigan to the Standard Station, where we cleaned up. My shoulder didn't look very good in the mirror, but it never really hurt that much. It was good that he was a small cop. Stella took longer than I did. When she came out of the restroom, she had no makeup, she never wore any, but her face was enthusiastic for life. We found my car and drove north for breakfast; she had toast and eggs, which for some reason she hadn't expelled from the more sentient category of life. I kept up with my diet of meat. I had to order the meals to go because she had lost her sandals and couldn't go in barefoot, so we ate in the Camaro.

I was very worried about her innocence and the way the world would take advantage of it. I told her I'd drive her to Madison and pay for a room until the University opened. She told me she wasn't going back to school; she had important work to do in the Rockies. On the way back to Grant, I tried to interject arguments against her going anywhere with Danny. Even walking into the Park I was persisting and she was resisting.

When I saw her friends in the usual spot, I grabbed her in some vain attempt to stop the inevitable. She pulled my arms down and took my hands in hers. "Seeker, I wish I could stay with you and help you attune yourself with the Love-essence, but I can't. Danny needs the essence much more than you do, and there's important work to do in the mountains."

She turned away and walked to the other four. A moment later they were heading south to where I assumed their station wagon was in hiding. Stella gave me a little smile and a wave; I waved back.

After the Weatherman faction split from SDS and engaged in bombings as a form of revolutionary protest in Chicago, New York City, San Francisco, and Washington, D.C., I was afraid the name of Sandra Marshfield or Morris Winters would come up, but they didn't.

I never heard of any microwave tower bombings, either.

I took the John F. Kennedy Expressway to the Edens Expressway and traveled I-94 home. Outside the city I gassed up at a station that was off to the north at least a quarter mile. I also got a few snacks for the trip. Then I just drove. The afternoon turned to evening, the evening to night. Robert F. Kennedy was beatified at the Convention; I was unaware. Humphrey and his running mate Edmund Muskie tried to fire up the Democratic faithful for the campaign ahead; I was oblivious. I forced my mind away from thoughts and memories and drove the Camaro out of rote.

When I noticed my gas gauge, I had passed through the Twin Cities and left St. Cloud behind. Midnight had come and gone; stations were closed. Panic forced me to think about sleeping at a rest stop. Suddenly, I saw a huge, well-lighted Texaco sign extended high into the night sky. Saved by the Texaco Star.

I had been working on the house I had bought in Menninger, and the bedroom was a mess, so I was staying with Mom and Dad. As quietly as possible, I unlocked the side door and crept upstairs, where I fell into bed, breathed a prayer of thanks, and slept.

But not for long. A light went on. My Dad had come upstairs after hearing noises. I opened my eyes. "Oh, it's you, son; welcome home." He turned off the light and went down the stairs. I knew he'd check to see I'd locked the door before he went back to bed with Mom.

Mark Twain was one of my favorite authors. I had read the jumping frog short story, of course, and two novels—*Tom Sawyer Abroad* and *Tom Sawyer, Detective*—which weren't very good:

In *Tom Sawyer Abroad*, Tom, Huck, and Jim become accidental passengers on a hot air balloon owned by a mad professor and set sail, flying east of Missouri, with Huck Finn as the narrator. When the professor gets drunk, he falls overboard into the Atlantic, but he has taught Tom how to navigate the balloon. They eventually reach North Africa. They land on the sand, and a lion chases Tom and Huck. In the air again they witness the ambush of a camel caravan by robbers and save a child from being kidnapped. The next day they see the mummies of the men, women, and children who had been in a caravan that had been caught in a sandstorm years before. Later they are attacked by lions and tigers at an oasis. They witness a caravan being buried in a sandstorm, and they reach the Pyramids, the Sphinx, what Tom says is Joseph's granary from the Bible, and Mt. Sinai before their trip ended.

Some of the banter between the characters was well-done, as well as Twain's comments on American society, but as I read the novel, I kept comparing it to *Huckleberry Finn*, and not in a good way. In *Huckleberry Finn,* Huck and Jim float south down the Mississippi, and Twain's narrative contains some of the most memorable scenes in American fiction. In *Tom Sawyer Abroad*, the characters float east in a balloon, their adventures and the writing is less than memorable. And whoever heard of tigers in North Africa?

Tom Sawyer, Detective is also narrated by Huck Finn. He tells about how he and Tom Sawyer were on their way down river to visit Tom's Uncle Silas and Aunt Sally when they discover that a man has stolen some diamonds from his former gang, and they are looking for him with the intent to kill. Tom and Huck decide to help the man, but he gets off the boat with the man's former partners in hot pursuit, while Tom and Huck are delayed and fall behind. Despite a meeting with a "ghost," a suspected murder, a sleep-walking uncle, and a courtroom scene where Tom Sawyer explains everything, the novel plods on to its conclusion. It was all just too hokey and contrived for me.

In college I read a collection of short writings edited by historian Bernard DeVoto and published as *Mark Twain Letters From the Earth*, many portions of which satirized religion, so I wasn't too keen on them, but I liked his comments on writer James Fenimore Cooper.

I also read his major works—the somewhat autobiographical *Life on the Mississippi,* and the novels *The Adventures of Tom Sawyer* and *The Adventures of Huckleberry Finn.*

To me *Tom Sawyer* was one of the great novels. Twain managed to weave into it the major themes of a boy's childhood—friends, young love, buried treasure, school days, Sunday School, adventures—all with the twists that made them so real to me. I had read *Tom Sawyer* more times than any other book.

Two of Twain's writings—*Life on the Mississippi* and *Huckleberry Finn*—were good half-books.

Life on the Mississippi started out well: "*...the basin of the Mississippi is the* BODY OF THE NATION." I agreed and saw the river as a giant aorta, carrying commerce just as the bloodstream carries corpuscles. I liked Twain's thumbnail sketch of the river's European explorers—De Soto; Marquette and Joliet; and La Salle; the portion about the fight between two river characters with their exaggerated bragging and their total lack of action that Twain was going to put in *Huckleberry Finn*, but never did; and the actual autobiographical part about young Sam Clemens and his steamboating days. However, much of the writing just seemed to be padding to add more pages and make it book-length.

Ernest Hemingway said that all of American literature was derived from *Huckleberry Finn*. That was probably an exercise in hyperbole, but the first half of the novel could bear up under the weight of that praise—the description of despicable Huck's father; Huck in disguise and his conversation with a woman; Huck and Jim exploring the wrecked steamboat; Huck with the Grangerford family and the feud with the Shepherdsons; the continuing relationship of Jim and Huck and their conversations; Jim's description of how he learned his little daughter was deaf; the unforgettable "Duke" and "King"—all these confirm at least some of what Hemingway alluded to. Then Tom Sawyer shows up and the novel goes downhill from great literature to farce.

Hannibal had about 20,000 people, but most of it was hidden by the rolling topography and the trees that lined the highway and lived in the yards. Most of the houses were set back from the highway. I began my descent into the Mississippi River Valley on a curve and curved again, coming out in a business district. I went right, got on Broadway, and passed through a residential area with the houses much closer to the pavement. Many of the homes had low concrete or stone retaining walls protecting their yards. Concrete steps interrupted the line of the walls. The houses were older, but I didn't think any of them had been around when Sam Clemens was young.

I passed the Blessed Sacrament Church on my right, a brown brick building with a large rose window and a cross above it and a four-story bell tower topped with another cross. A left-hand curve and a main business section. I passed a red brick church on my left; a Catholic school; and Holy Family Catholic Church with two front doors separated by a huge stained glass window above four smaller ones on my right.

The Marion County Courthouse bulked up on the left, looking like a massive Greek temple with four gigantic columns and capitals that looked Corinthian, but weren't. They supported a large portico roof. The building was topped by a huge gray dome and a single brick chimney that looked out of place.

A two-towered Methodist Church appeared on the right, and a three-and-a-half story stone building that could have been the setting for a Gothic tale of murder loomed up on the left.

I passed Central Park on my left, with another church across the street, but I couldn't see the name. I was heading on a slight downhill toward the river, but not before I passed another Greek temple—that time it was labeled the Farmers & Merchants Bank, but I don't think it was a bank anymore. It boasted four columns with capitals that were a sort of Ionic, but with additions that might qualify them as a form of Composite.

I was thinking about the great satire Mark Twain could compose in describing the "Greek temples," and about what he, as an atheist, must be thinking about the large number of churches in his hometown. *Maybe an atheist can't think anything after death.*

Then I saw it—the "Father of Waters," "Ol' Man River," the Mississippi.

I accelerated on a green light, crossed two sets of railroad tracks which I assumed were the old Burlington and the Wabash, and parked. I walked out on a breakwater and looked around.

Halley's Comet was in the sky when Samuel Langhorne Clemens was born in Florida, Missouri, a little spot on the map some twenty-seven or twenty-eight miles southwest of Hannibal. When he died in 1910, the comet was also there. Sam's family moved when he was four or five, so Hannibal was where he grew up. I tried to imagine a white, postage-stamp size village built almost to the water's edge with some buildings running up the bluffs; a ferry landing; warehouses; and a steamboat puffing black smoke, anxiously waiting to be unloaded at the wharf.

Now in 1970 I could see the Mark Twain Memorial Bridge to the north; there was no need for a ferry. The railroads had replaced the steamboats. Except for a great white grain elevator complex, some railroad buildings and structures, and a couple "boat ride on the Mississippi" concessions, Hannibal had been moved back off the river.

Gone forever were the wooden sidewalks in front of the false-front stores; the whittlers and tall-tale spinners sitting in splint-bottomed chairs; pigs, horses, mules, and wagons in the dust-laden streets; piles of freight on a lonely wharf; women in long dresses and scoop bonnets; Africa-dark slaves; a town drunk; Huck Finn sleeping in a sugar hogshead. A modern town stood in their place.

I marveled at the way capitalism, the free market, the profit-and-loss system, whichever term you prefer, built on a solid foundation of the natural rights of life, liberty, and property, continued to be the most efficient mechanism for the recognition of diminished demand and the elimination of no-longer-needed capital, and the introduction of new capital to supply an increased demand and satisfy changing consumers' wants. Communism, Socialism, Fascism, the Mixed System, any form of central planning have all proven themselves failures beside the giant engine of free enterprise.

I went back to Broadway, turned right onto North Main, and drove between brick buildings on either side that would have been at home in almost any small town in the Midwest. I pulled over at Hill Street, which was blocked off, and walked up the street. Toward the west end I saw what I was looking for—Tom Sawyer's house; actually Mark Twain's house; well, actually John and Jane Clemens' house, but what tourist would go there under that name?

The house was a white, two-story frame building with three windows on the second story and one on either side of the front door which was one step up from the sidewalk.

A female tourist with a guidebook told me that the Becky Thatcher house was across the street. I went across and met disappointment. Becky's two-story house was bigger than Tom's: it had two front doors and eight front windows, but while it wasn't ramshackle, it could not compare with Tom's well-kept house. I walked back for another look at Tom's.

Stretching down toward the river, the famous fence that Tom conned his friends into whitewashing stood in all its alabaster-white glory. A sign indicated it was not the original fence, but I could tell that: it was much too short, and Tom's friends would have had their work done in twenty minutes, including two coats.

I went around back where an addition perpendicular to the original house doubled its size. Tourists were walking in and out, but I had to get going. There was a museum in the gray stone building next door: I didn't go in there, either. Before I walked down to my bike, I pretended I was Tom, looking for an adventure: as soon as he stepped out of his front door, he would see the Mississippi to his left and from his backyard he could see tree-covered Cardiff Hill.

I drove a block to North Street and dismounted to see the statues of Tom and Huck at the base of Cardiff Hill. There were concrete stairs leading to the top and I took them, walking past a small gray house on my right. Tom and Huck had gone looking for buried treasure in a haunted house located in a valley on the other side of the hill, but there was no treasure or even a big old house there now. The hill itself was smothered by trees, bushes, a couple power poles, some lights, a few signs, and a lighthouse.

Twain had written that the Mississippi was a mile-wide at Hannibal, but it must have shrunk to a half mile. A sign pointed to Tom Sawyer's Island, tree-covered and a couple dozen yards from the Illinois shore. I could see why some critics asked why the runaway slave Jim just didn't swim from the island to the free state of Illinois, but I guess that would have made for a very short novel with not much of a plot.

As I started down, I noticed an old couple looking at the statues. When the woman saw me, she said something to her husband and moved over to their car, a Platinum Gray 1960 Cadillac Eldorado Seville hardtop coupe with its magnificent pair of fins, fins that just fit the car, not the flamboyant ones that made the '59 look like a flying machine that had fallen to earth. The Eldorado would easily run you seventy-five hundred for the privilege of getting fourteen miles to the gallon.

I took one last look up the hill and started for the Honda. The old man said, "Excuse me," and held up his hand to reinforce the fact he wanted me to stop. He walked over. "I'd like to introduce myself. My name is Glen Gray...not the Big Band leader, and I don't smoke." He chuckled. Mom liked Big Band music, so I knew that Glen Gray had led the Casa Loma Orchestra and that their theme song was "Smoke Rings." We shook hands.

"I'm Chris Cockburn."

"Where do you come from, Mr. Cockburn?"

"A small town in North Dakota."

"And what do you do in North Dakota."

"I work in a school."

"Oh, a teacher, eh? Well, I guess we need them, although I never got out of the eighth grade myself." He turned. "Mother, come over here; I told you he was a nice man." The woman with impossibly dark hair shuffled toward us, her steps punctuated with a cane. "Mr. Cockburn, this is my wife Doris. Mother, this is Mr. Chris Cockburn. He teaches school in North Dakota." I didn't correct him: I had been a teacher.

"How do you do, Mr. Cockburn. I didn't really think you were a bad person; it's just that so many these days...the long hair and beards...the drugs...." Her voice trailed off.

"Yes, I understand you have to be careful."

We exchanged a few minor pleasantries, and I said I had to be going. They waved as I drove off. I circled a few blocks, looking for a place to eat. Finally, I decided on a drive-in, the kind where you called in your order and a carhop brought it to you. I was trying to figure out where the tray would go when I heard a car horn and a voice calling my name. It was Glen and Doris Gray and they were waving me over to their Eldorado.

Mr. Gray got out and motioned me into the back. The interior was red and the upholstery was red leather. The color gave me a warm feeling. "Please allow us to buy your meal, Mr. Cockburn; we didn't mean to insult you."

I assured them they hadn't, but I accepted the invitation because it would be nice to have company. Mr. Gray asked where I was headed. After I told him New Orleans, he said he and "Mother" were going there, too, before taking a ship to Venezuela. They would ship the Eldorado to Caracas, also. Mr. Gray had owned a tool and die business in Detroit ("Pretty good for a man who never finished eighth grade"), but sold out and retired. A friend told him that he might want to invest in petroleum production in Venezuela, so they were going down there to check out the investment situation.

I knew the country had a lot of oil, but Venezuelan politics or Latin American politics, in general, would have made me leery of sinking my life savings into anything that could become volatile very quickly.

I remembered in 1958 Vice President Nixon was in Venezuela on a good will visit when his car was attacked and damaged by a crowd of student radicals. With possible nationalization of the oil industry, anti-Americanism, and Fidel Castro lurking in the background, Venezuela would not be my first, or even my twenty-first, choice to secure my retirement nest egg. I hoped the Grays knew what they were doing.

We talked a little about our families (their two daughters had given them four grandchildren); they told me how they had met at a barn dance, and she thought he was the clumsiest dancer she had ever known, but she wouldn't have missed the fifty years they had spent together for any amount of money or for Rudolf Valentino, either. I supposed that was an inside joke for after she had said it, they looked at each other and laughed.

Finally, we were done with our food and our conversation. Mr. Gray and I shook hands; I bent down to say goodbye to Mrs. Gray; I started my bike and rode away amidst smiles and waves.

I headed south on 79. Sometimes the limestone cliffs on either side were so close if I had moved over to the shoulder, I could have touched them. The Mississippi was on my left, but the trees and cliffs barred my view until I came to a break where there was a little 19th century village and café, then I saw the silver river rolling south under a cloudy sky.

I turned off on 453 and a quarter mile brought me to Mark Twain's Cave, which was a big disappointment. The made-up cave in *Tom Sawyer* was huge and cavernous; the real cave had narrow passages where sometimes my shoulders brushed against the limestone walls. I was glad to leave.

In the parking lot two old men were jawing. I sat in my saddle and listened as the older one dressed in a long-sleeved checked shirt and Big Mac overalls and wearing a straw hat and brown, scuffed boots took up the conversation.

"Ah know we got big winds in Missouah, but the gran'daddy of 'em all wus when Maw an' me lived over in Kansas. We wus bringin' in the winter wheat, an' the straw was so long the headers plugged so bad that it took us three weeks ta do a fiel' that we would've done in a day.

"Well, sir, the sky blacked up, an' the win' started howlin', an' Ah tol' the boys ta head for the cyclone cellar. They wus all down the hol' by the time Ah got in the yard. Jus' then the cyclone hit. The win' was so pow'ful that the rain was fallin' straight up. I saw it an' couldn't believe it; not a drop hit the groun'.

"Ya know how some o' them winds can drive a straw right through a board. Well, that was one of 'um. Jus' as Ah reach'd down fer the cellar doah, Ah seen one of them long straws headin' right fer ma face. It woulda kilt me sure, but Ah wus saved by a turkey.

"We'd been raisin' this ol' Tom Turkey fer Thanksgivin', but he wus like a fren' ta me, so Ah couldn't chop offen his head. He looked up at me from the choppin' block, an' Ah swear he had love in his eye.

"After that he'd foller me 'round the yard makin' sweet sounds. Oncet a skunk snuck up behin' me an' that ol' Tom chase'd him right off, a-flappin' his wings and carryin' on like it was the Judgment Day. Ah like' ta uv hugged him, but Ah couldn't go near 'im fer a week 'cause of the stink.

"Anaway, that ol' Tom had waited ta see if Ah was safe afore he lit out hisself. He seen that killer straw a-headin' fer me an' flappt up an' swallered the whole straw. It straightened him right out in mid-air, an' he was daid by the time he hit the groun'.

"Ah grab'd him, but Ah had a hard time navigatin' the cellar stairs, they wus so narra and ol' Tom was so stiff. Ah'm not ashamed ta admit Ah cried, sittin' down there in the dark. The boys thought Ah wus scairt, but Ah was sheddin' tears fer ma fren'.

"When we come up, we seen how lucky we wus. None uv the buildin's wus hurt; only the outhouse got knock'd off plumb, and the wood pile wus gone.

"Purty soon a neighbor come and said ma woodpile was at his place, so we druve over ta get it. There it wus, all stacked and with the axe right on top where Ah lef' it. 'Thank-ee, neighbor,' Ah said. 'Fer what?' 'Fer stackin' ma wood so nice.' 'Ah didn't; tha's the way the wind lef' it.'

"Wal, we carted 'er home and stack'd 'er. After we he'ped sum less-fortunate neighbors, Ah said goodbye to ma fren' ol' Tom. Ah sure hated to eat that bird."

I felt happy: Mark Twain lived.

I checked my map. I could have taken a route over the bluffs and hills, but the roads were so windy that I didn't think I'd save any time, so I went back to Hannibal and picked up 61, which was a four-lane highway until just past New London.

The wide median divided the highway. I passed small businesses; signs and billboards; small house and mobile homes; a large sign announcing the Pike County Fair, but it was almost a month out of date; and plenty of trees. Everything except the trees thinned out after I went down a hill and crossed over the Salt River.

When they put in the divided highway, they bypassed New London. There was a turnoff to Business 61, which was the old highway, but I didn't take it; I wondered how many drivers did.

After New London, 61 became two-lane. The trees along the highway thinned out considerably. I rounded a curve and Frankford zipped past on my right. On either side of the highway, small outcroppings of layered and weathered limestone started to appear. They had been exposed by the construction of the highway after being laid down in a shallow, warm water sea over three hundred million years before I saw them.

Around a curve and down into a valley, and the limestone formed a layered wall on both sides of the pavement with grass, bushes, and trees growing on top and sometimes in crevasses eroded into the ten to fifteen foot battlements.

Across Peno Creek and onto a valley floor. Just before a curve, the limestone reappeared as a hill to the right of the highway; there was no counterpart on my left. Some of the fields appeared to be terraced, but farms weren't very evident. Maybe they were hidden by the trees.

Around a curve and a limestone hill appeared on the left, then an even larger one, cut back during the highway construction. Nature had formed the limestone over millions of years; Man had reshaped it in a matter of weeks.

I went down into a valley and crossed Gailey Branch. I knew I was getting into the South when a stream or creek was called a branch. Trees closed in on the highway, but backed off as I climbed out of the valley.

I saw one of my Martian water towers, started passing ag-oriented businesses, and then I was in Bowling Green, Missouri, population 2650. How many Bowling Greens were there in the U.S? Just after I passed an ugly green building with a rounded roof, I crossed a bridge over the Gulf, Mobile and Ohio Railroad. In the 1967 film *In the Heat of the Night*, Sidney Portier as detective Virgil Tibbs arrived in Sparta, Mississippi, on a GM&O train. For that reason I would have loved to see one on the tracks below, but I didn't.

Eat, drink, gas up, buy-some-land, tractors-for-sale, tires-batteries-lubricants, insurance, feed-seed-fertilizer, spend-the-night—peoples' dreams wrapped up in boxy buildings, waiting for customers.

A red and black sign told me I was in the Home of the Bobcats. Another informed me that if I lived in Bowling Green, I'd already be home. I rounded a big curve to the left and a third sign thanked me for coming and sent me on my way with a "Hurry Back!" Although it seemed like a nice community, I doubted that I would.

The sky had cleared, the land really flattened out beyond Bowling Green, and there were no trees near the highway. Most of the land was under cultivation. When I did start through some highway cuts, if there was any limestone, it didn't show. A right-hand curve and I passed the little community of Eolia, which couldn't have had more than four hundred people. Then the land began to alternate between forest and farm. A bridge took me over the Cuivre River, a light coffee-color under the span. The Cuivre River State Park with all its trees was off to my left.

I passed Troy on my right and then Moscow Mills on my left. The forest-farm alternation continued until I reached Wentzville, a couple thousand people living on Interstate 70.

I swung onto I-70 which was clotting with cars and trucks. At first, a frontage road separated me from the businesses on my right, but then the businesses disappeared, to be replaced by a limestone outcropping, grass, weeds, shrubs, and trees. The businesses reappeared and the trees backed off. Debris cast off from vehicles started to appear in the median or along the shoulder: a shoe, a curled piece of licorice which was actually part of a tire, a dirty blue shirt, a failed muffler, a 2 by 4.

An interchange led to O'Fallon. I had a feeling that I was surrounded by thousands of houses, but the trees blocked my view. Businesses, then trees, then businesses, trees, and houses all glommed together, and I passed the interchange to St. Peters.

Traffic was getting fierce and fast. I hoped I could handle it. St. Charles. Auto dealers on both sides. A semi blew past me. A sign for a hospital. I might need one. Semis roared by me. Cars zipped past. I moved over to a slower lane. A St. Charles police car sat on the shoulder. No one minded. The highway headed down. Lots of trees ahead. A sign. Missouri River. A long bridge.

Through the girders I saw the Big Muddy, but its water was blue, reflecting the sky. Only on the edges where the trees cut off the sky did the brown color appear.

After St. Charles I traveled that portion of I-70 known as the Mark Twain Expressway, which fishhooked through northern St. Louis to the Mississippi and joined I-55 near the Jefferson Expansion Memorial site to complete the barb of the hook. I passed signs for Bridgeton, St. Ann, Woodson Terrace, Belridge, Ferguson, Normandy, North Woods, and Jennings, places I'd probably never visit.

Curving south with the hook, I passed under the St. Louis Avenue bridge and off to the left Gateway Arch emerged from behind a building. After the Madison Street bridge, I pulled over to the left to make my exit, under a railroad bridge (I thought it was the old Wabash line), under another bridge, and there stood the Arch, looking like the lower part of a wishbone.

I exited onto North Broadway and parked as close to the Old Courthouse as I could. I bought a ticket and walked a couple blocks and crossed over by the Old Cathedral onto the Arch Grounds. Only about five years old, the "Gateway to the West" Arch was stainless steel, 630 feet tall and 630 feet wide at the base. Its simple, clean lines would have appealed to Jefferson, I thought.

I took the tram to the top and the view was spectacular and depressing. I could see the curve of the river, the green of the park, Busch Memorial Stadium, but my view of Illinois was disturbed by the presence of East St. Louis, and my view to the west was marred by the tall buildings and the urban sprawl of modern St. Louis. The Wild West of Lewis and Clark was completely civilized. Mountain men Boone Caudill, Jim Deakins, and Dick Summers were lost on the streets of St. Louis.

New York had the Empire State Building, San Francisco the Ferry Building, but the Arch was the symbolic essence of St. Louis, so I didn't search for any other specific structure that captured the Spirit of St. Louis. I just rode the 750 around the downtown blocks and looked. I did see a couple of interesting buildings on Olive: the seven-story S.G. Adams Stationery store at the corner of Olive and 10th, its red sandstone contrasting nicely with the light colors of the buildings around it and another red sandstone at Olive and 8th in which hundreds of windows and the ones on the top floors reflected the sun and caused the building to burst into apparent flame.

I worked my way north, looking for a sign directing me to the Interstate. I got onto Cass Avenue, made another wrong turn, and found myself in the ghetto, actually one of several St. Louis ghettos. Both sides of the street were lined with two-story, red or brown brick apartment houses, all with front stoops and all populated by Negro families.

I was surprised by the number of men who seemed to have nothing to do but sit on their stoops in their undershirts. Then I found out they had at least one other thing to do: yell at me. "Hey, white bread, you lost?" "Betta git yo white ass off'n my street!" "Damn cracker!" "Yo, honky sonuvabitch!" "Goddam fag!" and the ever-popular one in which I was accused of having carnal knowledge of my mother.

I passed a vacant lot, waist-high weeds protecting dead cans and bottles, and crowned with one of those Studebakers from the early Fifties, the ones which at first glance you couldn't tell the front end from the rear. It had no wheels; it was flat on the ground.

A green light turned red. Cross traffic filled the intersection. I noticed some young men with dark skin leave their stoops and head toward the intersection. Some smaller boys followed them and then some girls. I was praying I wouldn't kill the bike when the light changed. The amber came on in the light to my right. The young men started to run. I prepared to defy any late-arriving traffic by leaving early, but the light changed, my start was right out of the manual, and curses and one rock rained down on my shoulders.

I turned south and fled out of town as fast as I could after finding a sign that pointed me to Interstate 55. I pushed the needle five miles above the speed limit. It was irrational: my tormentors didn't have motorcycles or cars, but I was scared. Then I added another five miles per hour and began weaving in and out of tight spots.

The river, barges, warehouses, and storage tanks appeared on the left, then the highway swung to the west, and I crossed the shrunken River Des Peres and after ten miles of adventurous riding and angry car horns, the wider Meramec River. A sign said Jefferson County, and I slowed down to the speed limit as I passed the Arnold interchange. I was still in suburbia, but the number of houses was diminishing.

Limestone topped by bushes and trees began showing up in the highway cuts again. I could see the layers, and sometimes there were dark vertical discolorations from the runoff. The highway twisted like a slow snake past Imperial. Sometimes limestone on both sides of the Interstate made little canyons. Trees greened everything. Through the gaps in the trees, I could see hills off to the right. If they were the Ozarks, I was not impressed.

I curved between two high cliffs of limestone and glimpsed the Mississippi off to my left and passed some hills on my right. I went over the Frisco tracks with a train on it, but I couldn't see the locomotive. (The Frisco was actually the St. Louis-San Francisco Railway, but its tracks never made it to the West Coast, reaching only to the panhandle of Texas.)

I took the Pevely exit and gassed up at a Phillips 66. A lot of semis were parked near a restaurant, so I walked over. I'd heard truckers knew where the best food was. I ordered a slice of blueberry pie alamode and asked what kind of pop they had. My waitress, a forty-year old bottle blonde with Revlon Red lips said, "Pop, dahlin'? Oh, ya'll mean soda." The Midwest was changing into the South. She began to list the flavors, but I stopped her at Dr. Pepper.

I liked listening to the talk of the truckers—where they had been or were going, the cheapest places for diesel, where to look out for Smokey, road construction delays, and sometimes about their families or how many days they had been out or how many days it was until home and they could hardly wait. And there was friendly banter or sometimes teasing a younger trucker. I left the place with a warm spot for truckers, a bunch of friendly guys helping to keep America running.

Back on the Double Nickel I met up with my old friends, the limestone cliffs. I crossed over Joachim Creek, passed by more limestone and emerged into an area with businesses and housing and signs reading Herculaneum, Festus, and Crystal City. When I saw Festus, I thought of the character Festus Haggen, played by Ken Curtis on TV's *Gunsmoke*, one of my Dad's favorites.

About a mile-and-a-half past the Festus interchange, I-55 ran out. I could see construction further south, but signs directed me onto Highway 61.

Trees, bushes, and power lines closed in on the pavement. I crossed the Missouri-Illinois tracks. Traffic had thinned considerably, which was good because after the Interstate I found the regular highway extremely narrow. It was rolling land, so there was generally a solid "Do Not Pass" line for one or both lanes. Every once in awhile there was an opening in the trees which revealed a house or a road leading to a house hidden by the trees.

The trees thinned and I passed under a double bridge being constructed for I-55. Just beyond there was a huge outcropping of limestone and then I was in the trees again. I started running over the shadows they cast in the late afternoon. I passed through a brief canyon of weathered limestone and the trees weren't as thick anymore. There were more houses and roadside businesses.

I went into a slow curve to the right; sometimes the trees were thick and crowded the highway and sometimes they were thinned out and allowed civilizing grass on the shoulders and houses offset from the pavement. I passed under some power lines and came to county road TT. The map showed that the Interstate was a quarter mile or so to the right and construction had stopped there, but I couldn't see anything because of the trees.

The trees gave way and a cornfield appeared on my right. I crossed Isle du Bois Creek and entered Ste. Genevieve County. I passed through treed areas, treeless areas, low rock outcroppings, past houses, places to get gas or to eat, while the power lines kept me company.

More buildings began to show up, both commercial and residential. Through the gaps in the trees, I could see tree-covered hills across a broad valley to my right. I obeyed a sign and slowed down. I passed an elevated two-story white house with a front porch, picket fence, and a set of steps leading down the embankment to the highway; then other houses; then the village of Bloomsdale with a couple hundred people and a miniscule business district. At the edge of town, there was an actual farm, one of the few I had seen, and a large cornfield. I passed over farms, more fields, and by some houses of people who wanted a rural view.

A lazy left-hand curve and I began a slow climb, passing between my old companions, the limestone cliffs. Near the summit of the hill, I passed some houses and two large vertical tanks. There were more houses hiding in the trees on the way down, most of them modest in size and appearance. I crossed a short bridge with cement guardrails over North Gabouri Creek and ran past a cornfield on my left. I went through the trees into a snaky curve—right, left, right—and passed a semi in a "No Pass" zone, the driver honking at me.

I went over South Gabouri Creek and into the outskirts of Ste. Genevieve. I pulled into a McDonald's; I was in a hurry; the day was dying.

Unfortunately for me, a Little League team had just started ordering, so all three tills were busy. Finally, I ordered a Big Mac, large fries, and a large Coke and found a seat. The kids were all excited about defeating Farmington, and I enjoyed listening to their talk of triumph.

After I used the facilities, I fired up and rolled onto 61. Businesses lined the highway and I wondered if there was a downtown shopping area. I passed a motel and hit a residential area with no sidewalks: the grass lipped the pavement. A mixed commercial-residential area, a cornfield, and I was out of town.

Around a curve and heading southeast, I had to turn on my headlight away from the town. The big river was a mile to my left and the Frisco tracks about four hundred yards in that direction. I couldn't see the river, but there was a train on the Frisco, pushing its light ahead of it just as I was doing.

There were lots of trees on my right, and fields to the left. The highway moved to the left and the tracks were there, right across a ditch, but I had left the train behind. I rolled over a couple dark creeks and found the trees again. The rails and pavement diverged, then got back together. Another creek. Thick trees. The highway went up a hill, and I could see the tracks below, then they disappeared in the trees.

I passed a stone retaining wall at the base of a hill as I curved around it, then houses and street lights appeared. A two-story white house ghosted on the right behind a retaining wall; its construction with a porch, railings, and lattice reminded me of 19th century Hannibal. More old Hannibal-type houses, the railroad again, an elevator and grain-storage facility, a dilapidated business section, a few more houses, and I had passed through St. Marys.

A sharp curve to the right, scattered houses, mobile homes, ag-related businesses, and lots of trees. Some curves and small hills and ag-land replaced most of the trees. I saw yard lights from farms and lights in houses. Then more lights ahead and I drove through the small community of Brewer, where the houses were scattered and there were no streetlights or sidewalks.

My headlight stabbed its way through the dark; I passed cornfields, farms, and houses until I came to more lights—Perryville. It was hard to be sure, but it looked to be a town of four or five thousand. At least it had sidewalks and street lights. The blocks seemed to be set at an angle to the highway. I went over a small depression with a pond reflecting the moon and I was out of town. Up a low hill, past a sign advertising "Livestock," and into the trees. Downhill between cuts bordered by jagged rock faces. A meadow in the moonlight. A curve and uphill into the trees again. Across a creek, but I missed the sign.

The highway snaked right-left-right-left-right-left with fields on both sides and then into more trees. I had to find a place to camp.

When I emerged from the trees, I had a visitor—a semi was on my tail. He pulled up behind me, but didn't pass. I couldn't understand that because the highway was straight. I motioned him around; he didn't take the hint. Trees appeared ahead and we curved into the village of Longtown. I complied with a sign and slowed; the semi's bumper was almost on my rear wheel. I passed a brick church on my left with a lighter colored steeple; I suppose I should have prayed.

A right-hand curve; a left-hand curve; then a straight shot out of town; houses in the moonlight, looking like they belonged in *Tom Sawyer*, but I doubted any of them were haunted; I should have pulled off and let the semi go by.

A derelict barn with an open door and a crippled grain auger protruding looked like a giant wrinkled bull elephant charging me from the trees. I should have taken the hint.

Down a little hill, around a curve, and I picked up speed. So did the semi. Trees, fields, farm, houses, the semi, and me. Another curve, then another, then the highway appeared straight; I motioned the semi to pass. He crept up even closer, so close I didn't dare slow down.

Into more trees and past a curve sign; the semi swung out. *What is he doing?* He shaved me close and pulled in quickly, then he slowed. I pulled out to look for the curve and the blackness exploded: the driver had tossed a cherry bomb at me. I got off the gas; he sped away, his taillights darting ahead in the dark like red fireflies. *I have to find a place to camp. Damn truckers.*

I passed a few houses, some in trees to the right, and then into a right-hand curve. A farm passed by on the left, a big house behind a hedge on the right. *Find a place.* A left-hand curve. No ditch. A cover crop. A line of trees fifty yards to the right. I drove through the field and parked under the overhang of the trees.

Some friends in the National Guard had told me that when they went to Ft. Leonard Wood in Missouri to train, they had been warned about the brown recluse spider, a sneaky little devil whose bite could make a person very sick or even die. I didn't know if they inhabited tree lines or not, but I was tired and would have to take my chances.

I placed the poncho so the bike would be between me and the highway. I got my gear out, brushed my teeth, and drank from the canteen. I looked out from under the leafy canopy and saw the stars. I worked on my journal and wrote out two post cards. I took out my Testament and skimmed the Psalms until I found Psalm 56, which read, in part: "Mine enemies would daily swallow me up...What time I am afraid, I will trust in thee...In God have I put my trust: I will not be afraid what man can do unto me...For thou hast delivered my soul from death: wilt not thou deliver my feet from falling, that I may walk before God in the light of the living?"

That made me feel good, but then I went too far—I read a little Jeffers, specifically his poem "To Death":

"I think of you as a great king, cold and austere;

The throne is not gold but iron, the stones of the high hall are black basalt blocks, and the pavement also,

With blood in the corners:

Yet you are merciful...And after a time you give us eternal peace."

I flipped off the flashlight and said my prayers of thanksgiving, not to Jeffers' Death-god, but to my God.

DAY FOUR

When I woke up, the leaves, grass, and cover crop were dew-covered. I didn't feel as though a brown recluse had visited me, but there were dozens of spider webs running from the lower branches to the grass. I shook out my boots, packed up, and started the 750. Immediately, large spiders ran up the webs. I knew they weren't the brown recluse, but it was still creepy. I was glad to get onto the pavement.

I went over a short bridge with cement guard rails spanning a trickle of water. Trees and fields alternated along the highway; there were occasional houses until I reached the outskirts of the small village of Uniontown, where the most prominent features were a large white barn on the north end, a two-story white house with green shutters in the middle, and a two-story brown brick house topped with five lightning rods and a TV antenna on the south end.

A curve took me into more trees which alternated with fields until I passed Old Appleton, even smaller than Uniontown. Apparently 61 had been moved a hundred yards or so to the west, by-passing most of the village, so the back ends of buildings were toward the highway, including that of a little red outhouse.

I crossed Apple Creek with its sharp-cut banks and entered Cape Girardeau County, went up a hill, passed a large white barn with a farmer sliding the door open, and left Old Appleton behind. Up and down a hill; sparse trees; a horse pasture to my right; over Poor Creek, which was almost dry and a poor excuse for a creek; and a left-hand curve. Over a trickle of water; up a hill and down; across Hughes Creek, tree-lined, but drying up; the land not looking very good to me.

I passed an old barn which was falling apart and a curve took me up a hill. More poor land, then over little Buckeye Creek with farm buildings on a hill off to the right, two silos towering over them. I rolled over the land; there weren't many trees. I passed a large ag business—the Shawneetown Feed & Seed Company. The trees with houses and mobile homes in the early morning shadows.

Fields, farms, curves in the highway, occasional thick growths of trees, then a big dogleg to the right and houses began to appear, owned by those who wanted to live in the country, but without farming. A brick church. More houses, more traffic, businesses, and the village of Fruitland. About a mile south, 61 tied in with I-55 and I opened her up.

Unlike 61 the Interstate was fairly level, and as I passed through a highway cut, my old friend, limestone, appeared, but the outcroppings were small and disappointing. After a ways I passed more outcroppings and they were much more prominent.

Billboards began advertising the various wonders on which I could spend my money in Cape Girardeau. There were several exits and some of the signs were insistent about which exit I should take. More poor limestone. Thick groves of trees. Then the city limits and the trees were gone.

I-55 was somewhat new to Cape Girardeau, and businesses were slowly moving out to meet it, so I decided to take the old business loop into town. I crossed Cape LaCroix Creek, passed a motel, and saw a little hole-in-the-wall pancake place.

There were only four windows in the front, so I had to take a chance and hope no one vandalized my bike or stole anything.

I ordered the Man-Sized Breakfast, and it was—three large pancakes (two buttermilk, one oatmeal), two eggs, four strips of bacon, hash browns, a biscuit, and coffee, which I didn't take since I don't drink it. I had a large milk. After my waitress Mae took the order, I took my kit into the bathroom and quickly cleaned up.

Mae was a friendly old soul, maybe sixty-five and gray-haired, but she knew waitressing. She worked rings around the younger waitress and was very friendly. We talked a little, and when she found out I was from North Dakota, she said she never wanted to go there because it was so cold. I wished I had more time to defend my state.

My neighbors were talking about the St. Louis Cardinals, who had finished fourth in the NL East the previous season and looked like they weren't going to improve in 1970, despite having the great Bob Gibson as their best pitcher. Two of the men thought manager Red Schoendienst needed to be gone: he had won the 1967 World Series, lost the '68 Series to Detroit, and had gone down from there. Speedy Lou Brock, Joe Torre, José Cardinal, and second baseman Julian Javier were praised; they were neutral on shortstop Dal Maxvill—good fielder, couldn't hit; but power-hitting Dick Allen and pitcher Steve Carlton were deemed troublemakers and should be dealt just like the Cards had gotten rid of Curt Flood, the little cry baby.

I wanted to say something about how the Cards had handled the Red Sox in the '67 Series because I didn't like the Sox, but then the men might start asking questions and if I had to say I was a Yankee fan that might not go over too well, so I was prudent and kept my mouth shut.

When I had first walked in, the smell of old cigarettes hit me, but no one was smoking. After the four men finished eating, they all lit up. Two of them were Marlboro men, one a Camel smoker, and one went for the menthol taste of Kools. I hated tobacco smoke and hurried to finish my breakfast.

At the till I inquired where the post office was. Mae asked if I had something to mail and I showed her the postcards. "They goin' ta yer folks?"

"Yes, and my cousin."

She smiled and said, "The post office is way over yonder on Franklin, but Ah'd be glad to mail 'em for ya'll when Ah git off." There were around thirty thousand people in Cape Giradeau, and I figured I didn't have the time to try and locate Franklin, so I took up her offer. I thanked her and was glad I'd left a nice tip.

A man in an army uniform passed me as I reached the door. I heard Mae say, "Clayton, how ya'all doin' this fine mawnin'?"

I drove back to 55 and headed south, merging into heavy traffic. The soldier Clayton had reminded me of my cousin Rory O'Connell. We'd graduated high school together, then I'd gone to Minot State, and he went to NDSU in Fargo. He was going with Holly Lawrence, a girl in our class he'd saved from drowning. She went to the University of North Dakota in Grand Forks and the distance between them hadn't made her "heart grow fonder."

In an attempt to keep things going, Rory transferred to UND at semester time, but it wasn't any use. I hadn't told Rory, but I never thought Holly would stick with him. She had joined a sorority; Rory joined ROTC. She married a banker's son from the Twin Cities a month after they graduated; he entered the Army and went to Vietnam. The war was heating up and he said his country needed him.

To understand the conflict in Vietnam, its origins need to be seen in a historical context, as a geopolitical piece in the playing out of empires.

Human beings have always tried to make their social groupings stable and to do that governments were formed, but many times the governments became so powerful that they began to dominate their own citizens and sometimes attempted to enhance their own power by conquering other social groups, creating empires. Egyptians, Babylonians, Assyrians, Chaldeans, Persians, Athenians, Romans, Mongols, Aztecs, all ancient peoples and all formed empires.

More recently the major European powers tried their hand at empire-building. The Portuguese and the Spanish were the first, but the other nations soon caught on. Africa was especially vulnerable and soon only two independent countries were left—Liberia in the west and Ethiopia in the east.

Bolivar, San Martin, O'Higgins, and others soon liberated the Spanish portions of the Americas, and the United States finished the job in 1898. The Spanish Empire was almost a ghost.

World War I was the destroyer of empires: the German under the Hohenzollern family; the Austro-Hungarian under the Hapsburgs; and the Ottoman. The war also weakened the Russian Empire.

World War II ended the weak Italian Empire, Mussolini's pride, and the Japanese Empire, and severely weakened the British and French empires, while the Russian Empire expanded to the west under the Soviet banner.

Independence movements in Asia and Africa wrested the British and French empires apart in the Forties, Fifties, and early Sixties. After Gandhi led India out of the British Empire, the English people had had enough and other portions of the empire were allowed self-government. The French had no Gandhi to suck the spirit out of them, so they resisted with more force than the British, especially in Indo-China and Algeria.

The sun was shining in a gloriously blue sky, the trees and the grass along the Interstate were green, and the Honda was eating up the gray-blue pavement. I crossed Ramsey Branch, barely a trickle of brown water. I went over the Highway 74 bridge and then over the Frisco tracks. Mud-flats, trees, the Headwater Diversion Channel, a curve, the Cape Girardeau Regional Airport, and I skirted by Scott City, a town of maybe two thousand, lying mostly east of the highway. The Interstate curved to the right, went over the Frisco tracks and Ramsey Creek, which looked a little bigger than Ramsey Branch, but not much, and then straightened out for a nice southward run. I checked my odometer.

When Rory left for Vietnam, we were all so proud of him. He looked very much the soldier in his uniform. My brothers Boy and Tom had fought in Korea, but I couldn't remember them in uniform, even though I must have seen my brothers wearing them. Rory made up for that. Aunt Mildred said she just couldn't go to Bismarck to see Rory off, so they said a private goodbye. Uncle Daniel, Rory, his brother Liam, and I drove down in one car, and Dad and Rory's sisters Mary-Margaret, Kathleen, and Maureen were in our car. Mom stayed home to comfort her sister and help with Rory's younger siblings Kevin and Theresa. Kevin was ten and not happy that he couldn't go along.

I was powering over land that ran flat and pavement that ran straight. I eased her over the speed limit and flew over Ramsey Creek again. *How many twists does that creek have?* Some farms and fields flew by, but the trees hid a lot of the countryside. Then blamed if I didn't cross Ramsey Creek again. Then a trickle of water went under the Interstate, but it was unnamed. I passed the Benton interchange. Benton was off to the right hidden by trees.

Rory had been back to Menninger twice. The first time he was pretty depressed. I had asked him why he had volunteered for Vietnam, and he told me he had been inspired to do something for the United States when he was a college senior and he read *The Green Berets* by Robin Moore, which was a novel about the jungle war we were fighting in Vietnam. And then the song "The Ballad of the Green Berets" by Staff Sgt. Barry Sadler came out and that clinched it for him: he had to serve, although not as a Green Beret. Communists were the enemy; he had to kill Communists. But even as more Commies were killed, the war was not going well.

The highway ran straight with thin lines of trees or sometimes no trees on both sides, blocking or revealing cropland. In my U.S. History class in college, I learned that the northern part of Missouri supported slavery and the South during the Civil War, while the southern part of the state was anti-slavery and pro-Union. Some of it had to do with the Ozarks not being conducive to slave-agriculture. I looked to the west for any sign of the Ozarks, but I didn't see anything. The land I was on stretched out flat. Did the people living on it in Civil War days support the South because the land wasn't hilly or were they pro-Union? I wished I knew Missouri state history.

In late 1857 French Emperor Napoleon III sent troops to Vietnam to protect Catholic missionaries who were being attacked. A twenty-five year war ensued which the French won in 1883. After some initial resistance, most Vietnamese settled down to a peaceful coexistence with the French. The blanket of peace started to fray in the 1920s and in the 1930s to shred. Ho Chi Minh became the leader of the Vietnamese Communist Party and attempted to bring the Leninist form of Marxism to his native land.

Ho's attempted insurrection failed, he was imprisoned, and Emperor Bao Dai became the titular head of the country, but behind the scenes the French held the power. With the fall of France to the German Army in 1940, Japan, a German ally, stationed thirty-five thousand troops in Vietnam, a situation the Vichy French had to accept.

Not so with Ho. He crossed the border from China and helped set up the Viet Minh, a Communist front. The Chinese Nationalist government knew Ho was a Marxist, but helped build up the Viet Minh militarily because Ho said he would attack the Japanese. He also received help from the American OSS (Office of Strategic Services), a forerunner of the CIA, in order for him to launch attacks against the Japanese.

In March 1945 the Japanese took control of Vietnam from the French, but it was too late: in August the atomic bombs at Hiroshima and Nagasaki drove the Japanese to the peace table. Ho saw his hour had arrived. Disguising his Communist ideology under the blanket of nationalism and anti-colonialism, Ho ordered the Viet Minh to seize control of Vietnam. The power shown by the Viet Minh gained public support for that group because the majority of Vietnamese generally wanted to be on the side of the winners. Support grew as the Viet Minh liquidated prominent opposition figures.

In September 1945 French troops returned to Vietnam, occupying the southern portion of that country where the Viet Minh were weak. Eventually, the French moved to the north, coming into conflict with the Viet Minh. In December 1946 Ho and his followers were driven out of Hanoi and took refuge in a rugged area near the Chinese border. Guerilla warfare ensued.

In 1949 the Communists led by Mao Zedong took control of China. Ho now had a strong Marxist ally, and that ally gave his men weapons, training, and indoctrination in the principals of Communist thought.

President Harry Truman recognized the dangers of a Communist thrust into Indo-China and the toppling of the first domino which could lead to other dominos falling, especially those with Communist insurgencies: Burma, Malaya, Indonesia, and the Philippines. In 1950 he insisted that Congress pass a bill to help fund the French resistance to Communism in Indo-China.

The war between the Viet Minh and the French dragged on. Casualties ran high on both sides, but it was the French who blinked. The French had been winning and had moved into the northwest corner of the country, where they found themselves surrounded in a small valley, Dien Bien Phu. The Viet Minh were suffering from low rations, sinking morale, and dwindling support from the peasants; Ho decided to go all in.

With supplies from China and the Soviet Union, the Viet Minh slowly closed the noose around Dien Bien Phu. Ho asked China to send in troops; Mao refused, but made it appear that he would, bolstering Viet Minh morale and sending French morale south. France asked President Dwight Eisenhower for aid by bombing Viet Minh positions. "Ike" was willing, but backed down when the British refused to join a coalition. On May 7, 1954, Dien Bien Phu fell; Indo-China was out of the French Empire. North Vietnam was Communist; South Vietnam was not.

I bridged over the Missouri Pacific tracks and a highway. The little village of Blodgett was off to my left behind some trees, but there was no interchange. I crossed over a dry run; there was no sign. The trees pulled away from the highway and I saw some farmyards. On regular highways farms are right there, just off the shoulder, and a lot of them look pretty inviting with their barns and animals and people, but farms are generally set back from an Interstate and the distance makes them sterile. I went under highway H.

In September 1954 the United States induced the United Kingdom, France, Australia, New Zealand, Pakistan, the Philippines, and Thailand to form SEATO, (Southeast Asia Treaty Organization) to protect that region from Communist aggression. In addition, to counter the weak Emperor Bao Dai, a forceful anti-Communist, Ngo Dinh Diem, had become the premier of South Vietnam, and his brother Ngo Dinh Nhu, another anti-Communist, became his chief advisor. The Ngo brothers believed that Western-style democracy was not compatible with Vietnamese culture and employed an authoritarian governing style which the peasants would respect and which would be able to try reforms and fight Communism without being impeded by democratic institutions. This style alienated many urban intellectuals who wanted democracy and civil liberties and who hated Diem because some of his reforms had cost them privileges and property that they had held under the French. Diem also became a target for the French, ever mindful of the loss of their colony.

Signs and billboards started popping up. I went under an interchange, passed a squared-off, man-made pond, and went over another interchange. Around sixteen thousand people lived in the town of Sikeston two miles to my right. Almost immediately I was in New Madrid County, the northernmost of the three counties known as the "Missouri Bootheel."

CIA Director Allen Dulles send operative Edward Lansdale and a twelve-man Saigon Military Mission to South Vietnam to support Diem and help him against the Communists, just as Lansdale had helped Ramon Magsaysay put down the Communist-led Huk rebellion in the Philippines. Lansdale helped Diem with propaganda and organizational skill, but Diem and he differed on the question of more democracy in South Vietnam. Plots, many of them French-inspired, were formed against Diem, but none got past the planning stage because Secretary of State John Foster Dulles and President Eisenhower backed Diem.

However, the American government did pressure Diem to allow more dissent and open the government to more opposition voices. No past Vietnamese ruler had acted in such a manner, and Diem thought it would make him lose face, so he ignored American wishes.

Instead, he began to crack down on his political enemies: the Binh Xuyen gang of criminals and two religious sects, the Hoa Hao and the Cao Dai. The Binh Xuyen reacted by attacking a police headquarters, a National Army headquarters, and some Army troops, but a counterattack by the Army threatened to wipe out the Binh Xuyen until the French intervened to save them.

Finding the opposition to Diem so strong, Dulles and Eisenhower panicked and agreed Diem should go, but Lansdale told them only Diem had the personality and capability to lead South Vietnam, so when another attack with tacit French support was launched against Diem, the American government flip-flopped and backed Diem, whose men won a massive victory. After consolidating his power against the pro-French Emperor Bao Dai, the Hoa Hao, and the Cao Dai, Diem asked the French to remove their troops from his country; the humiliated former colonial masters of Indo-China complied. Diem then turned his attention to the Communists, the Viet Minh.

The thinner stands of trees or sometimes the lack of trees allowed me to see more farms and the rural houses of non-farmers. I crossed over a waterway that must have been man-made, it was so straight. I came to a slight curve to the right. I checked my odometer: I had come thirty-nine miles without a curve. I crossed the man-made ditch again, curved straight south, and went under the Matthews interchange.

Ruling from Hanoi, Ho Chi Minh had established a Communist dictatorship in North Vietnam with the help of the Soviet Union and Red China. Uncle Ho had withdrawn some of his troops from the South, but had left others there, in violation of the treaty that separated the two Vietnams. Those Communists went underground and prepared for the day Ho would give the order to attack. Diem was determined to drive them out or kill them. With Lansdale's support, Diem succeeded in severely weakening the Communists in the South. Diem also rejected Ho's call for a National Unification Election because he knew more people lived in the North and that he would lose such an election.

In 1956 Nikita Khrushchev, leader of the Soviet Union, tried on the mask of Peaceful Coexistence, seemingly abandoning Marx's call for a world-wide revolution of the proletariat. It was a ploy, but to make it look real, Khrushchev had to rein in some of his more enthusiastic believers in the forthcoming Socialist Paradise, and Ho Chi Minh was near the top of the list. Nikita told him to cool it for the time being and not foment trouble in the South. Nikita's mew attitude infuriated both Uncle Ho and Chairman Mao, and a split between the Soviet and the Chinese version of Marxist thought developed, Ho siding with Mao. However, Mao cautioned that the time was not right to invade the South, mainly because the Korean War had hurt China's military and economy, and Mao needed time to rebuild and couldn't afford to aid Ho in his Marxist march.

From 1956 to 1959, Ho worked at turning North Vietnam into a Workers' Paradise, which worked well for the Army and the Communist Party apparatus (they always ate well), but not so good for the peasants, merchants, or intellectuals, all of whom suffered from repression, imprisonment, or death. Peasants lost their land, all private businesses were nationalized, and non-Marxist intellectuals disappeared.

Diem was also busy. He strengthened the Army. His soldiers and police crushed the remaining Hoa Hao resistance (their last leader, Ba Cut, was beheaded) and suppressed the Communists (fifteen to twenty thousand were detained in re-education centers). He survived a Communist assassination attempt in 1957, and became friends with the new American military advisor Lt.-General Samuel Williams, who helped upgrade the forces of South Vietnam.

Diem's government also instituted land reform, breaking up large estates in the Mekong Delta by buying land holdings over one hundred hectares and selling the land to peasants who received interest-free loans. With American aid, economic development stimulated agricultural production and to a lesser extent the business community, so that South Vietnam began to prosper, while the North, bound in the chains of Marxist economic dogma, languished.

Diem allowed a modicum of democracy, but of the type easily controlled by him. He also allowed his sister-in-law Madame Nhu to use her influence to have laws passed in the Assembly which would recognize more rights for women; this angered the upper class.

When Diem spoke to the U.S. Congress and met with Eisenhower and Dulles, he was treated as a Vietnamese hero.

By the summer of 1958, Ho Chi Minh, weighing his chances of gaining control of the South, began champing at the bit to attack Diem, but Mao told him to hold off for a little longer. Ho gave in on overt attacks, but instigated more assassinations of pro-Diem leaders and teachers in the South.

In early 1959, Ho decided it was time to move against South Vietnam. The Soviets cautioned against such a move, but Mao was supportive. Ho's military engineers marked out what became the Ho Chi Minh Trail by which supplies could be shunted to his fighters in the South. Southerners trained by Ho's Communist soldiers and known as Vietnamese Communists (Viet Cong) began infiltrating South Vietnam.

In September 1959 the first armed incursions and battles with the South Vietnamese Army and Civil Guard took place in Kien Phong Province on the southern border with Cambodia. The VC had struck.

Lines of trees, usually thicker to my right, shut off my view, but every once in awhile there were treeless stretches that revealed fields of a low row crop, dark green in color. I went under the 704 interchange. Large fields of the row crop spread out on either side of the highway. A small gray steel grain bin appeared on the right, but the farm it belonged to was hidden in some trees. A farm road that had paralleled 55 turned off into a field; four red diamond signs marked the turn. Trees, bushes, the row crop fields, and then I went under the Kewanee interchange and came out to meet more trees, bushes, and row crop fields.

In January 1960 the Viet Cong launched their second major offensive in the new insurgent war. Attacks in Tay Ninh Province on the Cambodian border northwest of Saigon produced a modicum of success, so conventional war tactics spread into the Mekong Delta. However, fearing a major American military response to the large-scale attacks, Ho ordered them cut back and told the Viet Cong to adopt guerilla warfare with smaller units and to use more assassinations, kidnappings, disembowelings, and beheadings. Ho also told the VC to soft pedal Marxist-Leninist ideology since the peasants seemed immune to it and often resented being forced to listen to it.

The VC set up a shadow government in the South which redistributed land, collected taxes, gathered information, and recruited young men to be soldiers. The South Vietnamese Civil Guard and Self-Defense Corps seemed powerless against the VC, especially when the Americans cut off funding to the Self-Defense Corps. The peasants, always attracted to strength, began to tilt to the VC side.

Sensing the danger, Diem moved regular Army units into the fight against the VC. While they did a better job than the Civil Guard and Self-Defense Corps, they lacked adequate anti-guerilla training, and the VC were not stopped, which led to recriminations between Diem and the Americans and even between American officials.

Diem wanted the U.S. to fund an additional 20,000 Vietnamese soldiers and more equipment, as did General Williams. Ambassador Elbridge Durbrow opposed such an expenditure and blamed Diem for the lack of progress. Durbrow did agree to let the U.S. Special Forces train the Civil Guard, but he allowed the Self-Defense Corps to die on the vine.

When eighteen South Vietnamese intellectuals issued the "Caravelle Manifesto" (named after the Saigon hotel where it was written) condemning Diem for the suppression of democracy and the repression of the intellectuals, Durbrow used the document and an unauthorized raid by the South Vietnamese Army into Cambodia to attack Vietnamese Communists hiding there to undermine Diem. However, back at the Pentagon Edward Lansdale learned of Durbrow's opposition to Diem and convinced Eisenhower and Dulles to back Diem. William Colby, the CIA chief in Saigon, also backed Diem against Durbrow.

In November a military coup came close to toppling Diem, who was almost killed as bullets riddled bullets riddled his bedroom his bedroom which he had just left. Durbrow took a neutral stance on the events, thus further alienating him from Diem, but Diem reluctantly did agree to allow more political freedoms, including an opposition party.

In December at the behest of the ruling Communists in the North, a group of sixty Communist Party officials in the South formed the National Liberation Front (NLF), which represented itself as an independent organization dedicated to the overthrow of Diem and to bring civil and political freedom to the people who would then be liberated in South Vietnam. In reality, the NLF was a propaganda weapon wholly subservient to the Communist North.

All-in-all 1960 was a good year for the Viet Cong, but there was a disconcerting development: Diem's troops had begun to interdict the Ho Chi Minh Trail, bringing more hardship to the insurgents in the South.

The North decided it had to rebuild the trail outside of Vietnamese territory, completely inside Laos, a country that was supposed to be neutral under a 1954 agreement. Instead, North Vietnam began pouring troops into Laos to help the Pathet Lao (Laotian Communists) in their fight with the government, thus making the rebuilding of the Ho Chi Minh Trail more secure.

I crossed over the abandoned St. Louis & Southwestern line, a railroad known as the Cotton Belt Route. A right-hand curve took me to the New Madrid interchange. I knew the name was not pronounced the Spanish way, accenting the second syllable (Ma-DRID), but was pronounced MAD-rid. The town was about three miles south.

In late 1811 and early 1812, a series of four earthquakes near New Madrid liquefied soil, warped and fissured the ground, damaged houses in St. Louis, temporarily reversed the flow of the Mississippi, and created a new lake. It was reported that one of the earthquakes caused church bells in Boston to ring. Worse, New Madrid was destroyed. The earthquakes were the worst ever recorded in the U.S. from the Mississippi Valley eastward.

The earthquake zone was still active, so I couldn't understand why nearly three thousand souls would chose to live so close to death. There were very few earthquakes in North Dakota, and the ones we had were rarely felt.

On January 20, 1961, John F. Kennedy became the thirty-fifth President of the United States. Kennedy was an anti-Communist, but didn't believe in the Eisenhower strategy of massive retaliation to halt a Communist advance. Instead, he adopted a plan put forth by General Maxwell Taylor, one of flexible response, which Kennedy believed fit the concept of limited war and which would help the U.S. avoid a nuclear confrontation with the Soviet Union or China.

To help implement "Flexible Response," Kennedy gathered a group of intellectual advisors on national security around him: Robert Strange McNamara, Secretary of Defense; Dean Rusk, Secretary of State; McGeorge Bundy, National Security Advisor. McNamara flooded the Department of Defense with young intellectuals determined to approach each situation as a problem that could be solved if only enough statistics and logic were used.

After a visit to South Vietnam, Edward Lansdale briefed the new President on the dire conditions facing Diem. Kennedy and McNamara were impressed, and Kennedy moved away from the Eisenhower policy of keeping military aid to South Vietnam on the short side. Instead, Kennedy allotted money to increase the South Vietnamese Army by 20,000, strengthen the Civil Guard, and authorize increased activity by the CIA.

Even though Diem controlled only forty percent of his country, Kennedy was more concerned with the Communist advances in Laos. In March he went on national television in an attempt to gain public support for American intervention in Laos, but in April he suffered the embarrassment of the failure of an American-inspired invasion of Castro's Cuba at the Bay of Pigs and decided to seek a diplomatic solution to Laos. He turned his attention back to Vietnam and ordered the number of American advisors to increase from 685 to 785.

In May Vice President Lyndon B. Johnson flew to Saigon and handed Diem a letter in which Kennedy pledged American support in the South Vietnamese fight against Communism.

After a build-up of men and material, the Viet Cong opened a major offensive in September. Defense Secretary McNamara and the Joint Chiefs wanted to send American troops into Laos to close down the supply lines; former New York Governor and Kennedy advisor Averell Harriman urged caution; Kennedy listened to Harriman. He did, however, dispatch his special military advisor General Maxwell Taylor to observe the situation in South Vietnam.

Delivered in November, Taylor's report indicated South Vietnam was weak militarily, but that the U.S. must continue to back Diem, who inspired deep loyalty. Taylor also recommended that Kennedy dispatch eight thousand American troops to Vietnam.

Already an admirer of Diem, Kennedy agreed to continue American support for him, but declined to send in American troops, and, in fact, denied publicly that Taylor's report called for such an expansion of the war. His advisors, such as Montana Senator Mike Mansfield, Averell Harriman, and Ambassador to India John Kenneth Galbraith, backed the President's decision.

However, Kennedy was cognizant of the possibility that South Vietnam in Communist hands would be the first domino to fall; with Chinese aid Laos, Cambodia, and Thailand would be next, followed by Malaya, Singapore, then the prize of Indonesia, and possibly the Philippines, Taiwan, and Burma, with the plum of Japan hanging in the future, waiting to be plucked. Kennedy authorized more aid, equipment, advisors and administrators for South Vietnam. He sanctioned the limited use of defoliants on jungle trails and crops in VC-held areas. He appointed Lt. General Paul Harkins as the new U.S. military commander to join the new American ambassador Frederick E. Nolting. He also ordered that news about the American buildup be kept from his political enemies, the Republicans; the press; and the public.

In October North Vietnam halted its offensive, fearing American intervention and preferring to wait and see what Kennedy would do.

Missouri was green and flat. Corn fields joined in with the row crop fields. I headed southwest on a straight course, keeping up with and even passing semis and cars, and went under a rusty bridge carrying the St. Louis & Southwestern tracks off towards Lilbourn. I saw the New Madrid water tower and said a prayer for the safety of the people there. I went under the interchange that took Highways 61 and 62 into New Madrid.

At a press conference on January 15, 1962, President Kennedy was asked if Americans were fighting in Vietnam. He said they were not. In point of fact, however, Americans were flying combat missions in prop-driven planes painted with South Vietnamese markings, and American advisors were accompanying and sometimes engaging the enemy alongside South Vietnamese troops. In late December 1961 James Thomas Davis became the first American killed in Vietnam.

The American press corps in Saigon, stonewalled by American and South Vietnamese government officials, began getting their information from the Vietnamese intellectuals, most of whom hated Diem.

On February 27 the Freedom Palace, with Diem inside, was bombed and strafed by two South Vietnamese fighter-bombers; the sole casualty was a maid, who was holding the baby daughter of Diem's brother Nhu. Reports that the pilots had been inspired by articles in *Time* and *Newsweek* embittered Diem against the press even more. Two reporters—Homer Bigart of the *New York Times* and Francois Sully of *Newsweek*—were expelled from the country.

January and February saw the Viet Cong, now numbering between 20,000 and 25,000, gaining in military power in the countryside, but by spring the South Vietnamese with better leaders, better training, and more American aid and advisors, had turned the tide against the VC.

They also adopted the strategic hamlet program in which villages would be protected by eradicating the surrounding jungle to provide free-fire zones against attackers, bamboo and barb wire fences, deep ditches or moats, large earthen mounds, booby traps and sharpened stakes. The renewed Self-Defense Corps and the Republican Youth defended the villages from within, and the Civil Guard patrolled between the hamlets. The fighting men who defended the villagers also helped them with medical care and farm work. The villagers had to help with the constructions projects, and some complained because they were not paid, but most supported the government's efforts.

In June Madame Nhu pushed for her "Social Purification Law," which the Diem brothers put into effect. It was designed to restrict divorce, smoking, underage drinking, dancing, prostitution and other evils Madame Nhu blamed the Americans for introducing to the Vietnamese. The law angered the merchants, the Americans, and the reporters.

The Communists continued to build up the Viet Cong and to support the Pathet Lao against the neutralist government in Laos. President Kennedy responded by dispatching the Seventh Fleet to the Gulf of Thailand and by sending three thousand American soldiers to the Thai-Laotian border, which he soon withdrew when Soviet leader Khrushchev guaranteed that the Communists would no longer attempt large-scale military activities in Laos, another Communist lie.

In Geneva Averell Harriman worked out an agreement to put Laos under a coalition government and to have all Communist troops withdrawn from the country. Any Americans would also be removed. At first Diem refused to sign, but when Kennedy convinced him that the Soviet Union would enforce the agreement and that the U.S. would never work for a neutralized South Vietnam, the Diem government signed.

At the prodding of General Harkins, the Diem government pushed its military into high gear and won some big victories against the Communists. Most people were impressed, but not the American reporters in Saigon. *Newsweek* was especially critical and verbally sparred with Madame Nhu, which led to Diem banning the magazine in South Vietnam. He then expelled an NBC correspondent. The press protested that expelling journalists violated freedom of the press; however, South Vietnam had never had any freedom of the press. New replacement reporters were generally young and inexperienced. This included twenty-five-year-old Neal Sheehan of UPI and twenty-eight-year-old David Halberstam of the *New York Times*. Both young men came to Vietnam determined to "get the story come hell or high water" and damned be anyone who stood in their way. At the same time in late 1962, the two reporters were strongly anti-Communist.

I continued on a direct southeast line. The Mississippi was maybe a half mile to my left, but trees blocked my view. I liked the greenness of the trees, bushes, grass, and even the weeds, but the taller vegetation left me wondering what the rest of Missouri looked like. I passed between rest stops, each with a couple small buildings. A ways down the road, I passed some more buildings and the town of Marston sprang up to my right, 600 or so people, and I went under an interchange.

In late 1962 the American press split, with some reporters becoming very critical of the Vietnamese war effort and others finding much to praise. Halberstam and Sheehan were among the former. The young reporters came under the influence of Col. John Paul Vann, who had his own interpretation of how the war was going, and it wasn't good. Vann was especially critical of Diem, an attitude that was soon taken up by Halberstam and Sheehan. More positive reactions to what they saw in Vietnam came from reporters such as Richard Tregaskis (author of the famous World War II book *Guadalcanal Diary*), Kenneth Crawford of *Newsweek*, and Harold Martin of *The Saturday Evening Post*.

Toward the end of 1962, Diem's troops' fighting ability and the success of the strategic hamlet program gave the military edge to South Vietnam, an edge even Halberstam and Sheehan had to acknowledge. Although Laos was a precarious neutral, a status not helpful to the South Vietnamese war effort, and the continuous resupply of the Viet Cong via the Ho Chi Minh trail, President Kennedy saw enough of Diem's fighting spirit to continue to back him.

On January 2, 1963, South Vietnamese troops and their American advisors attacked a strongly fortified Viet Cong stronghold at Ap Bac. The ensuing battle caused heavy casualties on both sides, including three dead and six wounded Americans, and both sides fought bravely until the VC were forced to retreat. Speaking to the press after the battle, Col. John Paul Vann emphasized the failures of the South Vietnamese commanders and their troops, which reflected on Diem, and covered up his own battlefield failure in landing the reserve company too close to the enemy lines. Halberstam and Sheehan sent their stories of the battle State-side, where the American public could read about a major defeat (it wasn't) inflicted on the government troops by the VC because of the ineptitude of the troops' leadership and ability. When General Harkins said Ap Bac was a success because the hamlet was taken from the VC, the American reporters could barely contain their contempt, not recognizing the fact that Harkins was trying to help the South Vietnamese save face, a very important commodity in Asia.

In April Laos hit the headlines again as the Pathet Lao and North Vietnamese troops captured control of a portion of the Plain of Jars. Kennedy refused to send in ground forces, but did authorize some air strikes. Harriman conferred with Khrushchev, who said the Soviet Union had no control over the Pathet Lao; Khrushchev lied. The military action gave an even safer march down the Ho Chi Minh Trail for reinforcements and supplies.

In May organized Buddhist protests demanded more religious freedom in South Vietnam; the American journalists threw their weight behind the Buddhists and condemned Diem as an oppressor. Stanley Karnow, David Halberstam, and Neil Sheehan began basing their stories on information they gleaned from a South Vietnamese Colonel, Pham Ngoc Thao, and an employee of Reuters, Pham Xuan An, both of whom were secret Communist agents. The leader of the protests, Tri Quang, was a Communist or a Communist sympathizer who believed that Communism and Buddhism were compatible. Averell Harriman and Roger Hilsman of the State Department pressured Diem to grant more religious liberty, which he did reluctantly. Tri Quang was not satisfied.

On June 11 a seventy-three-year-old Buddhist monk, Quang Duc, sat on the street outside the Xa Loi pagoda in Saigon, other Buddhists doused him with gasoline, and he lit a match, setting himself on fire. American journalist Malcolm Browne, who had been alerted to be there, snapped pictures. One of the pictures spread like wildfire in the media, turning many people against Diem. Harriman and Hilsman reiterated their demands that Diem capitulate to the Buddhists, but President Kennedy, who was furious that he had not been informed of the demand ahead of time, ordered a stop to the action; then he turned his attention to the civil rights problem in the American South before taking a trip to Europe.

Lying low a few days, Harriman and Hilsman emerged and ordered Acting Ambassador William Truehart to make contact with opposition leaders. An agreement between Buddhist leaders and Diem was announced, and almost immediately violent protests led by Tri Quang and Communist agents shattered the peace. Truehart continued to insist that Diem must accommodate the Buddhist demands.

On July 7 some policemen roughed up journalist Peter Arnett, who was covering the Saigon police trying to halt a Buddhist procession. David Halberstam, Neil Sheehan, Malcolm Browne, and Peter Kalisher of CBS protested the action in a letter to President Kennedy. An American protest was lodged with Diem. The reporters were not placated: Halberstam, the most influential of them, wrote an article for the *New York Times* in which he falsely stated that the Americans wanted a change in the government of South Vietnam.

The next day General Duong Van "Big" Minh, General Tran Van Don, and several others told Lou Conein of the CIA, they were ready to topple Diem if the U.S. approved. Conein reported the conversation to his superiors, but nothing came of it because the American officials saw that those generals who spoke with Conein were in the minority; however, the grease was being applied to the skids for the downfall of Diem.

I passed under some high tension power lines, the towers supporting them looking like they'd been built from a giant's erector set. The low row crops peeked through gaps in the trees lining the highway. A small group of single-story houses appeared on my right, nudged the Interstate, and disappeared again. If it was a village, I didn't know its name. Soon the trees and a few buildings marking the village of Conran showed up almost a mile to the right. I continued straight for almost five miles, saw a short freight on the Frisco tracks a half mile to the right, then swung left and went under the Portageville interchange, with the town of 2500 still clinging to the Frisco tracks. I passed a sign that informed me that Memphis was 109 miles, crossed over an almost dry watercourse called Portage Open Bay, and entered Pemiscot County.

Ambassador Frederick Nolting had been kept in the dark while on vacation in Europe by Truehart; all he knew about Vietnam were the bad things he read in the newspapers. Upon his return to Saigon, he was surprised to learn that Diem had actually acceded to many of the American demands for allowing more religious and political freedom. Nolting expressed his support for Diem; Roger Hilsman continued to oppose him, ignoring the turning of the military tide against the Viet Cong, and the fact that Laos was an open sore in Diem's side, about which the U.S. was doing little.

In August hardline Buddhists kept up their militant protests against Diem; more monks burned themselves to death. On August 18 a massive protest, aided by Communist agents, was staged outside the Xa Loi pagoda. Diem lost face.

That evening ten Vietnamese generals met to discuss the predicament the government was in. "Big" Minh, General Don, General Nguyan Khanh, General Le Van Kim, and General Ton That Dinh were among them. The generals went to Diem and recommended the imposition of martial law and the clearing out of all people gathering in pagodas. Diem agreed.

Without informing the Americans, the generals, many of whom were Buddhists, sent their troops to surround Xa Loi pagoda in the midnight hour of August 21. After physical confrontations that led to some hospitalization, the pagoda was cleared, as were many others. In some, weapons and Viet Cong documents were found. Diem had gained face.

Everyone seemed satisfied, except the militants, the Communists, and the American press. David Halberstam almost broke a blood vessel venting his spleen against Diem in a series of articles replete with lies and false information on the pagoda raids. Not surprisingly, the articles won Halberstam the Pulitzer Prize.

International outrage erupted after the articles appeared, so much so that the UN investigated the raids. Halberstam had written that thirty Buddhists were killed; the UN found that no one had lost his or her life.

Halberstam was unmerciful in his condemnation of Diem, his brother Nhu, and his wife. He suggested that "Big" Minh would be an admirable replacement for Diem.

The Americans began an investigation, and some of the generals involved in the raids turned against Diem, Nhu, and his wife. General

Kim even stated that Nhu had tricked the Army into imposing martial law. While none of the generals wanted Diem removed (they recognized him as the most capable man South Vietnam could have as a leader), many of them were implacable in their hatred of Nhu and Madame Nhu.

Based on the investigation, at the State Department Averell Harriman, Roger Hilsman, and Michael Forrestal (Harriman's adopted son), prepared a memo for the new ambassador to South Vietnam, Henry Cabot Lodge, whom Kennedy had appointed because Lodge was viewed as having a good chance of gaining the Republican nomination for President in 1964 and the ambassadorship would clear him out as a possible opponent to Kennedy's reelection.

The three State Department men adopted the Halberstam line as to the cause of the pagoda raids. They utterly condemned Nhu and said that if Diem didn't oust his brother, then it was time for him to go. They had the Voice of America broadcast that Nhu was responsible for the raids, not the military, and they instructed Lodge to inform the generals that if Nhu was not removed, the U.S. would no longer support Diem and would support a replacement.

When Harriman and Hilsman presented the memo to Under Secretary of State George Ball, he endorsed it. The three then phoned the President. Kennedy, a little distracted because he was enjoying the weekend at Cape Cod, listened to the cable and approved it if Secretary of State Dean Rusk and Acting Secretary of Defense Roswell Gilpatric agreed with it.

When Rusk was contacted by phone, he was not told that the President's approval of the cable was contingent on his own approval, only that Kennedy had approved it. Rusk quickly approved. Gilpatric, also not informed of the contingency involved in his approval, agreed with the cable. Pro-Diem men, such as CIA director John McCone, Secretary of Defense Robert McNamara, and Chairman of the Joint Chiefs of Staff Maxwell Taylor were not contacted, for obvious reasons. The cable went to Lodge that night.

When Lodge had originally arrived in South Vietnam, the very first group he rushed over to see were a group of reporters standing on the tarmac of Tan Son Nhut airport. He had private dinners with Halberstam, Sheehan, and Browne, all of whom became his ardent idolizers. Lodge loved the press and the press loved him.

Unlike his predecessors, Lodge didn't go out into the country to see first-hand what conditions were like; instead, he had the journalists meet him in Saigon and learn their opinions, which became his own.

Some older journalists such as Joseph Alsop, Keyes Beech, and Marguerite Higgins rose to the defense of Diem, and ripped the reporters who were attacking him; Lodge didn't listen. The younger American journalists hated Diem; therefore, Lodge hated him, also. When the cable arrived, it merely reinforced Lodge's position on Diem and Nhu. He had the contents of the cable made known to the South Vietnamese generals. Coupled with the Voice of America's broadcasts of a possible cut-off of aid, the cable spelled doom for Diem and Nhu.

The grass between the two sides of the Interstate had been mowed recently and occasionally I caught that new-cut smell. The grass on the sides of the highway hadn't been cut yet and was thick and still summer-green. The pavement made a left-hand curve and pointed south. I passed a farm with a small white house, shaded by a tree at least seventy feet high, four or five old grain bins, and a long, low barn with a metal roof. The trees began thinning out, so I could see the row crops. An electrical substation went by on the right. I crossed over a small drainage ditch, and then under the Wardell interchange.

Back in Washington, D.C. Kennedy, upon reflection, saw how damaging the cable was to the fight against the Viet Cong and North Vietnam. He called a meeting of his advisors. McNamara and McCone were seething with anger, and Taylor was furious that they had been side-stepped by the cable-writers. Kennedy himself was angry and verbally attacked the three men. Forrestal offered to resign, but his offer was refused. The other two seemed unrepentant. Kennedy blamed the reporters in Vietnam, particularly Halberstam, for the idea behind the cable. Surprisingly, however, when asked if the new policy contained in the cable should be cancelled, not one advisor said it should be: they were all concerned that such a quick turnabout would make the U.S. seem uncertain of itself in Vietnamese eyes and lose face.

In Saigon the generals promised the CIA a coup within a week, but many of them were on the fence. Rather than opposing the coup, Kennedy gave it a partial blessing and began watching events in South Vietnam closely. His advisors were split: Harriman and Hilsman continued to be rabidly anti-Diem, George Ball less so, while former ambassador Nolting stood up for Diem as the only man who could keep South Vietnam together.

Kennedy cabled Lodge, asking him his opinion on the projected coup. In an answer sent on August 29, Lodge pushed for it, saying the U.S. was committed and couldn't turn back. Kennedy agreed, reluctantly, and authorized Lodge to inform the generals the U.S. would not support Diem and Nhu in case of a coup.

Nhu, hearing of the proposed coup, put the Special Forces on alert; the generals wilted and the coup was called off. On August 31 John H. Richardson, the CIA's Saigon station chief, told Washington the coup was dead, and the U.S. had no choice, but to turn back. Kennedy ordered every cable sent or received back to August 24 destroyed.

Years later the cable men claimed the document caused no harm; that was not true. It convinced Lodge that Kennedy could be manipulated into supporting a much-needed coup against Diem and Nhu, and it informed the generals that the U.S. would countenance such a coup.

Small houses and mobile homes began appearing in little groves of trees. I crossed another drainage ditch. A small pond appeared on my right and then a larger one on my left. A slight curve and I was under the Highway P bridge. Three low white buildings off to the left were called Concord; beyond them was a line of trees which either marked the Mississippi or where the river used to run, I couldn't tell.

In September Lodge, Harriman, Hilsman, Forrestal, and Ball continued to attack Diem, but they were outgunned by the pro-Diem forces—McNamara, Taylor, McCone, Nolting, Attorney General Robert Kennedy, CIA Far East Division Director William Colby, and Vice President Lyndon B. Johnson. Kennedy saw merit on both sides: Diem needed to make democratic reforms, but he was also an outstanding leader and anti-Communist. Kennedy decided to take a middle position, along with Secretary of State Dean Rusk, but he did voice some harsh criticism of Diem in an interview with CBS anchor Walter Cronkite. Kennedy also dispatched two men—Marine Corps General Victor Krulak and State Department official Joseph Mendenhall—to investigate the military situation in South Vietnam.

Krulak's report stated that the war was going well, and that there was no serious call for the removal of Diem. Mendenhall's stated that Nhu had to go or the Diem government would fall. CIA Director John McCone backed Krulak. Hearing the diametrically opposed reports, Kennedy was in a quandary.

Ambassador Lodge wasn't: he continued to pressure Diem to remove Nhu. Madame Nhu did leave the country, but Diem refused to consider the removal of his brother. Lodge continued to threaten Diem with the loss of American support. After a meeting in which Diem adamantly opposed any move against his brother, Lodge was determined to back another coup attempt and sent a cable to that effect to the State Department on September 11. The State Department decided to adopt a wait-and-see attitude toward Diem, but Lodge continued to advocate a coup until John McCone told Kennedy of his anti-Diem intrigues. The State Department then told Lodge to knock off such activities.

Feeling isolated, Lodge turned to the young journalists for information and advice. All of it was anti-Diem. General Harkins, however, continued to support Diem, as did CIA station chief Richardson. Having learned of Richardson's high praise for Diem, Lodge requested on September 13 he be removed as station chief; McCone refused.

Two days later Halberstam wrote an article saying that by supporting Diem, Richardson was out of touch with the rest of the CIA, which was not true. As October began, Richard Starnes of the Scripps-Howard syndicate said the CIA in Saigon had refused to carry out direct orders from Lodge (not true) and named Richardson, thus blowing his cover. Either because of that incident or because of Lodge's continued calls for his removal, Richardson was replaced by the CIA. Lodge was ecstatic.

Kennedy had become upset by Halberstam's biased reporting and asked the *New York Times* to replace him; the paper refused. Kennedy then dispatched McNamara and Taylor to investigate the situation in Vietnam. Lodge, alarmed, said the visit wasn't necessary.

During a dinner with Diem, McNamara confronted him by saying the American public was losing faith in him as a leader and of the war in general. Diem condemned the inaccurate reporting by the American press. McNamara countered that Diem had to make concessions to the Buddhists or American support might be withdrawn.

McNamara and Taylor reported to the President that the war was going well, that in the short run the Buddhist problem would not hurt the war effort, but that Diem had to make reforms within two to four months or American aid should be cut. Kennedy adopted the policy recommendations and decided to cut aid. He also told Lodge to make clandestine contacts with possible coup leaders. The aid cut made Diem lose face, and he became even more intransigent.

Kennedy and Lodge exchanged messages on a possible coup. Lodge said "Big" Minh would lead a coup if he was assured of American aid after the toppling of Diem. Kennedy told Lodge to stick to the two to four month deadline; to keep secretly in communication with possible coup leaders; to assure the leaders of continued aid if the coup succeeded, but not to appear to be too enthusiastic about a change of government; and to tell Minh the official U.S. policy would be to remain neutral vis-à-vis Diem and his opponents until Minh could present a thoroughly worked out plan.

Lodge obeyed only a portion of his orders: he told Minh the U.S. wasn't necessarily opposed to a coup and would continue American aid, but he did not hide his enthusiasm for a coup, and he did not inform Minh that he needed a more concrete plan. The generals began making plans for a coup.

The "Missouri Flats" continued. There were few trees near the Interstate, and the houses and other buildings didn't block my view of the countryside for long, allowing me extended looks to the horizon: this was my kind of land. A mile or so north of Hayti the Interstate ended and I was on Highway 61 again. I passed along the eastern edge of the town of 3700 and continued my southerly journey.

The October war effort against the VC was going fairly well, and the strategic hamlet program was proving itself as an effective weapon against the Communists.

On the evening of October 22, the plotters against Diem received a shock when General Harkins told General Don he had heard of an alleged coup, and that he opposed such a move since the South Vietnamese military was fighting so well.

Shaken, Don reported to the other generals who had set the coup for October 26. The coup was postponed. A few days later General Don spoke with Lou Conein of the CIA, who assured him that Harkins was speaking privately, that American policy had not changed, and that

President Kennedy would not stand in the way of a coup and would not cut off aid if it proved successful. Don reported to Conein the next day that the coup had been reset for November 2.

Lodge, fearing that Harkins would communicate the plot to Taylor, began informing the President of the conspiracy. The news was a bombshell. Not only had the coup been moved up several months from what Kennedy had envisioned, it was clear that Lodge had been working behind the President's back to speed the plotters along. McNamara was furious; he wanted Lodge removed, and Conein, too. Kennedy refused to recall Lodge because that would put Lodge in a strong political position to gain the Republican nomination in 1964.

Instead, the President had National Security Advisor Bundy send a strongly-worded message to Lodge to back off on his encouragement of a coup. Lodge argued back that the coup would bring in a government more conducive to change than Diem's, and any attempt to stop a coup would cause resentment against the Americans.

On October 27 Lodge and Diem got into an argument after a dinner; neither man would give in on any of his stands on political reforms. On October 29 Lodge reported to Washington that a coup was about to happen and that the U.S. could not stop it, short of giving the information to Diem and Nhu. Basically, the Americans were powerless.

Lodge was lying: he knew a threat by him that American aid would cease with a coup would stop the generals in their tracks.

On October 29 Kennedy met with his advisors. William Colby of the CIA, Robert McNamara, and McGeorge Bundy seemed non-committal about the coup. Averell Harriman and Dean Rusk pushed for the coup, but Bobby Kennedy, Maxwell Taylor, and John McCone supported Diem. President Kennedy tentatively sided with them. Bundy was told to contact Lodge and inform him to tell the generals a coup was not advisable at that time.

Lodge's response was that the coup could not be stopped and, further, he refused to contact the generals. On the same day General Harkins sent three messages to the White House, condemning Lodge for not keeping him informed about the plot and reiterating that there was no suitable replacement for Diem. Not wanting Lodge in the U.S. and running for President, Kennedy did not sack Lodge. Instead, he repeated that Lodge should discourage any coup that didn't have a high chance of success, but then copped out and let Lodge decide if the coup could succeed.

On October 31 General Don approached Diem and Nhu about the cabinet posts he and General Dinh had requested. He was informed the appointments would not be forthcoming. The coup was now definitely on.

When Diem met with Lodge on November 1, he told the ambassador that there were rumors of a coup. Dissembling, Lodge told him there was nothing to worry about.

General Don obtained the equivalent of forty-two thousand dollars and a radio from Conein that put him in contact with the CIA, then at 1:45 P.M. the coup began. Captain Ho Tan Quyen, the naval commander and loyal to Diem, was the first victim, shot in the head. Fighting broke out between loyalist troops and the plotters' men. Diem and Nhu took to the basement of the Presidential Palace to monitor events. At 3:30 they contacted General Don and offered to negotiate. Don refused.

At 4:30 Diem called Lodge and asked what the American position was on the coup. Lodge feigned ignorance and said he didn't know. He also urged Diem to surrender and offered a plane to fly him to the Philippines. Diem shouted that the U.S. would bear the responsibility for whatever happened to him.

The fighting continued outside the palace, but forces friendly to Diem were too far away or had their access routes blocked, so they could not provide reinforcements. At 8 P.M. Diem and Nhu escaped the Palace through a secret tunnel and went to ground in the home of a friendly Chinese in the suburb of Cholon. The fighting continued fiercely as only the fighting in a civil war can, but there were no reinforcements for the dwindling number of troops loyal to Diem. At 6:45 A.M. November 2, Diem ordered his Presidential Guard to surrender.

Diem and Nhu sought safety in a church, from which Diem contacted Lodge. The ambassador said he would give the brothers asylum, but withdrew his offer to provide escape to the Philippines. With the success of the coup, Lodge feared that Diem would try to set up a government-in-exile.

Diem called the generals and arranged to surrender after an agreement was reached that he and his brother would be given a safe escort to the airport. An armored personnel carrier and two jeeps were dispatched to the church, Diem and Nhu were bustled aboard, and the vehicles headed toward Saigon.

At a railroad crossing the convoy stopped, two soldiers armed with a machine gun and a pistol shot Diem and Nhu from behind, then hacked and stabbed their bodies with knives. The generals put out a release that the brothers had committed "accidental suicide."

I saw a line of trees off to the right marking the St. Louis & Southwestern tracks. I was on about a six-mile straight run to the south, crossing a drainage ditch, passing a few buildings known as Canady, and seeing plenty of nice, flat fields, but hardly any farmyards. I took a curve and headed southwest, but the result was the same: many fields, few farms. I crossed two more ditches and saw the town of Steele to the right on Highway 164, white buildings peering out of green trees with a water tower overlooking everything. Two miles south and 61 joined I-55 again. I took a couple more ditches and jogged to my left. I headed straight south, passed a sign that said "Memphis 77," and on into Arkansas.

The most influential American newspapers jumped to support the coup. Lodge, John Kenneth Galbraith, and Harriman could barely contain their enthusiasm at the success of the plotters. However, when President Kennedy was informed of the deaths of Diem and Nhu, he ran from the room, his face distorted by the shock.

On November 5 the new government was announced: General Minh was the President, General Don was the Minister of Defense, and General Dinh the Minister of Security. They immediately promised to liberalize Vietnamese society.

On November 22 President John Fitzgerald Kennedy was shot by a professed Marxist in Dallas, Texas. Vice President Lyndon Baines Johnson was sworn in as the thirty-sixth president. Johnson supported Kennedy's commitment to South Vietnam and to that end kept most of Kennedy's advisors. He did, however, fire Roger Hilsman for his role in promoting the coup and would not listen to Averell Harriman. He did not fire Lodge, the most culpable of the Americans, because he feared it would lead to a Lodge candidacy for President.

While the generals did institute some political reforms, they began to withdraw them when they saw they led to more instability, not less. They were adopting Diem's outlook on Vietnamese politics.

More Buddhists burned themselves in protest in the next four months than in all the years of the Diem regime.

The generals removed many Diem loyalists from positions of political and military leadership, weakening the government and the army at a time when the Viet Cong stepped up their attacks. The strategic hamlet program went into a tailspin.

President Johnson began to rely on Robert McNamara, Dean Rusk, and McGeorge Bundy as his closest advisors on Vietnam. Even though Henry Cabot Lodge continued to make blunders in his official capacity as ambassador and was barely on speaking terms with General Harkins, Johnson refused to recall him especially when the polls were showing Lodge to be the leading contender for the Republican presidential nomination.

In 1964 conditions in the fight against the Communists deteriorated. The generals began to bicker among themselves. General Nguyen Khanh staged a coup on January 30 and took over the government. While Khanh was a good military leader, he was lacking in political expertise and sought the help of Henry Cabot Lodge, who recommended he make appointments from as many diverse groups as he could. Khanh took the advice and ended up with officials who had no talent, but who were diverse. He also replaced some officials with the pro-Diem supporters fired by the generals. However, when the Buddhists protested, he backed down and fired them. Khanh lost face.

Back in November Kennedy had ordered Lodge to protect Ngo Dinh Can, Diem's ailing brother who had surrendered to the Americans. Instead, Lodge had turned Can over to the plotters. He had languished in jail ever since. The Buddhist Communist Tri Quang urged Khanh to execute him. Lodge, who was beginning to see Tri Quang and the Buddhists as the troublemakers they were, asked Khanh not to kill Can. To no avail: Can was tied to a post and shot by a firing squad.

Arkansas had the same open spaces and low, green row crops that were in Missouri. I pulled into an independent gas station and filled up. Just to the west of the station, I saw the low crop. I went over and looked and then walked in to pay. I asked the white-haired owner what the crop was and he replied, "Soybeans. They grow good." He smiled. I'd heard of soybeans and now I knew what they looked like. On the wall there was a picture of a young man in uniform; it was surrounded by black crepe. Underneath the picture were the words: "U.S. Army Private John Philip Joyce, 1948-1968. Died at Khe Sanh, South Vietnam, in the service of his country. A great friend. An even greater patriot. BHS Class of 1966."

I looked over at the owner. "My son. A good boy. Damn him." He wasn't smiling. I hurried out of the building, fired up, and hit 55.

In the North, Ho Chi Minh's health was beginning to fail, and many governmental powers had devolved to Le Duan, who was much more a believer in the ideology of Red China than Ho and who led a cleansing of those officials who were less than enthusiastic about China's ideology and wanted a slow buildup of forces in South Vietnam. Le Duan pushed for large-scale attacks. To hasten such battles, the Ho Chi Minh Trail was widened and improved, so it could handle trucks and build up supplies in southern Laos. When the Joint Chiefs asked President Johnson for permission to enter Laos and destroy the supplies, the State Department argued that was a violation of the Geneva agreement that stated Laos should be neutral (overlooking the North's violation of the same agreement), and Johnson concurred. The North Vietnamese Navy also began sneaking supplies into the South.

Bolstered by their burgeoning supplies and urged on by Le Duan, the Viet Cong launched major attacks in the spring of 1964. The weakness or sometimes even the absence of leadership in Saigon allowed major Communist gains. Johnson and his advisors decided to launch OPLAN 34-A, limited covert action in the North; it was a major failure. General Harold K. Johnson, the Joint Chiefs of Staff, and John McCone of the CIA argued for air strikes and American ground forces against the North. They were rebuffed by Johnson, whose advisors told him such action would have little effect on the VC. Also, Johnson wanted to keep the lid on Vietnam until after the November elections.

When even General Khanh began arguing for a more aggressive American role, Johnson told his advisors in May that if diplomacy failed to halt the fighting, he would authorize strikes against the North, but only after November. Not knowing of Johnson's plan, Khanh kept up the drumbeat for American action.

In July Maxwell Taylor replaced Henry Cabot Lodge as the American Ambassador to South Vietnam, and General William Childs Westmoreland took command of the U.S. military advisory mission from General Paul Harkins.

I gunned the Honda to eighty; I had to get away from the old man and his love mixed with gall. Blytheville, a town of almost 25,000, whizzed by on the right. Highway 61 had gone through the town; I-55 bypassed it. Would the people still prosper? I slowed a little on a curve and gunned it again. South of town I humped over an interchange with old Highway 61 below. I saw a police car with a light bar, so I slowed down. I went into a lazy left curve and tried to enjoy the country.

On July 31, 1964, in the Gulf of Tonkin, the U.S. destroyer *Maddox* passed some South Vietnamese commando boats that had just bombarded a North Vietnamese island. The *Maddox* continued on what was a routine intelligence gathering patrol in international waters off the coast of North Vietnam. Fearing an attack, Ho Chi Minh ordered a retaliation if the Americans fired. On August 2 Le Duan ordered a military attack; Ho countermanded that order, but too late. Three PT boats fired torpedoes at the *Maddox*, but none hit. All three boats were damaged by the American response and withdrew. General Khanh and Ambassador Taylor urged a strike on North Vietnam, but Johnson refused. He did have the Navy send the destroyer *Turner Joy* to help patrol.

On the night of August 4, radar indicated enemy vessels were approaching the two destroyers, so planes and the destroyers' guns attacked the positions. Actually, no enemy action had occurred, but many sailors and airmen thought they had seen ships and reported it. The reports were sent to Washington, and Johnson, McNamara, Rusk, and Bundy, trying a policy of "limited war," decided on a small-scale air strike against the North. Johnson called in Congressional leaders to ask for their support; luckily it was forthcoming because the raid had already been authorized by Johnson. Around thirty torpedo boats, some torpedo boat bases and an oil storage facility were destroyed at the cost of two American planes, with one pilot killed and one captured.

Johnson and McNamara pushed Congress to pass authorization for the President to use any measures necessary to stop attacks on the U.S. military and aggression in Southeast Asia. The Gulf of Tonkin Resolution passed in the Senate 98-2. It passed in the House 416-0.

Backed by the Congress, Johnson then drew back from the precipice: he stopped the naval patrols and covert operations in the North and refused to authorize any more air strikes.

Sensing an opportunity, General Khanh seized more political power and drafted a new constitution giving him additional power. Tri Quang and the Buddhists, student groups, and Communist agents erupted in protests that became violent and anti-American. Khanh then gave in to some of their demands, thus losing face. The agitators became more emboldened. Khanh's dismissal of some military and civilian officials the Buddhists didn't like weakened the war effort.

By late August American officials such as Westmoreland, Taylor, McGeorge Bundy, William Bundy, and General Harold K. Johnson were asking for bombing of the North and in Laos and even more American troops in Vietnam. The recommendations scared the bejesus out of Johnson, who got the Joint Chiefs to nix the proposals.

Seeing a lack of American response, the North Vietnamese interpreted that to mean the U.S. was not committed to a defense of the South. Adding to that belief was Johnson campaigning for the presidency as the "peace" candidate as opposed to his opponent, Republican Barry Goldwater, whom he painted as a "warmonger."

At the end of September, General Nguyen Chi Thanh, a member of the North Vietnamese Politburo, was dispatched to the South to lead a major strategic change in the war: North Vietnam would try to conquer the South, not by stealth and attrition as in the past, but by bold military action.

Events in South Vietnam showed the deterioration of the country: a coup against Khanh failed, there were strikes and then a general strike, riots, demonstrations. Lack of support for Khanh remaining as leader led to his replacement as head of state by an old man, Pham Khac Suu, and as prime minister by Tran Van Huong. Khanh became commander-in-chief. Johnson's "limited war" response was reaping the whirlwind.

The engineers who designed I-55 must have liked straight lines: for the next thirty-seven miles I didn't have to correct or change my steering, except to pass vehicles. If enemy planes ever caught columns of people trying to flee or the military trying to advance on 55, they would have a strafing holiday. The land was flat, the farms near the Interstate were few, the soybeans were plentiful, and the drainage ditches were full of weeds, reeds, and small trees. Finally, I swung right, passed under the Turrell interchange, made a left-hand curve to the south, and then another one to the southwest.

Just past the witching hour of November 1, 1964, a Viet Cong mortar company launched a surprise attack on the Bien Hoa air base north of Saigon. Four Americans were killed, thirty were injured, and twenty-seven airplanes were damaged or destroyed. The Joint Chiefs demanded concerted retaliation against North Vietnam and in Laos. Johnson rung his hands: what should he do with the election only days away? He had his Special Assistant, Bill Moyers, call political pollster Lou Harris to see if a lack of response would hurt him at the polls. When Harris responded that it wouldn't, Johnson declined to authorize any American military action. To keep the generals and admirals from attacking Johnson in public just before the election, McNamara assured them that retaliation would come soon, not just yet.

The lack of action secured the North Vietnamese in their belief that Johnson was a paper tiger. They celebrated when Johnson defeated Barry Goldwater on November 3. The 325th North Vietnamese Army Division was ordered to invade northern South Vietnam via the Ho Chi Minh Trail. The 320th Infantry Regiment and several battalions were also ordered into the South. The North Vietnamese discarded their regular uniforms and donned black pajamas and rubber sandals, just like the Viet Cong and the peasants they hoped to be mistaken for.

After Tran Van Huong assumed power in November, he cracked down on the Buddhists and their Communist allies. Demonstrations were broken up; censorship was imposed. The Buddhists became more violent. Unlike Khanh, Huong did not back down. With a forceful leader behind them, the South Vietnamese soldiers rallied and morale and recruitment increased. However, the Communists were making gains, especially in Binh Dinh province.

Faced with two options, overwhelming response or gradual escalation, Johnson and his advisors, who favored the latter, found themselves opposed by the Joint Chiefs. However, on November 29 Johnson announced that gradual escalation was the new American policy.

On December 14 Operation Barrel Roll was the opening gambit in that policy: four American jets would attack the Ho Chi Minh Trail and Communist bases in Laos twice a week. The Joint Chiefs and the Laotian prime minister Souvanna Phouma pleaded for more attacks, but to no avail. The U.S. was committed to gradual escalation. The

CIA analysis later confirmed that Operation Barrel Roll was virtually worthless.

Then another political crisis: General Khanh and some younger generals dissolved the High National Council and arrested eight of its members. The government teetered on collapse. Khanh had not informed Ambassador Taylor of his plans for the Council, so Taylor demanded a meeting with Khanh, who refused to go. Instead, he sent generals Nguyen Van Thieu, Nguyen Cao Ky, Nguyen Chanh Thi, and Admiral Chung Tan Cang. Taylor gave them a severe tongue lashing for their actions against the Council. Then he went to see Prime Minister Huong.

Huong seemed to side with the generals, so Taylor went to General Khanh's office. An argument ensued and Khanh said he would consider resigning. Instead, he began denouncing the Americans and Taylor in particular in the public press. Taylor tried "to make nice" with Khanh, but by that time Khanh had begun communicating with the Communists.

On Christmas Eve the Viet Cong blew up the ground floor of the Brink Hotel in an attempt to kill comedian Bob Hope. Hope escaped because he had been delayed at the airport.

Taylor and the Joint Chiefs demanded strong action against the North for the hotel attack, but Johnson, on the advice of McNamara and Rusk, declined to order any American action. Expecting American retaliation, but seeing there was none, the Communists were convinced that Johnson would not expand the war; in fact, he would probably pull American troops out of the South.

I was on another straight-line run, this time of fourteen miles, with just one slight deviation to the west. I crossed over a small stream and wished Arkansas would put up signs naming its rivers. The land was still flat, but corn began to show up in the fields. I crossed over the little stream called Fifteen Mile Bayou, and the Interstate made its slight move to the right. Even so, enemy pilots would still have a field day attacking anything on that road. I passed by Marion, several thousand people stretched out along the Interstate.

I bridged over the Missouri Pacific tracks, swung into a left-hand curve, and passed over the Frisco tracks. West Memphis, the "Crossroads of America," lay hidden beyond the trees to my right, but there were businesses along the highway, and I could see some houses, but mainly I had to watch my driving because the traffic had thickened up.

On January 6, 1965, Tran Van Huong formally took control of the government, with the generals receding into the background. Tri Quang and the Buddhists denounced Huong and organized demonstrations that turned violent. The dissident generals refused to put down the anti-Huong, anti-American attacks. On January 27 after making a deal with the Buddhists, General Khanh, General Nguyen Van Thieu, General Nguyen Chanh Thi, and Air Marshal Nguyen Cao Ky seized power. Almost immediately the Buddhists reneged on the deal which would have sent Tri Quang and some other militants out of the country. Khanh caved in to the Buddhists.

Worried, Johnson sent McGeorge Bundy to Saigon to ascertain what was going on. While Bundy was there, two surprise attacks by the Viet Cong in Pleiku province killed nine Americans and wounded seventy-six. Johnson had had enough: on February 7 Operation Flaming Dart went into effect with forty-nine American planes bombing North Vietnam. Back home Bundy recommended a continuation of the air assault, but to gear it to Viet Cong activity: more VC action, more American bombing; fewer VC attacks, fewer American bomb runs. Although John McCone argued for a stronger and continued American response, Johnson went with Bundy, and authorized Operation Rolling Thunder, which went active on March 2. He also sent two Marine battalions to Da Nang to protect the air base there. He further agreed with the proposal of the Joint Chiefs and Westmoreland to have the Seventh Fleet interdict all North Vietnamese ships carrying supplies to the coast of South Vietnam. However, he refused to order the mining and blockading of Haiphong and the North's other harbors.

The replacement for Huong, Dr. Phan Huy Quat, was controlled by the Buddhists. On February 19 another coup shocked the capital, but its object was to get rid of General Khanh, not to form a new government. Khanh was forced to flee to the United States. Quat then prepared to do the Buddhists' bidding, including purging many anti-Communist officers in the military.

Sensing the weakness in the Saigon government, the Communists made major gains on the battlefield for a month. However, Johnson refused to follow the recommendations of Taylor, McCone, and the

Joint Chiefs to amp-up Rolling Thunder. Privately he admitted he didn't "know what the hell to do!" He sent General Harold K. Johnson to Vietnam to determine what should be done.

On March 15 General Johnson, North Dakota-born, reported that the U.S. must dispatch ground troops, as many as 500,000, to aid the South in the fight: South Vietnam could not defeat the Communists alone. Westmoreland and the Joint Chiefs concurred; Maxwell Taylor did not. Support came from an unexpected source; Robert McNamara informed the President that American troops were needed, so on April 1 Johnson authorized the introduction of two more Marine battalions and 20,000 support personnel. He also agreed to negotiate an end to the war with the North, an offer that was rejected out of hand.

When a defector from the North told his interrogators that entire North Vietnamese divisions were operating in the South, McNamara was able to convince Taylor that additional troops were needed because of an impending major Communist offensive. When Taylor agreed, the number of American troops went from 33,000 to 82,000. The new troops arrived in early May. On May 11 the Communists launched their spring offensive, backed by a surprising (to the Americans) number of heavy weapons.

In June near the beginning of the monsoon season, the Communists began a major offensive in the highland areas of northern and central South Vietnam. Early victories by the Communists convinced the U.S. and even the South Vietnamese themselves, that South Vietnam could not win the war without considerable American help. General Westmoreland requested troop levels be raised to 116,000. McNamara recommended limiting the number to 95,000. Johnson went with McNamara.

Than a double whammy—the Saigon government suffered a crisis over some high-level appointments being made by Premier Quat, who was considered to favor the Buddhists, and the Viet Cong attacked a district capital, Dong Xoai, north of Saigon. The heavily armed VC pounded the living daylights out of the South Vietnamese. The South Vietnamese Army's 7th Airborne Battalion alone lost almost two-thirds of its men. South Vietnamese reserves were nearly exhausted. General Westmoreland dispatched a battalion of the U.S. 173rd Airborne Brigade to Phuoc Vinh, eighteen-and-a-half miles from Dong Xoai and requested authorization to send them into combat.

McNamara woke Johnson up at 2 A.M. to tell him of the developments and of the request. Johnson decided to let Westmoreland make the call, but the weather cleared over Dong Xoai, so American air power was able to drive off the VC.

As the battle was proceeding on June 12, Premier Quat was replaced by Air Marshal Nguyen Cao Ky. General Nguyen Van Thieu took over as the leader of the generals' committee. The two generals were united in their hatred of the Communists and in their insistence that the Buddhists were weakening the country. They imposed censorship, curtailed some civil liberties, and reinvigorated civil administration.

Meanwhile, the VC and the North Vietnamese were continuing their onslaught in the central highlands. While some South Vietnamese units fought bravely, their strength was being steadily reduced. Johnson asked McNamara and Under Secretary of State George Ball to prepare plans for a new American strategy. Ball's report recommended keeping the American commitment at 72,000 troops and negotiate a peace. McNamara consulted with Westmoreland and his report called for 150,000 American troops and the addition of troops from allied nations. William Bundy also submitted a report that called for 85,000 troops.

Dean Rusk backed McNamara; McGeorge Bundy supported the plan submitted by his brother. Johnson hung fire. By mid-July the Communists had taken control of six district capitals, although one was subsequently retaken by the South. Johnson was depressed; he sent McNamara to Saigon on July 15 to confer with Westmoreland, who showed the Secretary of Defense a two-part plan for using American units. Phase I would require 175,000 troops; in Phase II an additional 95,000 troops would turn the tide of battle against the North. However, Westmoreland had no plans to stop infiltration along the Ho Chi Minh Trail. McNamara rallied behind the plan.

On July 21 and 22 Johnson conferred with his advisors, but made no decision. On July 23 an intelligence report indicated that Operation Rolling Thunder would be more effective if it was expanded to hit oil facilities and transportation lines up to the Chinese border. Gradual escalation was a failure. Johnson then made his decision to send more troops to Vietnam—186,700. He would not mine the harbors of the North. However, to "fake out" Congress into believing its members would have some input in the (already made) decision, he consulted with Congressional leaders on July 27.

On July 28 Johnson announced he was sending 125,000 additional troops to Vietnam; he did not mention 186,700 because he thought the backlash would hurt passage of his domestic effort—the Great Society—by which the federal government's role in American life would be metastasized.

What he did do was put American lives in the crosshairs of an enemy who was given safe sanctuary in Laos and Cambodia and whose major infrastructure would not be touched.

I passed motels, restaurants, gas stations and all the accoutrements of the modern American highway system. On my left I-40 split off or joined I-55, depending on which direction you were traveling. I weaved in and out of traffic and passed both buildings and green spaces on the left and right until I came to a long bridge over a railroad, but I couldn't tell if it was the Frisco or the MP. I came to a rather barren area which I took to be part of the Mississippi flood plain. A sign said "Mississippi River," and I headed over a concrete and steel bridge with two railroad bridges to the left. Soon I was over the channel with some barges floating downstream. Where I crossed the river was almost half a mile wide. The Memphis & Arkansas bridge was a cantilevered truss span. Almost as soon as I left it, I went into a left-hand curve. I was in Memphis, Tennessee.

Chuck Berry recorded his song "Memphis, Tennessee" in 1959. I thought it was O.K., but then Lonnie Mack did a guitar version in 1963, which perked the song up quite a bit, and in 1964 Johnny Rivers came out with what I considered the best version, fuller and with a great vocal: "Long distance information, give me Memphis, Tennessee; help me find a party that tried to get in touch with me." I kept record charts back then, not as early as 1959, but Lonnie Mack's version peaked at #6 and Johnny Rivers topped my charts on June 14. Now I was in Memphis, but not to find the home that the little girl in "Memphis" lived in "on the south side, high upon a ridge, just a half a mile from the Mississippi bridge," but to see Elvis.

When we came back to college in the fall of 1965, Pete and I were certain that Nguyen Cao Ky was the man to lead a victorious campaign against the Communists in Vietnam. He was a dynamic leader and wore a purple scarf, setting himself apart from everyone else. We each made a copy on poster board of the South Vietnamese flag, which was easy since it was yellow with three horizontal red stripes and wrote the words "Kill Communists" below the flag. Pete had one in his apartment and I hung one up in my dorm room.

On August 18 the U.S. Marines went after the 1ˢᵗ Viet Cong Regiment dug in on the Van Tuong peninsula nine miles south of the Marine air base at Chu Lai. Operation Starlite, an air and amphibious assault, was a great victory: the VC lost 614 of 1500 men, while the Marines suffered fifty-two deaths and over two hundred wounded.

On November 14, the 1ˢᵗ Battalion Seventh Cavalry of the U.S. Army flew into the Ia Drang Valley, west of Pleiku and took on the 32ⁿᵈ and 33ʳᵈ regiments of the North Vietnamese Army. The campaign cost over three hundred American lives and over five hundred wounded, but the two North Vietnamese regiments opposing them lost 1500 men killed, three thousand wounded, and were annihilated. The Communists had to rethink their strategy of meeting the Americans in open battle.

The U.S. military embarked on more "search and destroy" missions by small units. In a gesture toward peace President Johnson announced a cessation of bombing in the North on Christmas Day. On December 31, 1965, there were 200,000 Americans serving in Vietnam.

Almost as soon as I had crossed the Memphis & Arkansas Bridge, I was on Crump Boulevard, named after "Boss" Crump, a politician who ran Memphis for almost the entire first half of the century. I didn't feel honored to be running my wheels over his pavement. I swung a right at the sign that said "Interstate 55 South Jackson, Miss." I went under Wisconsin Avenue and between what was either a commercial or industrial section to the left and a residential section to my right. It was hard to tell because there were so many trees. I passed over a railroad and West McLemore Avenue. A sign informed me I was on the W.B. Fowler, Sr., Expressway. *Who is he?*

High cement walls guided me down, and I passed under a railroad, Riverside Boulevard, Trigg Avenue, Olive Street, and the South Parkway before emerging in the Riverview area, houses on the left and trees on my right. I curved through an industrial-commercial area with the Illinois Central tracks to the left. Eventually, I passed over them and then cut right onto Highway 3.

Before I left Menninger, I had written down how to locate several places I wanted to see. I had missed the Jesse James house, had seen John

Wayne's house, and now I was close to Graceland. Maybe I'd see Elvis walking on the grounds. Or maybe he'd be out front, talking to his fans.

In January 1966 bombing resumed against North Vietnam. Anti-war protests built up steam in the U.S.; draft cards were burned. On December 31, 389,000 Americans were serving in Vietnam, including my cousin Rory.

I passed gas stations, motels, and other businesses, with power lines and street lights strung along both sides of the pavement. And then I was where Graceland ought to be, but there was a wall and a gate and I couldn't get close to the mansion which was hidden somewhere up a little rise of ground by a curtain of trees. And then Graceland was gone. No Elvis. Not even his hair. It wasn't until I was in New Orleans that I saw a newspaper story that Elvis was in Las Vegas, rehearsing for a new show.

In April 1967 Dr. Martin Luther King, Jr. led a massive march against the Vietnam War. In October an even bigger march against the war took place at the Pentagon. On November 30 Robert McNamara resigned as Secretary of Defense, his war strategy of gradual escalation in tatters. On December 31, 485,000 Americans were serving in Vietnam.

When Elvis first came on the scene, I was in the sixth grade, but he didn't make much of an impact in Menninger until it was announced that he was going to be on the Ed Sullivan TV show. Some of the girls in my class had an Elvis party because they knew all about him, but most of us boys didn't know squat, except his songs on the radio.

They weren't like any other songs out there. When Mom had the radio on, I'd hear things like the plaintive "Let Me Go Lover" by Joan Weber; "Sincerely" by the McGuire Sisters, which I liked more on television because I had a huge crush on Phyllis McGuire; "The Yellow Rose of Texas" by Mitch Miller; the Four Aces' "Love is a Many-Splendored Thing"; "Sixteen Tons" by "Tennessee" Ernie Ford; "Memories Are Made of This" by Dean Martin; and "Rock and Roll Waltz" by Kay Starr. Lotsa slow; lotsa schmaltz. Plus there was a slug of instrumentals—"Cherry Pink and Apple Blossom White" by Prez Prado, "Autumn Leaves" with the piano styling of Roger Williams,

"Lisbon Antigua" by Les Baxter, and "Moonglow and Theme from 'Picnic'" by Morris Stoloff. There was one song that did pound out a rhythm and sharpen an edge that separated us from the "old folks"—"Rock Around the Clock" by Bill Haley and His Comets, but Mom turned the station whenever that song came on.

Then came Elvis. Man, what a ride! "Heartbreak Hotel"—Joan Weber wouldn't even dare walk the lonely street in front of that place. Bopping with "Blue Suede Shoes" and "Money Honey." Showing he could actually sing with "I Was the One" ("I was the one who taught her to kiss, the way that she kisses you now"); "I Want You, I Need You, I Love You"; "Any Way You Want Me" ("Well, that's how I will be"); "Love Me" ("Treat me like a fool; treat me mean and cruel, but love me") "Is It So Strange? ("Oh, if you tell a lie, you know that I'll forgive you, though you say our love is just a game, and when you hear my name, you say I'm from a strange world, but is it so strange to be in love with you?") and "Love Me Tender." And the double-sided hit: "Hound Dog" and "Don't Be Cruel."

The girls all went ape, and I think we boys were jealous, especially when his first movie, *Love Me Tender*, came to the Blackstone. I didn't think much of his acting; Richard Egan was better, but he wasn't as bad as my friends and I made out.

The movie played on a Sunday afternoon, the time when the various church youth groups met. As my group, the Young Crusaders, left the theatre and made our way to the church, the girls kept up a litany of "Elvis is the greatest" comments. We boys flitted around the girls, trying to jab and poke Elvis, but to no avail. They were hooked and no one could dislodge Elvis from their hearts.

Elvis improved his acting. He was better as Deke Rivers in *Loving You*, even better as Vince Everett in *Jailhouse Rock*, O.K. as Danny Rivers in *King Creole*, Tulsa McLean in *G.I. Blues*, and Glenn Tyler in *Wild in the Country*, and I really liked him as Pacer Burton in *Flaming Star*, but after that his acting car careened downhill.

But the songs—loud and wild like "All Shook Up," "Jailhouse Rock," "Hard Headed Woman," but too few and then none at all. Catchy tunes—"Paralyzed" ("All I could do was stand there paralyzed"), "Teddy Bear" ("Baby, let me be your lovin' teddy bear"), "Flaming Star" ("Every man has a flaming star, a flaming star over his shoulder"), "Return to Sender" ("I gave a letter to the postman; he put it in his sack;

bright and early next morning he brought my letter back"), "Devil in Disguise" ("You look like an angel, walk like an angel, talk like an angel, but I got wise, you're the devil in disguise") "Suspicion" ("Every time you kiss me I'm still not certain that you love me"), "Easy Question" ("Do you or don't you love me, such an easy question, why can't I get an answer?") And the mellow songs that showed maybe the soft Fifties weren't that bad, and we weren't as rebellious as we had thought—"Peace in the Valley," "Loving You" ("I will spend my whole life through, loving you"), "Don't" ("Don't, don't, that's what you say, each time I hold you this way"), "Fame and Fortune" ("Fame and fortune, how empty they can be, but when I hold you in my arms, that's heaven to me"), "Are You Lonesome Tonight?," "Can't Help Falling in Love," "Soldier Boy" ("Soldier boy, why feel blue, don't you believe she will be true?"), "She's Not You" ("Her hair is soft and her eyes are oh so blue, she's all the things a girl should be, but she's not you"), "It Hurts Me" ("It hurts me to see him treat you the way that he does; it hurts me to see you sit and cry"), "Crying in the Chapel," and "That's Someone You Never Forget" ("The way she held your hand, the little things you planned, her memory is with you yet, that's someone you never forget"). And then a wave from England broke over our coast line and the Beatles, Rolling Stones, Animals, Dave Clark Five, and so many more with their repackaged rock and roll swept Elvis out of the Top Ten. By the late Sixties, I wasn't listening to Elvis anymore, but I'd never forget what he had been.

Noting the anti-war fervor developing in the U.S., Hanoi decided to gamble. On January 30, 1968, during the Tet holiday, when a cease-fire had been agreed to, the Viet Cong launched surprise attacks on Hue, Danang, Hoi An, Ben Tre, Saigon, and over a hundred other cities. The fighting caused tens of thousands of wounded and killed South Vietnamese civilians, South Vietnam's army had 2788 killed and eight thousand wounded, and the U.S. and other Allies had 1536 killed and over 7500 wounded. The VC and the North Vietnamese executed thousands of teachers, policemen, government officials, and professionals living in the cities.

Quickly, the Communists were killed or driven back, except in Hue, where fighting continued for a month. Between 75,000 and 80,000 Communists became casualties. The back of the Viet Cong as a fighting force had been broken. The South had won.

However, the American media saw it differently. They played up the destruction of Vietnamese villages, the loss of civilian life, battles in the city streets, refugees, and American boys dying. Communist failure to hold any ground, their terrorist actions against civilians, their huge casualty numbers—not so much.

Walter Cronkite, the CBS-TV anchor, made a trip to Vietnam and reported with sad cow eyes on February 27 that the war could not be won, that the U.S. had to negotiate a peace. Actress Jane Fonda, who was pro-Viet Cong, pro-North Vietnam, pro-Communist, and who had called American soldiers "war criminals" and even sat in a North Vietnamese anti-aircraft battery while smiling for the cameras, concurred. So did most of the media. So did the majority in Hollywood. So did the loud mouths in academia.

On February 28, General Westmoreland requested an additional 206,000 troops.

On March 31, Johnson declared on TV he would not seek reelection to the Presidency.

Rory came home the summer of '68 before he went back for another tour of duty. He had flown into Sea-Tac, and as he walked through the concourse, a bearded man in a Nehru jacket and wearing love beads came up to him, snarled "baby killer," and spat on his uniform. Rory said it took all his discipline to keep from killing the guy, or at least teaching him some better manners.

We talked a lot during his stay, and the thing that continued to bother him was the misinformation that the American media were passing off as fact. Tet was an American-South Vietnamese victory. The Commies lost.

He said he was joining a pacification program that was working to destroy the combined political and military apparatus—the Communist Party in the South and the NLF—that supported the Viet Cong. Such destruction would eliminate much of the Viet Cong infrastructure. He also said that if the American public, the Congress, and the President continued to back the American military, there was no doubt in his mind that we would be victorious.

He also had no doubt that American involvement in Vietnam in 1965 had kept two dominos from falling: Thailand and Indonesia.

Thailand had suffered from Communist infiltration since 1962, but in early 1965 Communist activities began to increase with help from Red China, North Vietnam and the Pathet Lao. When American troops landed in South Vietnam, the Thai government was convinced that America would help them in their fight to defeat any Communist insurgency, that Thailand would be safe from any Communist takeover and that assurance helped them take the fight to the Communists.

The dictator of Indonesia, Sukarno, was a leftist who was drifting closer and closer to the Red Chinese in the early Sixties, much to the dismay of the Indonesian military. When Johnson ordered American troops into South Vietnam, it convinced the Indonesian generals that they could count on the United States in a battle against Sukarno and the Indonesian Communists. The army crushed the Communists, and, while the generals allowed Sukarno to remain in the government until 1967, his power was broken.

On November 6, 1968, Richard Nixon was elected President. On December 31, 535,100 Americans were serving in Vietnam.

After my disappointment in not seeing Elvis, I headed south, passing burger joints, chicken places, restaurants that advertised catfish (*no, thanks, I've seen you just pulled out of the water, all whiskers and slimy skin*), furniture stores, jewelry stores, drug stores, gas stations, car washes, motels, and dozens of other businesses to satisfy consumer demand and occasionally the empty building where the owner didn't anticipate changing demand or lacked the ability to compete in the market. I was surprised there were no restaurants that advertised peanut butter and banana sandwiches, Elvis' favorite. Power poles and light poles stood like thin soldiers guiding me out of the city.

I went left on East Shelby Drive, passing both commercial and residential areas, and joined I-55 again. A minute-and-a-half later I was welcomed into the State of Mississippi and De Soto County. Little pockets of suburbia kept appearing or were indicated by signs until I got the feeling that most of De Soto County was just a vast bedroom for the Memphis middle class.

The trees thickened toward the southern end of the county, the traffic lessened, and I opened up the 750. Jackson 176 miles. I passed over or under occasional roads that headed off east and west through the woods. Once in awhile I saw corn or soybeans when there was a gap in the trees. The last mile or so of the county was a tree-grower's paradise. I came to a long bridge over the Coldwater River, which had a wide flood plain, and entered Tate County.

On January 25, 1969, peace talks began in Paris between the North, the South and the Americans. On March 17 President Nixon authorized Operation Menu, bombing inside Cambodia to reduce North Vietnamese supply areas along the border. In June American troops peaked at 543,000 as President Nixon announced the "Vietnamization" of the war. On September 3 Ho Chi Minh died. On November 15, 600,000 people attended an anti-war rally in Washington, D.C.

Trees and the flood plain, then just trees, then the Coldwater interchange and a turn to the southeast. Over Hickahala Creek, its surface reflecting the blue of the sky and the green of the trees that overhung its banks. Past the exit to Senatobia with signs calling me to gas up or eat; I kept going. A turn to the south, under an interchange, and then a slight curve to the southeast. Into the trees again. The highway split and trees grew in the median, then the lanes came together. Into Penola County. Past the Como exit. Four miles later the highway split again and the median trees were taller than those along the shoulders. The Sardis exit, most of the town tree-hidden off to the right. More thick trees, then over the top of Belmont Road. A mile-and-a-half of median trees, over Highway 35, a half mile of median trees, and the Batesville exit. I had to make a decision. About forty-five minutes west lay Clarksdale. Going there and back would cost me two hours of time. Two hours later getting into New Orleans. Did I really want to see the crossroads where bluesman Robert Johnson had sold his soul to the Devil?

On April 30, 1970, President Nixon announced the invasion of Cambodia by American troops to destroy Communist bases. On May 1 to 4, anti-war demonstrations were held on the campus of Kent State University. On the 3rd the R.O.T.C. building was burned. On the 4th the Ohio National Guard fired into a crowd of demonstrators, killing four people. On May 14 police shot and killed two anti-war demonstrators at Jackson State College in Mississippi.

On June 24 the U.S. Senate, already getting ready to "bug-out" of Vietnam, repealed the Gulf of Tonkin Resolution 81 to 10.

American troops victorious; American politicians wetting their pants. The outcome of the war hung in the balance.

I took the Batesville exit and headed through town, over the double-tracked Illinois Central, and out into the countryside. I went over the Tallahatchie River, but there was no one on the cantilevered bridge, not even Billie Joe McAllister. Besides, the bridge in Bobbie Gentry's song "Ode to Billie Joe" was further south. The trees opened up and I could see the large flood plain of the river. Then the trees closed up on the right, but were thinner on the left. They were set back from the highway, so there was a lot of green grass in the relatively shallow ditches. I passed a white gas station, but I didn't see what brand it sold. The road was straight, the traffic was thin, and I gave her the gun ten miles over the speed limit. I crossed into Quitman County and over a bridge. The stream was muddy and unnamed. Two-and-a-half miles and I swung a left; three miles and I swung right. Another bridge: the Coldwater River looked like creamed coffee. I went over the IC tracks and came to a stop sign. The town of Marks was completely hidden by the trees to my left. I passed through a huddle of buildings known as West Marks and into a gentle left-hand curve. The highway went straight for nine miles, and I covered it in seven minutes. Another coffee-colored stream—Big Creek. I came to a sign that indicated U.S. 61 and U.S. 49 were the same road. I was confused.

Robert Johnson was born in Hazelhurst, Mississippi around 1911. As a young boy he lived a pillar-to-post existence while learning to play the harmonica. He also tried the guitar, but was terrible. Determined to make a living as a musician, Johnson moved to a plantation to work and practice guitar. One of his teachers, Ike Zinnerman, was rumored to have picked up his style by visiting graveyards at midnight. Intrigued, Johnson was determined to do something similar.

After two years he came back to town with an entirely new and "bluesy" style. A rumor began that he had gone to a crossroads at midnight where he met the Devil in the form of a huge black man. The Devil tuned Johnson's guitar, played some songs, and made a deal with the young man: his soul for a great blues style. Done.

I had never heard of Johnson until I read a 1966 article in *Down Beat* magazine about him. I scrounged the album *King of the Delta Blues Singers* from a used book store in Minot and listened.

Blues and Delta Blues, in particular, cry out as the voice of someone being down, but to me it's not a voice of despair because the song itself is an affirmation of life, rough as it may be. I don't claim to be a big blues fan, but every once in awhile when I'm feeling down, I listen to Bessie Smith, Billie Holiday, Ray Charles, Janis Joplin—not the purest blues, but at least they have the voice for it, edgy, gritty, some people say a whiskey voice. Pat Boone and Doris Day can't sing the blues.

If I want real blues, I turn to the blues harp (harmonica) and vocals of Sonny Boy Williamson, the second one, the one that died of a heart attack, not the one that was killed.

I'd turn out the lights and listen to the jaunty "Let Your Conscience Be Your Guide" and "Don't Start Me To Talkin'" about domestic abuse, and songs that had the following lines:

"Bring It on Home"

"Baby, baby, I'm gonna bring it on home to you;
I done bought my ticket, I got my load,
Conductor done hollered, 'All aboard.'" Take my seat
and rode way back,
And watch this train move down the track."

"Sad To Be Alone"

"So sad to be lonesome,
Too much inconvenient to be alone,
But it make you feel so good,
When your baby come back home."

"Help Me"

"You got to help me,
I can't do it all by myself;
You got to help me, baby,
I can't do it all by myself."

"Born Blind"

"You talk about your woman,
I wish you could see mine;
Every time she starts her lovin',
She brings eyesight to the blind."

So I had wanted to see the crossroads where Johnson made his deal with the Devil, not because I especially enjoyed his music, but just because of the supernatural aura. I had pictured a lonely country crossroads darkened by midnight, with wind in the surrounding trees, maybe some lightning and thunder, and a huge black man trailing soot. Instead, it looked like the crossroads was in a town.

I knew it wouldn't be to the south because the highway wasn't there in Johnson's time, so I went under the interchange and into town. Clarksdale appeared as a bunch of trees, but I could see a water tower and some tall structures above an agri-business by the railroad. I came to a stop sign and decided to go left. I was skirting the town, but the highway sign said 161, so maybe it used to be 61. The pavement curved right. I passed a corn field and then was in town. A stop sign; the usual small town businesses, some showing their age and some dead; a little turn to the right and then one to the left; and then an intersection with signs reading 49 and 61.

I was already through the intersection, so I went around a long block and came back. I saw an old Negro walking in front of Abe's Bar-B-Q, which claimed to have been around since 1924, but the building didn't look that old. When I pulled up, the man gave me the snake-eye, but when I said, "Excuse me," I guess he felt better because he came over.

"Can you tell me if this is the crossroads where Robert Johnson sold his soul to the Devil?"

He pointed at the intersection. "Right here."

I must have looked disappointed.

He chuckled. "Yuh don' really b'leve that stuff, do yuh?"

"I don't know."

"It's good for the tourist trade. Tha's all. Good foh draggin' in suckahs." He walked away, still chuckling. Even if I waited 'til midnight, that crossroads would still be as tame as a new-born lamb looking for its mama's milk—no lightning, no thunder, no sooty black man.

I felt like a sucker. I hauled out of town and set a new speed record getting back to the Interstate. As I turned onto 55, I was some twenty-three miles west of Oxford, the former home of novelist William Faulkner, who had died the year I graduated high school. Most of his novels and short stories involved the imaginary town of Jefferson, which he modeled after Oxford, and the fictional county of Yoknapatawpha, which he fashioned out of Lafayette County, where Oxford was the county seat. I was driving into the Mississippi which Faulkner's fiction populated with race, class, greed, miscegenation, incest, bestiality, murder, lynching, prostitution, mental retardation, hunting, and death, everything that makes a novel worth reading.

Regardless of the dark side painted by Faulkner, Mississippi was a pretty state, so green, and the trees were thick along the highway. I passed over Eureka Road and started to notice that Mississippi didn't have a lot of small towns along the Interstate. I went over Shiloh Road and the lanes split with tall trees on both sides and in the median. It was like a one-way track through a forest. I went over McNeely Road that led off to Courtland on my left, but the town was a mile away, and the trees were too thick. After almost two miles the lanes rejoined. I crossed over Long Creek, which they may just as well have named Dry Creek. The trees receded, but I still couldn't see Courtland. I went over Hentz Road and back into the trees.

By the time I got to college, I had read Hemingway's major works, but not many of Faulkner's. After my American Lit. class in my sophomore year, I decided I needed to improve my knowledge of American writers and chose Faulkner.

I liked Hemingway's clipped sentence style, so it took me awhile to get used to Faulkner's, which ambled on, so much sometimes, that I forgot what the point was. In *Absalom, Absalom!* I counted one of his sentences: 157 words. That would have sent Hemingway spinning.

With Hemingway it doesn't matter the setting of the novel or short story you want to read—Michigan, Spain, France, Italy, Africa, on a boat off Cuba—you'll find good things in all of them. With Faulkner, however, you can forget just about everything not set in Yoknapatawpha County—novels such as *Soldier's Pay*, *Mosquitoes*, *Pylon*, *The Wild Palms*, *Old Man*, and the dreadful *A Fable*.

I'm not saying I enjoyed all Faulkner's works, but I eventually read them all.

The Sartoris family is one of the six most important families in Faulkner's fiction, so a good beginning would be to read *Sartoris*, Faulkner's third novel and the first one set in Yoknapatawpha. John Sartoris lived four miles outside Jefferson. His wife died in childbirth, his younger brother Bayard was killed in the Civil War, his mother-in-law was killed by some lawless poor whites, and Sartoris killed two carpetbaggers. Sartoris built a railroad to Memphis, but had a falling out with his partner and was killed by him. His son Bayard Sartoris had a son named John, who had twins, John and Bayard. Young John is shot down by German planes in World War I. Young Bayard comes home from the war, depressed over his brother's death. He takes to driving a high-powered car, and when he takes Grandfather Bayard with him on a high-speed drive, he crashes the car, and his grandfather dies of a heart attack. Young Bayard flees north and dies in the crash of an unsafe airplane he was testing in Ohio. *Sartoris* has enough death in it to rival a Russian novel. If every family in the post-bellum South suffered that many deaths, none of them would have survived. The book is episodic, but it's a start.

Grenada 29 miles. *I'd better stop and eat.* I passed under the Pope Water Valley Road. The topography of the country had ceased being flat for quite awhile, but the contours in the land were now becoming more noticeable. A slow left-hand curve took me under the Enid Dam Road, and almost a mile later I crossed into Yalobusha County.

The Sound and the Fury is the story of the Compson family—Jason and Caroline Compson and their children: Candace (Caddy), Quentin, Jason IV, Benjy, who is described as an idiot, and Caddy's daughter also named Quentin. I was thrown at first because the novel begins with Benjy describing a game of golf: "Through the fence, between the curling flower spaces, I could see them hitting. They were coming toward where a flag was and I went along the fence. Luster was hunting in the grass by the flower tree. They took the flag out, and they were hitting. Then they put the flag back and they went to the table, and he hit and the other hit." The novel has no compact plot, but is composed of four sections:

In Section I, Benjy and his Negro nurse Luster look for a quarter Luster lost; without it he can't go to the carnival in town. They don't find it and go back home, where Benjy sees Quentin, Caddy's daughter, sitting on the porch swing with a carnival man. Benjy cries. Luster's grandmother gives Benjy his birthday cake; he is thirty-three. Jason and Quentin have an argument and later Luster and Benjy see Quentin sneak down a pear tree by her bedroom window.

In Section II, Quentin is at Harvard. He is consumed by the knowledge that his sister Caddy had been seduced, resulting in her daughter Quentin. He finds a small Italian girl who seems lost, so he tries to take her home to her family, but is accused of kidnapping her. Some friends save him from the girl's brother, and Quentin goes on a picnic with his rescuers. At the picnic he attacks one of the men, Gerald, who had helped saved him, for no apparent reason and is beaten up. His thoughts reveal that he had tried to beat up Caddy's seducer, but failed, a failure that has haunted him. His attack on Gerald was a recreation of that fight. We also learn he had tried, without success, to convince his father he had incestuous relations with Caddy, so that her moral failure would, at least, remain in the family. Quentin then commits suicide by drowning.

In Section III, Jason Compson loves one thing—money. He hates Caddy because she had married a banker, which would have given Jason access to a lucrative career, but the banker divorced her. Jason believes the cause was her daughter Quentin, so Jason hates her, also. Jason has become Quentin's guardian. He has allowed Caddy, who no longer lives in Jefferson, only one opportunity to see her daughter and that was for one minute when Quentin was a baby. And Caddy had to pay him a hundred dollars. He tries to control Quentin, so she won't follow her mother's moral laxity. He sees Quentin with the carnival man, they have a verbal fight, and Quentin is locked in her room after supper. Later, Jason loses almost everything when the cotton market drops.

In Section IV, Dilsey, the Negro cook and the only character who really loves Quentin and Benjy, knocks on Quentin's locked door to get her to come down for breakfast. When there is no answer, Jason opens the door to find that not only is Quentin gone, she managed to jimmy open a money box and all his cash is gone, too. He rushes out in hot pursuit. Dilsey, her daughter Frony, and her grandson Luster take Benjy to an Easter service in a Negro church. After the service Benjy cries and will not be comforted because of the disappearance of Quentin. Dilsey has Luster drive into Jefferson, but when they come to the town square, Luster sees some of his friends and turns the horse to the left to go around a statue. That was an unforgivable breach of etiquette: everyone had to pass the statue on the right. Benjy knows what Luster did was wrong and sends up a howl. Jason has returned from his futile search just in time to see Luster's violation of tradition. He leaps up, clubs Luster out of the way, and forces the horse around to the right. He hits Luster again and then punches Benjy, telling him to shut up. Jason yells at Luster to get everyone home. After they get into familiar territory, Benjy settles down.

To Benjy and his brothers Quentin and Jason the world is "full of sound and fury, signifying nothing," but Dilsey, full of compassion and love, can overcome such loneliness.

I zipped under Pope Road and off to my left I saw a cow pasture and beyond that a long earthen dam on the Yocona River and behind that lay Enid Lake, according to the map, but I couldn't see it. I started up a hill and went left as the Interstate split, and I enjoyed about a mile-and-a-half of median trees. I went by the Charleston exit and over Highway 32.

As I Lay Dying was one of my favorite Faulkner books, almost Gothic in its telling. Addie Bundren made her husband Anse, a white trash farmer, promise to bury her with her relatives in Jefferson when she dies. Despite a loveless union, the Bundrens have five children: Cash, a thirty-year old carpenter; Darl, twenty-eight; Jewel, eighteen and the result of an affair Addie had with Whitfield, the preacher; Dewey Dell, seventeen and the only daughter; and Vardaman, nine.

As Addie lay dying, she hears Cash building her coffin outside the window. When Addie dies, Anse's comment is "God's will be done… now I can get them teeth." After her death, a storm breaks, and it is three days before they get the coffin onto a lumber wagon and on the road. A bridge was out so they backtracked to a ford, where the rushing water drowns the mules, Cash breaks his leg, and Jewel has to save the coffin from being carried away. Anse bartars for a new span of mules.

The main road is out so they take a longer route. On the way they make a cast out of cement for Cash, whose leg swells and turns black. Dewey Dell tries to buy some abortion pills. Addie's body is decomposing and smells, so when they stop for the night in a barn, Darl sets fire to the building to destroy his mother's body, but Jewel saves the coffin and what's inside.

After nine days the family arrives in Jefferson and digs Addie's grave with some borrowed shovels. Cash goes to the doctor, who tells him he'll be a cripple; Darl goes to an insane asylum, either that or jail for arson; and Dewey Dell again tries unsuccessfully to obtain abortion pills. Anse uses the money Dewey Dell's lover had given her for the abortion to buy a new set of dentures, then he marries a pop-eyed woman.

Anyone with doubts about Faulkner's imagination must read *As I Lay Dying*.

Grenada 19 miles. The afternoon sun heated up the air, but on the bike I didn't notice much. I passed under Highway 211 and the bridge was discolored by the exhaust of the big rigs. Back into the thick trees, then a break, then thick trees, over Tillatoba Creek, shallow brown pools overhung with tree branches. A split in 55 with over two miles of treed median, bisected by Highway 216. A slight left curve and past the Tillatoba exit and over Tillatoba Road.

Faulkner novels I could take or leave included *Sanctuary*—After a car wreck, college student Temple Drake ends up in a gangsters' lair, where a retarded man, Tommy, acts as her protector. Popeye, a Memphis gangster, kills Tommy, rapes Temple with a corncob since he is impotent, and puts her in a Memphis whorehouse. Red, a young criminal, takes an interest in Temple, so Popeye kills him. Lee Goodwin is tried for the murder of Tommy, and Temple testifies he killed Tommy and raped her. Goodwin is found guilty, but a mob breaks him out of jail and burns him to death. Temple is taken to Europe by her father. Popeye is executed for killing a man in Alabama, which was impossible because on the night of that murder, Popeye was killing Red.

Light in August—I liked the title, but could hardly finish it, it was so long and wordy. Basically, Lena Grove arrives in Jefferson, looking for her lost lover on the day spinster Joanna Burden is discovered in her burning house; she had been murdered. Joe Christmas, a man with Negro blood and who has been having a three-year affair with Joanna, is implicated as the murderer and arrested. Lena gives birth, but her lover jumps on a train and leaves. Christmas breaks jail and tries to hide in the kitchen of Gail Hightower, a defrocked minister, but a mob finds him there and a young deputy shoots and castrates Christmas. Lena leaves Jefferson, still looking for her lover. Joanna, Christmas, and Hightower all lived lives isolated from the white, Protestant, Southern culture around them, but only Hightower lives to see how important it is for individuals and communities to interact with each other in positive ways.

Absalom, Absalom! is the story of Thomas Sutpen, who grew up poor in the mountains of western Virginia. When the family moved to the coastal area, the rich planters looked down on them, something Sutpen never forgot. He decided he would create a dynasty and be like the rich planters, but he discovered the woman he married had Negro blood and would never be accepted in Southern society, so he divorced her and left her and their baby son in Haiti. He moved to Jefferson, built a mansion (which remained unfurnished three years after its completion), brought in a wagonload of Negroes, and borrowed seed for his first crop.

Sutpen married Ellen Coldfield from a very respectable Jefferson family, and they had two children: Henry and Judith. Henry made friends with Charles Bon at college, and when he brings Charles home for Christmas, Ellen pushes for a marriage between Charles and Judith. A year later the marriage plans are still in the works until Sutpen tells Henry the wedding can't take place because Charles is his son. Henry doesn't believe his father and accompanies Charles to New Orleans, and later they enlist in the Civil War together.

At the war's end Henry and Charles return to Jefferson, but Henry now believes Charles is Judith's and his half-brother and shoots him so the incestuous marriage can't take place. Henry then runs away. Sutpen returns from the war to find his plans for a dynasty in ruins; his wife has died, his son has fled, and his daughter is a spinster. Desperate for a son, Sutpen proposes to his sister-in-law, Rosa Coldfield, but she rejects him. He then impregnates the granddaughter of Wash Jones, a white trash handyman, but the baby is a daughter. Jones then kills Sutpen, his granddaughter and her baby, before being killed by a posse.

Judith and Clytie, her half-sister as a result of Sutpen's relations with a slave woman, live in the mansion. They hear that Charles Bon had a son named Etienne, but both Charles and the boy's mother died, so Clytie goes to New Orleans and brings Etienne to the planation to live.

Even though Etienne could pass as white, the women raise him as a Negro. He marries a very dark-skinned woman and they have a son,

Jim Bond, who is an idiot. Etienne and Judith die of yellow fever. Henry sneaks back and lives in the mansion with Clytie and Jim Bond. Rosa Coldfield discovers a very ill Henry in the run-down house and sends for an ambulance, but Clytie thinks people are coming to arrest Henry for killing Charles fifty years before, so she burns down the house and both she and Henry die. Jim Bond is left crying in the remains of the house, Sutpen's "dynasty."

The story is told by four narrators, each with his or her version of the truth, and even when you put the four together, it's difficult to say if what you have left is the truth. In that way it's akin to Japanese director Akira Kurosawa's 1950 film *Rashomon*, in which four different characters describe their versions of a murder and rape.

The Unvanquished is an easy read. It's made up of seven sections which describe members of the Sartoris family, Southern aristocrats, during and after the Civil War, sometimes humorously, sometimes sentimentally.

Intruder in the Dust is partly a detective story and partly a morality tale. Lucas Beauchamp, an old Negro, but his grandfather was white, is arrested for killing a white man, Vinson Gowrie. Lucas is considered to be "uppity" by the white people in Jefferson, and they can hardly wait for the Gowrie family to come into town and burn Lucas alive. A sixteen-year old white boy, Chick Mallison, owes Lucas because the old man helped him when he fell into a creek. Chick hates to be indebted to a Negro, so he keeps looking for a way to even out the score by helping Lucas. Lucas tells Chick it was not his Colt 41 that killed Gowrie. Chick tries to tell his uncle Gavin Stevens, Lucas' lawyer, but Stevens will not listen.

Chick, his Negro friend Aleck Sander, and an old maid Eunice Habersham dig up Gowrie's grave, but the body is that of lumber dealer Jake Montgomery. The three get the sheriff and Gavin, but when they check the grave, the coffin is empty. They search and find Montgomery's body in a shallow grave and Gowrie's in four feet of quicksand. The shot that killed him was from a Luger, a gun that Vinson's brother Crawford owns. Lucas tells the sheriff that Crawford had been stealing lumber from the mill he and Vinson operated, so Crawford killed Vinson and then Montgomery, who was trying to blackmail him, and then framed Lucas.

Arrested, Crawford commits suicide in jail and Lucas goes back to his "uppity" ways.

I think one of the reasons I enjoyed the novel was because Mom and I had seen the 1949 movie version on late-night TV. Juano Hernandez was outstanding as Lucas (I'd also seen him in *Young Man With a Horn* as Art Hazzard, as Uncle Famous Prill in *Stars in My Crown*, and Eddie Yeager in *Kiss Me Deadly*; later on I saw him as Bugs in *Hemingway's Adventures of a Young Man*, Mr. Smith in *The Pawnbroker*, and Uncle Possum in *The Reivers*—always a good performance). Claude Jarman, Jr., played Chick; Will Geer, one of the more likeable Communist fellow travelers, was the sheriff; the always dependable Elizabeth Patterson played Miss Habersham; and David Brian was adequate as the lawyer named "John Gavin Stevens" in the movie version.

I went over an unnamed water course which was just some brown mud holes. Grenada 12 miles. Jackson 117 miles. I was going to get to New Orleans late. Trees continued thick, but then opened up on the right, where it was difficult to see anything in the clearings because there were high banks on either side of the Interstate. I passed over the IC line and over Highway 55, which revealed a glimpse of buildings called Scobey to the left. A lazy left-hand curve, two-and-a-half miles of trees and I crossed into Grenada County. Over Hardy Road, a mile-and-a-half of tree-covered median, over Highway 333, a lazy right, over Highway 51, past Geeslin Corner, and then an exit. *Should I take it? No.*

Under Paper Mill Road; a mile-and-a-half median with thick trees, but thinner stands on the right; over a dried-up water course and then over the Yalobusha River, gray-brown, except where the sky made it blue or the shadows of the trees turned the water black; and then the Grenada exit.

Faulkner's writing that I liked:

The Snopes Trilogy, which was three novels that began strong, but then tapered off; it dealt with the theme of the poor-whites replacing the old Southern aristocracy.

The first and the one I enjoyed the most was *The Hamlet*, in which white trash Flem Snopes rises from almost nothing to a man of importance in Frenchman's Bend as a result of sharp dealing and marrying wealthy Will Varner's daughter Eula, who was pregnant by another man. Eula is a very desirable woman. First, Flem edges Will's son Jody out of the Varner store and then basically out of the family.

Other Snopses then move into the Bend—bank robber Byron Snopes; blacksmith Eck Snopes; Ike Snopes, who is mentally retarded and has sex with a cow; I.O. Snopes, a swindler; clerk Lump Snopes, Mink Snopes, a murderer; Montgomery Ward Snopes, who deals in pornography; hog farmer Orestes Snopes; grocer Wallstreet Panic Snopes; and Watkins Products Snopes, a carpenter. The Bend has been conquered by the lower class.

The Town sees Flem move his family to Jefferson, where he advances up the social scale from restaurant owner, superintendent of the power plant, vice president and then president of the bank, the moves again based on sharp dealing. Eula becomes the mistress of Manfred de Spain, the mayor and subsequently the bank president. Linda, Eula's daughter, grows up. Flem uses his knowledge of Eula's affair against her by getting her father, Will Varner, to oust de Spain as president, so Flem can take over. Rather than let her affair become known to Linda, Eula commits suicide. De Spain leaves Jefferson and Flem and Linda move into his mansion. Linda leaves for school in New York, and Flem, now wanting social acceptance, helps rid Jefferson of his Snopes relatives, who have followed him there.

In *The Mansion* Flem is wealthy, respectable, and a deacon in the Baptist Church. Mink Snopes is in prison for murder, but Flem is afraid Mink will get out on parole and kill him, so he arranges for a prison break, but one about which the authorities are informed, so Mink is given another twenty years. Linda Snopes returns to Jefferson. Mink gets out of prison two years early, gets a pistol in Memphis and kills Flem. Linda, who aided in obtaining Mink's early release, helps him escape.

Faulkner's last novel was *The Reivers*. Lucius "Boss" Priest buys an automobile to spite the bank president in Jefferson. Boon Hogganbeck, Boss's hired man, loves the car and gets to drive it occasionally with Lucius Priest, Boss's grandson, as a passenger. When Lucius' grandparents and parents leave for a funeral and will be gone up to ten days, Boon persuades Lucius they should drive the car to Memphis, which they do. Ned McCaslin, Boss's Negro coachman, rides along as a stowaway. Boon and Lucius stay in a whorehouse where Miss Corrie, Boon's girlfriend, works. Ned trades the car for Lightning, a race horse. Ned is convinced he can get Lightning to run, defeat a horse that's beaten him twice, and win back the automobile.

Lucius has a crush on Miss Corrie and defends her honor against Otis, her young relative who is also staying at the house. Otis attacks Lucius with a knife and Lucius cuts his hand getting it away from Otis. Miss Corrie and Boon break up the fight, and when Miss Corrie finds out Lucius was cut defending her honor, she promises to give up her life as a prostitute.

At the race track Butch, a deputy, makes trouble for Boon and Ned and puts the moves on Miss Corrie. Lightning loses the first of three heats, and Butch gets into a fight with Boon, so Boon and Ned are arrested. After Ned and Boon are released the next morning, Boon finds out it was because Miss Corrie had sex with Butch, so Butch would order the release, and the horse race could go on. Boon loses his temper and beats up Butch and hits Miss Corrie. Lucius is very upset that Miss Corrie would go back on her word.

In the second heat of the race, the other horse, Acheron, runs out of the track, so the race is Lightning's. Lightning also wins the third heat as Ned works some magic with a sardine to get him to run faster than ever. Boss shows up, another race is run, Lightning loses because Ned doesn't do the sardine trick, and Boss has to pay $500. Ned had bet on the other horse, so he cleaned up. They all leave for Jefferson, where Boon and Miss Corrie get married and have a son named Lucius Priest Hogganbeck.

Seeing the movie earlier that year only increased my enthusiasm for the book. Steve McQueen played Boon just liked you'd want your big brother to be. Sharon Farrell, whom I'd seen on TV, was innocent and sexy at the same time. Rupert Cross was another TV actor who jumped to the big screen as Ned McCaslin and was a great counterpoint to Boon. Lucius was played by Mitch Vogel, whom I had only seen on one episode of TV's *Adam-12*. He was totally believable, and I thought he had a great career ahead of him. Clifton James was the greasy Butch. Will Geer as Boss and Juan Hernandez as Uncle Possum stood out in minor roles.

I remembered hearing of Grenada during the Civil Rights marches in the mid-Sixties. James Meredith, Dr. Martin Luther King, Jr., and comedian Dick Gregory had been in Grenada, emphasizing voter registration. I wondered if it took.

Driving into the town, Grenada reminded me of an amoeba: most of it was two miles from I-55, but many of its businesses were stretching out along the pavement toward the Interstate, just like the pseudopod the one-celled creature sends out for movement or absorbing nutrients. I passed burger joints, pizza shops, and hit plenty of traffic lights. I wanted to see the old town, so I kept going. The road curved left and went down a slight slope. I turned onto Highway 51, also called Commerce Street. A few blocks later there was a sign: CAFÉ. I pulled in.

The large tablecloths were white and draped down over the sides of the tables, but I picked a booth near the door. There were six or seven customers, all near the back.

"Hi, sugah." A middle-aged waitress with black hair from a beauty shop or bottle put a menu and water glass down and left to bring some orders to the back. When she returned, I ordered a hamburger deluxe, hush puppies (something new I wanted to try), and a Coke. "What flavor?"

"What?"

"Yore Coke. What flavor?"

I didn't understand. "What flavors do you have?"

"Well, there's the regular, root beer, orange, cream soda, Dr. Pepper, 7 Up...."

"I'll have a Dr. Pepper, please."

"Where y'all from, sugah? Ah know it's not aroun' heah."

"North Dakota."

"Is that in the United States?"

"Yes, up by Canada."

"Well, Ah nevah been north of Memphis, so Canada may's well be the moon."

As she walked away, four young men probably in their mid-twenties came in. They had crew cuts, either flat top or regular, which was not the style after the Beatles. They wore t-shirts or short-sleeve shirts, and one of them had a Confederate flag tattooed on his forearm. Jeans and work boots completed the swagger. They sat in a front booth across from me.

The burger was outstanding, and I liked the spicy hush puppies with their taste of corn and either onion or garlic. I left a good tip and got up to pay.

"Hey, Jack, you see sompthin' needs a hair cut?"

"Yeah, and a shave, 'fore it 'sociates with white folks."

I stood at the counter, waiting for the waitress, who had told me her name was Shirley.

"Hey, hippy, ya'll better skedaddle outta town 'fore a dog catchah comes by."

Shirley came up and took my money.

"Hey, faggot, Ahm talkin' to you. Get outta our town. We don't like queers, Negrahs, druggies, nohow."

Shirley turned. "Bramble, you and yore fren's hush up or git out. This man ain't botherin' you."

"Yes, he is. Jus' his looks turn my stomach."

Shirley yelled, "Al! Trouble!"

A rather large man with a chef's hat and an apron appeared from the kitchen, carrying a meat cleaver. Bramble and his boys got busy reading their menus. Shirley said, "They don' mean any real harm; they kinda funnin' with you." She gave me my change. "Thank ya, sugah."

Before going out, I turned and Bramble extended his middle finger to send me on my way. I half-expected to see my bike destroyed, but nobody had touched it. They hadn't known it was mine when they passed it.

I fired it up and headed onto 51. I turned onto the Avenue of Pines and drove through a clean middle class neighborhood. I passed a little girl and her Dad out for a walk and waved. She returned my wave; he didn't.

I went back to 51 and then to Govan and a less affluent section of town. A turn left on Franklin and I was in a neighborhood of dark faces. No one waved at me and I didn't wave at anyone. I turned right on Bryant and went over the double-tracked IC. I kept going and then I heard a train horn. I turned into Bogue Alley, took a left at Brick Alley, and wondered why I had gotten myself in that rough section of town. A short right and a left and I was on Railroad Avenue. Across the fence a big orange and black IC diesel grumbled by. I hoped it was the *City of New Orleans*, but it was just a long freight. I went right to the 3rd Street corner and watched the cars roll and squeal by.

A teenage Negro stepped out from behind two power poles. He said something I couldn't hear because of the train. I saw some more Negroes coming up the street. The caboose growled over the crossing. The kid stepped in front of my bike. "You lost, white bread?"

He wore a black turtleneck and over it a military jacket with the sleeves cut off. He was trying somewhat unsuccessfully to grow a mustache. He wore glasses with dark lenses and a black beret, but it was riding high because of his Afro.

"Hey, crackah, I ax you if you lost?"

"Leave him alone, Gerald; he ain't done nothin' to you." A rather pretty girl moved into the street. The other people who had come up stayed by the power poles.

"I tol' you, my name ain't Geral'; tha's a slave-name. Mah name is Cinque."

"Dohn mind Gerald, mistah; he jus' think he H. Rap Brown, but he jus' li'l ol' Gerald Allen Lincoln from li'l ol' Grenada, Miss'ippi."

The kid pulled a knife from his pocket and a blade switched out. He did look like Brown, a radical member of SNCC, the civil rights group, and the "Black Power" advocate who said violence was as American as apple pie. "Ahm gonah cut this ofay." He moved toward me, but the girl grabbed his arm and pried the knife loose.

"You git home now, Gerald; Mama wants you to go to the stoah. Don't worry, mistah; he won't hurt you."

She pushed him off the street and the group started back the way they had come. Gerald or Cinque or whatever shot a glance at me, and I thought I could see tears on his cheeks. I geared the bike and started to turn the corner, when I saw movement to my right. The kid was in the street with his sister in pursuit; he raised his left arm and a "bird" was flying my way.

I humped it over the tracks and headed for 51, ignoring every person I saw. I turned left on 51 and fled toward 55, having angered both white and black citizens. Crossing the interchange, I was going too fast, so when I turned left, I went too wide, and I had to cramp to the left, stick out my right boot and push it into the curb. It must have helped because the bike straightened out and I merged with the traffic.

The late afternoon sunlight deepened the green of the trees and grass. Mississippi was a beautiful state; it was too bad some of its people didn't like me. I-55 split and the trees were tall and thick on the median and the right shoulder. Jackson 104 miles. I went under Sweethome Road and the highway came together, only to be divided by another wide median. The Carrollton Avenue bridge, a two-mile long tree-covered median with Harris Road cutting through it at an angle, and the Elliot interchange. I had come eight miles since Grenada; I realized Mississippi hadn't wasted a lot of money on interchanges. In some parts of North Dakota we had an interchange about every two miles.

I crossed into Carroll County and five miles later into Montgomery County. For fourteen miles I skimmed along, paralleling the county line, under the Winona interchange, and then went into Carroll County again.

There were medians, roads, bridges, trees, and traffic. The Vaiden interchange and I-55 ended. I took the exit, passed a couple gas stations, and a couple miles later rolled onto 51. The going was slower, the trees sometimes crowded the highway, but it was nice to see houses, yards, and people.

I picked up the IC line on my left, and every once in awhile I could see the tracks through gaps in the trees. Sometimes there were fields, but almost all of them to my right. Holmes County. Yazoo County. Madison County. Over the Black River, which was turning black in the late afternoon sun. Halfway through Canton a sign told me I-55 was up and running, so I went right and two miles later I was back on the good old Double Nickel.

Four interchanges later I was speeding through the eastern edge of Jackson. On the south side I merged with I-20 for a ways, went over the Pearl River, made certain I stayed left, crossed over the IC tracks, and I was on my way again, with a minimum of problems with traffic, except for a pickup that kept tailgating me.

That was enough of an upset that I pulled off at Byram and stopped at a Chevron station to fill up and use the facilities. As I was leaving, the attendant switched on the neon. I was 260 miles from New Orleans and night was approaching.

After Byram, I-55 bypassed the little towns that suckled off Highway 51: Terry, Crystal Springs, Hazelhurst, Wesson, Brookhaven, Summit, McComb, Magnolia, and then I was in Louisiana.

I had flipped on my headlight a ways back. The trees made it a little darker, but I could tell when I went over or under a bridge, I just didn't know the name of the stream or the road. Sometimes I could see lights when there were breaks in the trees. I went over Highway 38 at the Kentwood interchange and saw the lights of the town on both sides of the Interstate, but mostly on my left, then into the trees again.

I passed exits to Tangipahoa, Arcola and Roseland, Amite, Independence, Tickfaw, but I rarely saw any lights because of the trees. I did see Hammond because 55 was coming to an end, and I had to get onto Highway 22 and head east. I curved into Madisonville, had to stop at a stop sign, and crossed the Tchefuncte River—I could see its name by the street lights. I curved out of Madisonville and then curved right. The trees weren't as thick, and the moon was waxing toward full, which it would be in less than a week.

I took the West Causeway Approach and curved toward the south. The Causeway was a toll bridge, so I had to get in line and pay at the booth. And then I was on the longest bridge in the world. Actually, it was two parallel bridges with two lanes each; the second bridge had been completed the year before.

I couldn't have asked for a better way to enter New Orleans for the first time. Riding a motorcycle, the dark water of Lake Pontchartrain on both sides, and the moon dancing along like a bright dolphin for company.

It was a long ride, something like twenty-three miles, but the glimmer of New Orleans was like a beacon. The glimmer became a glow which became a radiance and then individual lights. I almost hated to leave the Causeway, but I had started for New Orleans and I was there.

I took I-10 and followed the portion called the Pontchartrain Expressway into downtown New Orleans. I exited onto Calliope Street, turned on St. Charles Avenue, and went half a block to Lee Circle. In the raised middle of the Circle, General Robert E. Lee stood proudly atop his white tower-monument.

I parked in front of the ten-story YMCA and went in. There was no one behind the front desk, so I pushed the buzzer. No one. Then again. A young man, not overly enthusiastic, appeared. "Wanna room?"

I thought that was obvious since I was carrying my gear, but I was polite. I registered and paid. He didn't offer to show me to my room, just gestured to the elevator. He did say I couldn't park out front.

The room was barebones adequate, but I was worried about my bike. I went down and started it, not knowing what to do. St. Charles had turned into a one-way, so I couldn't leave the Circle that way. I went around and exited on Andrew Higgins, then took a left onto Camp Street and another left into a parking lot behind the "Y." There was a small alley between the "Y" and the smaller building next door, and it angled so anything parked in the alley couldn't be seen from the street or the parking lot. I drove the Honda into the angle, locked the wheel, and prayed.

I bothered the clerk again to buy some soap and shampoo. I had never felt a hot shower do so many good things for me as the one that night. It was a communal shower, just like the ones in Forge Hall had been, but there was no one else showering, so I took my time.

Back in my room I was worried and tired, but I wrote in my journal. Jeffers and the Bible would have to wait. I fell into a somewhat fitful sleep, my mind on my bike, which I had left in the hands of God in my prayers.

DAY FIVE

I was awake early, threw on my clothes, and condemned the elevator for being so slow. When I turned at the angle, my bike was still there. I breathed another prayer.

The telephone book and map I borrowed from the front desk showed that the closest Honda dealer was out I-10 nearly five miles away, but what could I do?

I bought some New Orleans postcards and a box of detergent at the desk and threw my dirty clothes in the washer.

A warm shower and some time to compose what I wanted to say to my folks and Theresa. I put a towel around my middle and threw everything into the dryer.

For no reason I read "Be Angry at the Sun" by Jeffers:

> "That public men publish falsehoods
> Is nothing new. That America must accept
> Like the historical republics corruption and empire
> Has been known for years."

Well, I did get angry when the government lied to us, but right then I wasn't going to argue with Jeffers that I shouldn't be upset. I turned to the Bible:

I skimmed the pages until I saw the word "thanks" and read Ephesians 5, verse 20: "Giving thanks always for all things unto God and the Father in the name of our Lord Jesus Christ." I realized I hadn't been paying much attention to God's protection, so I knelt by my bed and prayed, thanking Him for His love and for protecting me on my journey.

I felt better, got my clothes, and got dressed. At the desk I asked for the nearest post office and the man said, "Up on Loyola" and pointed it out on the city map, so I took Howard up to Loyola, bought enough stamps for several cards, and mailed the two I had written. Then I shot over to Canal and had breakfast. I ordered ham and eggs, buttermilk biscuits, and a tall orange juice, then on a whim, some grits.

In the next booth four men were arguing over the Super Dome, which was being built. One guy was totally obsessed with putting the Dome down because of the buildings that had to be razed to make room for it. The Old New Orleans was good enough for him. One man was enthusiastic, but the remaining two cautioned him that it would take a lot more than a dome to make the Saints a playoff team. They'd only been around since 1967 and didn't have a winning season yet. With aging Billy Kilmer as quarterback and a kicker, Tom Dempsey, missing half a foot, I didn't think their chances in 1970 were very good.

I left a good tip, although the waitress was so busy we hardly spoke. I walked over to a bank and cashed some traveler's checks. Outside, I knelt as if I had to tie my shoe, even though my boots had no laces, slipped the bills in my sock, and headed for the Honda shop. I had to go a block over to Common to get onto I-10. And the traffic was fierce. I didn't have much time to look around, but I did see the tall Texaco Building down Canal; it was multi-windowed and looked like a giant cheese grater standing on end.

Eventually, I reached my exit and found the Honda dealership. I walked into the main lobby and talked to a salesman, who directed me to the service door. I drove there and asked if they could change my oil, look at the chain, and make certain the bike was ready for a long trip. Just as the foreman was wheeling the bike inside, a manager came out and said, "Y'all know you gottah pick it up tomorrah. We got no room for storin'."

"Yeah, I know. I'll be here," I lied. I wasn't parking my bike in the angle anymore.

I was five miles from the "Y"; I had to get started.

Some of the neighborhoods I walked were mostly populated by dark-skinned people; some were almost all light-skinned. I just kept walking and no one bothered me. Sometimes I'd meet people, and dark or light, I'd nod and keep going.

At one point I came to where an alley joined the street. A car was partially in the alley and partly on the street, so I had to walk around the front. When I looked through the windshield, I saw two girls locked in an embrace, kissing. *Well, that's something you don't see every day in Menninger.*

It was a clear sky and the sun was mean. I stopped by a neighborhood store and went in. A Negro man was by the cash register. I said, "Hello."

"How do, sir. May I hep you?"

"I'd like a Dr. Pepper, please."

"Step over to that cooler. Ovah there." He pointed. I pulled out a bottle and came back. I put down a dollar and he counted the change.

"Do you have an opener?"

"Somewhere." He bent down and reached around under in the counter. Two Negro girls came in laughing. When they saw me, they stopped. He handed me the opener.

"Thanks." I popped the cap and drank. The girls began looking at the candy.

"You ain't from around here, are you, sir?"

"No, North Dakota." The girls giggled.

"I could tell. It's not customary fo' white folks to enter my store."

"Is it against the law?" The girls giggled even louder.

"No, just customary."

I finished. I put the bottle on the counter. "Can I leave this here?"

"Certainly."

I put a dollar on the counter. "Give the girls what they want."

"I wouldn't do that, sir. If their Daddies find out, you will be in a whole mess o' trouble."

The girls were still giggling when I left with my unused dollar.

Walking isn't so bad if you get your mind off what you're doing. I thought about what I was going to do and what I had done.

Suddenly, I realized I was in the Vieux Carré, the French Quarter. I headed for Bourbon Street. It was a one-way, and I was walking against the traffic, but the thing that really struck me was its narrowness.

What a place. It was like a little City of Abandon in a hundred square blocks, San Francisco in a cracker box. Even in the afternoon there were tourists, hippies, cops, guys on the make, and even some people from the Canal Street businesses hurrying or wandering.

A lot of the buildings were three-story brick with metal fire escapes webbing up the front or side. I was especially intrigued by the large metal balconies that wrapped around the buildings that stood on the corners.

Not everything I wanted to see was on Bourbon Street: Antoine's Restaurant was on St. Louis, four stories, a wrap-around balcony, and painted pink. It had been established in 1840 and I'd never eat there; I just wanted to see it. Preservation Hall was at 726 St. Peter, and it looked as if it had been there since St. Peter walked the Earth: there was a large entrance, gated at that time of day, with two wooden doors of two panels off to the side, each with a diamond-shaped hole near the top; the doors didn't look used; a balcony with three wooden doors of two panels, again unused and with no diamonds. The whole thing looked run-down like a building left over from the French Revolution.

I also noted Pete Fountain's Club at 800 Bourbon and Al Hirt's Club at 501 Bourbon.

The Old Absinthe House at Bourbon and Bienville had a sign saying something about the pirate Jean Lafitte and 1807. The outside looked like it had been painted by hippies: pinks, golds, greens, and purples. The shutters were green and it had a wrap-around balcony.

I saw buildings with signs shouting that they were the Club Sho-Bar, the Panda Bear, the Teriyaki Cafeteria, the Bourbon Apartment Hotel, Rizzo's Restaurant, the Hotel Bourbon, the 809 Club.

The Gurn Boutique, Bourbon Novelties, and the Mask Factory shared a baby blue building.

One building had a Confederate flag, the Louisiana flag, and a couple I didn't recognize, but no American flag, flying from staffs leaning out over the sidewalk. Next door was the S/HE Unisex clothing store. The items they featured in the window were hot pink, chartreuse, lavender, and lemon yellow—plenty of things for SHE, not anything for HE, if the HE were me.

Dixie's Bar had a cloth awning and a tuba with the bell pointing up attached to the balcony, on which there were plants that looked like yucca in orange-brown pots.

The 500 Club was an interesting two-story building of gold brick with a wrap-around balcony. A sign bragged that the Club featured the

Cat-Girl, the World's Most Famous Exciting Dancer. Across an alley or small street was the Jazz Danspierre 600.

The Famous Door Bar had a porch that extended over the sidewalk with five black posts near the curb and two white and black posts on the side. Across the street was the Peoples' Grocery with a balcony that swept around the corner.

The Royal Sonesta Hotel was at 300 Bourbon; it was four stories with two wrap-around roofed balconies, and ten dormer windows along the roofline.

I had to get to the "Y" and rest up: I wanted to explore the French Quarter at night. I walked Bourbon; went a block south on Canal; turned and crossed it, a wide street divided by a median which had streetcar rails; and turned at St. Charles. I walked to Lee Circle. Despite my excitement, sleep came easily.

When I got up, I found a "greasy spoon" where I ate supper, the type of place where even if you don't order onions with your burger, it tastes like onions anyway, and the grease from the fries coagulates on your plate. Such food, like "Fair Food," can't be good for you, but life without them once in awhile would pretty tasteless.

Down Canal I saw what looked like a huge pile of old clothes, but they were all black. I wondered why they were on the sidewalk, but didn't investigate. I crossed Canal and walked Bourbon just to see the people. As I passed Pete Fountain's and Al Hirt's, I went in and bought tickets for the next night's shows.

It was still early evening, but two sailors were drunk and holding each other up as they lurched along. Three teenage girls walked by dressed in blouses that exposed their midriffs, white leather vests, hip-hugging bell-bottoms, and sandals. Love beads abounded. *Where are their parents?*

Two younger men, probably early twenties, stood on the corner of Bourbon and St. Louis near Al Hirt's. They were both dressed in black slacks, black belts, black shoes, and white dress shirts. As I passed, I saw one had diastema, with a very wide gap between his upper central incisors. The other one had long, black sideburns that slid down his cheeks and became a beard.

A family of five headed my way; the kids were probably young teens. Why would any parents bring their children to Bourbon after dark? There were barkers outside the clubs demanding, begging, cajoling people to come inside for a topless, bottomless show. The pictures of the women left little to the imagination, and I saw the two young sons shoot stealthy eyes at the barely legal pictures they had never seen in Iowa, Nebraska, or wherever.

People were eating, drinking, and laughing on some of the balconies, and the whole street was a binge of noise.

I walked down to St. Peter and waited for the doors to open. The inside of Preservation Hall was bathed, or I should say, sprinkled with a dingy light. I sat in a chair and waited. Soon some old Negroes wandered onto the stage and played a few notes. Their instruments were the trumpet, sax, trombone, stand-up bass, banjo, piano, and drums. I wondered if the old geezers were up to it. Abruptly, they were off. I like New Orleans jazz, where all the instruments play simultaneously. I also like Chicago style, where the various instruments take a solo turn. The modern progressive jazz leaves me cold; a lot of the time, it's cold.

But that night those seven old cats were blowin', New Orleans style, Dixieland, call it what you will; they were hot.

The entire audience, most of whom probably knew more about jazz than I did, were rockin' the place. And the old geezers—I regretted calling them that—blew the lights out. We even got a couple encores from them.

I walked into the night air thinking the whole long trip was worth it, even if I went home tomorrow.

I strolled down Bourbon again. I noticed "gap-tooth" and "beard" arguing with a girl in a tight red blouse and black mini-skirt. It wasn't my affair, so I kept going. On my way back the trio had disappeared. A little further on I saw a bright yellow neon sign on a building: "DESIRE."

I crossed Canal and the pile of black clothes had moved. I had to walk right by it, and then I saw it wasn't clothes at all, but a large Negro woman sitting in a wheel chair beside a grocery cart. Evidently all her worldly goods were in the cart and covered by a black cloth. She was completely hidden in the black clothing. She must not have had much schooling because she had misspelled a couple words on her cart: the sign read "Privat Property. Hands Of. Mama Calbasa."

She appeared to be asleep with an empty King Edward's cigar box open on her lap. After Preservation Hall, I felt so good, I dropped a five dollar bill in the box.

She never moved. "Thank yuh, sir. Mama Calbasa thanks yuh."

"You're welcome."

I wrote in my journal, filled out two postcards, and read.

I skipped Jeffers because my happiness might not survive his poetry, which was generally a downer.

I read Psalm 146, part of which is "Happy is he that hath the God of Jacob for his help, whose hope is in the Lord his God: Which made heaven, and earth, the sea, and all that therein is: which keepeth truth forever."

I was happy that God had made men who could play jazz the way I'd heard it that night. I thanked Him in my prayers.

DAY SIX

The morning was lush with sunshine, humidity, and anticipation. I walked to Canal and had breakfast. Mama Calbasa was not around. Neither were the Super Dome men.

I took a cab to the Chalmette Historical Park with its Chalmette National Cemetery and the site of Andy Jackson's victory over the "bloody British" at the Battle of New Orleans in 1815. I was surprised to learn that only one grave was that of a soldier who had actually fought in the battle; most of the thousands were from the Civil War.

I toured the Malus-Beauregard plantation house that was antebellum and redolent of a time with magnolias, cotton, and slaves singing as they worked, although I knew that wasn't a true picture. A large white obelisk stood as a monument to the battle and the men who fought it.

I'd been to Custer Battlefield in Montana, all hills, gullies, and the small white gravestones of death. The New Orleans battlefield was fairly flat, so the British attackers were easy targets for the Americans entrenched on the far side of the Rodriquez Canal and some earthworks.

Sometimes I would think about the poor guy who was killed just prior to the 11th hour of the 11th day of the 11th month of 1918, the end of the First World War, and think "What a waste." But the Battle of New Orleans was fought after the peace treaty ending the War of 1812 had been signed, so the deaths of the dozen or so Americans and the hundreds of British, including General Pakenham, were really a waste.

I wandered around the field for a long time, trying to recreate battle scenes in my mind. I was upset that a Kaiser Aluminum plant was spewing pollutants nearby.

The taxi ride back was filled with thoughts of admiration for the bravery of soldiers and the futility of their deaths.

After I rested in my room, I wandered over to the French Quarter and walked down St. Peter to Jackson Square. I avoided the blandishments of dozens of fortune tellers, mystics, seers, tarot card readers, and palm readers. The square was about the size of a city block and dominated by the bronze equestrian statue of Andy Jackson and the three-spired St. Louis Cathedral. Along two sides of the square on St. Peter and St. Ann were four-story, red brick structures known as the Pontalba Buildings. The ground floors contained shops and restaurants, and the upper floors were apartments. The lower of the two balconies was covered with green plants and colorful flowers. There were a lot of magicians, jugglers, and musicians working the streets.

I walked down to the levee and climbed it. When I saw the Mississippi River, it was higher than the land I had walked up from. That didn't look like a good situation.

Kerouac had called the Mississippi River "My beloved" and "the great brown father of waters rolling down from mid-America like the torrent of broken souls." He also wrote of "old New Orleans at the washed-out bottom of America."

The river was brown, but was New Orleans the catch-basin of broken souls?

"Another one of God's majestic miracles."

I hadn't heard the noise of anyone approaching, but a Negro stood next to me. He was in his late thirties, maybe early forties, but his hair, mustache, and short goatee were cotton white. He had on a black suit, gray shirt and a clerical collar.

"Yes, it is."

"The Bible says that God created the waters first, and then commanded them to let the dry land appear. The same thing here. The river brings down earth from the north and we get the delta." We both looked out at the brown rush. "I'm Rev. Ebenezer Saunders of the African-Christian Church of God, Jesus, and the Holy Ghost. We are a small congregation, but filled with the spirit and love." He extended his hand.

I took it. "I'm Chris Cockburn from North Dakota."

"Proud to make your acquaintance, Chris. Are you here on vacation?"

"Sort of, before I go back to work in the school."

"Oh, you're a teacher, then; a mighty fine profession."

"No, I used to teach; now I'm a custodian." The word burned my lips and he must have seen my discomfort.

"There is nothin' wrong with being a custodian, as long as you're a good one."

"Thank you, sir."

"So there really is a North Dakota. I was born and bred in Nawlens. I've never been out of Louisiana, except to Mississippi. I've heard of it, of course, but the name always conjures images of the Wild West, buffalo, Indians, cowboys. In my mind you should have a holster, six-gun, ten-gallon hat, chaps, and cow pony. Or if it's winter, wearing a big thick coat and fighting huge snow drifts in a gigantic blizzard."

"Yes, we have bad blizzards...and tornadoes in the summertime."

"And we have hurricanes. Every section of our nation has some natural phenomenon that the Father has allowed so as to test our faith."

"I guess."

"I would like you to meet my family, Chris, if you would want to."

"Sure."

We walked down to where a woman was emptying the contents of a hamper onto a red and white checked tablecloth spread on the ground. She wore a yellow dress that was high on her neck, brown hair and eyes, but what I really noticed was her beautiful light brown skin, flawless.

"Chris, this is my wife, Jacqueline Fleur Saunders; she's Creole, so if she gets uppity you'll know why." He had a little laugh that showed me he was joking.

She nodded. "Hello, Chris. You can call me Jackie."

"How do you do...Jackie."

"Very well, thank you."

"I've invited Chris to share our meal."

"Oh, how nice. Doubly welcome, Chris."

"This is my son Ebenezer, Jr., my daughter Lizette, and my other daughter Nicole."

The boy was about eight, the girl a couple years younger, and the baby was just a pair of big dark eyes in a stroller with a sun-shade doing its duty. The two older children bowed and said "Hello" as if on cue. They were dressed as if they had just come from church.

The meal was delicious fried chicken which came from a recipe way back in Creole history. There were tangy sweet potatoes, pickled snap beans, buttermilk biscuits, and pecan pralines for dessert. When I complimented her on the "praylines," she was a little embarrassed to correct me: in New Orleans it was "prawlines."

About the only talk during the meal was the kids showing good manners in asking for something, my compliments on everything I ate, and Rev. Saunders apology for having just water to drink.

When the meal was finished, the kids went up the levee, and Mrs. Saunders began putting things away, declining my offer of help.

"So what are the great topics they are discussing in North Dakota?"

"The war, of course, and Kent State."

"Yes, both of them sad commentaries on the use of violence instead of love to achieve an end. The late Dr. King would be dismayed at the way his beliefs are being trodden down."

I had to agree on Kent State—two innocent kids lost their lives. But if the National Guard felt their lives were threatened…

The kids came back and sat down quietly; I had to contrast them with the noisy tourists' kids darting all over the square like banshees.

"Sometimes you have to march and take a stand against something you disagree with, but you do it with love and non-violence in the manner of Dr. King. Even to the point of prison."

"My Daddy's been in jail."

Mrs. Saunders had come back. "Hush, littler Eb." The boy looked down, but quickly raised his head; his smile told me how proud he was.

"The present state of the civil rights movement since the passing of Dr. King is not pleasant to comprehend. Black Power, the Black Panthers, Stokely Carmichael, Malcolm X, they are heading in the wrong direction. Even if they win some small victories, their methods will betray them, and the resentments in the white communities will linger for decades. We have to return to the teachings of Dr. King and even as far back as Booker T. Washington to live at peace with our white brothers and sisters, and use that love to prove we are good neighbors. Build the local communities and then move out from there."

Jackie echoed her husband's ideas as she joined the conversation.

I didn't have much to say about his ideas: they sounded good to me. There was some small talk about our families, then I thanked them again, he invited me to their church, and I left. I turned back once and Rev. Saunders and his wife were walking hand-in-hand down the levee;

he was carrying the hamper in his other hand. Little Eb was behind the stroller and Lizette was walking beside him.

I wandered the French Quarter, away from Bourbon Street, out with the Voodoo shops; the head shops; the shops with no names and unknown items for sale; the empty shops, some with their sorrowful signs that had failed to tempt enough customers. Out into the high rent, low rent, and no rent districts, at least I wouldn't have paid any rent to live in the rats' nests that passed as buildings. Passing the street people, the broken down, the left out, the unwashed and unwanted, the hookers who couldn't make it pay on Bourbon Street anymore, the druggies, the vagrants, the insane, and the old ladies with their inevitable bags.

As I headed back to Bourbon, I passed the African-Christian Church of God, Jesus, and the Holy Ghost. It was located in a store-front.

I went over to Pete Fountain's and waited for the first show. I walked into the semi-darkness and sat at the bar. There were tables all around and a stage with drop curtains in back and a canopy. The bartender stood in the dim light from above the bar. "Yours?"

"I'll have a large milk."

He never batted an eye; just walked away and came back with it. I paid the exorbitant price and gave him a dollar tip.

After an introduction Pete Fountain came on stage with his band. Artie Shaw and Benny Goodman had always been my favorite clarinet players, but I had heard Fountain on TV and on some of Mom's LPs. I was surprised by his looks: he was bald, but had a dark beard. He looked like an egg with hair glued to one end. On his album covers he had wavy black hair: was it a toupee? He was dressed in midnight blue and so was the band.

The crowd cheered and clapped enthusiastically for the Dixieland versions of "Do You Know What It Means To Miss New Orleans," "St. James Infirmary," "When It's Sleepy Time Down South," and "St. Louis Blues." There were others I didn't recognize, but the applause was just as loud for those numbers, so I guess the other people knew the songs and appreciated the playing. Either that or they had drunk so much, they'd applaud anything out of a horn.

The one song I was disappointed in was "Stranger on the Shore," which Mr. Acker Bilk had written for his daughter Jenny. It had been big my senior year of high school. I didn't care for the lower tone of Fountain's version or the little runs and trills he played. I like Bilk's cleaner version, one I thought had more emotion poured into it, but I guess a musician could do that if he was playing for his daughter, rather than a bunch of people in a bar.

Fountain was up on the stage, separated from the people, and even though he was amiable, smiled at the customers, and laughed a lot, I didn't feel much of a connection.

After his encore, I hustled over to Al Hirt's Club. I was early so I stood outside and listened to people, but all they talked about was where: where they'd been, where they were going, where the best food was, where the best drinks were.

The setting in the club was different than that of Fountain's. The brown wooden stage was low and round and close to the first row of tables. The tables were in concentric rows around the front half of the stage and looked down on it. An introduction and this huge bear with a brown beard and wearing a brown suit bounded on stage, carrying a trumpet. His band, also in brown and matching the color of the stage, followed.

What a performer! Hirt played some Dixieland favorites, but I really liked his other numbers better—"Sweet Lorraine," Ziggy Elman's theme "And the Angels Sing," Bunny Berigan's theme "I Can't Get Started," "Java," "Sleepy Lagoon," "Alley Cat," an old standard "Stardust," "Sugar Lips," and "Cherry Pink and Apple Blossom White," among others.

Between songs he was always leaning toward the audience near him, talking and laughing, or yelling out to those of us higher up. He had two encores.

I left the club feeling like Al Hirt really enjoyed people.

I moved down the ruckus of Bourbon Street and met "gap-tooth" and "beard" with the girl, now in hot pink and black and an older man. "DESIRE" burned yellow in the background.

The ubiquitous Mama Calbasa was in a different spot on Canal. I dropped a five. "Thank yuh, sir."

"You're welcome."

I wrote in my journal, composed my postcards, and read.

In Jeffers, I read "Shine, Perishing Republic," with its lines—

"But for my children, I would have them keep their distance from the thickening center;

"Corruption has never been compulsory, when the cities lie at the monster's feet there are left the mountains."

Bourbon Street certainly had its corruption, but didn't people like Al Hurt leaven it a little like good people everywhere?

I read some in Second Peter: "And turning the cities of Sodom and Gomorrha into ashes condemned them with an overthrow, making them an ensample unto those that after should live ungodly…(For that righteous man dwelling among them, in seeing and hearing, vexed his righteous soul from day to day with their unlawful deeds…)"

I wished I had spoken with Rev. Saunders about how he handled the corruption that surrounded his church. I included the Saunders family in my prayers.

DAY SEVEN

A glorious Saturday morning in the Big Easy. I walked over to Canal and had a sunshine breakfast of ham and eggs (sunny-side up, of course), wheat toast, hash browns with onions, orange juice, and milk. I kidded with Lorraine, my waitress. Efficient, friendly, and forty. She had started calling me "Dakota." I left a big tip.

I thought maybe I could walk from the French Quarter over to the St. Claude area and see Desire Street, but I'd heard the streetcar there had been replaced by a bus, so Tennessee Williams drifted from my mind.

I caught the St. Charles streetcar at the stop on Lee Circle and got off at Jackson Avenue. The streetcar was olive green with red trim and connected by an umbilical cable to the electric line above the tracks. The passengers were a conglomeration of white, black, and brown, so any former segregation had ended. The ride was smooth and I got off at Jackson Avenue in the Garden District.

Magazine, Camp, Chestnut, Coliseum, Magnolia, Clara, Willow, Washington, and all the streets 1st through 4th. I walked every one. I even went over to 8th and looked at the home of author George Washington Cable, a friend of Mark Twain's, but I had never read anything by him. It was a two-story white house with the upper story and its balcony with six columns seeming to crush the lower story into the ground.

I walked under the column-supported porch of the Commander's Palace Restaurant. Two stories of blue and white with a Victorian "tower" on one corner and a couple dormer windows on top. It was a famous place, but I didn't go in. Plus, they probably had a dress code. There were shops and cafes on Magazine, but I avoided them, also.

An older building looked like a large Victorian home with a red roof, gray sides, and a rounded, columned front porch, but it was the Latter Branch Public Library. Most of the antebellum mansions were fenced off, so I had to look at them at a distance, sometimes through wrought-iron fences, sometimes through both fences and bushes.

Huge houses, balconies, verandahs, some spires, numerous columns, spectacular architecture packed into a few blocks. I had read that some of the architecture was Greek Revival, some was Italianate, and some of it looked Victorian to me, but I didn't have a guide book, so I was at a loss. I assumed the ones with the large white columns were Greek Revival.

One place I didn't have to make any assumptions was the huge Lafayette Cemetery #1—all its guests were dead. The graves were actually above ground. I had heard that was due to the high water table. The remains were sealed in small marble houses of the dead with slanted or rounded roofs, some with crosses, and some with doors, which I figured were one-way.

While I walked, every once in a while I'd be overwhelmed by the fragrance of flowers. Then I walked slower or stopped and enjoyed the scent and the beauty surrounding me. This was August, and it smelled good. In North Dakota when the plum, chokecherry, crab apple, mountain ash, and some other small trees, and lilac and honeysuckle bushes bloom in the spring, it's a wonderful smell, but by August North Dakota air smells like air.

As I boarded the streetcar, I regretted not having a camera, but I was certain if I had brought one, it would have been broken or lost.

I went to a seafood place on Canal and had a late shrimp dinner, then after writing in my journal before some of the Garden District images faded, I rested in my room.

At dusk I headed for Bourbon. I dropped a five dollar bill in Mama Calbasa's box. "Thank yuh, sir."

"You're welcome."

I wandered the streets of the French Quarter and avoided the panhandlers and druggies and their begging.

Bourbon was rocking. Tourists were spending money as if it came out of a water faucet. The girls were hot and the beer was cold. The barkers were loud and the cops were few. I noticed a lot of college t-shirts—Illinois, Kansas State, Texas, Ohio State, UCLA, Florida State,

Notre Dame, St. Bonaventure—what were those Catholic kids doing on Bourbon?

What looked like a brand new Tulane shirt in Olive Green and Sky Blue bumped into me with an "Excuse me."

I crossed over after a few blocks and noticed "Tulane" shadowing me on the other side. I loitered against a building and after a few minutes "Tulane" crossed over. He approached furtively. "Excuse me, but are you new here?"

I admitted I was.

He stuck out his hand. "My name is Richard, Richard Wilkie. I'm new here, too."

I shook his hand. "How ya doin?"

"I…I was wondering if you had eaten yet."

I said I hadn't and wondered what was going on.

"Would you like to eat with me? I know a great place for sea food."

How lonely is this guy? Is this a pick up? "Yeah, I suppose so."

We walked down a side street and stopped at a sidewalk café. I figured nothing could happen if we ate outside, so I was glad when he suggested it.

While we were waiting for our orders, he told me he had arrived in New Orleans a week earlier to get ready for graduate work in History at Tulane. He had graduated from Iowa State in the spring, *magna cum laude*. He was from Mason City, Iowa; had three sisters and a brother, all older; his father was deceased, but had run a farm along with his mother, whose health was failing; he was a Republican who hated Nixon; and a big fan of the Vikings and Twins.

I edged in that I was from North Dakota and had graduated from Minot State. That was about all he could have learned about me because he did most of the talking.

I studied him. His hair was a thinning black that was short and combed forward on his head. He had brown eyes, which were his best feature. He had jug ears, prominent nostrils, rough skin that looked like he had had bad acne, tombstone teeth, and a dimple in his chin. I wouldn't call him ugly, just say he was unprepossessing.

The prawns and crawfish he had urged on me were great, so succulent, so Creole with cayenne, garlic, onions, celery, peppers, tomatoes over white rice. I had eaten crawfish before out of our river, but they were nothing compared to those that evening.

As we finished, Richard announced that he would pay, but I wouldn't have it. A guy paying for my meal—No.

I couldn't think of a reason to shake Richard so we walked Bourbon together. It seemed he had been in all the strip clubs, seen all the exotic dancers, the topless and bottomless girls, the intimate reviews. He would describe each club as we passed, asking if I wanted to go in. I'd seen enough in San Francisco, so I kept saying no.

Finally, we came to a club that featured belly dancing. He hadn't seen the show, so I gave in. We entered and sat at the bar that surrounded an elevated stage. There were other patrons at the bar and tables. I ordered milk and Richard had a Coke. The prices were exorbitant.

Some Middle Eastern music began, the lights dimmed over the patrons and brightened over the stage. A woman, maybe forty, with long dark hair came out, dressed in a red bra with silver trim; a sheer red skirt trimmed in silver, especially around the beltline; a red chiffon scarf on each wrist; and finger cymbals. Her feet were bare.

It's not really belly dancing; it's mostly hip movements with some movement of the rib cage and shoulders. Whatever it was mesmerized the mostly male audience. If that woman had wanted any of us to follow her to the Casbah, we would have.

Toward the second half of her dance, Richard nudged me. "This is great."

Then the woman started going to each patron at the bar, danced in front of him, kneeled, and pushed his face between her rather large breasts. She did the same to the next and the next. Eventually, she got to me. She danced. I tried to look into her eyes, but failed, and then my face was between her breasts.

A fusion of smells: her perfume, something musky, a whiff of perspiration, and almost hidden—a hint of harems.

But what was the most interesting thing was the hardness of her breasts. I had felt breasts before; they were soft, smooth, supple, lovely things. The breasts I felt that night were smooth, but they were hard, as if human skin had been mounted on a melon.

She stood in front of Richard, whose face tilted up expectantly, then she wrinkled her nose and passed on to the next man.

I couldn't look at Richard. When the dancer had finished the ring, we left. On the sidewalk, he just said, "Good night, Chris" and headed toward Canal.

What could I say? He'd probably been rejected by women before and, unfortunately, would be again. But if a Bourbon Street dancer won't let you smell her breasts for money, you are in a sad place.

"Good night, Richard."

I waited until the crowd swallowed him. After crossing Canal, I tossed a five into Mama's box, got my usual response, and finished my journal and cards. I neglected Jeffers, the Bible, and my prayers.

DAY EIGHT

There's a song (Bobby Darin did a version) that begins, "New York on Sunday; Big city takin' a nap." The same applied to New Orleans in August 1970.

I was out of bed early and walked up and down Canal Street, bustling six days a week, not so much on the Sabbath. They must have liked hotels in New Orleans because they had just about every flavor and variety, some in big new buildings, some in the smaller ones that were older, but looking more like Frenchified, balconied hostelries. Walgreen's, liquor stores, "Drink Coca Cola," burger joints, coffee shops, Chinese food, "Pralines," shoe stores, clothing stores, jewelry stores—all yelled out, "Don't spend all your money on Bourbon Street!"

I walked over to Bourbon. In the bright sunshine the patina of a happy, wild, "anything goes" atmosphere had fallen away, and I saw buildings in need of repairs, in need of paint, in need of owners. With the artificial light turned off, and the sunlight eliminating any shadows, much of Bourbon Street looked shabby and forlorn.

St. Louis Cemetery #1 was located at Basin and St. Louis. I went in. The vaults were above ground and I walked between them. There were crosses; plaques that read "MOTHER" or "FATHER" or other things; fleur-de-lis; urns; statues—angels, saints, the Virgin; some with fresh flowers, but most were disintegrating without floral tributes. There were a few vaults that had deteriorated so much it was difficult to say what they were. Some were surrounded by wrought iron fences, but they didn't keep the vaults from crumbling away any faster than the unfenced ones.

A Mass had ended at Our Lady of Guadalupe Church on Rampart Street, and as I left the cemetery, I was surrounded by the Catholic faithful. One older gentleman must have seen me at the gate because he stopped me.

"Are ya'll a visitor to our fair city?"

"Yes, I am."

"And Ah assume ya'll are interested in the tombs?"

"Yes."

"Remember they are above ground more from their heritage in Spanish and French tradition than because of the water table." He walked away without giving me a chance to question him.

The crowd thinned out as I made my way back to Bourbon. I turned toward Canal, and my daylight trip of disappointment continued as the sunlight exposed even more buildings, weary with age.

A street person approached; he was selling the *NOLA Express*, the New Orleans underground newspaper. I bought a copy. Like the other underground newspapers of the period, *NOLA* was filled with obscenities, pornographic drawings and pictures, anti-Americanism, anti-imperialism, anti-racism, anti-Vietnam War, anti-police, anti-establishment, ads for free food and housing for itinerant street people, veiled references to available drugs, protest times and places, the usual hippie, radical, druggie nonsense. I looked through it and threw the paper in a refuse container on Canal.

When I walked into my usual café for breakfast, I bought a Sunday *New Orleans Times-Picayune* and an out-of-date *New York Times*. After a little repartee with Lorraine, she left me alone to enjoy my pancakes and syrup, link sausages, crispy hash browns, orange juice, and milk. In between bites I read the newspapers. Jim Morrison of the Doors was being tried in Miami on charges of "lewd and lascivious behavior"; Steven Stills, who had performed with Buffalo Springfield and Crosby, Stills & Nash, had been arrested for drug possession; Patricia Palinkas had become the first woman to play professional football as a placekick holder for the Orlando Panthers, a semi-pro team; there was trouble in Northern Ireland and South Africa; in July a battle between the 101st Airborne and the North Vietnamese had ended, and Vietnam was relatively quiet; and a movie called *Patton* had opened in a theatre across the river. As I recall, it was the Tower Theater in Gretna.

I had read Ladislas Farago's *Patton: Ordeal and Triumph*, a biography mostly favorable to General Patton, but also depicting some personal flaws, during my senior year of college. He became one of my heroes, and I had finished a couple more biographies since then.

I hustled back to my room, freshened up, and headed for the Lee Circle bus stop. I rode a nearly empty bus across the Great New Orleans Bridge, got off, and still had some blocks to walk.

The theater building actually had a tower on the outside. I bought my ticket and went in. The movie was more than half over. A harried Army chaplain was talking with George C. Scott, who was playing General Patton. The General wanted a weather prayer so that the skies would clear and he could kill Germans. The chaplain was doubtful, but came up with one that began, "Almighty and most merciful Father, we humbly beseech Thee of Thy great goodness to restrain this immoderate weather with which we have had to contend. Grant us fair weather for battle." The clouds cleared away and the battle turned in favor of the Americans.

I loved it.

In the movie Patton's Third Army helps end the Battle of the Bulge. He heads toward Germany, but is halted as the High Command gives precedence to Patton's rival, British Field Marshal Sir Bernard Law Montgomery. The war ends; Patton is depressed. His friend General Omar Bradley, played by Karl Malden, tries to cheer him up, and they agree to meet for a meal. As Patton walks off with his white bull terrier Willie, the camera is on him, and there is a voice-over done by Scott: "For over a thousand years, Roman conquerors returning from the wars enjoyed the honor of a triumph - a tumultuous parade. The conqueror rode in a triumphal chariot, the dazed prisoners walking in chains before him. Sometimes his children, robed in white, stood with him in the chariot, or rode the trace horses. A slave stood behind the conqueror, holding a golden crown, and whispering in his ear a warning: that all glory is fleeting."

The movie ended; tears streamed down my cheeks. I was hooked.

I wiped my eyes, went to the lobby, bought a large popcorn and Coke, and walked back in.

If I thought it was a great movie before, the opening scene elevated "great" to "my favorite movie ever," surpassing John Wayne's *The Searchers*.

A huge forty-eight star American flag dominates the screen. Scott as Patton walks up some steps in back of the stage and comes forward. He is in full-dress uniform of dark brown jacket, lighter brown jodhpur pants, shined general's helmet and knee-length boots, beribboned, a chest full of medals and one around his neck, a brown swagger stick, holding black gloves, an ivory-handle pistol in his holster. This man is a soldier.

A bugle plays; Patton salutes. The bugle stops. "Be seated." There is a sound of moving chairs. Then Patton begins, "Now I want you to remember that no bastard ever won a war by dying for his country. He won it by making the other poor dumb bastard die for his country."

This can't be happening. An American movie that actually thinks America should win her wars. When we're getting ready to abandon South Vietnam.

Later in the speech: "Men, all this stuff you've heard about America not wanting to fight, wanting to stay out of the war, is a lot of horse dung. Americans traditionally love to fight. All real Americans love the sting of battle. When you were kids, you all admired the champion marble shooter, the fastest runner, big league ball players, the toughest boxers. Americans love a winner and will not tolerate a loser. Americans play to win all the time. I wouldn't give a hoot in hell for a man who lost and laughed. That's why Americans have never lost, and will never lose a war... because the very thought of losing is hateful to Americans."

This is great!

Patton takes command of the American forces completely humiliated at the Battle of the Kasserine Pass in North Africa. After rebuilding the troops in his image, he leads them to a victory over the German Afrika Corps of General Erwin Rommel at El Guettar.

As he watches the progress of the battle through binoculars and sees it turn in his favor, he smiles and says, "Rommel...you magnificent bastard. I read your book!"

Patton and some of his staff visit an ancient battle site of the Third Punic War in which the Romans obliterated the Carthaginians. Patton reveals his belief in reincarnation: "The Carthaginians defending the city were attacked by three Roman legions. The Carthaginians were proud and brave but they couldn't hold. They were massacred. Arab women stripped them of their tunics and their swords and lances. The soldiers lay naked in the sun. Two thousand years ago. I was here."

Patton and Montgomery engage in an undeclared competition to see who can do the most liberating of cities and territory in Sicily; Patton wins, and Montgomery bears a grudge. Patton is greatly affected by his battle losses and slaps a soldier suffering from battle fatigue, calling him a "yellow bastard" and a "god-damned coward."

For that incident and some undiplomatic references made during press conferences, Patton is removed from command. Afraid he will miss out on the invasion of France, Patton makes peace with Generals Bradley and Eisenhower and is given the command of the Third Army.

The Third Army charges across France, liberating cities, towns, and villages, but a lack of fuel halts it temporarily. Refueled just in time, his Third Army helps relieve the Americans holding out in Bastogne in the Battle of the Bulge. Patton drives on to Germany, but the war ends.

Patton hates the Soviet Communists and continually insults them. He gets in trouble at news conferences again, especially when he says former Nazis with experience and know-how should be put in positions to help rebuild Germany. He is relieved again and says good-bye to his staff in a scene with subdued, but real, emotion.

He avoids being killed by a runaway ox-cart and goes for his walk with Willie.

I stayed for two more showings. That afternoon and early evening, I lived on popcorn, Patton, and pop.

When I caught the bus, I was the only rider. I got off at Lee Circle and walked to the "Y." I wrote in my journal, but left the postcards, Jeffers, and the Bible until the morning.

I included in my prayers a plea for victory in Vietnam.

DAY NINE

I knew it would be a great day.

I looked for a happy poem by Jeffers, not an easy thing, and ended up reading "The Beauty of Things," which contains the lines:

"To feel and speak the astonishing beauty of things—
Earth, stone, and water,
Beast, man and woman, sun, moon, and stars...
The natural beauty, is the sole business of poetry."

The Bible was easier. I turned to the Psalms and read Psalm 64, the one Patton quoted in an voice-over in the movie. In part, it read:

"Oh, God, thou art my God; early will I seek thee: my soul thirsteth for thee, my flesh longeth for thee in a dry and thirsty land, where no water is...

My soul followeth hard after thee: thy right hand upholdeth me.

But those that seek my soul, to destroy it, shall go into the lower parts of the earth.

They shall fall by the sword: they shall be a portion for foxes."

I wrote out my two postcards, followed my routine of dropping them and the Saturday ones in the out box on the front desk, and hit the streets.

I asked Lorraine for ideas on a breakfast and ended up with a three-egg omelette, consisting of honey ham, apple-wood bacon, breakfast sausage, cheddar cheese; crispy hash browns; milk; and grapefruit juice for a change.

I walked down to 2 Canal Street and gazed up at the thirty-three story skyscraper that housed the World Trade Center. Inside were various foreign consulates and the Port of New Orleans headquarters.

Just up Canal stood the Rivergate, a recently finished, large reinforced concrete building. According to a brochure I picked up, architects from all over the world came to study its dual curved roof, which, viewed from a certain angle, made it look like a space craft out of science fiction to me.

I was more interested in the river. I walked a block, sat on the levee, and watched the water, the boats, the barges, the ships, some of the lifeblood of New Orleans. I was especially intrigued by the ones flying foreign flags and wished that I knew them all.

McDonald's was a few blocks up Canal, near my breakfast place. I felt like a good ol' American meal and ordered a Big Mac, large fries, and a large Coke. A lot of the talk around me was weather—there was a disturbance in the Gulf which they hoped would not develop into a hurricane.

After eating I walked back to the Quarter. I could tell my legs were a lot more muscular than when I started the trip.

The practice of Voodoo came to Louisiana after it had been established by slaves and workers from West Africa and Haiti. In Louisiana Voodoo blended with Catholicism, so the typical Voodoo beliefs in magic amulets, charms, herbs, poisons, and powders were intermixed with crucifixes, holy candles, holy water, and incense.

Over the years Voodoo had become a commercial success in New Orleans, with shops selling Voodoo dolls (the kind you stick pins in and your opponent gets sick or dies); amulets; "gris-gris" bags containing verses, sometimes from the Koran, and small objects unique to the owner and which can be used for good luck or as black magic against an enemy; and charms.

I visited Voodoo shops on Bourbon, Royal, North Rampart, St. Claude, Dumaine, and St. Peter, one of them even named after the Voodoo Queen, Marie Laveau.

Many of them had imported the figure of Baron Samedi from Haitian Voodoo in the form of a plastic skeleton in a top hat, tuxedo, dark glasses, cotton plug in his nostrils and sometimes with a cigar clenched in his teeth, and a glass of rum in his bony fingers.

Most of the shops were cluttered with things for tourists to take home and tell their friends to "Beware, that's Voodoo." I didn't think any of the places were authentically Voodoo. If any of the owners were trying to put a hex on me to buy something, they failed.

After a rest in my room and another McDonald's run, I went back into the Quarter.

It was a more subdued crowd than Friday's or Saturday's, and the whole show was starting to drag—nothing new, nothing worth seeing.

I was standing on a street corner when an accented voice said behind me, "How ya doin'?" *Is that accent French? Is it Spanish?*

"All right."

"gap-tooth" and "beard" closed in on either side.

"You not from here."

"No."

"Where you from?"

"Up north, North Dakota."

"Where you stayin'?"

"On Canal. Sheraton Hotel," I lied.

"You don' look like no Sheraton type." "beard" finally spoke.

Silence.

"gap-tooth" said, "You lookin' for action?"

"What?"

"Grass, smack, upper, downer, cotton."

I knew what the first four were. "What's cotton?"

"Cotton? You don' know what cotton is?" "gap-tooth" stared at me. "beard" sniggered. "Cotton is poontang, ginch, *cocotte*, a pro, a workin' girl, a whore. You, her, *aborder*."

"Oh."

"You want some cotton?"

"No, I don't think so. No, thank you."

"Don' make up your mind 'til you seen the merchandise." He nodded to "beard," who stepped into a bar and came out with the girl I'd seen with them the other night.

"Dis is Cherie. Cherie the Cherry. She be good to you. So good you tink you in heaven. Jus' fifty dollar."

Cherie was wearing high-heeled black boots almost to her knees, a short zebra-patterned skirt that revealed almost all of her thighs, a white silky blouse which showed she had no bra, a couple gold chain necklaces, and a couple gold bracelets. She was average height, but how much did the boots add? Thin, almost skinny. Her black hair was shoulder-length and what facial skin I could see had the same olive tint that Mrs. Saunders had. However, most of her skin and her lips were covered with so much make-up, she looked almost like a clown or someone trying to appear Voodoo to impress the tourists.

I tried to "look" beneath the make-up. She was pretty, not cute or beautiful, but a girl whose face men would respond to. No feature too big, too small, an attractive face. And then I studied her eyes. She was staring at me, almost defiantly, and didn't turn away when I stared back. I moved a little closer, and even in the neon lighting, I saw that she had ebony eyes.

When I mean ebony, that's exactly what I mean—black as black can be. Pick up a piece of coal and you'll know what I mean.

Her eyes were hypnotic. They were pulling part of my soul towards her…

"Well, fifty buck and she your playting for a half hour. How 'bout it?"

The girl's black diamond eyes stared at me, then stared down the street; she shifted her stance and repeated the process. She didn't care one way or the other.

I was torn. I didn't want to be with a whore, but I was attracted to her. There was some little thing under that crust of makeup…something I needed to see…to understand. Finally, I said, "No, thanks" and stepped into Bourbon.

"No big deal. Meybe some udder time when you in the mood. C'mon, *podna*; you, too, T-Cherie. We try anoder corner. *Allon!*"

The three of them walked to the end of the block and Cherie went into another bar. I stood across from them and watched. After a couple tries—success. A college student from Minnesota or so his shirt said took one look at the girl, and his hand was already on his wallet, until "gap-tooth" told him to put it away.

They walked to their original corner and I shadowed them. They turned and walked a couple blocks, "gap-tooth" was doing most of the talking, the kid answering in monosyllables. Cherie walked quietly with "beard," but brushed into the kid every so often. I was a phantom on the opposite side of the street, but close: I didn't want to lose them. "gap-tooth's" boisterous voice made me want a large dirty sock to shove down his throat.

They turned into a…—it wasn't an alley; it was more like a foot-path between buildings. I had to wait, then I squeezed my way down the path until I saw them at the back of a long, two-story wooden building that had once been white, but even in the moonlight showed up dappled white and black. A small yard with stunted trees and a tiny yard light and almost entirely enclosed by buildings completed the picture.

The four of them mounted the rickety steps, and every one of her steps brought more hate to my soul. There was a balcony with eight doors and windows. "gap-tooth" produced a key and they walked in. A light showed on the window shade, but even when I walked around a bit, I could see nothing.

Pretty soon "gap-tooth" and "beard" came out. "gap-tooth" locked the door. "Thirty minute, dat's all," he yelled. I squeezed my way back to the street, crossed over, and continued down the block. "gap-tooth" and "beard" laughed their way toward Bourbon.

I walked back and worked my way into the small yard. A lighted window. A locked door. Inside, a bed. I didn't want to think about it and fled to the lights of Bourbon.

"gap tooth" and "beard" had disappeared. I stood across from their corner and waited as the tourists passed on their appointed or un-appointed rounds. Maybe fifteen, maybe twenty minutes, and the two emerged from the bar Cherie had first been in.

"gap-tooth" shook his head, slapped "beard" on the shoulder and laughed. So did "beard." "gap-tooth" left. "*C'est bon?*"

"For true." "beard" lounged against the building. He pulled out a pack of cigarettes, green and white, probably Salems. He lit up, blew smoke into the street, and stood there. I couldn't leave.

Ten minutes later the Minnesota kid walked into the light, looking sheepish, like he hoped no one from his home town would see him and guess that he had been fornicating.

I ached across the street. Eventually, Cherie and "gap-tooth" appeared. "gap-tooth" grabbed "beard" around the shoulders and shook him, saying, "*Bon ami.*" Cherie disappeared into the bar.

I endured the same sad selling of a human being once more, but it was too painful, and I headed for Lee Circle. I gave Mama Calbasa ten dollars because I had missed her the previous night.

I walked past the neglected front desk, took the lazy elevator, and walked down the lonely hall. I wrote in my journal, but not much. Short postcards. A warm shower with plenty of shampoo and soap.

As I was getting out of the shower, a young man came in. He was the first guy who'd been in the shower with me the whole time I'd been there. "Hi, I'm leavin' tomorrow."

"That's nice." I dried off and went to my room. And thought. My brain wasn't working. Except for the image of ebony eyes.

I went back to the shower room, which was empty. I took a cold shower. Guys had told me it worked. It didn't. I went back to my room.

I sat on my bed in the darkness and tried to clear out all conscious thought. Ebony eyes faded. Everything faded. I don't know how long it was, but suddenly, I was Buddha under the Sacred Bo Tree—I knew. Something changed inside me. Jeffers ran through my head: "Corruption has never been compulsory." Somewhere in St. John, people confronted Jesus with a woman taken in adultery, a sexual sin. He said he did not condemn her, but that she shouldn't sin anymore. If Cherie stayed in New Orleans; she could never stop sinning. I had to get her out.

"gap-tooth" was waiting by the bar, but he wasn't conversing with prospective customers. He looked around the corner and Cherie and "beard" appeared. I quickly crossed the street.

I got close. "I think I'd like some cotton now."

A smile exposed his gap even more. "So you aks for cotton when the store she closed."

He stood there. Cherie and "beard" came up. I slumped my shoulders; he had all the good cards.

"You want somethin'?" He stared without smiling.

"Cotton...Her." I pointed.

He stared hard for ten seconds, pulling out and lighting a Winston, then burst into a loud laugh. "I jus' foolin'. She do extra tonight." Cherie didn't seem to care.

We walked a familiar route.

Her room was rectangular with the door and a window on one side and two windows opposite them. Worn, brown carpet; light brown paint, no curtains, just shades; an overhead fan with two lights, both with maybe sixty-watt bulbs, so the place was dim. A small table, two kitchen chairs, a little fridge and stove, an aged sink which I saw had rust stains. Something with handles and doors, which I guessed was her clothes closet. One corner had what must have been the world's smallest bathroom. But then the bed. It was huge, king-size, for certain. There was even a gauzy canopy. The pillows were large and plentiful, but the only covering on the bed was a fresh white sheet.

Overlooking the bed was a large picture—Cherie lying on her side, nude on the bed, smiling at the camera, exposing her breasts, but with the sheet strategically placed across her hips.

"You ready?" "gap-tooth" could have been "bull-horn." He looked at Cherie.

"Yeah." She went to the back where a partition had been arranged to make a small dressing area.

"beard" headed for the door. "gap-tooth" turned to me; his voice was quieter, but very firm. "Fifty dollar." He held out his hand. I paid with a Grant. He smiled. "Rich man, huh?"

"Not really."

He pointed to a large clock by the door I hadn't seen. "When we leave, the time she start. You have thirty minute. If you not done, two dollar a minute. No rough stuff, no biting, no hitting, no strangling, just about anyting else go; she even play nurse and wash your *bibitte* for you." His laugh filled the room.

"But if Cherie say to stop, you stop. Nowhere in dis city be safe for you, you not stop." He quickly pulled a knife and the blade switched open; he pointed it at me and smiled. "Time she start now." He closed the door, locked it, and two sets of footsteps receded.

There was some movement behind the partition, but no Cherie. I walked around and saw the back windows were padlocked with a lock and flange. *If there's a fire, she'll burn to death.*

"You're not ready; you're wasting time." She wasn't happy.

I turned and Cherie was standing by the bed. She'd turned a light on above the bed so everything was a pink bath. Her hair had been combed, the makeup was garish with dark blue eye shadow and shiny, redder-than-blood lips, and she reeked of some kind of perfume they didn't sell on Fifth Avenue. She walked toward me, at least a foot shorter than my six-two.

She wore a diaphanous pink whisper that revealed a lot more than it covered. I could see she was braless. She had on the briefest panties I'd ever seen, pink, of course; and she was wearing pink high heels.

She was a little unsteady on the heels, but she made it and took my hand. "C'mon, baby. I'll be good to you." She led me over to the bed. "What do you want?" It was a hard voice.

"What?"

"What kind of sex turns you on? Regular, oral, anal, 69? Anything you want, baby." More grit had been added to her voice.

"Let's go, slow poke. You only got twenty-five minutes. Get your boots off." She was sounding like a drill sergeant.

I sat there.

"What's wrong? Do you like boys?"

"Yeah, I mean no, I mean not that way; some of my best friends are boys."

"Well, what is it then?"

"I want to talk to you."

"Oh, *merde*, another missionary."

"I'm paying. What do you care?"

"You're right. Seven minutes gone already, and I didn't have to do a thing. Keep goin', cowboy."

I turned so we were face to face. "I like you. I think we should get out of this place."

Her face retained its hardness.

She leaned away and I saw her bare breasts, small, but perfectly shaped—evoking mystical promises, nameless joys, and the entrance to a feminine world experienced in a separate universe of soft love; giving solace and strength to the infant, the lover, the husband, the ill, the lost, the aged, the dying; a soft strength in a hard world.

Except the mysteries and joys could be lost or maybe not experienced at all. Lonely souls walked the earth continually without love.

I thought for Cherie the promises could still be fulfilled: she could go home and start anew, renewing her soul, renewing her life.

But not as a whore.

I took her hands in mine. Soft, smooth. I bowed my head. Tears dropped on her hands.

She tried to take her hands back, but I wouldn't let her. "Let go!"

I looked into her eyes. "I like you, Cherie. I want to get you home."

A glacier will push down a valley to the sea, and when it reaches the sea, it doesn't stop. Some of it starts to hang over the water, and it's still part of the glacier, but then an inch more, a fraction of an inch, some little thing, and it breaks off and it's something else, an ice burg, and it goes its own way. All it had to do was break off.

Ebony eyes were looking at me and the face they were in, the mask of paint and pain, crumbled before me, and she was crying in my arms.

After she stopped, she said, "I do want to go home." Her voice was soft and unsure; all hardness had melted with the tears.

I told her I had a plan and I'd get her out the next night. I lied; I had no plan.

We had sixteen minutes left, and she talked to me as intimately as if I had been her best friend, a trusted relative, but I was certain she had no one.

Her name was not Cherie; it was Marcéline Marie Jarreau, and she had grown up in Pointe Coupee Parish, northwest of Baton Rouge. After she graduated from high school, she wanted to become a beautician and someday own her own shop. Her father had died, and her mother wanted her to stay and help with three younger siblings, but her mind was made up. She was going to New Orleans. Her mother suggested the smaller cities of Baton Rouge or Shreveport, but no; it was New Orleans or nothing.

She took a bus, leaving a family of four in tears. So was she.

Learning came easy, and she was hired the day after graduation. No one in her family could afford to come.

She started sending money home, and she exchanged letters with her mother and two sisters. Then she lost her job: the shop was closing.

Her next job paid less; her money home was periodic; her letters less frequent. That job ended, too, when the owner died in a car accident.

She took a job as a waitress on Canal Street. She took a much smaller apartment. She was so busy and so shy, she had no friends,

One evening "gap-tooth" and "beard" came in. (She called them Etienne and Louis, but those names are too good for those bastards, which she also called them.) She waited on them. The next night they came in again and asked for her. She was a little flattered. A week later "gap-tooth" came in by himself. He said after she got off, he could show her the French Quarter; he knew it well. Foolishly, she went with him, against all her instincts, but she was so lonely.

He said he had to get some money from his room, so they came up to the very room we were in. As they walked in, "beard" stepped from behind the door and put his hand over her mouth.

"Those Cajun bastards gagged me, stripped me, and took turns...I was a virgin." She was choking on tears; I had my own to deal with.

"They fixed everything up with my boss; they collected my last pay check and told him I had decided to work for them. They got my address from my mother's last letter, still in my purse, and brought everything over here.

"After they did everything sexually possible to me and hit me every day in my belly and kidneys so it wouldn't show if the cops came, I knew I was ruined, not fit for any man, except the trash that comes in here. I was filth, as bad as the men who paid for me.

"One night after they made me be with a man and a woman at the same time, I was in this bed, thinking of home, and I actually, physically, felt my dreams die...Is that possible?"

"Maybe, but they can live again, if you are strong and have faith. We'll find them."

"Time's up!" We both jumped. The key went into the lock. "Marci-Marie" scooted into the bathroom. (I had decided to call her "Marci-Marie"; "Cherie" was a ghost of the Past.)

"Done, I see. *Bon*. And all dressed. Was she worth it?"

"Yeah."

"What?" He looked to his left. Marci-Marie had come out of the bathroom, still in her "working outfit." "gap-tooth" yelled, "*Pouponer!*" and pounded on the wall. Marci-Marie disappeared.

"My fren', you have to leave." He shoved me toward the door. "Maybe you like my Cherie agin sometime? Tink about it."

I waited in the yard to make certain he wasn't beating on Marci-Marie, then I walked to the "Y" under a full moon and fell into bed with my clothes on.

I had to come up with a plan.

DAY TEN

I woke up with a headache. And a head full of hate.

I couldn't have eaten breakfast if it were my last meal. I sat on the bed with my head full and my stomach empty.

Finally, I decided to go legal. I found a police station on Royal and reported my story to a detective. He looked preoccupied, or maybe he was just amused and had no time for me.

"So you say you spent fifty dollars to talk to a young woman in sexy lingerie for a half hour?"

"Yes, but that's not the point. I paid for sex." I could see this would not be good.

"Did you have sex?"

"No."

"But you want me to file a report there is prostitution on Bourbon Street."

"Yes, because there is."

"The men, Etienne and Louis."

"Yes."

"Their last names?"

"I don't know."

"Their addresses?"

"I don't know."

"The address where the alleged non-sexual prostitution occurred?"

A half dozen detectives who had been listening burst out laughing; the detective smiled at his own wit.

"I don't know, but I can show you."

"O.K., sir. When you're next on Bourbon and you're propositioned, report it to one of our patrols there. The officers are fully trained and will be glad to help. Thank you…Good morning." He turned his swivel chair, showered by more laughter.

I crossed Canal and walked to the federal building on Lafayette Square. I waited two hours to talk to an agent, and all I got was—"I'm sorry, sir; if it was prostitution the way you described, it's not a federal crime. Try the local police."

I decided to go civic. I walked along Camp to the Chamber of Commerce building. After waiting half an hour, I was ushered into an office with a large desk, large chairs, and a large window. I declined a cup of coffee and went into my story. The large man behind the desk was aghast. My tale was unbelievable; he was certain I was mistaken. When I stuck to what I had reported, he said, "The Chamber really can't get involved in such matters. Please see the local police." Ushering me out, he offered me some free tickets which I declined.

I was on my own.

I picked at a hamburger steak dinner I shouldn't have ordered.

"Not feelin' well, Dakota?"

"I guess not." I left most of my food and a tip.

At the cash register Lorraine gave me a small pack of Pepto Bismol.

In my room I came up with a plan: when "gap-tooth" and "beard" took us up to the room, I'd pull out my machete and hack them to death. I threw that plan away: I wanted justice—eye for eye, tooth for tooth, life for life—but they hadn't killed Marci-Marie, at least not technically, so the justice was missing from the plan.

At two to one, overpowering them and stealing Marci-Marie seemed improbable; that plan wilted.

Something in their drinks, they fall asleep, we run away—*but I never see them drink.*

I couldn't think; I lay down.

After a rest I walked down to the banana docks and watched the men work, and the Mississippi roll on to the sea.

Back in my room I took out my Testament. If Jesus were confronted with my problem, how would He react?

I had to discount any miracles. He could have turned the Cajuns into pigs and sent them over a cliff or withered them away like the fig tree, but miracles were beyond my capabilities.

Maybe He would have spoken about turning the other cheek, loving your enemies, forgiving those who sin against you 490 times, but that wasn't going to happen. Where would that leave Marci-Marie?

He made a whip of cords and chased the moneylenders and animal sellers out of the Temple. That was a good start, but a whip wouldn't stop the Cajuns.

After His cousin John the Baptist was beheaded, Jesus did nothing more than ask his Apostles to accompany him to a quiet place. No actual retribution—the killers got away with it. Maybe the Cajuns would lose it all on Judgment Day, but Marci-Marie was never going to have to turn another trick.

I put the Testament away.

Would Mickey Mantle not play through pain? Would John Wayne run away from a fight? Would General Patton retreat?

I went to Canal Street and ate four large slices of pepperoni pizza and hot peppers. It was going to be a long night.

I took a different way to the brothel, approaching it from the opposite direction. I squeezed into the yard and walked to the backside of the building. Wooden ladders dropped from the windows of each room, poor substitutes for fire escapes.

A plan developed: after "gap-tooth" and "beard" left, we would pack Marci-Marie's things, break a window, climb down the ladder, and make our way to the "Y." I'd sneak her in; we'd be safe for the night; and we'd go out to the Honda shop in the morning. I'd take her home to her new life.

I approached my plan from every direction. If the Cajuns left, it was perfect.

I went over to an Arcade and played pinball, wasting time. Then I watched other guys waste time. Then I took my turn wasting time again. And so it went.

As dark began shadowing the streets, I walked the narrow confines of Bourbon. "gap-tooth" and "beard" weren't in their regular trolling site, so I waited. The tourists and street people all had a certain familiarity by then.

The Cajuns came around the corner laughing. They took out their red and white and green and white packs and lit up. They laughed some more and strolled toward Canal Street. I ran in front of a car, got the horn and a curse, and caught up with them. "Etienne!"

The bigger man turned. "How you know my name?"

"Uh, Cherie told me last night."

"That little *cowan* talk too much, *grosse beuche!*"

"Meybe we fix?" "beard" could speak sometimes.

"I want some cotton. Fifty for Cherie tonight."

"You too late; she busy." He started to walk away; "beard" followed.
I moved in front of them. "I'll wait."

He smiled. "You wait long time. She pullin' a train tonight."

"beard" sniggered.

I stood in his way. "Ten professors from that 'versity in Austin. Then she get a break. No more tonight."

I felt an urge to kill him right there, but I had no weapon. My pocket knife and boot knife wouldn't be that effective. He saw the hate in my face. He took a big drag on a Winston and blew the stream of smoke from his gap right into my face. He was not afraid.

He must have seen something else because he spoke to "beard" and the Cajuns reversed direction. "See us tomorr' night, *bon ami.*" He smiled.

I watched them turn the corner. I followed and wormed my way between the buildings. They were seated at the foot of the stairs, smoking, joking, and laughing softly.

They were on guard.

I couldn't look at the window on the second floor where I knew Marci-Marie was...

I didn't want to think about it.

Loneliness. People. Neon. Streetcar tracks. Five dollars. Fewer people. Less light. Emptiness. She's dying inside, and so am I.

A cactus clot of desperate sadness clawed the inside of my chest all night.

DAY ELEVEN

D-Day or Die!

 I decided it was a better idea to leave the bike where it was and we could go get it. If I brought it to the "Y" and parked it, it might be stolen or "towed" by the cops.

A big breakfast and a happy Lorraine. She made me feel so good, I doubled her tip—it would be my last one.

I tried to walk off the worry about the one flaw in my plan—what if the Cajuns didn't leave? I was keeping away from the Vieux Carré and had just left getting a closer look at the Texaco Building when I chanced upon an older building with a plaque on it. The plaque indicated I was on the outskirts of Storyville, the old New Orleans red-light district from pre-World War I days. Many early jazz men had frequented the cat houses, and when they were shut down, the men and jazz moved with the Black Migration north to Kansas City, St. Louis, and Chicago.

I didn't need any reminding about prostitution. I walked to Congo Square, formerly a place for slaves to enjoy themselves and set up their own markets. I lost myself on the grass and in the trees. Watching the Negroes and their children, I could see how they were a community unto themselves: their speech, their music, some of their kids' games, but especially the togetherness that seemed much closer than that of white groups I had seen.

That group-solidarity was, I thought, probably a good thing, but could whites be included without destroying, or at least modifying, what made it "black"? Could we ever have a Martin Luther King-color blind society?

Back on Canal, I went to the bank and cashed in all my traveler's checks. I was glad Mom had insisted I take more than I thought I needed—Mama Calbasa and Marci-Marie I had never figured on.

Late afternoon; a supper of four large slices of pizza and hot peppers, my power meal; early evening; time dragging; dusk.

Mama had made her nightly appearance across Canal and near St. Charles; I crossed and dropped a five. "Thank yuh, sir. You is considerate."

"I guess I won't see you anymore. I'll be leavin' tomorrow."

"Well, good luck, son. Mama give yuh luck to hep yuh on your way. Here." She held out a child's toy, a small black cat. "Touch it." I obeyed. "Now Mama really bring yuh luck."

"Thank you, Mama." I dropped another five, but she just smiled.

I worked my way to Bourbon. Wednesdays were slow, but the neon beckoned the unwary tourists. I took up a position opposite the Cajuns' corner. They weren't there, but I didn't expect them to be out that early—they were like bats and didn't see the light of day, or maybe they were vampires and sunlight would kill them. I chuckled at my wit, but quickly stopped because a woman tourist stared at me and because the situation I wanted to end wasn't funny.

Time passed. The sky grew darker, but the lights seemed brighter. People came and went. But not the Cajuns. I walked down the block— maybe they were on the other corner—but I tried to keep an eye back where they might appear, and I didn't want anyone to beat me. No Cajuns.

I started to panic. *What if they don't show?* I hustled back. Time dragged. I hated it. People laughed. I hated them.

Then they were there.

I ran across Bourbon. "Etienne!"

"Ah, *bon ami*. You wait for T-Cherie, huh? She your *beb* now?" "beard" laughed. "I think she work *cunja* on you, huh?" The laughter was louder. I hated it and them.

"I have fifty."

"But, bon ami, Cherie work so hard last night; meybe we give her rest, huh?" He smiled.

I stood there at Kerouac's washed-out bottom of America wanting to smash the Cajuns into a pulp with a sledge hammer. What would Jesus do? What would Martin Luther King and Rev. Saunders do?

"Jus' a joke. You got money; we got girl." He nodded at "beard," who went into the bar and came out with…Marci-Marie…or was she still Cherie—she was in electric blue and black, gaudy makeup, and looked sullen.

They walked ahead of me; the men smoked. At the little passageway, "gap-tooth" stood aside and said, "*bag daer*" and pointed. It was like he thought I'd never been there before.

We single-filed it through, crossed the weedy yard, and climbed to Cherie's room.

Marci-Marie went behind the partition and there were soft noises.

"gap-tooth" held out his hand. "Fifty." I paid and he folded the bill and put it in the breast pocket of his black leather vest. The small noises continued. He looked at the partition. "*Ca viens?*"

"*Bon.*"

He moved to the door where "beard" waited. He motioned me to follow. "beard" went out, but "gap-tooth" stood there until Marci-Marie came around the partition. "Thirty minute…and I tink we wait outside." He winked. "*Laissez les bon temps rouler.*" He locked the door.

The one thing that could go wrong had gone wrong. If I broke the glass, they would hear it and bust in.

I walked over to Marci-Marie. "Pack up."

"You have a plan?"

"Yes."

"Will it work?"

"Yes."

"Because if it doesn't, Etienne will cut our throats. He told me he's done it before."

"Get packed. One suitcase. Just what you need. And whisper." She walked to her closet. I went to the window. If I had brought a screwdriver, I could have taken the screws from the flange or maybe pried it up, although it looked like the screws were long ones. "Do you have a screw driver?" I whispered.

"No. Do you need it for your plan?"

"No, keep packing."

I took out my boot knife and tried the wood. It was dry and old. I started pushing the knife in and popping pieces of the wood out. Cutting, hacking, jabbing, slicing, thrusting, the ancient wood gave way. I could see the sides of the screws, but I still didn't dare try to pop the flange with my knife and chance breaking the blade.

Marci-Marie stood beside me, an old-fashioned metal suitcase with reinforced corners and a large handle that would never break off in her hand. She had a large purse or handbag with a long strap around her neck. "Hurry."

Wood chips, then wood chunks, then we were free. I tried to force the window up. It was stuck. *It can't be painted shut.* When I had checked, there was barely any paint anywhere on that entire side. I tried again. Nothing. I edged all around the window with my knife. I moved over. "Help me."

Marci-Marie put her hands on the wood. "Don't break the glass." She nodded. "On three." She nodded again. We pushed together and slowly the window inched up.

She went out first and negotiated the ladder to the ground. I followed with the suitcase, which was a lot heavier than I thought it would be.

No one on that side of the building or on the other. A run across the lot and then into the passageway. I checked the stairway—no one. The second-floor balcony was clear, also. Maybe they were both outside her door, waiting. I smiled. I took her hand. "Let's go." We sprinted across the lot—no cry of alarm.

The mouth of the passageway loomed black. Hellfire and little biscuits! It was the Devil himself. "gap-tooth" stepped into the yard, not comprehending, but reaching for his switchblade anyway and yelling, "Louis!"

I took the suitcase handle in both hands and swung it as hard as I could into his face. He went down and didn't move. We did.

If the tourists on Bourbon thought it unusual to see a man, a woman, and a suitcase running down the street, they didn't seem to care.

In the movies when someone is knocked out by a fist, a club, a gun, whatever, they're out for minutes, sometimes for hours. This wasn't the movies. By the time we reached Canal Street, the Cajuns were on our trail.

Luckily, the traffic wasn't that heavy, but we still had to weave our way across the broad strips of pavement and tracks. The Cajuns did the same and all of us were running on the sidewalk on the far side of Canal. If we turned on St. Charles and got away, they could figure out the one place we might be was the "Y" at the end of the street. We had to keep going.

Across Camp. Footsteps getting closer. Magazine was next. The Cajuns were gaining too fast.

"*Feet pue tan*! Stop you damn *galette*! You rotten *tortue*! You ugly *cowan*! I cut your face! I cut your *bibitte* off and feed alligator! *Pic kee toi*!"

We dodged around a big hump of black. Footsteps maybe ten feet behind. Loud in the night. Send her on ahead and make a last stand....

No footsteps; no cursing. I looked back. The Cajuns were flat on the sidewalk and not moving.

Marci-Marie came back. "What happened?"

"I don't know—a miracle?"

As we walked back, a woman's voice said, "Would yuh min' pushin' that trash inta the street?" It was Mama.

"But when they wake up, they'll kill you."

"Oh, I don't think so." She laughed and stood up. Out of two holsters attached to her belt, she pulled two revolvers; one had a long barrel like a Colt Peacemaker and one was a snub-nose .38. "Now hurry up. I got two fren's checkin' on me any minute."

Using my foot, I rolled "beard" into the gutter and turned to "gap-tooth" just in time to see Marci-Marie kick him in the face, then she kicked him in his groin. I grabbed her; she was crying. I pushed the body into the gutter.

"The young lady don' like him?"

"No." I stooped and pulled the fifty from his vest pocket. I also took out the Winstons, dropped the pack on the sidewalk, and crushed it with my heel. I handed Mama the fifty. "It's not stealing; it was mine."

"I got no questions; it's manna from heaven, but now yuh bettah git. I see mah fren's."

We thanked Mama and headed up the street. A police car passed us and stopped by the Cajuns. The officers got out and started talking to Mama. We turned onto St. Charles and safety.

The front desk was empty, as usual, but we went up the stairs, which no one used. I didn't feel so safe in my room, and neither did Marci-Marie: she had me jam a chair under the door knob.

I hadn't noticed before, but she looked attractive in a beige blouse and skirt, with tiny beige shoes on her feet. They did not have high heels.

We sat on the bed, and I held her while we recovered ourselves and could breathe normally. When I said we should get some sleep, she agreed, but then said, "I want to shower."

I explained the communal shower situation, but she insisted. I told her it was too dangerous, but she insisted—"I don't feel clean. After that place, I don't feel clean."

I checked the hallway; it was very early in the morning and normal people were in bed. I went into the hall, waited, then had Marci-Marie come out with a towel on her head. She went in and I stayed out.

Soon the water was running. I stood by the door. Five minutes. *Where is she?* Ten minutes. I opened the door. "Marci-Marie?" No answer. Just as I pulled my head back, I heard a door open and saw a man start toward me carrying a towel.

He looked a little nervous as he came up to me. I didn't smile. "Hello." A weak voice.

"You can't use the shower. Go up a floor."

"What's wrong? I can hear water."

"That's what's wrong. Go up a flight."

"But…"

"Look. There's a bad leak. A plumber's on the way. You can't use this shower room. Now either go up, or I'll call the front desk."

"O.K. O.K. Don't get sore."

He went away.

The water stopped. I waited for what I thought was a decent amount of time, then stuck my head in. She was ready and we quick-timed it to my room.

I jammed the chair in place and took off my boots and put my knife on the nightstand. She went into the little bathroom with a john and sink. When she came out, with no makeup, I saw what a pretty girl she was, but I also noticed a certain hardness around her eyes and her mouth, frail defenses against the unendurable. I hoped it would fade over time.

She was wearing some kind of cotton nightshirt, light blue with little ribbons. She laughed; I liked her laugh. "I haven't worn this since…." Her face iced up. "Anyway…."

She turned down the covers and slid under. I emptied my pockets, opened my pocketknife and placed it by the other knife. I got into bed, reached over, and turned out the lights.

Everything was quiet for awhile and then she started telling me a story about her childhood and some ducks. We talked about fifteen minutes about light and frothy things, then she said, "Chris, I'm scared."

"So am I."

"Not just about Etienne."

"What then?"

"About going home. About how I will tell…how I will explain… to my Mama."

"Shhh. She'll understand. It won't be easy, but mother's understand." I hoped her mother was like my mother.

"Chris, will you hold me?"

"Sure."

She came into my arms, just a little thing. We warmed each other.

"Do you think I'm spoiled…I mean for another man. In Catechism the priest told us…."

I stopped her. "For the right man, you will be perfect."

She cried for awhile, a little cry, just like she was little.

She put her hand on my thigh. "Chris, you can have me if you want."

"Go to sleep. That life is over. Go to sleep, Marci-Marie."

"I like it when you call me that." I took her hand off my thigh.

"Go to sleep."

I liked her; I didn't love her, and I wasn't going to deceive her by pretending I did. It would have been easy to have sex with her, but sex wasn't love, and love is what she needed, what she deserved.

Love was wound up in a big basket of Time. First, you learned to love someone, and when you both were ready, you expressed that love in a sexual way. After that, love would grow and develop in ways different than the love before sex, a deeper, more understanding, perhaps less romantic, but more solid love. I didn't love her; sex would be taking advantage.

Asleep, her breathing was light, but steady. A couple times she trembled and sounds like unborn words were in her throat, but I caressed her hair and told her everything was all right.

I lay in the darkness and thought about what my mother would do if Barbara or Marjorie had gotten into a similar situation. That reassured me. I could see Mom with her tears and hugs.

I couldn't read the Bible or say my prayers. I was a liar; I was a hater.

I stared into the darkness until I fell asleep.

DAY TWELVE

At a little past five, I woke up. I let Marci-Marie sleep; she was still nesting in my arm.

When she did wake up, it was time to get a move on. We dressed, or rather she did—I just had to put on my boots. I made certain everything was packed and ready, then I went down to the lobby. I called a cab. When it showed up, I asked the driver to wait and got Marci-Marie. No one even saw her in the "Y."

She wanted my arm around her as we headed out. She was amazed at the size of New Orleans as the driver made time on I-10. Despite living in the city, she knew little about it.

I paid my bill at the Honda shop; no one said anything about my being late.

It took awhile to get the poncho full of my stuff and her suitcase attached in such a manner that she could ride, but after I bought some cords inside, we got it straightened away.

She was excited; she'd never ridden on a motorcycle before. I told her to hang on tight.

She held on tight; her arms around me felt good. She leaned her head against me; that felt even better.

We cut through the early morning traffic, which was thick enough. We reached Metairie and turned off on the Expressway. As we approached the Causeway, she was telling me something. I turned my head, and she yelled, "I can't swim!"

We were laughing as we started across Lake Pontchartrain. There was an early morning fog, so the buildings of New Orleans quickly faded out.

I retraced my route and caught Highway 190 at Hammond. The morning air was cool and I could tell she was chilled. I pulled over and had her put on my jacket. She protested; I insisted. When I was riding, I rarely felt too hot or too cold. She put on the oversized jacket and got lost inside it. She hugged me with sleeves that had no hands.

The IC tracks were three-quarters of a mile to our right. The fog hadn't penetrated that far inland, so I hit the speed limit, but it was hard to hold it because the little towns were only a few miles apart. Clouds were forming to the south.

Thick trees, businesses, some residences, power lines paralleling the pavement. A large cemetery to the right, the graves all below ground, and across the road a few buildings and a lot of trees called Baptist.

At Albany I realized we hadn't eaten breakfast, so I pulled in for gas and suggested it. She smiled and said she was really hungry. We went to a little brick restaurant across the street. She took my hand while we were walking and refused to take off the jacket.

Marci-Marie had a healthy appetite. So did I. Pancakes, bacon and eggs, toast (white for her; wheat for me), orange juice. She even had a bowl of grits and teased me because I didn't.

She talked about her family a lot. She laughed at some of the things I said about my younger years in the Dakota winters. She had never seen snow.

She also smiled a lot, and when she did, ebony eyes softened as they looked at me. I was afraid of what was happening, but I smiled back.

She declared it the best breakfast she'd had since she left home. I left the tip and we were off. She held my hand as we walked to the bike and held me tight as we took off.

We came out of some trees and the IC line was right there, three diesel units and a hundred-car freight. "I like trains!" I yelled above the noise. I don't know if she heard me, but she hugged me tighter.

The little town of Holden and a junction with Louisiana 441. Mostly trees, but enough buildings that the speed limit dropped to 45.

I had been in trees before, but Louisiana was the king of trees. When they were between us and the railroad, the highway appeared even narrower than it was. I hated meeting semis.

We passed over a brown steam and hit a dense wilderness of trees until we came to Livingston, its businesses strung out along the highway.

I-12 was under construction a few miles south. When it opened, what would happen to the towns on 190?

More trees; a slight deviation south, which separated us from the railroad; the town of Walker, businesses stretched along the highway over a mile.

Denham Springs and a curve to the south on double lanes. Traffic congealed around us; big trucks; Marci-Marie seemed O.K.

We skirted around the eastern and northern spread of Baton Rouge and crossed the muddy Mississippi, a half-mile wide. She hugged me tighter and sometimes her hands felt like a caress.

I had studied my map, so I knew where to pull off to get to Oscar, Louisiana. We drove along what looked like the river, but what was actually a huge ox-bow. Residences and other buildings interposed themselves between us and the water.

Marci-Marie tapped my shoulder. "Here." I pulled off the pavement onto a tree-lined lane. Some of the trees were green, but many of them were dead. We passed a fuel tank up on stilty legs, but it didn't look like it was being used. A large tree hung over the lane. Another one cast a shadow over a small wooden cabin with a porch and a lean-to, painted maybe two decades prior. There were an aged chicken coop with a fenced-in run where the birds were pecking the ground; a shed with dead paint; and a car, green and out of the Fifties. I stopped.

We looked the place over; I hoped someone was home. I put down the kickstand and got off. She didn't. I held out my hand, and after hesitating, she took it. I unstrapped her suitcase and handed it to her.

"I'll need my jacket; it gets cold up north." I meant it as a joke, but tears flooded her eyes and rolled like tiny crystals of sadness down her cheeks.

She dropped her suitcase and threw her arms around me. "Stay, please stay."

"I can't." I released her arms, slipped off my jacket, and put it on. "You're home. You can have a beautiful life, just as beautiful as you are. I have to go home, too."

I handed her the suitcase. Her face was knotted as she tried to stop the crying. I turned the bike around and kicked it into life. The tears defeated her resistance.

A woman came and stood on the porch. I reached over and brought the girl to me. I placed her hand on my heart. "Marci-Marie Jarreau,

you will always have a place here." I pointed to the cabin. "And there."
I kissed her on the forehead. "Start your new life." I put on my helmet,
geared the bike, and rode away.

Fifty yards down the lane I stopped. A large human shadow stood
in the yard. A smaller shadow moved slowly toward it, then ran, and
then was lost in the arms that were extended.

It was a long time on the road before I knew where I was.

Highway 61 took me north out of Louisiana and into Mississippi.
It's a long, lonely road; at least I was lonely. Trees guided me along like
sentinels. There were a few little villages and towns in Louisiana, but
after I crossed into Mississippi, it was ten miles of trees barely broken
by a farm or a house which were like stationary boats in a green ocean,
until I reached the appropriately named Woodville.

Then it was off into the "forest primeval," green mile after green
mile. Over the Buffalo River; past a small indentation in the green called
Dolorosa; over the Homochitto River, tea-colored water with a sandbar
forming on a curve; bare earth for several hundred yards; then trees all
the way to Natchez, where I stopped at a Gulf Station.

The attendant said, "Sure is a change from yesterday." I didn't
answer. "The weather, I mean."

"Oh, yeah, you're right."

"You from North Dakota, uh? I read your license."

"Yeah."

"Nevah been there. Was in Washin'ton durin' the war, Ft. Lewis."

It could have been World War II, Korea, or Vietnam; the man
seemed to have no specific age.

I walked inside and used the facilities. I washed my face to get some
of the dirt tracks off; my eyes would have to take care of themselves. I
bought some candy, chips, and a pop; I knew the gas wouldn't be that
much.

He handed me the change. "Rain's comin'."

I thanked him for the change; it didn't look like rain to me. The day
was cloudy, but the clouds were white and light gray.

"Good luck."

"Thanks."

I headed out on 61. I passed a few scattered buildings called
Washington, more buildings and the junction with 553 and I was by
Stanton, and some more buildings and Cannonsburg was a memory.

All the time the forest was closing in on me.

After Fayette, some of the original Natchez Trace ran through the forest off to my left. Originally animal trails leading to grazing land, salt licks, or water, the Trace was used and expanded by various indigenous people and then used by white explorers, traders, and settlers. Parts of it also became dangerous as gamblers and gangs of robbers became denizens of the Trace. In October 1809 Meriwether Lewis died in an overnight shelter on the Trace, either by his own hand or by homicide.

Little white circles on the map—Melton, Lorman, Russum— drifted by.

At Port Gibson the Trace turned into the paved Natchez Trace Parkway and went off to the northeast toward Jackson.

I crossed the Bayou River, then the Big River, and ten miles later 61 turned into four lanes. The little towns of Cedars and Stout, and finally Vicksburg.

I passed through the city and drove out to the Vicksburg National Military Park.

During the Civil War, the North relied on three strategies:

Seizing the Southern capital at Richmond. I didn't think much of that idea. Napoleon had taken Moscow, to no avail. On the other hand, Hitler conquered Paris and French resistance ended. I didn't see the South surrendering just because Richmond was in the hands of the Union: Southerners were as much tied to their native states as they were to their nation.

The Anaconda Policy was much more effective; the Union blockaded Southern ports, starving the South to death.

The third strategy was to gain control of the Mississippi Valley, thus cutting off Texas, Louisiana, and Arkansas, and their resources, especially cattle, from the rest of the South.

Gaining control of the southern Mississippi in Louisiana up to Port Hudson and the northern reaches from Tennessee down to Vicksburg had been accomplished after Grant's victory at Shiloh. The two hundred mile stretch of river from Vicksburg to Port Hudson was a tougher nut to crack.

Vicksburg was the key, but it was strongly fortified and also had some natural defenses, so the battles really turned into a siege. Grant attacked in May and June 1862 and again in December 1862 and January 1863. Finally in May 1863 his third try was successful. Vicksburg surrendered on July 4, 1863, one day after General Robert E. Lee was defeated at Gettysburg, the most famous battle of the Civil War.

To say that Vicksburg was as important as Gettysburg is not to diminish the importance of the Northern victory south of the small town in Pennsylvania, but strategically, Vicksburg completed the severing of the South into parts and hastened the end of the war.

The battlefield was laid out like a large fishhook with the Visitors' Center in the middle of the shank. I left my bike in the parking lot and walked under the marble Memorial Arch with its two Doric columns and the carved inscription "Vicksburg National Military Park." To the north I visited the national cemetery with its rows of small white grave markers; the *USS Cairo* (a Union gunboat which was sunk during the siege) and Navy Monument; sites with cannons, redoubt sites, sites of forts, Grant's headquarters, all kinds of state and other memorials and markers (the guidebook said over 1300); to the south of the Visitors' Center were a fort, a redoubt, and more memorials. Signs kept reminding me that relic hunting was prohibited.

The Louisiana State Memorial featured a pelican feeding three young ones and two Confederate battle flags carved out of the rock. The Illinois State Memorial looked like a combination Greek and Roman temple with its six columns and round roof. The one I liked best was the 76th Ohio Infantry Monument, which depicted a single soldier with his cap off, holding his rifle, butt on the ground. He stood with his head bowed, and he was carved recessed in the rock which curved over him like it was protecting him. The word "OHIO" was carved in the rock.

Union gunboats sent 22,000 shells into the besieged city, and Union artillery added more than twice that number. However, less than a dozen civilians were killed because they lived in caves they had burrowed into the clay hillsides.

The last siege lasted forty-seven days, cost the Union over 4800 casualties and the Confederacy 3200. When Confederate General John C. Pemberton surrendered, so did 29,000 troops.

Walking the battlefield, or siege-site, was tiring, but I needed to stretch my legs. As I walked from site to site, I wondered if there were some way clashes of deeply held beliefs could be resolved without war. I couldn't come up with one.

As I left the battlefield, I saw the sky had darkened far off to the south. I found Highway 80 and crossed the Mississippi on a cantilevered bridge that also carried the IC tracks. I passed Delta, a handful of souls probably praying the levee would never break.

I crossed a wide Mississippi floodplain, a few buildings known as Mound, even fewer called Thomastown, a little jot named Barnes, and after nineteen miles, curved into the town of Tallulah. The only Tallulah I was familiar with was the actress Tallulah Bankhead, who was in the Hitchcock film *Lifeboat*, a late-night TV favorite of Mom and me, so the name intrigued me.

Most of the people walking or driving were Negroes.

It was past dinner time, so I looked for a place. Along the side of the road and sitting in an indentation in the trees stood a small building that looked like a Dairy Queen, but had no sign, except "EAT." I decided to give some business to a single proprietorship, rather than a corporation, and pulled onto the gravel parking lot.

There were a counter with eight stools, two tables, and two booths. Behind the counter was the kitchen area, as big as the seating area. The walls had hand-lettered signs: "We patty our own burgers." "We hand-cut our fries." "We make fresh hush puppies daily." "You can't beat our buns, made fresh daily." There were other signs in the same vein.

The customers in the booths were Negroes. A Negro man appeared from the kitchen. "How are you today, sir?" He handed me a menu and put down a glass of water.

"Fine."

"Come a ways?"

"New Orleans."

"Goin' far."

"North Dakota."

"Woo-ee. You got a piece to go."

He left. A woman looked at me from the kitchen and smiled. Her skin was dark.

The man came back and took my order. I looked around, but the other customers avoided my eyes. A couple came in, dropped their eyes, and sat at a table.

I felt uncomfortable until my food came. Then I began eating some of the most flavorful food I'd had on the trip. The burger was juicy and tasted like beef should taste. The fries, well, McDonald's are the best, but those fries were neck-and-neck with them. The bun was big, light, and tasted great. When I finished, I had a piece of their home-made pecan pie and a side of their home-made ice cream. I was stuffed with home-made goodness.

In high school I had read the short story "Quality" by John Galsworthy in which a German boot maker took his time making every pair because he wanted everything done right. As newer, faster methods came in, he continued in his old ways of hand-making quality boots, but customers wanted speed, not quality, and the shop was taken over by another firm, not as devoted to quality.

I hoped there was room in this world for both McDonald's and "EAT."

I left tips for both the waiter and the cook. He thanked me and wished me well on my journey. I walked out of the quiet café.

Two young boys, one dark, one white, were looking at my bike. Their clothes indicated their families were not well-to-do. One had short curly hair and one was a red-head. They could have been miniature versions of Jim and Huck.

"Well, I ride all the way to Vicksburg and see ma cousin and go to the movies."

"That's nothin'. I'd go to Nawlens and see Mahdi Grah."

The sky didn't look good. I had to interrupt their cycle dreams. "Excuse me, boys." I legged over the bike, upped the kickstand, and kicked the starter. On an impulse I took out by billfold and handed them some money. "Go in there and try the ice cream. It's great."

They had taken money from a stranger. Should they give it back? They looked at each other. They yelled their thanks as they scampered for the door.

I rolled onto 80. Heading west, I passed a lot of cropland, the floodplain soil providing the nutrients. The weak shoulders of the highway flowed off into shallow ditches.

I whipped by Quebec and Tendal, which was marked by the Tensas River, but without a map I wouldn't have known the little places were there. Waverly was a complex of agriculture-oriented buildings—bins and towers.

The Macon River, shadowy under the darkening clouds. I curved into Delhi; trees had reappeared on both side. The IC tracks were one block south of the main drag, the construction of I-20 a mile south. Again I wondered how the brave little businesses in Delhi would fare when the traffic went south. On my right a neatly kept cemetery sat behind a fence. One of the monuments was a ten-foot white obelisk.

I opened her up, rain threatening. Dunn, Holly Ridge, Bee Bayou, I didn't slow down.

I did slow down at Rayville, where I was greeted by large displays of farm implements, farm-oriented buildings, semi-trucks, and the IC line.

I turned left at the light onto South Julia Street and crossed the IC tracks. Some people kidded that the initials of the Illinois Central Rail Road stood for "I Can't Run Railroads." The tracks looked well-maintained to me.

No more lights, so I edged up my speed, slowed to get onto the on-ramp of I-20, and opened her up. Over the Boeuf, over the Bayou, small streams, trees leaning over the banks.

Through a forest, then farmland, then the city of Monroe. Across the Ouachita River, a couple football fields wide, some barges below the bridge, but looking pretty tame.

A nice looking city, that and West Monroe, but I didn't get too many looks because I was clawing my way through traffic, trying to beat the rain.

An exit to Calhoun and the first spatters. Under a highway bridge. Darkness on my left. Trees on both sides, thick. *Hold off rain. It's not going to hold off. Here it comes. I'm getting soaked. I have to get off.* A little indentation in the trees to my right. A shallow ditch. I slowed and nosed the bike down across the ditch and under the trees overhanging the back of the indentation. I was forty yards off the pavement, safe enough.

I set up the poncho. That and the trees were a good shelter. I set up camp under the poncho and listened to the rain. It showed no signs of quitting, so I wrote in my journal and filled out my last two New Orleans post cards, even though I planned to be home before they would arrive. I still couldn't read the Bible or say any prayers, and Jeffers would only make me feel worse.

I took off my boots and wet clothes. I hung the clothes on various parts of the bike. I crawled into my sleeping bag, surprisingly dry. The rain made soft sounds, and the traffic made wet sounds in the air. I drifted off…

Something was wrong. I woke up. The rain had lightened, but it was dark. There were just lonely cars. Something was crawling down by my leg. I could hear a little clicking sound. It was moving toward my head.

Is it a snake? They had copperheads and water moccasins, maybe even rattlers, I didn't know. *Do they have scorpions in Louisiana? What would move with a click?*

It was moving closer. *Is it an armadillo? Can they get rabies?*

Oh, Jesus, please protect me!

It was just off my shoulder. What if it stung, bit, ripped, or gnawed my face?

I reached over in the darkness, grabbed something—it had a shell with multiple legs all working slowly—and threw it as far as I could.

I stayed awake with occasional drops rolling off the poncho and the sounds of lucky drivers, safe in their vehicles as company.

Eventually, I figured I was safe, clutched the machete, and fell into a fitful sleep.

Sometimes you just have to reach out and grab slimy things and heave them out of your life.

DAY THIRTEEN

I woke up to a mist or light fog. After I got dressed, I looked for my night visitor, but found nothing. I packed up and rolled across the ditch and onto I-20.

There may have been nice views as I went west, but I couldn't see them. The misty fog even made the trees lining the highway a ghostly gray. Any vehicle that passed me sent up a spray. I hated fast semis.

Exits to Ruston, a few buildings formed in the mist; Grambling; Arcadia; Gibsland; Ada; and over something called the Black Lake Bayou; Minden; and Dixie Inn, which was the end of the line, or at least the end of I-20. I exited onto 80.

Fillmore; then Bossier City and more spectral buildings; I pulled over to read the map and locate I-20; across the Red River; Shreveport, other-worldly in the mist; Greenwood, well-named, but I was tired of trees; I was fleeing trees.

"Welcome to Texas." A large sign with the white lone star in the red, white and blue Texas flag; the mist dissipating. I pulled over for a quick clean-up and breakfast in Waskom. Gas up. Pay. "Will you please drop these cards in your outgoing?" "Glad to; have a safe trip." "Thank you." Back on the road. Sun coming out. Wind drying me.

I was fleeing across Texas. And there were still too many trees.

Steinbeck dreaded Texas: it was so huge and he had in-laws there since his wife was Texas-born. To Texans it's not just a state; it's a state of mind, an obsession, and a religion. It is also a contradiction: Texans fought for freedom against Mexico, but one of the reasons was they wanted to retain slavery which Mexico had abolished; its summers are hot enough to make everyone indolent, but most Texans are hard workers; rich men like to be thought of as "good ol' country boys" even as they attend the theaters and the symphonies available in the large cities; Texans elected conservative Republicans to national office, while sending liberal Democrats to fill the county and city posts.

To Steinbeck Texas was the most hospitable state in the nation. His wife joined him in Texas, and they drove out to a rich man's ranch for a Thanksgiving feast. The family dressed and acted like common people, but the ranch itself reeked of wealth.

Early in the morning Steinbeck caught four rainbow trout on four casts into a trout pool. The cook fried them in bacon fat and he had breakfast. He and his host and his host's dogs went quail hunting for several hours, but never raised a bird.

At two o'clock he had two drinks of whisky and sat down for a Thanksgiving feast with two turkeys, after which he went for a walk and took a nap.

The overriding question for Steinbeck to answer on his trip was "What are Americans like today?"

He concluded that despite their individual differences there are "Americans," a category that sets them apart from any other group. The specifics of his conclusion eluded him, except to say his view of "Americans" saw them as increasingly paradoxical.

Wrestling with that idea, Steinbeck ventured into the Deep South, which he faced with anxiety, knowing that as a white Northerner, he was not wanted.

He had read of a group of middle-aged white women nicknamed the "Cheerleaders" who would station themselves outside a recently integrated New Orleans school and yell obscenities at a small Negro girl and a white man and his child as they entered the building, escorted by U.S. marshals. He disguised himself as an old sailor and mixed in with the crowd of whites. The shouting and screaming was nauseatingly worse than he had ever imagined.

He knew New Orleans; he had friends in New Orleans, non-racist friends. Where were they, that they would allow such a degrading demonstration of wild fury against small children to occur?

What was worse was the feeling that the crowd and the Cheerleaders were there to a great extent to be on television and to be able to go home and watch themselves on the news.

Steinbeck was so affected by what he had seen and heard, he didn't stop at one of the great New Orleans restaurants; his stomach would not allow it. He grabbed a sandwich and headed out of town.

He stopped by the Mississippi, and soon an elderly white man with white hair and a neat white mustache came strolling by. They drank some strong coffee together and discussed the racial divide in the South. The elderly man believed that the Negro had been classified for centuries as a beast of burden, and that made it acceptable for whites to treat them as beasts, but now that Negroes were demanding to be humans, the old traditions were being undermined and were being defended in brutal ways. He didn't know how it would all end, but perhaps the whites and the Negroes would eventually produce a third type of being, one that has overcome the white feeling of hatred and fear of the Negro and the Negro feeling of resentment toward the white. Until then, all he could see was violence.

When the man left to go home and be taken care of by an elderly Negro couple, Steinbeck felt better, knowing there were such Southerners about.

He picked up an elderly Negro along the highway, even though the man was reluctant to get into a white man's vehicle. Steinbeck tried to engage him in conversation, but he only drove the man deeper within himself. Finally, the man asked Steinbeck to let him out, after which he continued to trudge along the highway.

He stayed in a motel that night, but his sleep was a restless one, with thoughts of the tension and the fear he had seen and experienced that day constantly intruding on it.

The next morning at breakfast a skinny, thirty-some white man with long blonde hair begged a ride. Steinbeck tried to be pleasant, but the man was a racist, and they got into an argument, at the end of which Steinbeck kicked him out of Rocinante, leaving the man on the side of the highway calling Steinbeck names with a racial overtone.

Steinbeck then picked up a young Negro, a college student who had participated in boycotts and sit-ins and who wanted direct action to bring about racial integration. Steinbeck tried to caution him and brought up the non-violent methods of Martin Luther King, Jr., and Gandhi. The student rejected them as too slow; he wanted racial equality in his lifetime. He got off in Montgomery, Alabama.

Steinbeck did not claim to have given a cross-section picture of the South, but he did say that the racial conflict was real, dangerous, and hard of solution.

Steinbeck wrote "...people don't take trips—trips take people." Near Abingdon, Virginia, Steinbeck's trip came to an end—he just got tired of the whole thing. West Virginia, Pennsylvania, and New Jersey were a blur, and when he hit the Manhattan traffic, he got lost.

As I rushed past Marshall and Longview, I was running away from something, too. I hadn't seen the racial animosity Steinbeck had witnessed; New Orleans had settled down from those days, but I had seen evil. It was vile and repulsive.

The sun appeared; was it bigger because I was in Texas? Names like Kilgore, White Oak, Gladwater, Tyler, floated by on signs, but the picket lines of trees blocked my view, and the houses and buildings went by unseen.

Evil will persist in this world, no matter how hard humans try to eradicate it. Our world is broken; humans are broken. The idea that human beings can create a society without violence, without evil, is vain arrogance.

Finally, the trees began to thin out. The land was flat—I was coming home.

The Interstate had been built to avoid the towns and cities, but businesses had sprung up along the highway, leaving the populated places behind. Maybe towns would develop around the truck stops, service stations, cafes, and motels that had mushroomed beside the pavement the way they had beside the railroads in the 19th century.

As kids when we saw a friend with his zipper down, we'd ask, "What's the speed limit in Texas?" If he hadn't heard the joke before and said "I don't know," we'd answer, "Wide open," and look down. Then he'd know he had some unfinished business.

I throttled her "wide open." This was Texas. However, when I hit a hundred, I cut back; there were speed limit signs, and I didn't know what the fines were.

The trees were in a dispute with the climate. Thick stands would thin out and then thicken again. The pattern would repeat and repeat again until just after the Van exit, then thick was losing. Thin stands of trees confirmed the drier climate.

One thing that did thicken was the traffic, especially semis and tankers. With the rolling land and the sparser number of trees, I could have felt I was back in North Dakota, except for the trucks.

I endured, mile after mile of movement, but like Steinbeck, my trip had been too long. I was hungry; dinnertime was long gone. Texas stretched out.

Should I eat before or after Dallas? At Mesquite I turned north and began to loop around the Dallas-Ft. Worth metropolitan area. I'd eat later.

I hooked up with I-35E and headed northwest, past Carrollton, Lewisville, Denton, blending with I-35W to form I-35. Flowing north with the traffic, but at least sometimes I could see all the way to the horizon.

I pulled off at Sanger and drifted along, looking for a place to eat. I pulled in at a sign that displayed a set of long horns and said "Great Steaks."

The place wasn't that busy; there were a couple tables and three booths occupied by men who looked like cowboys and women who looked like they lived in a big city.

My streak was 10 oz. and well-done, just as I specified. Smothered in onions. A slew of American fries. A half pint of green beans. A thick piece of wheat toast. A large glass of milk and one of water. I was all set.

The small talk I heard was a couple booths over: "There's no way in hell the Washington Senators will ever move to Texas."

I wasn't too interested; I was interested in my steak. Meat fresh off the range and not frozen—man, what a treat!

I used the facilities and left a Texas-size tip.

I got back on 35 and headed for Oklahoma. I could see to the horizon and I felt good.

I brushed by Gainesville. It looked like a nice community; the dome of its courthouse stuck out above the skyline, proudly proclaiming it was a county seat.

The bike went over a ridge, then started down, around a curve and onto a flood plain and then over the Red River, not doing too well as a river, with a large sandy, brush-covered island lengthening out from under the bridge and temporarily dividing the water, which actually looked light blue under the sky.

No big Welcome sign; no Oklahoma flag. Just "OKLAHOMA."

I tested the speed limit; the day was getting away from me. At Ardmore I-35 ran out and I had to slide over to 77 via 70 and go through town. That really slowed me down. I tried to regain time on the two-line highway, but then hit a series of curves through some lows hills called the Arbuckle Mountains. Some of the cuts revealed light-colored rock layers tilted up at odd angles, indicating some kind of tectonic activity in the ancient past.

Slowly I climbed up and out of the hills, but soon found I had to negotiate a hairpin turn, then another, and I was gliding past rocky formations on the shoulder of a valley, but the trees had closed in and I couldn't see it very well. I passed buildings scattered along the highway offering groceries, beer, curios. I went over Honey Creek, drying in August.

Some people had chosen to live in that rough land; fenced-in or walled-in yards; open yards; cabins for rent.

Across the Washita River, divided by a sandy island that ran out from under the bridge. Up and onto flat land again; I opened her up.

The highway, old-fashioned in its way, passed through Davis. An outdated gas station on my right—the owner's living quarters extended over the pump area, held up by two pillars; an addition contained two small service bays. Quick to the pump, friendly, but I didn't have the time to talk. "Thank you." On my way. I'm burning daylight, or what's left of it.

Over the double-tracked Santa Fe line that splits the town in half. Two blocks and turn north. Davis seems to be a nice town, but too slow. Open her up. More trees than before.

Crawl through Wynnewood, take a left, over some kind of man-made ditch, curving north, over the Washita again, the superstructure of the bridge over my head like a steel spider web. Miles interspersed with trees, then Paul's Valley. Obey the speed limit. I'm getting nowhere fast. A long slow through town, including a left-hand and a right-hand turn. A curve to the north and across the Washita, an old friend by now. Another island forming by the bridge.

I pick up the Santa Fe just to my right and we run together past farmland. The highway swings left just before Paoli. Across Owl Creek (shades of Ambrose Bierce and his short story) and into town. Only six blocks and I'm through.

More farmland. Open her up. The six blocks of Wayne, where I rejoin the Santa Fe, but trees separate us until we split apart south of

Purcell. Another agonizingly slow "stroll" through town, but then I-35 again. I really open her up.

Eleven miles, a jog to the right, across the Canadian River and I'm in Norman. Lights are coming on. Watch the traffic. Moore, Oklahoma City, Edmond, and I'm free. A swing to the right and 35 avoids the old city of Guthrie.

I look for a place to light. A little knoll appears to my right. Virtually no ditch. I drive over to the fence line and make camp, keeping the bike between me and the highway. I write in my journal and say a prayer of thanks for my safety—I'm on better terms with God on the flat land. The lights of Greater Oklahoma City pattern the clouds to the south.

I fall asleep wondering if Comanches ever camped on my knoll.

DAY FOURTEEN

W hen I rolled out from under the poncho, I looked to the south—the city lights were gone, replaced by gloomy clouds and every so often lightning. I couldn't hear any thunder, so the storm was still far off. I packed up in record time and hit the pavement.

Kansas was up ahead. Behind, I was being pursued by the Storm God. After I read about the Aztecs and the Spanish in *The Conquest of Mexico* by William H. Prescott during sixth grade, I went on to study the Aztecs themselves. Tlaloc, their god of rain, intrigued me with his bugged-out eyes and fangs. Whenever a bad storm hit, I would blame Tlaloc.

So maybe it was Tlaloc rushing at me from the south. But there was something else; it had been dancing around in my mind during the night, but always behind curtains. Even as I cursed myself for wasting time yesterday on a huge steak, I knew there was something I needed to discover, to bring out into my consciousness.

I passed over the Cimarron River and thought of Edna Ferber. The fictional setting of her novel *Cimarron* was supposedly that portion of Oklahoma around Guthrie.

The river was low, exposing much of its sandy bottom.

The old pitcher Satchel Paige once said, "Don't look back. Something might be gaining on you." Crossing over the bridge, I saw he was right: the storm had gained on me and I could see sheets of dark rain.

What could I do? Pull off and take shelter in Stillwater, Ponca City, or Blackwell, or go for it. I went for it.

The rain caught me ten miles south of the Kansas state line.

I could feel the wind getting stronger, then a few raindrops; I felt them on my hands first, then my face. I went faster. Then I was engulfed. Water was everywhere. The world turned gray—the highway signs, the grass in the median and on the shoulders, the fence posts, the trees, the bridge over the Chikaskia River, the river itself, the fields, the scattered buildings, all lost most of their color and took on aspects of gray as I passed.

The rain stung the lower part of my face and streamed off my visor. It puddled up on the pavement. Once you're completely wet, you can't get any wetter. I couldn't be any wetter. I was cold; I was saturated; I was almost eight hundred miles from home as the crow flies (they weren't flying that day); I was hungry. It couldn't get any worse.

I hit the Kansas state line and just beyond was the Kansas Turnpike. It did get worse: there was the first toll booth and I had no money ready. I had to stop and dig in my pockets. A friendly motorist thought it would help me if he sounded his horn.

I paid and splashed away. My friend caught up and passed, sending a sheet of water over me as a gift.

Coffeyville was an hour-and-a-half to the east. I had thought I could drop in on BethAnn. The rain washed out that senseless thought.

I persisted, traveling in a world of wet and gray. My one fear was a skid or hydroplaning, any little thing that would send me sliding across the pavement and off into a ditch. I wanted to keep ahead of my enemies, the semis, but my fear held me back, and the trucks drenched me, some drivers sounding their horns to cheer me on my way.

The surface of the turnpike was not good; it had been patched and repaired with asphalt and sand, making for a rough ride. A toll booth appeared: I was ready.

The odometer counted off the wet, weary miles. Over the Ninnescah River, the sign barely readable. Buildings, exits, streets, finally I was in Wichita, built on cattle coming up the Chisholm Trail from Texas to be shipped out on the Santa Fe, now a large industrialized city.

I negotiated a deal with the slippery pavement not to buck me off, and I would go slow as I split away from the Turnpike, looped around the west side and crossed the Arkansas River, mostly sand. I swung right and then turned north on a four-lane U.S. Highway 81. Leaving Park City, I was in farmland again. The rain slackened, then slowly dripped to a stop.

I pulled off at Newton, another old cow town and once called "the wickedest city in the West" because eight men had died in a gunfight there.

Wicked or not, I had to get dry. I took Highway 15 which became Main Street, crossed the Santa Fe tracks and searched downtown until I found a Laundromat.

I was lucky: there was a restroom. I changed my pants, shirt, and socks; bought detergent; and put the wet things in the washer. I crossed the street to a café and ordered a hamburger and fries to go. It wasn't that I distrusted Newtonians, but I went back to the Laundromat and sat by my washer for ten minutes. Then I went back, paid for my food, and returned to eat it. The burger tasted almost as good as the steak I'd had in Texas. I transferred my clothes to the dryer.

Then I decided to do a Steinbeck.

There were seven other people doing laundry. Two of them were Hispanic women in long dresses and somewhat clunky shoes. They sat over by the detergent, fabric softener, and bleach dispensers. I walked over. "Habla Inglés?" That was about the extent of the college Spanish that I could remember.

The two women squeezed together. One of them said, "No, no Inglés." Their united looks said "Go away." I wandered away from the aroma of American detergent.

An old man sat on a bench, staring out at the traffic. His clothes were clean, but very faded. "Hello, how ya doin'?"

"Nuthin' to complain about."

"Nice weather."

"If ya like nice…Say, ya gotta butt?"

"No, sorry, I don't smoke."

He lost interest and began staring at his shoes which looked like their last shine had been a celebration of the Cubs in the World Series.

There were two sets of two white women. Each pair sat together. While I was eating, I had tried to listen to their conversation above the hum and spin of the machines. Common themes were the rising prices of food, milk, clothing; family problems, especially with husbands; and health—no one felt healthy, not themselves, their family members, nor their neighbors. One duo was addicted to a soap opera and discussed the latest episodes.

Two of the women must have synchronized their washing and drying—both of them had just pulled their clothes from the dryers and were standing by the long tables folding. I admired their skill in turning a pile of jumbled clothing into smooth finished products.

"Hello, ladies. Nice day."

Both of them looked at me with blank faces. The larger one said, "If you want change, there's a bill changer over there by the detergent." She used her head to indicate where I should go. I stood there at a loss. "If you continue to bug us, I'll call the manager." I moved away.

The manager's office was down a hall and in the back. He was a large man, but stayed to himself and played the radio. I had heard songs playing in the background: "Patches" by Clarence Carter; "Hitchin' A Ride," Vanity Fare; "Ohio," Crosby, Stills, Nash, and Young; "I Just Can't Help Believing," B.J. Thomas; "In The Summertime," Mungo Jerry; "War," Edwin Starr; "Mama Told Me," Three Dog Night; "O-O-Child," Five Stairsteps; "Band of Gold," Freda Payne; and "Spill The Wine," Eric Burdon and War.

I finished my Coke and regrouped. I went over to the other duo. "So, you like the Soaps."

Two hostile faces looked up. The woman with rings on all her fingers and thumbs asked, "You been evesdroppin' on us?"

"No, I just...."

"Our husbands will be by any minute." She sneered. "They don't like us talkin' with other men, if ya know what I mean."

I went over to my dryer, doubtful that any irate husbands would appear. The women started guessing what would happen on Monday's episode. I waited while "Close to You" and "Make It with You" by Bread drifted in from the back.

When my clothes were done, I folded the shirt and socks inside the pants and headed to the door. Just before I reached it, a young couple came in. She carried the detergent and fabric softener; he had a big basket of clothing, but he opened the door for her. They came in laughing.

She was Kansas cute: straight ripe-wheat hair, a few freckles on a light skin, blue eyes, straight nose, pink lips; about 5'4" and pregnant. He was tall, dark, and not so handsome, but not ugly. I'm not into men.

I slipped my clothing into the poncho, secured it, and rode away. My mind was troubled—there was something about the young man opening the door for the girl. Something like a little cloud the size of a man's hand as the Old Testament says. Behind the cloud an idea was growing, trying to hatch into a thought.

I drove down a Main Street that was mostly two-story brick buildings.

At Main and Seventh there was a Methodist Church with a white cross that looked Byzantine tacked onto the roofline over a couple of stained glass windows; four Corinthian columns with an entablature resting on the capitals that made the entryway with two smaller Doric columns appear like that of a Greek temple; and a dome decorated with a green top—very unusual. I appreciated what I had learned in my Humanities classes at Minot State.

On the right and sitting back from the street, but dominating the entire block, was the one-story Harvey County Courthouse, a new building, brick and glass, utilitarian, no dome.

At the corner of Main and Eighth stood a church that looked like a church. St. Mary's Catholic Church was red brick with one corner devoted to a tall steeple that had a white cross on top. Another white cross was on the front peak of the roof. The structure was not utilitarian: it cried out for people to enter and worship.

I passed a black sign with the representation of a golden sunflower and "15" in the middle, so I was on the right route. I crossed an unnamed waterway which I assumed was a tributary of the Arkansas River. Was it "ARK-an-saw" or "Ar-KAN-sas." In that neck of the woods, it could be either.

Just before I hit the MP tracks, I took a forty-five degree turn to the northwest; the MP kept me company, twenty yards on the right. Seeing the tracks was comforting. So was the sun, which had burst open and showered the land as only a prairie sun can. I teased five miles above the speed limit.

This was farming country; even the stubble fields looked like they welcomed the rain. Some puddles still occupied depressions in the pavement.

The railroad and I crossed an unnamed stream—Kansas was stingy with signs. The tracks and pavement moved apart and sandwiched a farmyard between them, then moved together again.

It was beautiful country—flat, trees scattered so you hardly noticed them, the horizon always beckoning, and I could see for miles.

Speed up; have to get home. Across another nameless stream and slow her down for Hesston, almost four thousand people living in a town that owed its beginnings to the railroad. It was agriculture-based and a sign bragged of Hesston College, which I'd never heard of.

Hit the curves out of town and cut 'er loose.

A tiny bridge over a dry run. A larger bridge over what had become pools of water, unconnected. The railroad bridge was old, held up by wooden pilings and supports. A totally dry run; the pavement cracked and in need of repair.

Slow down for Moundridge, 1200 people; looks clean.

Over a little stream and hook up with the MP again. Four dry runs, one wet one, and a sandwich of buildings between asphalt and steel at tiny Elyria. Two dry runs and a bridge over unnamed water. An MP diesel in its "Dark Eagle Blue" color, a stylized white eagle and "MISSOURI PACIFIC LINE" in a red gear-wheel disk with a white border and another diesel unit tugged a freight of box cars and grain cars. I rolled to a stop on the shoulder just as the engine started on the bridge. I waved; the horn sounded; my day was made.

Thirty-three cars, and I gunned the engine.

Finally, McPherson, my kind of town: the Santa Fe, the MP, and the Rock Island all converged there. Highway 81 turned into four lanes and I headed for Salina on good pavement. I lost my railroad, but the dry runs continued.

Wonderful cropland. A split of the lanes and a median with trees that reminded me of Mississippi, but the trees weren't as thick. Another split and the median captured a rest area. The split stretched for over four miles.

The Smoky Hill River; a name to conjure with. Zebulon Pike, Pawnee, Comanche, Kiowa, Arapahoe, Sioux, gold rush, U.S. Cavalry, Smoky Hill Trail, Ellsworth and its cattle and crime. Somewhere I had read of the cow towns: "Abilene, the first; Dodge City, the last; but Ellsworth, the wickedest."

I kept going with thoughts of the Old West and the small cloud followed me. Twelve miles to Salina in nine minutes. Salina boasted the MP, the Santa Fe, and the Union Pacific, with a total of six lines entering the city. I could live there.

I slowed my way through the city, rode I-70 for almost two miles, and turned north on 81, a two-lane affair. Abilene was some twenty miles east; I didn't have time.

I crossed the Saline River, which still had water. A solitary light brown silo stood just off the shoulder. Was it still used?

I rushed north, over dry runs; past farmyards, most looking prosperous; over the Solomon River, trees pressing in on brown water;

past Bennington, barely visible a mile to the right and hidden by trees; over the UP tracks; a lazy left-hand curve; a right-hand curve and Minneapolis two miles to the west, a much smaller prairie version of its big city namesake.

Lindsey Creek, Pipe Creek, snaked their way through the prairie, soil and rock formations on top of the floor of a Cretaceous sea. Any glaciation, I tried to remember my geology, was fifty miles to the east.

I rolled through the middle of Concordia on Lincoln Street, seven thousand people living with the MP, the Santa Fe, and the old Burlington tracks. I passed McDonald's, Dairy Queen, and other reputable eating places, but I wanted an old-fashioned café that catered to railroad men.

I crossed a long viaduct. The huge elevators and storage bins to my right showed me wheat was king. On the other side of the viaduct, the town ended; I had to turn around and retrace my wheel tracks. I turned on Rust Road and found a family restaurant.

A teenage girl was my waitress; not very friendly. I think her boyfriend was at the counter and she could hardly wait to get back to him. The chicken fried steak and mashed potatoes were all right, but I couldn't see railroad men consistently patronizing such fare. The homemade roll was delicious as was the blueberry pie. The talk around me was about farm prices and a new store that had opened. I left a barely adequate tip.

I went back to Lincoln and gassed up at an independent station on the corner. Over the viaduct and out into the country. Across the Republican River, all sludged-up with sand islands separated by small channels. Thirty miles to Nebraska.

Flat farmland, some trees, a few farmyards right on the highway, farm machinery making up a large portion of the traffic, a curve to the right, a run through Bellevue, where I crossed the Rock Island on the north side of town.

Leadbelly sang:

> "Oh, that Rock Island Line is a mighty good road;
> Oh, that Rock Island Line is a road to ride;
> Oh, that Rock Island Line is a mighty good road;
> If you want to ride, you got to ride it like you find it."

I hoped the old folk singer was right. The longer I rode the prairie, the better things were between God and me:

> "Get your ticket at the station on the Rock Island Line;
> Jesus died to save our sins—hooray to God;
> We're going to meet him again."

A curve north; more trees lined into shelterbelts; a large dry run; and the Nebraska state line. A big welcome from the three hundred people in Chester off to my left; a smaller welcome from Nebraska. I crossed the Burlington/BN tracks, issuing from the grain elevators and disappearing on the eastern and western horizons.

Over Dry Creek, aptly named. A curve, another one, and over the Little Blue River, sand-choked. Into Hebron with its nice wide street with plenty of motels, gas stations, farm implement dealers, and restaurants to bring people into the modest community of 1600.

Speed up; the south fork of Big Sandy Creek, dry as the proverbial bone; Big Sandy Creek (just as dry as its fork) and the UP rails in quick succession; driving north, always north. Dry Sandy Creek, how appropriate.

A curve around a few blocks called Strang and over the Burlington/BN line. Through Geneva, population 2300. A nice wide street and businesses similar to those in Hebron. A two-story house has a porch with four white wooden columns just the ones on my old home in Menninger and so close to the street, I'd like to stop and rest on it. Some medians divide the street. Over the Chicago & Northwestern rails, out of town, and over a dry run.

On to Fairmont and the Burlington/BN, eight miles; McCool Junction, seven miles; and I-80 five miles.

I turned west on I-80. No small towns; everything flat and straight. Cops; I can't see any. Time to make time. That Japanese-made motor was humming.

Forty miles to Grand Island. Forty minutes? That's a laugh, but nobody would believe my time on a 750. I crossed over the Burlington/BN west of Aurora and the Platte River as I turned into town. What a disappointment—the Platte River, home of the Pawnee; route of the fur traders and explorers; route of the Oregon, California, Mormon, and Bozeman trails—reduced to a couple small channels. One large island had been there so long shrubs were growing on it in profusion. "Plat" is French for "flat," so I guess the old saying was appropriate for the Platte: "A mile wide and an inch deep."

I continued north on the Gold Star. I passed a cemetery on the right, shaded in the late afternoon sun. It covered several blocks and was the biggest cemetery I'd seen on my trip, except in New Orleans. I crossed the double-tracked Union Pacific rails—the UP had chosen to build west from Omaha and used the Platte Valley as part of its route on the first transcontinental railroad. I crossed the old Burlington again and was out of town.

North past St. Libory and I picked up a UP branch line. We traveled together six miles until the tracks crossed the highway to the west side. I couldn't remember the last time I had seen the railroad signs in the shape of an "X" in a rural area.

I passed over some little hills and picked up the tracks again. I crossed over the Middle Loup River; to my left the railroad did the same thing on five rusty trusses.

I skirted St. Paul and headed north again. Over the North Loup River. In the old days the Pawnee also lived along the Loup. Out of the Loup Valley, the soil drier; the vegetation showing brown.

The miles stretch out; traffic is almost non-existent. One of the loneliest stretches I've experience. Shadows lengthening and I need a place to rest. I keep an eye on both sides of the road, but there's no place.

Rougher country with road cuts. A good size one ahead. I slow down and much of it is in front of the fence line; I wheel into the ditch and up. I stop on top of the cut. The waning moon comes out as I make camp.

I write in my journal and read "Their Beauty Has More Meaning" by Jeffers, which begins "Yesterday morning enormous the moon hung low on the ocean." Its message isn't pleasant, despite the imagery: he, Jeffers, and the whole human race will be "rubbed out," but nature will endure.

I counter that with Psalms 104. In part—"Bless the Lord, oh my soul. O Lord my God, thou art very great; thou art clothed with honor and majesty. Who coverest thyself with light as with a garment: who stretchest out the heaven like a curtain…He appointed the moon for seasons: the sun knoweth his going down. Thou makest darkness, and it is night…O Lord, how manifold are thy works! In wisdom hast thou made them all: the earth is full of thy riches."

I feel better.

I listen to the night and think that if I died on top of that cut, it might be weeks or even months before my body was found. How many people would care? A hand-full.

I get into my sleeping bag, say a prayer of thanksgiving for safety for me and my family and for a new life for Marci-Marie, and try to sleep.

Just as sleep invades my body, the little cloud in my head fades, and I see what it has been hiding.

In a political science class in college, we had studied Alex de Toqueville's *Democracy in America*, published after the Frenchman had made a trip to the United States in 1831.

Much of it was dated: he saw an America maintained by its having no strong neighbors, no great wars, no high taxes, no large armies, and no great capital city that controlled the country. He believed that state and local governments could help control the central government.

But he did see the tendency of Americans to accumulate possessions, and he made some points I liked: a condemnation of slavery, an emphasis on religion, and freedom of the press.

But the idea that had been clouded in my mind, that had been enclosed like a chick in the shell, was now revealed, was now hatched. In that enlightened second, Stubb could have said of me as he said of Captain Ahab in *Moby Dick*, "…the chick's that's in him pecks the shell. 'Twill soon be out."

I couldn't recall Toqueville's exact words that night, but I looked them up later:

He wrote, "Religion is often unable to restrain man from the numberless temptations of fortune; nor can it check that passion for gain which every incident of his life contributes to arouse, but its influence over the mind of woman is supreme, and women are the protectors of morals…

"No free communities ever existed without morals; and…morals are the work of woman. Consequently, whatever affects the condition of women, their habits and their opinions, has great political importance in my eyes."

Toqueville explained that women in America are products of religion, political liberty, and democracy, and, as such, have to rely on their own guidance at an early age. The American woman has barely left childhood before she "…thinks for herself, speaks with freedom, and acts on her own impulse." The world is early disclosed to her. The vices of the world and the dangers of society are revealed to her. Clearly, without illusion, and bravely, she confronts them, relying on her own strength and confidence.

The American people, knowing they could not repress a woman's passions, determined that they would teach her how to control those passions within herself. Rather than allowing her to mistrust herself, they sought to enhance her belief in her own strong character. Rather than hiding women from the sordidness of corruption, Americans allow them to see it, and then train them to avoid it.

This type of education is based on religion, but also on reason. This education helps the American woman entering into matrimony adapt to her loss of freedom and use it to build a solid marriage and family. Unlike Europe, American marriages are freely arrived at, so the woman does not feel trapped and does not turn to her passions as a way out.

In American marriages the roles of the two sexes are clearly laid out, but the domestic duties of an American wife do not reduce the equality she shares with her husband. Many American women show a strength in raising a family that is totally lacking in European women who feign as to how weak and timid they are.

American men see women as refined and virtuous; this respect is so great "…that in the presence of a woman the most guarded language is used, lest her ear should be offended by an expression."

American men also hold the virtue of women is such high esteem that "In America, a young unmarried woman may, alone and without fear, undertake a long journey."

The American woman's honor and independence are so precious to all Americans that capital punishment is applied to the man who forcibly deprives her of them through rape.

Toqueville closed his chapter by writing: "…if I were asked…to what singular prosperity and growing strength of that people [Americans] ought mainly to be attributed, I should reply, To the superiority of their women."

I fall asleep with variations of these words as signposts pointing to one thing my trip showed me.

In Nebraska I don't have to worry about wet, hard-shelled, legged creatures trying to share my sleeping bag.

DAY FIFTEEN

The day broke dewy and with a whisper of fall. Down the fence line a Western meadowlark sent a paean to the early morning sun behind the trees at my back. It was Sunday, and I wasn't in church, but I felt as though I were. I agreed with Emily Dickinson when she wrote:

> "Some keep the Sabbath going to church;
> I keep it staying home,
> With a bobolink for a chorister,
> And an orchard for a dome."

Of course, I didn't have a bobolink or an orchard, but I'd take a meadowlark and a home on the prairie any day.

I packed up and came down off my little hill, rolled across the ditch, and started up the Gold Star. Across a dry Spring Creek and past Greeley, five hundred people living in the middle of nowhere. Across the Burlington/BN tracks, past the Sacred Heart Cemetery, and up a long rise of ground. I met a semi coming down, the first traffic of the early day. The rolling topography stretched out ahead of me. Hay land, pastureland, soil not looking very good where it was exposed. Shelterbelts. Sporadic farms.

Hillier land. Long runs up ridges. Some places highway engineers had to cut through. Was this land ever homesteaded? If it was, did the people give up—"In God we trusted; in Nebraska we busted."

Finally, some signs of life—the greenery of the Cedar River Valley, not much, but something. Up into more hills, ridges, and rolling prairie.

I speed up; five miles over; I have to get home. I wish I knew the geology of Nebraska.

The land flattened a little. In the distance a white car. The 750 is humming. The car is closer. It's waving a long antenna from the rear left fender. It's closer and a light bar rides the top. I slow down, but don't dare brake. The Nebraska State Patrol car passes.

I watch in my rear view. The car whips around; I'm counting my money mentally. Lights flashing; I pull over.

The officer gets out, leaving the lights on. A red car passes; the first one for a half hour and just to embarrass me. He asks, "Where ya goin'?"

"Home. North Dakota."

"Where ya been?"

"New Orleans."

"That's quite a trip. What d'ya do?"

"Work in a school."

"Teacher, huh. You don't look like one, if you don't mind me sayin' so."

He took off his hat and looked the bike over.

"How much is the fine?"

"What fine?"

"I was going a little fast."

"That's all right. Just hold it down some." He started back to his car.

"Where's the ticket. I'll mail it in."

"No ticket. I get so lonesome out here on the road that I just like to talk to people. Have a nice trip."

"Thanks." I waited until he turned with a wave and went south. I fired up and took off north. I waited five miles and sped up.

I passed the village of Bartlett. The hilly, knobby, ridgey land continued. Where were the people? A turn to the northwest and the land pancaked. It was my kind of land again, but I needed to have it populated. North again; I had to get out of the "moonscape with vegetation."

Across the Elkhorn River and into O'Neill, almost four thousand people who don't know how lucky they are.

I bump over the C&NW tracks; a brown depot sits on my right. A block-and-a-half and I cross the Burlington/BN tracks. I lazy through the business district, looking for people, but see few. The town looks like it's doing all right. The highway turns west and then north, and I pass through both commercial and residential areas. It's too early for the Protestants, so the people I see in cars are probably early Mass-goers. Regardless, I am thankful.

Leaving town. Large, well-cared for O'Neill Cemetery on my right. Twenty-five miles to South Dakota. Rolling land, but probably better farmland than what I'd been through. Down there it was so dry that the mud had dust. White horses in a pasture. A jet's contrail painting its way across the sky. A ridge showing white in a highway cut. Cropland more evident, shelterbelts, but where are the people, the farms?

Suddenly, rough land; ridges angle up from the highway; a descent into a wide, angular scar cut into the prairie; a tributary of the fabled Niobrara River, famous in geology for giving its name to a chalk and a limestone formation laid down in Cretaceous seas; trees suture themselves to the banks.

Out of the valley; more farmland, but no people. Another descent; another scar; it's the Niobrara River itself, but to the left a power dam has tamed the old bull buffalo; the Spencer Hydro plant uses it energy for electricity. South of the dam there is a trailer park; lots of people; recreation time.

Out of the valley; rougher land; a curve to the west, skirting a river. Slow down on a curve and go through Spencer. Church people. Across the Northwestern tracks and Ponca Creek. Out of the valley, heading north, then east; I begin to see lots of trees off to the left. The C&NW line is running on my right. Stubble fields; plowed fields; a dip down a little valley; a curve to the left; a bigger valley—it's the Missouri.

I cross the Big Muddy on the Ft. Randall Dam, reservoir on my left; narrow river to my right; the wild wolf of the prairies tied down and neutered.

Pickstown; through trees, by deer crossing signs, under hydroelectric lines, over some rough country, but then out onto the flats. Skim by Lake Andes on a curve, over the Milwaukee Road tracks, then past the lake itself; drive east, passing the few blocks of Ravinia on the south; turn north.

Gun it; I'm hungry; slow through Armour and over the Milwaukee Road tracks; slow again on a left-hand turn; then a right-hand turn and slow again at Corsica. Why do they put these little towns on the highway? The Milwaukee Road keeps me company on my left.

Past farms, around Sunday drivers, every revolution of the wheels brings me closer to home.

Stickney, and the Milwaukee Road ends. But I don't. Five minutes and I'm on I-90. Eighteen more and I'm looking for a place to eat in Mitchell.

I exited onto West Havens, but drove all the way to East Havens before I pulled in to a gas station, filled up, and used the rest room to make myself presentable.

I backtracked to a Dairy Queen because I wanted to top off my meal of burger, fries, and Coke with a chocolate-covered cone. There were a few single customers like me, but most came in two's or small groups. I heard about Hurricane Dorothy that had killed at least forty people in Martinique. The Soviet space probe *Venera 7* that had been launched and would make the first soft-landing on Venus. Two men in black and gold windbreakers hoped that the Mitchell Kernels football team would trounce the Huron Tigers. Rev. Thornberry's sermon was outstanding or so a woman declared. Peoples' jobs, health, and families all came up before I finished my cone.

I went east on I-90, crossed over the Milwaukee Road tracks, and two miles later hit the daily double—I crossed the Jacques River and another set of Milwaukee rails and saw the railroad bridge below the Interstate bridge. I reversed directions at an interchange and on my way back noted how much the Jacques had grown over the miles from Menninger. It was the furthest south I'd ever seen my river.

I hustled back to the Gold Star. Over the Milwaukee Road tracks. Past white buildings, then a white farm house and out onto some beautifully flat land which my eyes probed all the way to the horizon. I passed over several drying or dried water courses and some shelterbelts. I saw this was corn country and that white was the dominant color for farm buildings.

There was some traffic and a lot of farm implements being moved on the highway. I waved whenever I saw a farmer and invariably got one in return. The miles rolled by under my wheels. I headed north, truer than a compass.

I crossed the Milwaukee Road branch going to Wessington Springs. Curved a little through a small valley caused by an unnamed stream and headed true north again.

Kenneth C. Gardner, Jr.

A few acres of rough land caused by a water course, now dead. Hay bales in the ditches. White farms. The Milwaukee Road tracks across the highway are guarded by signal lights which are not warning of any approaching trains. I look back to my right anyway and bump across. The pavement curves immediately to the left and Highway 14 heads east to Huron some ten or so miles away. Speed up.

The town of Wolsey, some four hundred people, slows me down. The predominant color of houses is white; all the faces I see are white; the water tower is silver.

I cross the Northwestern tracks going east and west; I curve out of town and pick up the Milwaukee Road, which has been accompanying me since Highway 14.

More farms now. I'm in pothole and slough country. Past the eastern edge of Tulare, eight blocks long and gone. Lakes, sloughs, a curve, and I'm over the tracks; the Milwaukee Road heads to Redfield; the Gold Star angles northwest, then continues north to Redfield, three thousand people served by two railroads. As I go through town, the houses are mostly older ones, but kept up well. I curve and cross the Northwestern tracks. A large brown brick church to my left and the Spink County Courthouse to my right, looking like a large Quincy-box schoolhouse.

St. Bernard Catholic Church on the corner. Light brown brick. A slim tower with a gold dome and white cross, a peaked roof with a white cross, a large steeple and bell tower under a gold dome and white cross. Unique.

I turn the corner and head north again, go over Turtle Creek, and open 'er up past white farms and black cattle. The Gold Star is flat and straight with no towns and just one little jog east of Mansfield. I fly over water courses, some wet, some dry, all unnamed.

I skirt the west edge of Aberdeen and cross the Milwaukee Road on a large bridge. A few jogs, but mostly straight, and I'm in North Dakota a half hour later. My home state welcomes me; so does the town of Finch.

The west side of Finch looks clean; fifteen hundred people; I shoot quick glances up and down Main Street as I pass; some empty buildings; "For Sale" signs on empty houses, probably some population loss; big elevators to the west; large white house needs paint; city limits. I missed the court house, the school, the college.

The Milwaukee Road accompanies me north; level farmland, shelterbelts, farms with the ubiquitous white paint; a curve to the northwest. Pothole country; more shelterbelts; farm houses that are brown, gray, pastels; the Soo Line tracks with gates up, but I check left and right although on the flat, I'd spot a train a mile away; the village of Magoffin, a hundred people trying to hang on.

A turn north; the city of St. George; nine hundred people; elevators rule the skyline. Flatland farms; shelterbelts; I'm making time despite the farm equipment on the highway.

Up ahead it looks like an accident. I haven't seen one on my entire trip. A car, several motorcycles, and some people sitting on the shoulder of an intersection. I slow down.

A dark-haired girl runs out, waving me down. I stop. She's wearing cut-offs and a shirt that's tied so her midriff is bare. She comes up to the bike, smiles, puts her hand on mine, and says "Wanna party?"

"What?"

"We stop bikers and ask them to party. They always have grass or pills or something. What d'you have?"

I wheel my bike off the pavement and look around. The car's a four-door, a Daddy's car, with all the doors open on a summer afternoon and four girls dressed for summer, looking out and smiling. Six motorcycles are parked on the shoulder, and six guys and two women in various stages of decline lounge in the grass or on the pavement, their preference. A couple of them make the Satan's Slaves look human.

A blonde girl from the car joins her friend, her shorts even shorter and her midriff even more bare. "Whatcha got for us?"

"Nothing."

"Quit teasing. You're a biker; you must have something. Bennies?"

"No, nothing."

The girls look at each other. The first one says, "Aw, that's all right. You can party with us anyway. Just another bike or two."

The blonde says, "Yeah, you're cute. Maybe you and I will party." She smiles, all innocence and heedless daring. I want to put them in the car and find their parents, but all I can say is, "You shouldn't be here; you should go home before you get hurt."

They both laugh. As they walk away, the blonde says, "You don't know what you could have had." They slip into the car and start talking to their friends, who begin laughing between puffs on their cigarettes. They look at me.

The bikers are oblivious.

I fire up and roll away. The road curves and I meet a semi and two cars, but no motorcycles. The pavement curves back and sitting on an approach is a car marked "County Sheriff." I pull alongside and explain what I saw and what I fear might happen. The sheriff agrees, saying he thinks he knows who the girls are. He hits his lights and spins out. I follow.

I am right behind him when he clears the curve, and five seconds later the motorcycles are gone in two different directions. The sheriff wheels his car in front of the four-door and begins talking to the girls. I straddle the 750 and wait.

The sheriff backs his car up and the girls go by me; five fingers fly the bird. I'm used to it.

After the sheriff thanks me, he says he'll follow the girls and inform their parents, for whatever good that would do. He pulls away and I start back up the Gold Star.

I power north over land that has not changed in any significant way since the end of the last ice age. Yes, the potholes and runs and little streams filled or died, crops were planted and were harvested, bales of hay sat on the land and then were hauled away, but the land remained.

Seventeen minutes and I'm on the outskirts of Kingston. I ride into the Jacques River Valley and follow the highway through the center of town, passing the Basilica, now empty. I cross the BN tracks and head up onto the drift prairie, running past the farms, the villages, Caseyville, the final familiar sixteen miles, and home.

As I rode, I took stock of my trip.

It wasn't like Kerouac's. I didn't travel from place to the next place, looking for the next high, the next drink, the next woman, and find that you needed to do it all over again, the journey on the road becoming the purpose because "the road is life."

If Kerouac was with me, I'd remind him of the 1950 Kirk Douglas film *Young Man with a Horn*. Douglas plays Rick Martin, a gifted trumpet player, but one who can't keep a job with the dance bands of the time because he always wants to improvise, to play the music he hears inside himself, just the type of musician Kerouac saw and wrote about. Martin marries Amy North, an emotionally unstable woman played by Lauren Bacall. They begin quarreling, he begins drinking, and she wants a divorce.

Martin's life begins to deteriorate. He even turns on his old mentor Art Hazzard, supremely played by Juano Hernandez. After a fight, Hazzard is killed by a car and Martin sinks ever lower. At a recording session with Jo Jordan, a singer in love with him played by Doris Day, Martin steps up for a solo on "With a Song in My Heart." However, he completely loses it when he can't hit the notes he hears and smashes his trumpet.

His life spirals downward and he becomes an alcoholic. He ends up in a drunk tank, where his friend Smoke, played by Hoagie Carmichael, finds him. Smoke contacts Jo Jordan, and together they help Martin back to sobriety and to the music he loves.

In the course of the movie, Martin is improvising and blowing just the way Kerouac loved; but his dependence on booze ruins his ability to reach the notes he wants.

That's what I would tell Kerouac: At the end of the road, there ain't no such notes. The road, especially on booze or drugs, will not give you ultimate peace. You stop on the road, and you have to get going again. You need to find a place to stop, get off the road and learn to love—your family, your friends, someone special. That's what I would have told Kerouac if he had lived.

Was it like Steinbeck's?

I saw that American taste was becoming homogenized. Clothing was similar, if not the same, wherever I went. Radio played the same songs. McDonald's Golden Arches were everywhere.

I agreed that Americans were Americans, more alike than different and with more in common with each other than with people of other countries. But I could see a fraying of that unity: racist people who wanted to live in the past (white) or in a future Utopia that would never exist (black); also there was ethnic hesitancy to adopt a new language.

I saw that people felt comfortable in their own small groups, sharing things with their friends, but reluctant to talk to strangers, except in jocular, non-intimate ways. Unless maybe if you were teenagers. The one bar I went into, the men were intent on the dancer, not in expressing opinions, so, unlike Steinbeck, I didn't see any fistfights where men publicly displayed their values. I did hear a political conversation in Iowa, but it had begun before I arrived and stopped when the speakers saw I was listening.

Upon reflection, I had seen America in the Republican River I had crossed with the sand islands exposed. Our people were like the islands, little groups above the surface, but separated from other groups. If some event caused the water to rise, the islands would be submerged and flow into each other, making one. That might be our destiny, although I found it unlikely.

Or maybe the water level would drop, and the islands would become permanently separated by little puddles and rivulets. If that happened, would it still be a river? Would it still be a society?

More importantly, I learned that we—men and women—have to make a society where our girls and women are safe and can develop their lives in a moral environment, free from intimidation and violence. Free, strong women will set the tone for American morals and values.

Menninger, my home, showed up across the melt-water channel. I raced down, took the curve, and went up the overpass. The well-traveled streets, the familiar houses, and then my place. I pulled in and unloaded. I'd see Mom and Dad after supper.

A hot shower, clean clothes, and a chance to sit down, not on a motorcycle seat. Around the corner of the living room and Mom and Dad were on the sofa. Then Mom was up and hugging me, and Dad was waiting to shake my hand and welcome me home.

I ate supper with them; Mom insisted. Both of them also insisted I tell them something about my trip. I told them the censored version.

Dad thanked me for the postcards. Mom said, "Chris, I almost forgot. Aunt Mildred wanted to talk to you as soon as you got home. I'll call her."

I talked to Dad while I waited. *What could Aunt Mildred want?*

She came in with a hug, then she exclaimed, "Chris, guess what? Theresa went up town by herself and brought home some milk!"

I was shocked. It probably doesn't sound like much—a twelve-year old girl walking three blocks uptown and back, but for my cousin Theresa to have done it was amazing. After she had been molested, she kept to herself and refused to go anywhere unless someone was with her.

"And it's because of you!"

"I don't understand."

"Those postal cards you wrote to her about your trip. She was the only one in our family that got any. They made her feel...well...special. She'd be worried and happy and excited for you, and she prayed for you every night. Then one day she asked if I needed anything uptown. You could have knocked me over with a feather. I made up that I needed milk. When she took the money, she said, 'If cousin Chris can go to New Orleans all by himself, I can go uptown.' And she did. And she's gone other places, alone or with her girlfriends. And she wants to tell you something tomorrow, if it's all right."

Of course, it was all right.

I said grateful prayers that night.

DAY SIXTEEN

I n the morning I walked over to the school and talked with Tommy
and Clyde, writing out a schedule to finish up the work before
classes started.

Just after dinner, the phone rang. It was Theresa, asking if it was
convenient for her to come over.

A couple minutes later she knocked. After our greetings, she asked,
"Cousin Chris, would you like to have an ice cream with me. My treat."

"That sounds great. Should we walk or should I fire up the Honda?"

"No, I think I'd like to walk. Motorcycles scare me."

We walked the two blocks down Lamborn, talking about little things,
but after we ordered, she wanted to know all about my trip. I told her as
much as I thought she needed to know over two large hot fudge sundaes.

The ice cream was long gone before I had finished.

She started looking through her little purse for the money. I reached
for my billfold, but she insisted on paying. I said I'd get the tip and she
said that would be all right.

On the way up the hill, we didn't talk much, some about her family
and about how she hoped she would like seventh grade. I was recalling
how much she had meant to me when she was little, and how I would
carry her around and she would hug me. Then she was molested and
withdrew into a world where men were people who hurt you, and she
didn't want me around. I thanked God she was coming back.

She walked up to the door with me, and when I turned to say
goodbye, she hugged me and said, "Chris, you're my hero." She turned
quickly and headed up the sidewalk.

If sunshine ever gets inside a man, that was what I felt.

EPILOGUE

That night on the news there was a report on a bombing in Madison at the University of Wisconsin. A young man was killed in the Army Math Research Center. I thought of Stella Starfall and her friends and Morris Winters and their idealism, red with blood.

A couple weeks after I returned, my friend Dotty had a son. She named him Charles Christopher after me and asked me to be his godfather.

School began and I could watch out for Theresa without being too obvious.

Everyone in the family was thrilled when she said she was going to the Homecoming Dance, especially since it was with a group of her girlfriends. "But I'll dance with a boy if he asks."

I was glad they had done away with the Initiation and its dance. Not really the dance, but the initiation of the seventh graders would have been too brutal for Theresa.

One Saturday I took the Honda out east of town for a run. Afterwards I stopped at the O'Connells' house. My twenty-two year old cousin Liam was home. We talked and reminisced for an hour.

When I went outside, Theresa was standing by my bike, rubbing her hand back and forth across the seat. Teasingly, I asked, "Wanna ride?"

She hesitated, her crystal blue eyes wide…"Yes."

"Ask your mother." She dashed into the house.

Aunt Mildred, Uncle Daniel, and Liam followed Theresa out. "Chris, is it safe?"

How does a motorcycle rider answer that question? "Yes. I'm a safe driver."

"Well, I guess it'll be all right."

Theresa was bare-armed. I put my fringed leather coat around her; she was lost in it.

I kick-started the bike and helped her get on. I geared the bike with my foot.

"Hang on tight."

"I will."

Her small arms were strong around me.

Printed in the United States
By Bookmasters